MARY NEALY

TEN X PLAGUES

A NOVEL

BARBOUR
PUBLISHING

ISBN 978-1-60260-684-5

Cover credit: Studio Gearbox, www.studiogearbox.com

Published by Barbour Publishing, Inc., P.O. Box 719, Uhrichsville, OH 44683, www.barbourbooks.com

Our mission is to publish and distribute inspirational products offering exceptional value and biblical encouragement to the masses.

Member of the
Evangelical Christian
Publishers Association

Printed in the United States of America.

DEDICATION/ACKNOWLEDGMENTS

In Corinthians 12:8–10 is a list of the gifts of the Holy Spirit. As I read the list it was very familiar. I'd heard this list many times before and had heard of people with nearly all these gifts. Wisdom, knowledge, prophecy, faith, healing, performing miracles, discerning spirits, speaking in tongues, interpreting tongues. But this once, as I read, I was struck by the gift of discerning spirits. I wondered what that would be like. What if you could walk up to someone and immediately know that they were good or evil, or even discern evil spirits—demons—within them?

When an idea comes to me while reading my Bible, I try to pay very careful attention to that, because I believe God sometimes speaks to us in a voice so still and small that it amounts to not so much a voice as an idea. From this idea a book was born. I'm dedicating this book to the God who gives me ideas.

CHAPTER ONE

*With the staff that is in my hand I will strike the water of the Nile,
and it will be changed into blood.*

A cold chill of evil sleeted through Keren Collins's veins.

Wind howled like a tormented soul between the Chicago tenements. Goose bumps rose on her arms. Her hair blew across her eyes and blinded her. Being sightless made the evil more powerful, as if it cast her into the presence of a blackened soul.

She felt an impending doom so powerful her hands shook as she twisted her mass of unruly curls into a messy bun and anchored it with an ugly but functional leather contraption.

She had parked her Impala a half block away from the decrepit brownstone she was watching. The front stoop and the young punks gathered there were visible. She looked around, listening. Did the evil have a source? Could this feeling be coming from inside that run-down building?

No way was Keren going in alone to find out. Chicago cops were about as popular in this part of the South Side as the Cubbies. She sat in her car, and waited and itched.

O'Shea, why'd you pick today of all days to be late?

To keep from fretting over this strange premonition, Keren pulled her notes out to reread what she had on Juanita Lopez, reported missing two days ago. Keren and O'Shea had done some preliminary checking yesterday that had led Keren to this old hangout of Juanita's. No one had seen the young woman for a week. Keren had read about two sentences when she snapped the little book shut and jammed it back in her blazer's inside breast pocket. She couldn't sit still when things felt this wrong. Pushed to action and against all common sense, she reached for her door handle.

Pounding footsteps drew her eyes to the left and behind her car. A man raced down the sidewalk on the far side of the street. The beat of his sprinting feet made Keren's heart speed up. He raced past her, straight toward that cluster of thugs Keren figured for Juanita's old gang. They saw the man running and straightened like wolves scenting blood.

The runner went up the brick steps right between some of the meanest scum in the city. He collapsed against the wall, gasping for air. Keren narrowed her eyes as he lifted a small piece of. . .something. . .and pressed it to the side of the door, sliding it sideways and jamming it into a crack he must have found. A sign maybe, brown wood, a foot or so long and half as high. If it had a picture or words on it she couldn't make them out. Just as he pressed it against the wall one of the gang members slapped a hard hand on the man's shoulder, ripped the sign out of his hand, jerked the door open, and shoved him inside.

That sense of evil grew, but Keren didn't have to be a genius to know that the guy who'd just been shoved inside could be in big trouble.

A half-dozen Hispanic boys erupted from the brownstone and took up positions in front of the building as if they'd been assigned guard duty.

Keren slumped low in her seat, sitting on her backside while someone was being killed. But she couldn't take on a gang alone. Minutes ticked by.

"O'Shea, where are you? C'mon."

She couldn't stand it anymore. She reached for the door handle and her phone at the same time.

An explosion blasted bricks loose from the building's foundation. The kids standing guard were mowed down by shrapnel.

Keren's car rocked on its axles. Its car alarm went off and the airbag deployed and punched her in the face.

A blast of heat hit next and gritty dust enveloped the car. She leaped from her car and charged toward the crawling, bleeding boys.

Running and stumbling, she was blinded by the billowing smoke.

Another explosion knocked her down. She could hear glass shattering to her right. Flames shot out of the windows on an upper floor, cutting through the gritty air.

Bits of pulverized brick whizzed overhead. Choking dust coated the inside of her nose and throat. She covered her face and waited until the buzzing debris from the new explosion passed. Forcing herself to her feet, she tripped and went down and realized she'd stepped on a boy.

She caught the shoulders of his jacket. "Get up!"

He looked up at her, dazed.

"Get up and run!" She dragged the boy. She knew she shouldn't move him, but another brick slashed inches from her face and she knew this was kill-or-cure time.

"You've got to get away." She thrust her face close to his, hoping to penetrate his daze.

Blood trickled down his forehead. Cinders rained down.

Keren staggered as she tried to haul the kid upright. "Run. Now. Move! Move! Move!"

He shook his head. His eyes cleared and he gained his feet and stumbled away. Keren moved forward and fell over shattered brick. This time she stayed down and crawled. The rubble on the ground cut her hands and knees. She reached another victim. This one was already trying to stand. Over the crackling flames and crashing stones, she shouted, "Run, get out of here!"

A falling brick struck Keren in the shoulder and she fell flat on her face just as someone ran out of the building.

"How many are in there?" she yelled.

The kid didn't answer as he ran past.

Keren saw a dark lump off to the side, crumpled on the ground, and she got to him and yanked at another fallen, dazed teenager. The kid's face was shredded from brick fragments, his eyes glazed. Keren dragged him to his feet. She suspected only pure survival instinct made him move in the direction she shoved him. She saw two other boys crawling in the right direction and let them go it alone.

She was close enough to the building to see a young child hovered against the side of it. He was frozen, his eyes wide with terror. She crawled toward him.

A stream of staggering, screaming people came out of the building. The man who'd gone running up to the building right before it exploded—tall, dark-haired, commanding, covered with blood and gray soot—brought up the rear, shoving at two kids, yelling and urging them forward like a general on the battlefield. "Get out, go, go, go!"

As the man ran down the steps, the door he'd just charged out of blew off the building and whizzed inches from Keren's head. Flames raged out of the opening. The man threw his arms around both boys and dove under the shooting flames. They skidded across the cruel pavement.

The air turned white hot from the new blaze. It was alive with glowing embers and toxic smoke. Choking, Keren struggled on toward the little boy. A blaze flared out of a broken basement window and enveloped her. She dropped to her belly and wrapped her arms over her head, afraid her hair would catch fire. The instant the burst of fire ebbed, she crawled forward on broken bricks and glass.

When she reached the child, she caught him to her. Bricks rained down. She forced the child away from his hideout. He got the idea, wrenched away from her, and ran.

She looked at the inferno that engulfed the front entrance and every window in the building. There was no way to get inside to search for survivors. Turning away, she saw the man was on his knees, beating on the flames devouring one of the boys.

The man's face was coated. His clothes and hair were gray with ash.

Keren charged in, snagged one of the boys by the back of his sweatshirt, and jerked him to his feet. Something solid slammed the man to his knees beside her. A stream of blood cut through the grit on his face.

He staggered to his feet when Keren would have expected him to be down for good. "The whole building's coming down."

He tore at the boy's burning jacket. The panicked boy fought him, but the man ripped the coat off.

Keren shoved the other boy forward then turned to help the bleeding man. Turning to her, his eyes blazed with life in the midst of death. His spirit hit her almost as hard as the bricks. His square shoulders, and the honor and compassion in his eyes, didn't match with this soul-destroying neighborhood. What was he doing here? Besides bleeding. She reached to help him get away.

9

The old building howled like an angry monster. Flames reached for the heavens. The buildings on both sides were engulfed in flames and near collapse, too. The man glanced back. Keren's gaze followed his. Through the choking grit, she saw someone lying unconscious at the corner of the building, near the alleyway.

"Chico," the man said. "Please, God, not him."

She heard the true prayer in his voice.

The whole building, now engulfed in flames, shifted forward.

She turned to order the man to get away before she went back for the boy. But he was gone, running toward the boy, right into the teeth of the fire, toward certain death.

Another boy burst through the solid wall of raging flames that blocked the front door of the condemned brownstone. He screamed and beat at fire that had turned him into a human torch. He ran down the stoop of the tenement and plowed into Keren, shrieking and writhing in pain, and she staggered back as he fell at her feet. He rolled and flailed at the merciless flames.

Ignoring the white-hot raining ash, Keren tore off her blazer and smothered the fire. She slid her arm under the boy's shoulders. The stench of burned flesh was overwhelming.

The boy screamed, but he was conscious enough to get to his feet with her support. As she moved away from the raging fire, she looked back at the building. Her heart clutched. The man scooped up the fallen boy and turned to run, but he was out of time. Bricks rained down on his shoulders and he vanished as he was buried alive.

Then, through the smothering clouds of smoke, she saw the man rise up, with what seemed like superhuman strength, and shed the bricks on his back. He had the child's limp body cradled in his arms.

The boy beside Keren fell. She couldn't abandon this teenager to go help the man. Her heart wrenched as she turned away from the man and virtually carried the wickedly burned boy toward safety.

She glanced back and saw the man run sideways down the street, trying to get past the collapsing building. Falling bricks and tortured metal clawed at him. Rocks and cinders pelted him with every step.

"God, help me. Help us save these boys. Help that man." She looked back. Something slammed into the man. He staggered then fell against the side of a stripped car. Keren knew that last blow was one too many. The man had no strength left.

As Keren hauled the semiconscious boy around a corner to shelter him, she risked one more look back into the blizzard of shrapnel. Hundreds of bricks hurtled straight at the man. Then he was swallowed up by the choking dust of the explosion. Buried under tons of stone. Keren cried out at the heroic man's failure. When he vanished, the evil she'd sensed earlier swept back, and Keren could swear she heard Satan laugh in the face of the horror that surrounded her.

Trying desperately to keep functioning, she fumbled for her phone and called 911.

CHAPTER TWO

A doorless wreck of a car materialized in front of Paul Morris.

He slammed into it, realized what it was, shoved Chico in, and jumped in after him just as bricks battered the roof with brutal fury, caving it in.

Paul threw himself over the child.

The noise was deafening. Smothering dirt blinded Paul. He felt the roof press against his back. He fumbled in his pocket for his phone. When he flipped it open, the display light pushed back the terror enough that he could dial 911 in the choking dust. "There's been an explosion." He gave the operator the address. "There's a fire. We need ambulances. Dozens of people hurt and killed!"

"Please stay on the line, sir." The woman's calm voice gave the whole thing a nightmarish quality, but Paul knew he was wide awake.

The car's roof vibrated with the thudding bricks, rapping out an ugly song on Paul's spine. He dropped the phone on the floor, leaving it open so he could see, and slid onto his knees beside the little boy, ready to drag Chico onto the floor, too, though there was next to no space. Blood coursed through the silt coating Chico's face. The car held what was left of its shape as the bricks buried them alive. Paul felt for a heartbeat and found one, weak but steady. With only inches to move, he struggled out of his zippered jacket and covered the boy's mouth and nose to protect him from breathing grit.

The first siren was audible through the bricks. He picked up his phone and said to the 911 operator, "I hear them coming. Thank you."

"Sir, wait until—"

Paul hung up but left the phone open for the light as he turned back to Chico. He could make out a black streak on Chico's face that had to be blood. He pressed on the fast-bleeding cut with the jacket.

Paul's phone rang. He remembered the 911 operator had told him to wait. "Hello, I'm sorry, operator, I didn't mean—"

"I'll try to get the evil out of her before she dies, but there is so much. She's so filthy."

The voice that had started all this.

Paul fought back the brutal, ugly, satanic words he wanted to say.

"I gave you the car."

Paul shook his head. A voice came from everywhere and nowhere. It surrounded him and comforted him. It sheltered him, just like the car he'd fallen into.

He bowed his head and saw blood dripping down the front of his torn, dirt-coated T-shirt. "You gave me the car?"

A crooning voice spoke in his ear, "I saw you trying to save those evil men."

"Boys, not men. They're just boys." Paul gripped the phone, coating the keypad with bloody fingerprints.

"They're old enough to be evil. When you saved them, you missed your chance. Now Juanita will suffer the first plague. The plague of blood."

The connection broke off.

He had to get to Juanita. Now.

Paul shoved at the space where the car's door should be and found bricks. Chico stirred beside him, but Paul thought of Juanita and kept digging, shoving. He knocked a hole in the stack of bricks, and they clattered to the pavement as he squirmed outside into blinding grit and ear-piercing squalling sirens. He stumbled over debris covering the street and fell to his knees. His hands landed on shards of glass and jagged brick. He was only distantly aware of the pain.

He stared, curious about the spreading stain of red on the ground around him. An echo deep in his head told him it was blood, and the blood was his. A plague of blood.

Juanita. Those pictures.

A man emerged like a phantom from the cloud of smoke and grit and crouched beside Paul. "Sir, let me help you."

The letters EMT on the man's chest blurred. "I'm not the one who needs help. In. . .in the car. A boy." The letters faded completely. "And Juanita. I have to save her."

Paul saw the ground rushing up to meet him.

He had the presence of mind to thank God for the car.

Keren dropped to her knees beside the boy. He didn't move. Whatever strength he'd had to get this far was gone. She slapped at sparks that still ate at the remnants of his clothes. A piece of the boy's crisp, blackened skin slid away. Tears cut like acid through the grit in her eyes as she pulled her hand back.

"God, please, don't let me hurt him any more." She reached for his neck to feel for a pulse then stopped. He was so badly burned on his upper body she didn't dare touch his throat. She caught his wrist. She couldn't find a pulse. He wasn't breathing. His chest was burned black. She gritted her teeth, tilted his head back to open his airway, and began chest compressions. An ambulance, siren wailing, whizzed past Keren and skidded to a stop. Two men climbed out.

She looked up, pressing rhythmically on the boy's breastbone. "He doesn't have a heartbeat."

They gently moved her aside and took over as another ambulance screamed up. She stared at the boy's blackened flesh where it had peeled away from him and stuck to the palms of her hands. Blood seeped through her fingers.

"Let me help you, miss. You're bleeding." A woman pulled Keren toward the ambulance.

She shook off the hands. "I'm Detective Collins, Chicago PD. There are a lot of people here who need help more than I do." Teenage boys, bleeding and moaning, were collapsed all along the street.

More ambulances arrived with glaring lights and screaming noise. Keren yelled over the cacophony, "A man, over there, and a little boy." She started to lead the woman there.

O'Shea came lumbering up to her. The medics headed toward the right spot, and she saw that a couple of paramedics were already lifting someone into their ambulance. She couldn't bear to see that heroic man and that little boy, crushed to death.

"Keren, what happened? Are you all right?" O'Shea pulled a handkerchief out of his pocket and pressed it to her forehead.

Mick O'Shea had taught her nearly everything she knew about being a cop. He'd saved her when she came close to being busted off the force by an arrogant, grandstanding superior officer, and Mick was lead investigator on the Juanita Lopez case.

She brushed his hand away and saw the handkerchief was soaked with blood. "Where've you been?"

"I got hung up in traffic," O'Shea said. "There was an accident on the Dan Ryan Expressway, and I was the first cop on the scene."

The EMT drew a sheet over the burned boy's face. She pressed the handkerchief back against her head wound and let her bloody hands cover her eyes.

The fire department arrived, and more police came. The rubble crawled with rescue workers. Keren turned toward the chaos. Her steps faltered. She looked at the sky-high cloud of billowing grit. It wasn't the sight of the carnage that stopped her—the air was so clogged with dirt that she couldn't see any details—but Keren knew evil. From her earliest memory, she always had. She was almost overwhelmed by what she sensed about whoever had done this. Usually she had to be in the presence of someone before she could discern their spirit. But this was more powerful than anything she'd felt before.

She saw a rescue dog whining and digging at shattered bricks. She and O'Shea exchanged a grim look and plunged into the madness.

⟵

Keren was a tough cop. She liked to think she was a little tougher than most.

So those weren't tears running down her face, soaking the dust mask she'd been issued, salting her lips. It was grainy air that made her eyes run. She ignored it and kept working. She was grateful for the cover of night, even though it meant she'd been working nonstop for twelve hours. The whole block had burned out. The buildings were all condemned, but there were homeless people living in them. Many had gotten out, but with terrible injuries. Keren knew there had to be many more trapped inside and most likely dead.

Keren had a gift for sensing the difference between simple,

human evil and a demonic hand. Her father had told her it was a gift given to her by God, to discern spirits, both good and evil. It had been her cross to bear all her life. In this tumult she felt an overpowering sense of the devil at work.

A boy, not older than six, hung limp in her arms. Keren hugged his dead body close, unwilling to flinch from his blood and crushed bones. Tears flowed until they streaked the coating of gray ash that encrusted the boy. She did her best to avoid numbing her feelings. This little boy deserved the respect of Keren's horror. She let his face burn into her mind, even though she knew it would haunt her for the rest of her life.

She lay the boy gently down on a spread-out body bag and left him. Let someone else zip the bag closed; she'd give him his last minutes in the air. As she straightened, she heard the sad whine of the cadaver dogs as they began to resist hunting through the wreckage of the apartment buildings. Their handlers urged them on with coaxing voices that sounded as depressed as the hounds. She knew how the dogs felt. She was about ten minutes away from curling up on a pile of jagged bricks and going to sleep.

O'Shea grabbed her empty arms. He gave her a long look. From behind his dust mask he said, "Cap wants us at the hospital. It sounds crazy, but this explosion may have something to do with the Lopez case."

"We can't leave." Keren's voice broke.

"Orders, Keren." O'Shea took her arm and started dragging her over the jumble of bricks.

It was a testimony to how exhausted she was that she let herself be manhandled. "How could this have anything to do with Juanita Lopez's disappearing act?"

"They've got someone there, just now waking up, who claims he knows what happened and the two are related." O'Shea kept dragging her and she kept letting him.

"Could he be responsible for this?"

"The guy in the hospital?" O'Shea asked.

"No," Keren said sarcastically, "the captain. Of *course* the guy in the hospital."

"I don't know. I barely caught his name. I don't even know if what I've told you is right. I probably made part of it up, 'cuz Cap was yelling his head off and shouting orders at everybody. I got the basics and ran like a scared rabbit."

"Smart man." Keren let O'Shea into her five-year-old Impala then went around to her side. Her car was blue somewhere under its coating of gray grit.

She caught sight of herself in the rearview mirror and was appalled. She pulled the dust mask off and it was worse. Her eyes, which she called light blue, looked gray to match the car and her clothes and the whole rest of the world. Her hair sprung out in a hundred directions. She looked like a science experiment gone horribly awry.

"We should clean up first. We'll probably get kicked out of the hospital."

O'Shea snorted, which was as close as her partner came to a laugh most of the time. "Everyone there's gonna look the same. We'd get kicked out if we were clean."

"Still, I'd hate to drip brick fragments into some guy's newly sewn-up head."

"We'll risk it. Drive."

Keren obeyed him. Amazing what a little trauma will do to a person. "What's the name of the guy Cap said to question?"

Keren eased her car into the street.

O'Shea checked his notebook. "Paul Morris."

Paul Morris! Keren's stomach took a dive. No, it wasn't that uncommon of a name. It couldn't be the same guy.

"Where is Paul Morris?" Keren yelled over the din in the emergency room.

A harassed nurse actually balled her fist. Keren got ready to duck.

"Find him yourself! I'm busy!" The nurse walked away before Keren could threaten the poor woman into cooperating.

There were bleeding people everywhere. Some injured. Others, obviously worried family, crying and dragging on the arm of anyone who looked official. Every cubicle was jammed with cots.

"How, in all this chaos, are we supposed to find anyone?" Keren shook her head at the chaos.

O'Shea shook his head, then he shook it again as if he were trying to shake out the vision of bleeding, weeping, grieving people. "You start in the cubicles. I'll start asking around out here."

"Okay, that should only take ten or twenty hours," Keren said.

"I'm open to suggestions." O'Shea glared at her.

"If that means I have to use my brain, forget it. I'm sucking fumes. Just start. Even if we could get a nurse to talk to us, she probably wouldn't know where he is in this mess."

O'Shea waded into the crowd. Keren heard him asking, "Do you know a Paul Morris? Is one of you Paul Morris?"

Keren sighed and went into the first cubicle.

It was over an hour later when she found him. She peeked between two poorly closed curtains and saw a man sleeping on a gurney, amid five other occupied beds.

It was him. The man who'd run up to the tenement building with that wooden sign and been shoved inside. The man who'd risked his life to save those kids.

She was surprised at the strength of the image she had of strangling him with her bare hands. The neck brace wouldn't save him. Not if she threw herself into it.

With the same insight that had washed a demonic presence over her at the bomb site, she knew she was looking at a good man. Sometimes she got a mild impression of good or evil dwelling inside a person. Sometimes it hit her so hard it almost knocked her to her knees. Right now, she was taking a hit.

Paul Morris, whatever he had been when he'd stomped Keren under his heel, was now a man of powerful faith. She found herself moving into the room—drawn to him, even in his sleep, wishing she had as strong and bold a spirit.

He was wearing the tattered remains of sweatpants, and Ace bandages where his shirt should be. Besides the neck brace, he had a bandage covering half his head. One of his arms was in an inflatable cast, strapped to his chest with a blue sling. Bruises blackened his face. Stitches lined his temple, jawline, and lower lip.

Keren stared at him and felt forces clashing inside her. She wanted to talk to him, share her faith, and learn about his.

She wanted to break his other arm.

Was Morris even going to remember her? He'd done all his damage long distance, taking down several young detectives when he'd stormed through their lives. Keren was the only one who had put up with the reprimands and suspension and stayed on the force. Now, she could sense the goodness in him. It was completely at odds with the glory-hogging, career-destroying rat he'd been. So, maybe he'd changed, or maybe he'd always had both goodness and cruelty in him. Keren had never before gotten close enough to him to get a positive impression.

There was no point in dredging up the past. If she did mention it, he'd probably demand another police officer. Keren wondered if he really knew anything now, or was he just in the right place at the right time? He'd left the force. Maybe he missed having his name in the paper.

She stepped out of the cubicle and waved to get O'Shea's attention over the crying and shouting injured. O'Shea nodded. She went back for one more look before she schooled her features into neutrality for O'Shea's benefit. She sucked in a deep breath and tried to remember it wasn't Christian to hate someone's guts. She'd take Morris's statement then get back to real police work.

Paul Morris was the guy who'd run into the building, and that meant he hadn't set the bomb. She'd just lost her prime suspect. She had hoped to find a man on whom she could blame this whole mess. It wasn't going to happen.

O'Shea slipped into the cubicle.

Keren had never told O'Shea about Morris and why she'd been assigned to the evidence locker. After six months of pushing paper, she'd helped O'Shea crack a case, and he'd asked for her to be assigned as his partner. She wasn't about to go into it now. "Paul Morris?"

His eyes popped open so quickly, and his focus was so clear, Keren doubted he'd been sleeping.

"Yes. Pastor Paul Morris, Lighthouse Mission."

Pastor? Keren checked the ceiling to see if pigs were flying overhead. "I'm Detective Keren Collins, Chicago PD. We got a call that you had information about today's bombing."

"At last." A sigh of relief almost wiped the pain and concern off his face. Almost. "I've been asking to talk to the police. I have some idea what happened this morning. I mean, I don't know who did it or anything."

"Of course he doesn't," O'Shea muttered. "Life just isn't that sweet."

"I was at the gang hangout this afternoon," Keren said. "I was looking for Juanita Lopez when the building exploded."

"Juanita." Morris's eyes closed. "Poor Juanita." He shook his head and flinched with pain. "Sorry, some of it's a blur."

Keren said, "Tell us what happened."

"I got this phone call." Morris raised his uninjured hand to his head. "But before that, a delivery man dropped off a package. Or no. . .pictures. He dropped off pictures of Juanita, and a sign."

Morris shook his head. "I'm not making sense. I'm sorry. The doctor has given me some pain medication. I'm not thinking too clearly."

"Just start at the beginning, Pastor Morris. Tell us what happened first."

"I was just back from my morning run. Before I got inside, a delivery man came up to me with a large manila envelope. I went into the mission and ripped the envelope open. I found. . ."

⌒

The beautiful writing was done with ink too coarse to be a marking pen. Paint of some kind. It made Paul uneasy, for no reason he could define. He slipped his thumb under the flap. The paper ripped open. He reached inside just as his cell phone rang.

He answered. "Hello?"

"I'm an artist, you know." A man spoke, his voice so smooth and quiet he purred. "I've given you something priceless."

"Who is this?"

"Wood isn't my *favorite* medium, but I'm very good with it. Every new creation is like a child. And who can create a child? A father. Or God."

God?

Paul realized at the same moment the man spoke, that he held

TEN **X PLAGUES**

a piece of wood in his hands. It was a rectangular plaque about an inch thick, sanded satiny smooth, stained to a dark brown.

"Are you the one who sent this wood carving?" Paul turned his attention from the gift to the caller. It wasn't that unusual to receive gifts from people who supported his mission.

Pravus was etched in a delicate script in the lower right corner.

"It would be worth a fortune if I'd gone into art as a living." The voice was soft, almost singsong, with a tone that made the hair on the back of Paul's neck stand up.

"Who is this?" Paul repeated. "I'd. . .uh, like to send a thank-you note. This is beautiful."

And it was. There was delicate carving across the front. Letters that spelled words Paul couldn't read, although they struck a chord. *Natio.* That was Spanish maybe, which he spoke adequately but couldn't read. *Natio* meant "nation" or maybe "tribe."

"My true creation is in the photographs." A sigh of ecstasy hissed across the phone lines.

There'd been a time when Paul's instincts had kept him alive. Those instincts kicked in hard. Paul dropped the envelope on the table and used a pen to tip it. Polaroid pictures slid onto the table. The instant he saw them he knew what kind of paint the caller had used to write the address.

Blood.

"What have you done?" It had been five years since he'd been a cop, and he no longer had the detachment he needed to survive this kind of thing.

"Isn't she beautiful?"

Sickened by the pictures, Paul forced himself to study them, desperate to understand what this caller wanted. Then his eyes fell shut. He whispered, "Juanita."

"Yes, that's right, Juanita. I'd forgotten her name. She's just

23

canvas to me, not as nice to work with as wood."

"What have you done to her, you. . ." Biting back rage, Paul knew then he could turn back into a cop. All the reflexes were still there.

"Now, now, Reverend, I expected better from you than that. We're in this together."

Gripping the phone until his fingers ached, Paul asked, "What are we in together? Why are you calling me? Where is she?"

"She's going to stay right where she is unless you deliver a message for me, Reverend."

"Message? What message?"

A scream sliced through the phone line.

"No," Paul roared. "Don't hurt her. I'll do what you want."

The screams increased. Paul couldn't think. Not as a pastor. The old coldness that at one time had cost him his faith, his family, and almost his life, settled on him. "Tell me what you want, Pravus." Paul heard the level tone of his voice and couldn't believe he sounded like that while his heart thundered with fear.

"Take the sign to the address I included in the envelope. Don't call the police. Don't talk to anyone. Hang it on that building and wait for me to phone."

"Hang it on the building? Wait! How do I do that?"

"That's your problem, Reverend. When you have delivered your message," Pravus cooed, "I'll tell you where to find this harlot."

Juanita's cries increased, broken by screams of pain.

"I'll do what you want, and then, if you want to survive this, you'll give me Juanita."

There was an extended silence on the phone. Pravus said, "You sound more like a policeman than a man of God. Why doesn't that surprise me?"

CHAPTER THREE

There was an address in the envelope. I found it and I ran." Paul studied Detective Collins as he muddled through to the end of his story. She was filthy. Her hair looked like a bale of straw had been given an electric shock. Then all of her had been liberally coated with white dust. He vaguely remembered a woman at the explosion helping him, but he never would have recognized her.

"I called 911. All I remember after that is thanking God for the car."

"Okay, Reverend," Detective Collins said. "Now, I have a couple of questions."

An hour later, she flipped her notebook closed. But she wasn't done talking. The woman never got done *talking*.

"And as far as you know, the sign this man who identified himself only as Pravus gave you burned up with the tenement?"

Detective Mick O'Shea grunted as he scanned his notes.

"For the *fifth* time," Paul said, "as far as I know, it burned or is buried in the rubble. I don't know. What about Juanita?"

Detective Collins gave him a glowering look, like he was a hostile witness. Had he been this tedious and annoying when he was a cop? Not possible.

"Whichever kid took it away from me might have kept his hands on it when he ran. I could identify most of the gang members I saw, and you could question them." Paul had been as cooperative as he could, and he'd deliberately waited until the end to ask his own questions. "You don't have any idea how many of them got out, do you?"

"No," Detective Collins said briskly.

Paul looked at her under the dust and grit. Both she and O'Shea were so filthy he doubted he'd be able to pick them out of a lineup if his life depended on it. She'd been treating him like a suspect, and he'd had to fight to control his temper. Paul might not have succeeded if he hadn't seen what looked like the tracks of tears cutting through the dirt on her face.

Detective O'Shea said, "We had a body count of twenty last I knew. Most of them were vagrants living in the adjacent buildings, which also collapsed. The buildings were all condemned, so it didn't take much to bring them down."

Paul closed his eyes as he thought about the people he'd come to love. The oddballs, the outcasts. Losing them, some of them before they'd had a chance to turn to God, left him with a crippling feeling of failure.

"There was a little boy, Chico. I carried him away from the building. He was bleeding badly. I think they transported us in the same ambulance...it's all pretty foggy after the medic came—" Paul's heavy eyelids dropped closed with the weight of this defeat.

O'Shea interrupted, "We just don't know, Pastor Morris. We nosed around the ER, looking for you, but we saw a lot of kids—"

"This one was young, early elementary, Hispanic."

"You just described every child in the place," Collins said with a dismissive shrug. "It was a Hispanic neighborhood."

"I know what neighborhood I was in." Paul clamped his mouth shut to stop yelling. It also helped his control that yelling hurt. He closed his eyes against the pain then found he couldn't get them open again. "If you could just check." The sound of his desperation echoed inside his head.

He tried to sit up straighter so he didn't lose his train of thought. His ribs punished him for the shift of his weight, and his neck sent a razor-sharp jolt of pain all the way down his spine.

"Reverend Morris," Collins said, "don't move. You'll only make it worse."

A note of compassion had sneaked into her voice, the first she'd shown him. Paul forced his eyes open. *Thank You, God, that I'm no longer a cop.* Her penetrating look was common to all cops. But he had a sense that there was more to it. She didn't like him for some reason.

If only he could make her understand. "I know you're busy. I know you're tired." He fumbled for the edge of his mattress. "If I could only get to my feet I could do it myself. These cracked ribs will quit aching once I'm on my feet."

She caught his hand before he could get a grip on the mattress. "They'll quit aching unless you breathe or walk or talk. I've had cracked ribs. I know how they feel."

He squeezed her hand until he was afraid he was hurting her, but thinking of Chico was driving him crazy. And what was he doing worrying about one boy when there were so many hurt? What was he doing lying here when there was so much need? What about Juanita?

"It's just that I felt like God was guiding me when I ran." Tears burned at Paul's eyes and he tried to pull away from her. "Surely God didn't do that and then let the boy die."

The lady detective had a grip like iron. "You're near collapse, Reverend. Let me ask the doctor if it's time for more pain medication. There's nothing more you can do tonight."

She wouldn't let him up, even if he could have managed it, which he doubted. Paul shook his head, or tried to. He wasn't sure if he got it to move. He had to tell her he wasn't tired. Sure, he was banged up, but it was only cuts and bruises and a sprained wrist. The IV drip and the neck collar were all part of the doctor's fiendish plan to keep him prisoner. He had no internal injuries, no broken bones. He was one of the lucky ones. He had to get out of bed and comfort these people.

He'd tell her that, if only he could get his eyes open.

"We'll ask around, if you'd like." She leaned close. "We'll find out about the little boy."

Paul's brain fuzzed but he forced his eyes open. The world seemed to go all soft focused on him, and suddenly the riot of curls swirling around her head fascinated him. She had his right hand held tightly, so he reached his injured left hand unsteadily toward her, lifting the blue sling away from his body. His fingers closed over a handful of corkscrews. He felt the grit, saw how dirty it was, and still it was soft and silky.

He stared at the hair he held. "Pretty."

He saw something other than compassion flash in her eyes. She pushed his hand away roughly and stepped away from his bedside. He knew it was rough because it made his sprained wrist hurt like crazy. Of course, breathing made his sprained wrist hurt like crazy, too, so he couldn't be sure if she'd meant any harm.

"We've got to let you rest," she said. "Do you think you can remember the words carved on that sign? It might give us a place to start searching for Juanita. If you can tell us, we'll get out of here."

"How many times do I have to tell you, no. I don't remember the words." Paul struggled to control himself. His temper had always been his Achilles' heel. "I think it was Spanish, but I'm not sure. I told you the phone rang before I got a good look at it and, after the call came, all I could think about was getting to that building."

Something nudged his memory. He hated to admit her

badgering had actually shaken loose an answer. "Natio. . .I remember that word because I thought it meant 'nation.' I speak some Spanish, but I don't read or write it well."

O'Shea made a movement so sudden it jarred Paul. O'Shea thumbed through his notebook. "It didn't say, *"Pestis ex Sanguis,"* did it?"

"Plague of blood?" Paul asked. "Where did you get that?"

O'Shea yanked his head out of his notebook. "Plague of blood? That's what pestis ex sanguis means?"

"Yeah, it's Latin."

"And how would you know that?" Collins demanded. "Have you heard the words 'plague of blood'? They mean something to you?"

"Well, yeah, sure." Paul shrugged, which also hurt like crazy. Maybe when Detective Collins had shoved at his sprained wrist, she hadn't been all that rough.

"We thought it might be some kind of rap group. We didn't pay much attention to it," O'Shea said. "We've just started investigating Juanita Lopez's disappearance. She's been missing almost a week, but she wasn't reported right away, then we had a forty-eight-hour waiting period. What does it mean?"

"The plague of blood," Paul said, slightly more alert. "The first plague God sent to Pharaoh when Moses asked him to 'let my people go'. . .that's it!" Paul sat up straight and his ribs punished him for it. He groaned and sank back onto his bed. *"Eamus Meus Natio Meare.'* It's not Spanish, it's Latin. I was so panicked when I got the phone call from Pravus, I didn't understand what it meant. I learned it in seminary. It means 'Let my people go.'"

"The message Pravus told you to give to the gang?" O'Shea asked.

Paul nodded.

"You said 'first plague,'" O'Shea mentioned warily. "Weren't there...?"

Paul spoke into the silence as he saw O'Shea and Collins remembering the Bible story. "Ten."

"The ten plagues of Egypt." Detective Collins's knuckles turned white on her notebook.

Paul arched his eyebrows. "You know the Bible, Detective Collins?"

"I know the Bible." Her jaw tightened until Paul thought it might crack. "I know it very well."

Paul tried to control the pounding of his heart as he thought, one by one, of the plagues. "Then you know we need to brace ourselves for a plague of blood."

CHAPTER FOUR

Blood. Everywhere. Blood and the smell of death.

"I s'pose he used the blood to get our attention." O'Shea crouched down and reached his pen out to lift the hand that lay on the edge of the fountain.

"It worked." Keren watched the victim bob faceup in a small cemented pond within walking distance of the Lighthouse Mission.

It was the kind of park where you stepped around the discarded condoms and kept a wary eye out for used needles. One of its efforts toward beauty was in this modest fountain, twenty feet around and sunk into the ground like a little pond with its simple joyous spray of water.

The fountain was obviously circulating the same water over and over, because blood spurted into the air in a hundred fiery arcs. The bright crimson rainbows bled down on Juanita Lopez, who lay in some kind of white dress floating on the water. From here they could see the dress was marked with drawings.

"The ME concurred with Morris on the Latin," Keren said. "She knew from med school that *sanguis* is "blood" and *pestis*, "plague." That covers the carving we found hung over Lopez's door. The new words"—Keren pointed at the victim—"if Morris is right, mean 'Let my people go.'"

O'Shea stared at the paintings on the woman's dress. "Still no sign of that wood carving Morris got?"

"Nope, and we've questioned everyone." Keren had been frantic to track down any clue, hoping there was still time to save Juanita. "We've had city crews on that bomb site ever since it happened."

"That mess is the only reason we aren't swarmed with press out here. They'd have a field day with this, regardless of its connection to the explosion. But when they connect the two, we won't be able to take a step without reporters dogging us."

"Let's try to keep them away from it if we can."

"I'll talk to the ME's office and the CS unit. They'll work with us, but headquarters is another story. They can't keep a secret, and the mayor's office leaks like a sieve."

"We can't keep this under wraps anyway." Keren looked at the body, the young Hispanic woman, her dress, long sleeves floating out like the wings of an angel, long skirt with no waist, just loose all the way to the gathered neck. "No way this is a onetime deal."

O'Shea pulled his notebook out of his breast pocket. "Did you interview the gang members who were in that house with Morris?"

"We've got detectives and two FBI agents from the local office finishing up questioning them in the hospital. It doesn't look like any of them know who set that explosive. Their enemies are all more the guns-and-knives type. I talked to a few before you called me over here." It wasn't even noon yet and she'd already put in almost a full day. "Now I know how a dentist feels." Keren pulled her blazer close. "I spent all my time pulling teeth. Not a cop-friendly crowd."

Keren wished she'd worn a coat instead of her gray wool blazer. It was a warm summer morning, but she couldn't stop shivering. "If you're checking for a Latin scholar, try a Catholic priest, an old one who used to do the Latin Mass."

O'Shea shook his head in disgust. "Yeah, we were slow on that carving above her door."

This was their case. O'Shea was the primary. Between the two of them they had nearly thirty years on the force, and both of them had missed it.

Keren reviewed the facts. "Juanita Lopez. Missing. Female. No sign of a struggle. No sign of anything wrong at her place, except for a few words carved into a sign, hung over her front door in the hallway. In that ratty building, no one was even sure if the sign was new. Coworkers reported her missing. No one had seen her for four days. Even so, we didn't list her until forty-eight hours after they called."

"A lot of them turn up on their own, Collins. Most of them. You know the drill." O'Shea watched her intently. She suspected it was to check her for any sign she was a wimp.

"And then that call to Morris and the explosion. And now this." Keren shook her head. They had come up with nothing. Keren had spent Wednesday at the site of the explosion; this morning she'd questioned witnesses, including Morris, who was due for release from the hospital tomorrow. Nothing. She'd hoped some of the gang members had seen something, but they were all clueless and uncooperative. Keren was afraid the trail was ice cold.

And now this morning, they'd gotten this call about a floater. The first cop on the scene hadn't been able to translate the Latin words painted on the dress, but he'd heard about the missing woman and her connection to this neighborhood. Reverend Morris's story had circulated through the department like wildfire.

At last the fountain quit bleeding. Someone had figured out how to turn off the recycling water. They both studied the obscene sight in front of them. Dr. Deidre Schaefer, the precinct's most experienced medical examiner, pulled up in the county van.

Keren and O'Shea stepped away to give the forensics team room to work.

Dr. Schaefer pointed at the body and spoke softly to a photographer, who clicked away casually, as if he were taking pictures at a wedding.

Keren watched the professional behavior of the ME's team. "In all this craziness let's don't forget routine procedure. We could miss something by putting all our faith in the Reverend."

"You mean see if she's got an abusive boyfriend or gambling debts?" O'Shea said with thinly veiled sarcasm.

"Yeah, right." Keren looked at the bobbing corpse. "Routine."

~

Keren washed her face, then she washed it again. She scoured her hands until they were red and raw. She was so obsessed with scrubbing, it took her awhile to figure out that she was trying to wash away the sight of Juanita Lopez floating in the crimson fountain. It didn't make her feel less violated to realize what she was doing. But it did make her shut off the water.

She wasn't just trying to wash this morning's crime out of her head, she was also trying to wash away the desperate evil behind Juanita Lopez's murder. This was a killer driven by his own personal demon in the truest sense of the word. Even after only one death, she was absolutely sure. Another thing she was sure of—there would be more.

When she came out of the bathroom, O'Shea was sitting behind her desk. Reverend Morris was there with him, looking as battered as ever, but a whole lot cleaner. He had on black sweatpants and a dark-red sweatshirt with a white lighthouse and the words, "Jesus is the light of the world" across his chest. His hair was dark and long enough to brush his collar. All his bandages were gone, including the sling. The three lines of stitches on his face made him look like a kinder, gentler Frankenstein.

She tamped down hard on her knee-jerk resentment.

"I've found our expert, Collins." Mick jabbed his pen at Morris. "He's agreed to work on the Latin stuff for us."

Keren stopped so suddenly she almost stumbled over her own feet. She'd planned on a white-haired priest. Paul Morris wasn't even close. She felt again a level of honor in the man and she remembered him whispering "pretty" while he held her filthy hair.

It wasn't enough to override her hostility. Her antipathy was audible when she said, "You don't speak Latin, Rev. You thought that sign was Spanish."

Morris must have caught her caustic attitude. That didn't exactly make him a genius.

He raised his eyebrows as if he was surprised, even hurt, by her tone.

"He only thought that for a minute," O'Shea said. "Once Latin occurred to him, he figured it out. He learned it in minister college."

Morris, apparently a stickler for honesty, what with his vocation and all, said, "They taught me after a fashion. I have a Latin/English dictionary and I know how to use Google. What I can't translate, I can find." His gaze narrowed on her face. He studied her for a while. "Have we met?"

Keren ignored his question. "I don't think that's good enough, Rev. We need someone who is an expert. We could buy our own Latin/English dictionary."

"I'm a little better than that," Morris said mildly.

"You were supposed to stay in the hospital another day." Keren whacked O'Shea on the arm and he got out of her chair. "You look like you can barely sit up."

Morris massaged his left wrist and continued to study her face as if he were sorting around inside his head for a WANTED poster on her.

"The hospital was overwhelmed." He spoke mildly, pastorishly. "I checked myself out to open up a bed."

That was generous, courageous, and self-sacrificing. It only made her more annoyed. And knowing that wasn't fair only made her *more* annoyed.

"Then you should be at home resting." Keren slouched back in her chair. "Your translating will slow us down."

O'Shea gave Keren a look that would have made her squirm a couple of years ago. Now it only irritated her.

"I'm going to make arrangements for a new cell phone, one we can sync with ours and we can more easily record and trace," O'Shea said to Morris. "It'll have the same number, in case this nut calls you again."

O'Shea turned to Keren. "He's in. We've got to figure out why he got the phone call. So, he might as well be our Latin expert while he's at it. You two work this out."

He headed for his own desk.

She gave him an angry look that was wasted on his retreating back, but the reverend caught it clearly enough.

"I came in here to help, and Detective O'Shea said you were looking for someone to examine the paintings on. . ." His voice faltered. ". . .on Juanita's dress." He cleared his throat. "She's been violated enough. You don't need to bring strangers in to help if you don't have to. There's no reason I shouldn't be the one."

Keren opened her mouth to flatly refuse his offer then clamped it shut. She knew she wasn't being reasonable, although the reverend hadn't shown that great a skill with Latin. But it was possible that these days no priest spoke Latin, either. Or precious little more than Morris. If they didn't use the reverend, they'd need to go find a college professor. This was much easier, and the only reason she wanted him gone was because of their past history. A history that he apparently hadn't cared enough about to remember.

She couldn't figure out a way to get rid of him. "Fine. I suppose you're better than nothing. The autopsy's scheduled for this afternoon. Go home. We'll call you when we're finished, so you can examine the photographs."

"I'll just sit in on the autopsy."

The idea galled her. "You will not! I wouldn't let you within a hundred feet of that girl! You couldn't handle it."

"Wanna bet?" Something in his tone made the heels Keren was digging in slip a little. She studied his eyes. They'd gone a flat blue, as cold and dead as the nails in a coffin. She couldn't believe what a difference it made in him. It changed him into the cop who had run over her. And it reminded her of how much she disliked him. "I know you used to be a cop. But this still isn't where we need your help."

He gave her an extended look that seemed to worm right into her brain. "You knew I was a cop?"

"Yeah, I'm a cop myself," Keren said dryly. "I'm forever detecting."

"So what's your problem? You know I can help you with this."

The arrogance she remembered so well was right there. She longed to slap him down. "No problem, Rev. And you won't slow us down, because I won't let you."

His eyes narrowed, but he didn't respond.

"So you went from a cop to a reverend? That's quite a transition."

"Is it? It seemed natural enough to me at the time." He quit talking and studied her until she felt like a bug under a microscope.

He smiled in a way that told her he was deliberately trying to make her squirm.

"You know, Rev, it's not very Christian to enjoy making me feel uncomfortable."

"And you're such an authority on being Christian?"

Somehow it hurt that he hadn't sensed it in her. She wondered if that might be because she'd been relentlessly rude to him ever since they'd met. "Oh yes. Born and raised. I have. . ."

She almost told him about her gift. She was shocked at how close she'd come to blurting out the grim message she'd gotten from the murder scene. She'd learned very young never to talk about it. It had created too many awful situations when she'd seen demonic work in the oddest places. And it had ruined a relationship that she'd thought was ordained by God. She'd done some fast growing up and never mentioned her gift again. If the reverend understood, he'd be the first one who did.

She wondered why she'd come so close to telling him. Honestly, the man probably had his parishioners confessing things to him right and left.

"You have. . . ?" he prompted.

Keren couldn't imagine what in the world to say. The truth was not an option, and she had no intention of lying. The only thing she could think of was to snarl at him some more. A plan which appealed to her.

"And by the way, you can't be born a Christian. We all come into this world needing to make the choice for ourselves."

"I know that." A nice theological debate would get his mind off her slip of the tongue.

O'Shea came trotting up.

She took one look at his face and forgot all about her gift and her need to confess it. "What?"

"We've just had another missing person reported."

Keren knew what he was going to say next. She prayed she was wrong.

She wasn't.

"There's a carving over the door."

CHAPTER FIVE

*Aaron stretched out his hand over the waters of Egypt,
and the frogs came up and covered the land.*

This little carving was his gift to the world, not that the world deserved it. Uncultured, uneducated, unwashed, and completely unable to appreciate him. But they'd see his greatness. He dawdled and decorated the polished oak with his chisel.

EAMUS.

And enjoyed the work of his hand. The way she cowered and cried inspired him to greater heights.

MEUS.

He'd found new restraints that held her better. He talked as he worked, trying to make her understand the honor he was bestowing on her.

NATIO.

He'd brushed her hair and read to her from Mother's Bible. He even went so far as to show her the artwork he'd carved on his own body.

MEARE.

Still, like Pharaoh, she didn't see reason. Pravus held the power of life and death. Like God. No he wasn't *like* God, he *was* God. And this sinner had been given all the chances he was going to give her.

The beast within urged him onward to the second plague.

⟵

"You can come up to the apartment door, Rev, but you can't come inside. We can't let you touch—"

"I know the drill, Detective Collins." He breathed out anger and breathed in God. It was his own Christian version of counting to ten. He couldn't quite figure out how he'd gotten on the pretty detective's bad side, but he'd managed it—in spades.

"Uh, sorry, Rev. I keep forgetting you were on the force."

Paul had the distinct impression that Detective Collins never forgot a thing.

"Good. I don't want to carry the mantle of 'cop' around with me anymore."

She shoved at her hair as if she were swatting away a gnat. He remembered the wild tangles from his hospital stay. He towered over her as they walked into the apartment building. He was six one. He glanced at her with experienced cop eyes. She was five six, all lean muscle and coiled energy, hidden under the kind of cheap suit a cop could afford. She started up the outside steps of the apartment building at a fast clip. Paul tried to keep up and it hurt like blazes.

He was trying to like her, but his ribs were her sworn enemy. "I have better luck helping the people at the mission if they don't sense the badge."

She entered the building and started up the stairs to the missing woman's apartment. "Should you have shed the sling and collar so quickly? You look lousy. You'll probably end up back in the hospital."

Paul didn't answer her. He hadn't had time to breathe all his anger out yet. For him to do that, she would have to shut up and give him a little more time. He was tempted to ask her to do just that.

The apartment building they were in was just outside the neighborhood Paul served. Shabby, but hanging on to respectability by a thread. Paul tried to trot up the steps behind her, but every time he jostled his ribs, his chest hurt like a heart attack. He settled for watching her disappear around the corner of the stairs. Then the Stay Puft Marshmallow Man, O'Shea, passed him.

Paul trudged on, left in the dust of real cops. "Humility is the name of the game, isn't it, Lord?"

O'Shea turned around and looked at him. Detective Collins leaned over the railing above and stared down.

He looked back and forth between them. "Did I say that out loud?"

O'Shea gave him a disgusted look. Collins rolled her eyes. They exchanged a look, shook their heads, and started moving again. By the time he made his destination, the fifth floor, they had disappeared inside a room. The hallway was dismal—the paint old, the carpet stained. But there was no trash strewed around. The doors were all on their hinges. Only one stood open. Paul smelled mold and decades of cigarette smoke, but there were no bullet holes to be seen.

There was enough noise coming from the apartment to clue Paul in that they weren't the first ones there. He very carefully stayed out. Over the door he read, *Pestis Ex Rana*, carved in a beautiful script. Paul examined it, as he hadn't had time to examine the carving he'd been given.

The words were etched into a wooden sign the same size and color as the one Paul had received. Pravus could have hung it there in a matter of seconds.

Pestis ex rana. "Plague of frogs." Paul didn't know how Pravus intended to harm anyone using frogs. But, on the other hand, Juanita hadn't drowned in that ghastly pool of blood. Pravus had killed her before he'd thrown her in the water. Frogs didn't matter any more than the blood.

After he studied the carving, he stayed outside as bossy Detective Collins had ordered, but he began *looking* inside, snooping for all he was worth. There was a collection of pictures on a wall just inside the door.

"No!" He stumbled and would have fallen if he hadn't hit the wall across from the open door. Detective Collins was at his side before the pain in his chest could knock him down.

"What is it? Are you hurt?" He noticed she reached for the sprained wrist, checked her movements, and reached for the other arm. "You need to go back to the hospital."

She brushed his hair off his forehead. "I should never have let you come!" She leaned close. She looked deeply into his eyes.

He looked back. He hadn't expected this kindness. He hadn't expected the warmth in her mysterious blue-gray eyes. He hadn't—

She blinded him with a high-powered flashlight. "You probably still have a concussion."

He flinched away from the light and gasped from the pain flinching caused.

"I told you this was a bad idea." She talked to him like he was a slightly backward second grader. "Now we're wasting time with you when we should be—"

"Get that light out of my eyes," he cut her off. "I'm not sick." He sounded like a cop and fought to control it. "It's the pictures. The pictures in the hallway."

She snapped her head around, immediately forgetting him. "Those pictures hanging on the wall?" She dragged him along right into the apartment, forgetting her stern warnings to stay out of her crime scene.

"I know the woman in those pictures."

There were several of them, including group snapshots taken in casual settings, framed and hung with care, around a glowing picture of an ocean sunset with "Make a Joyful Noise All the Earth" across the bottom.

"Which woman?"

Paul reached up and, without touching the picture, pointed to LaToya. A young black woman with hope and humor shining out of her dark eyes. "Her. LaToya. LaToya Jordan, she's someone who spent a lot of time at the mission."

"Are you telling me..." Detective Collins broke off. When she spoke again Paul felt like her rigid jaw was grinding her words into dust. "...that you know both of the victims?"

Paul nodded. He had to tear his eyes away from LaToya's picture. He knew what was in store for her. The shock passed and he began panicking deep inside, shaking in his gut. "No, dear God. Not LaToya. Don't, please don't let this be happening to her."

Detective Collins wrenched him around to face her. "You know what this means, don't you, Rev?"

He looked into her tough cop eyes and wanted to drop to his knees and beg her and the other policemen here to tear Chicago apart looking for LaToya. "Yes, of course I know. It means someone I care about is right this minute living through a nightmare."

"No," Detective Collins snapped at him. She shook his arm. "Get ahold of yourself and think. Use your brain for a change. That's not what it means."

"Of course it is. You saw the carving above the door. LaToya didn't leave of her own volition." Paul pointed to the hallway.

"She's out there somewhere. She's—"

"What it means," Collins interrupted, "is that these murders aren't about the women."

"What kind of crazy thing is that to say? Two women are—"

"Remember who you used to be. Try for just one second to think like a cop. These murders aren't about the women, they're about you."

Paul wheeled away from her cold eyes and her heartless truth. He stared at LaToya in horror. Seconds ticked by as the possibility cut its way into his heart. Finally, he spoke to the picture in a whisper, "LaToya, I'm so sorry. This is my fault."

"We've got to interview you more thoroughly. We've got to hunt in your life for enemies. You deal with dangerous people at the mission."

"They're not dangerous. We've never had trouble—"

"Not dangerous, like Carlo, the gang member whose building you ran into just before it exploded?" she cut in. "He's got a rap sheet as long as your arm. If he wasn't a juvie, he'd be doing life."

"No, I'm not talking about Carlo. I mean—"

"We're not going to discuss this here. We'll take you downtown and start talking about people who might be crazy enough to want to hurt you." Detective Collins caught his arm.

Paul pulled away. "I'll do whatever you need to do, but what about LaToya? Every man and woman who wastes time talking to me isn't out hunting for her."

"Oh, we'll be hunting for her, all right," she said grimly. "We'll just be hunting inside your head."

She grabbed Paul's arm again and hauled him out of the apartment. He went along peacefully, feeling like he was being arrested but too upset about LaToya to care. She was right. Detective Collins had it figured out exactly right.

Juanita and LaToya had been killed because someone hated him.

It was true.

⤳

"It's a lie!"

After two hours of badgering in the interrogation room, Paul had it figured out, and he told Detective Collins that for the tenth time. "These murders aren't about me."

"You know they are." Detective Collins had her heels dug in.

Paul sat with his hands clenched together on the table in front of him. It was all he could do to keep from leaping over the table and shaking some sense into the pretty little tyrant.

"Just because they're both from my neighborhood, and I knew them both, doesn't mean this is about me. You're wasting valuable time. If you won't go out and hunt for her, at least let me."

"Rev, do you really think O'Shea and I are the only ones working this case?" she stormed.

"I know how it is when a crime gets committed on the South Side. It's not a priority."

"This one is. We've got forensics working on the pond, both women's homes, and the site of the explosion."

"That fountain." Paul's stomach twisted and he'd only seen the pictures. "He made a fountain flow with blood."

"Blood meal. It's a garden fertilizer. Available in every store that sells potting soil. All it really did was dye the water red. Just another thing we've found out while you say we're doing nothing." Detective Collins placed her hands flat on the table and leaned forward. "The ME is personally doing all the prelims for the autopsy. The forensics lab has pushed this case ahead of everything else. The FBI is running all the results we've got through their computer looking for similar crimes. We're tracking down the delivery man who brought that package to you. We've got people going through your records at the mission—"

"I shouldn't have let you do that," Paul interjected. "I should at least be there. Those records are—"

"—and hunting through your old case files from your cop days." She kept talking as if he were a buzzing insect. "We've got one poor schmuck going to every art supply and hardware store in the city, trying to identify the exact type of cutting tool Pravus used to make his signs. We're tracking down the name. Someone thought *Pravus* sounded Middle Eastern. I told them it was Latin, but still we're trying to rule out any terrorism. We're digging through the rubble of that building, tracking down the source of every incoming call on your cell. We're questioning everyone who might know someone you drove completely crazy!"

Paul inhaled sharply. Somewhere along the line, he'd done something to someone that had resulted in this. He scrubbed his face with his right hand, still coddling his left. He wanted to wash reality away. "I can't bear to think about it."

Keren caught his arm, his good arm, and pulled it away from his face. "Well, you're going to have to think about it! I don't have time to baby you while you—"

"Back off, Keren," O'Shea growled from where he leaned, with his arms crossed, against the wall off to Paul's left. "He's a witness, not a suspect." He'd mostly observed, throwing in a question now and then. Paul got a sense the two of them were doing a routine with him that they'd performed a hundred times before. But Detective Collins was losing her cool. That wasn't part of the routine.

She let go of his arm. After a few moments of obvious effort, she said, "Sorry, that was out of line."

"No, I'm sorry," Paul said through a clenched jaw. "I know you're trying to find a connection between me and this lunatic. But I've thought it over and we're on the wrong track. Yes, I know both of them, but lots of people know both of them. They were from the neighborhood. This guy could have come from here and been victimized by someone in this area."

"Pravus phoned *you*, Rev. He knew *you* and cared enough to track down *your* cell phone number and mail *you* that sign."

"But don't you see, he could have done all that without it being personal. I'm the logical one in that neighborhood. My cell phone number is no secret. I've got it posted on the bulletin board at the mission. He kept saying Juanita was evil. He said, 'I'll tell you where to find this harlot.' He might see me as someone who would join his twisted fight against all the ills around the Lighthouse Mission."

"Listen, Rev, you can speculate all—"

"Will you quit calling me Rev?" Paul lunged to his feet. His ribs punished his chest. His temper pounded in his wounded forehead. He spun away from the mouthy cop who wouldn't quit.

He needed to spend some quiet time in prayer. He knew he was fraying badly around the edges. His temper was hot, his impatience was boiling over. All his old cop instincts were fighting to emerge, and they were the worst part of himself. But even if he could get away from this nagging woman, he'd still dash around looking for LaToya instead of kneeling before his Savior, seeking peace.

Hang on. Don't lose it. Don't lose it.

Collins slammed a fist on the table. "We don't have time to argue about your *title*."

Paul lost it.

He whirled around to take her apart. She was fuming. Her

hands were clenched until her knuckles turned white.

"Why can't you cooperate?" she snapped. "Don't you care if we get this guy?"

"Not care?" Paul reached for her and grabbed her wrist with his good hand. He dragged her up out of her chair until they were nose to nose, with only the table keeping them apart. "How *dare* you say I don't care?"

She jerked against his hold. "Get your hands off—"

"All right." O'Shea slapped his hands on the table between them so hard he shoved the table a few inches and broke Paul's grip on the little shrew.

O'Shea's thunderous outburst brought dead silence to the room. "We're going to take a break," he said through clenched teeth. "We're not getting anywhere with you two snarling at each other."

"Are you nuts?" Collins asked. "We don't have time to—"

"Quiet!" O'Shea cut her off. His voice echoed against all four shabby walls.

"But—"

O'Shea jabbed a fat finger right at her nose. "I mean it, Keren. You're out of here if you say one more word before I declare this break over. I'll go to the captain and have you reassigned. You know I can do it. I'm going to the overpriced cafe next door and get some coffee. I'll meet you outside and we'll take a break and sit in the park across the street."

Anxiety pressed on Paul until he thought he might suffocate. "We're not wasting one second sitting in a park."

"You"—it was Paul's turn to get jabbed at—"are going to shut up right now."

Five years ago he wouldn't have backed down. He'd have ripped this blowhard's finger off and shoved it down his throat.

But he was a changed man. He didn't feel real changed right at this moment, but he remembered what he was supposed to act like and let O'Shea keep his finger.

"Let's get out of here. I'll buy us each a six-dollar cup of coffee and we can think about highway robbery instead of this case."

Paul looked across at Collins. She shrugged and opened her mouth—Paul thought to agree with him for a change, that they should keep working. O'Shea turned his blazing temper on her with a single look.

With an exasperated growl, she threw her hands wide and led the way out of the police station.

⟿

Paul leaned back on the park bench and drank the most outrageous cup of coffee he'd ever had. Caramel, mocha, cappuccino, latte, espresso, whatever.

Maybe all those things. The cup was bigger than his head. His coffee usually ran to a brew so strong it could open the eyes of a man hungover for the thousandth morning in a row, and so hot it could warm the frostbitten toes of a woman who had cardboard in her shoes on a subzero Chicago morning. That coffee was made in a one-hundred-cup coffeepot that burned along all day.

This coffee had whipped cream and chopped nuts on top. He sat drinking it while a monster acted out a plague on his friends.

They chatted idly about the green grass and the blue sky. Every time they got on the subject of the horror they were dealing with, O'Shea would growl and they'd change the subject.

Finally, O'Shea glanced at his wristwatch. "We've been here ten minutes. I'm going in. Your new cell phone should have been delivered by now. I'll round it up. You two are staying for another five. I want you to figure out why you've been snapping and snarling at each other from the minute we started working today. You both want this case solved. You both know you need to cooperate to get it done. If I didn't know better, I'd think there was something personal between you."

"Personal? Me and Rev? We just—"

"Will you quit calling me Rev? Why don't you—"

"I promise I'll lock you both in the lineup room if you don't work this out." O'Shea heaved himself to his feet. "We've got a murder to solve, and if I have to do it myself"—he turned on them—"because you two kids never learned how to work and play well with others—"

His voice rose to a shout. "There's gonna be payback for both of you." Then a roar. "That you'll still be stinging from, years from now." He stormed off in a huff.

The two of them stared after O'Shea in shock. Then they looked at each other.

"Did he just threaten to spank us?" Paul asked.

Keren looked at her coffee. Paul noticed she was fighting a grin. "Maybe. And that bit about the lineup sounds a little like being sent to our rooms."

"And this is definitely a time-out." Paul swirled his mocha-shmocha-cappa whatever, trying to keep the concoction mixed up until he was done drinking it and to give himself something to do besides talk to Keren.

Finally, she moved. He glanced up and saw she had her hand extended toward him. "Hi, my name is Keren Collins. It's nice to meet you. Call me Keren."

Paul shook his head then took her hand. "My name is Paul."

"Oh I'm sorry, I heard your name was Rev. Where did I get a silly idea like that?"

"Can't imagine. So. . .truce?"

Keren nodded. Then she said in a hesitant voice, "I know you're a good man, Rev. . .I mean Paul." She arched an eyebrow at him. "*Rev* really suits you."

"Paul or nothing." Paul realized he was still holding her hand and dropped it. He rubbed his hand on his pant leg to cool it off.

"I'm sorry I've been riding you so hard." Keren glanced up at him. "I can't even blame this case exactly. I mean, it is the case but. . ." She shrugged.

Paul saw her clench her teeth to keep from saying something. He wondered what it could be.

"O'Shea says I have good cop instincts, and all my instincts tell me we're dealing with an evil that is beyond. . ." Keren fell silent again.

Paul had been trained in counseling. He shouldn't put words in her mouth, but he was so sure of what she was going to say he had to do it. "An evil beyond what any human is capable of."

"Without help." Keren nodded.

"Do you believe in the devil, Keren?" Paul was amazed how many people didn't, even when they were faced with the evidence of him every day.

"You bet I do." She surprised him. "All that is wrong with this world isn't just the evil in people's hearts. I believe in the rebellion in heaven. I know Satan has been cast out, and now he and his minions walk among us. I know that's not the accepted idea these days. Even a lot of Christians don't believe in him."

"I've seen too many people lured away while I'm trying to lead them to God." Paul thought of Juanita and LaToya, two girls who hadn't been lured away. He prayed now for LaToya's safety and thought of Juanita, who was with the Lord, beyond earthly pain, beyond the need of any prayers.

"And I've felt Satan in myself, warring with God." Keren took a sip of her coffee. "Trying to infect me with greed and jealousy and anger."

"Oh, c'mon, when have you ever been angry?" Paul asked dryly.

Keren looked up and smiled. "I'll take the Fifth on that. . . Paul."

"Now that didn't hurt, did it?"

" 'Bout killed me." Keren stared into her cup for a long minute, then she said, "Do you know the verse that says Satan will be set loose on the earth?"

Paul quoted, " 'When the thousand years are over, Satan will be released from his prison and will go out to deceive the nations in the four corners of the earth.' It's from Revelation."

"I wonder sometimes if we're not living in that time," Keren said. "I wonder if Satan hasn't been released from his prison."

"Ask the people in Africa dying of AIDS, or the people in North Korea who are starving to death, or the people in Saudi Arabia who are being put to death for becoming Christians, if they think Satan isn't loose," Paul said.

"You may not need to go so far afield," Keren said. "How about we ask LaToya?"

"You really are a believer, aren't you?" Paul felt the assurance in his heart even before she answered. She wasn't the kind of Christian he was used to. She was too cold, too busy, too grouchy. Of course, they'd met under nasty circumstances. He hadn't exactly been on his best behavior, either.

"I really am." She stood. "I'll get rid of the cups, then we'll go see if our 'time-out' is over and Mick'll let us quit sitting in the corner and get back to work."

Paul wasn't perfectly satisfied with their new harmony. He knew there was something else going on. Her jaw never really relaxed. Her piercing eyes, so pale they were breathtaking, watched him until he thought she could have performed laser surgery with them. But she wasn't attacking him anymore, so he didn't push.

Paul handed her his empty cup. Her hand closed over his. He was bemused by the strength and softness of her hand. He glanced up and their eyes caught. A soft breeze blew one of those corkscrew curls across her gently sculpted cheekbone. She was so extraordinarily pretty and delicate. He towered over her, but her size didn't diminish her strength. Her white teeth bit nervously into her bottom lip. Her full lips held his attention.

They both dropped the cup at the same time. Paul jumped back. He told himself it was to avoid getting splashed with the nonexistent contents of his empty cup. He looked at Keren again, unable to stop himself. She was extremely busy picking up the cup. Silently, they walked back into the station house together. Paul weighed the pros and cons of going back to open warfare.

For the first time in the history of the world, war sounded like the most peaceful option.

CHAPTER SIX

She made peace with Paul and immediately began longing for a return to war. Or at least a demilitarized zone—that would keep him far away from her.

After that long look and the electric heat of his hand on hers, she'd have gone right back to fighting if O'Shea hadn't been keeping such a close eye on them to see if the cease-fire was real or phony. She was far more comfortable with her hostility than with the attraction. She'd learned in a terribly hard school to accept her lonely life. And she'd been content.

And now Paul had touched her and—as if that electricity had started a motor—suddenly she was alive and awake in a way she hadn't been in years. Her solitary life wasn't enough.

But solitary was safe. She liked safe.

"I got the hard copies of Detective Morris's case files." An eager young secretary rolled a cart in front of her, bearing the fruit of ten years of Paul's workaholic ambition. She gave Paul a completely unnecessarily friendly smile and said only to him, "Let me know if you need anything else."

Unable to stop herself from rolling her eyes, Keren turned to the mountain of paperwork.

He'd been a patrolman for four years, a detective for six. With a suppressed groan and grudging respect, she could see he'd been more prolific than a wheat field full of bunnies.

"Start with the computer. We can thin this down." O'Shea

nodded at Keren. She took over the cyber war portion of this mess.

Before they'd gotten a good start the phone on O'Shea's desk rang. After a few quick words he hung up. "The medical examiner is ready to autopsy our vic. Let's go."

Paul rose from his seat. "Can't you call her Juanita?"

"No, we can't," Keren said, marching out of the room. Paul caught up to her and opened his mouth, probably to nag, as he dogged her.

For once O'Shea took her side, cutting him off. "We can't, and you know why. It's our job to identify with the *criminal*, get inside *his* head. If we start thinking about Juanita, then we're inside the *victim's* head. We're not going to be able to solve this crime."

"But it's so—"

"Enough, Paul." O'Shea unrolled his shirtsleeves and tugged on his suit coat as they jogged down the stairs toward the parking garage. "You know how it goes. Especially on a case like this, where the facts are so nasty. We can't dwell on Juanita or get involved in sympathy. If we do, we can't function."

"I was a cop. I know how you rationalize your detachment. But from the outside looking in, you guys seem as cold blooded as the bad guys."

"Well, we're not," Keren snapped as she jerked her car door open. "Don't make this harder than it is. Detach as best you can, or you'll be useless to us."

Paul shoved his hands in his pockets and rode in silence in the backseat of Keren's car to the coroner's office.

As they pulled into the lot by the forensic lab, Keren caught his eye in the rearview mirror. "You don't have to do this."

He looked back with a sad kind of stubbornness. "Juanita died very likely because of an enemy of mine. I'm not going to protect myself by avoiding this."

Keren tried one last time. "But why watch, Paul? Watching won't make her any less dead. Any chance you have of remembering the vic. . .Juanita, when she was happy and whole, will be destroyed by witnessing her autopsy. You know how they are."

"Yes, I know. Believe me I know." He paused and looked at the Polaroid of Juanita that he must have lifted from the case file. It was the one Pravus had sent that Paul had left behind at the mission. He shouldn't have it, but Keren didn't say anything.

"This picture has burned itself into my memory. Seeing the autopsy won't make it worse. Nothing can make it worse."

"Don't be so sure of that," Keren warned.

〜〉

It was so much worse, Paul didn't even think of trying to sleep.

He went into the mission and found the usual crowd drinking coffee. There were several men sleeping in their chairs, dressed in clothes they'd found in the mission store. It was warm out so most of them wouldn't stay here overnight. They were mostly alcoholics, but too many of them drank to quiet the tormenting voices in their heads. Bipolar, schizophrenic, crazy, whatever the currently popular word was for mental illness. They came in for supper, some would hang around for a while, then they'd go back on the streets. But a few stayed here, and a few had let Paul help them find an apartment. And a few, like LaToya and Juanita, had gotten their lives in order and were on their own.

Paul tried to reach all of them, get them help, get them off the street, but mostly he just cared for them, made sure they had food and warm clothes. A reasonably clean bed on winter nights. He saw himself as a servant.

Turning to the small group that sat at a table, talking quietly, Paul saw the kind of thing that kept him going. Made him believe he was doing what God called him to do.

Murray, Buddy, Louie, five others. These men and a group of women who sat at another table made it all worth it. Rosita was one of them. She waved and gave him a smile.

Paul said hello to everyone then grabbed a cup of coffee and sat down by the men.

"How are you, Pastor P?" Buddy was bipolar, near as Paul could tell. He had a beard, weathered face, and gray hair. He had moved into a low-rent apartment just recently, since his meds had started taking effect and he was thinking more clearly. But he still came in for meals and sometimes to help out. He complained about the way the medication made him feel, but he'd been a long way down in the gutter, and at least for now, he seemed to want to stay out of it.

"I feel like a building fell on me." These men had all gone through plenty, and they liked hearing Paul had his own struggles. And gossip moved through this community like any other, so they knew what had happened to Juanita, how it connected to the explosion in Carlo's building, and Paul's part in it.

Murray nodded. "Find anything out?"

All eight men focused on Paul, and he weighed his words. He wasn't going to talk about the autopsy. That might be enough to send all of them into a tailspin. Telling the truth didn't mean telling everything he knew.

"The police want to keep working with me. I'm sorry I was gone the last couple of days. Looks like you got the meals served and everything cleaned up without me. I'm sorry to not be here to help."

"We managed." Murray had a full beard, black salted with

gray, that he hadn't trimmed in a decade. He was wire thin, full of barely controlled energy. He'd found a talent for playing the guitar and helped with church services and had good managerial skills. When Paul was gone, Murray took over, even preaching a sermon now and then. He had just found an apartment away from the mission, though he still came in daily to work.

"Murray can sing, but his idea of preaching a sermon is to yell at all of us that we're going to burn if we don't change our ways." Louie had just gotten out of prison after a five-year stretch and worked at the mission as part of his community service. The other men laughed softly. Murray was fervent for the Lord, no doubt about it.

"I'd like a turn preachin', Pastor," Louie added. "I'd especially like a turn passing the collection plate."

More laughter. There was no collection plate at the Light-house Mission. No one had a dime to spare. Louie ran a hand over his thinning dark hair and slouched in his chair. He was able bodied and did his share of the work and a little more, but he showed no interest in finding a job outside the mission. He'd be gone as soon as he'd put in his time here. Paul hoped he'd reached him for the Lord. Louie said all the right words, but Paul couldn't tell if the young man had taken salvation to heart.

Paul knew Murray could talk fire and brimstone, but he suspected Louie was reacting more to his own sense of guilt than to what Murray said. Louie had routine drug tests, and if he flunked one, he'd be back in prison immediately. So far, as near as Paul could tell, the young man was staying sober.

"Price of sitting through a meal," Murray said. His approach might well be the best one. Paul leaned toward love and mercy in his sermons.

The men spent a few minutes good-naturedly teasing each

other. Paul let their talk draw him out of the horror of sitting in on that autopsy. He should never have done it. He'd survived it by switching into cop mode. Now he was having trouble pulling out of it, and he let these men, his friends, his brothers in Christ, bring him back to himself. This day had reminded Paul of all the selfishness of the life he'd left behind. He settled back into his faith and rediscovered his servant nature while these men updated him on the day. By the time he finished his coffee, he was Pastor P again, and he thought he was exhausted enough to be able to sleep.

"The day's catching up to me. I've got to get to bed." The thought of walking up four flights was almost more than he could stand, but the elevator wasn't reliable, and he had no wish to spend an hour or two stuck between floors.

They told him good night. He walked away from the only friends he had—men who, if they succeeded in the mission, went away and if they failed, went away. As he climbed he thought of that moment when he'd touched Keren while handing over his coffee cup.

That touch made him realize that he was terribly lonely.

He showered and donned a clean pair of sweatpants and another Lighthouse T-shirt then sank into his bed, feeling sleep claim him as he lay his head on the pillow.

The nightmare bloomed instantly to life, jerking him awake. The day played through his head. He tossed and turned half the night, with the autopsy grinding its way into every cell in his brain. When he dozed off, he had nightmares about what LaToya might be going through right now.

It was almost merciful when he was awakened by pounding. He staggered out of his bedroom to answer his door, more exhausted than when he'd gone to bed.

He yanked the door open and saw Keren and O'Shea. Two other men stood in the hallway behind them. His stomach twisted. "You found LaToya."

Keren shook her head and the lopsided bun she always wore bobbed dangerously on her head. She held up a sheet of paper from her notebook. It said, "Shut up."

She jerked her head toward the door. He was obviously expected to follow.

Paul's living quarters shared this floor with the mission offices. She didn't speak, just waved her hand at him to follow. O'Shea stayed behind with the other policemen and Paul didn't even ask why. It didn't fit with the "Shut up" sign.

They jogged down the narrow flights of stairs, past the men's shelter on the third floor, past his newest project, a teen center on the second floor. The eating area, which also doubled as the church, was on the ground floor. The jog felt like someone was beating on his chest with a baseball bat instead of stabbing him with a knife. Sad to say, it was a big improvement.

There was a women's shelter in the basement for a few of their special residents. That area was carefully locked away from the men. Even Paul wasn't allowed down there. The women residents had suffered so much at the hands of men that many of them were incapable of relating to them in any healthy way, even with their minister. In order to make them feel safe enough to trust the Lighthouse Mission, their separation from men had to be absolute. They even had a separate dining room and their own church services led by nuns from the nearby Catholic church. Paul knew he should really move the women's facility to another building. Rosita had taken over a lot of that part of the mission, along with other women volunteers.

Paul was already breathing hard when he and Keren reached

the ground floor. Keren went straight outside and he followed, hurrying to catch up. With every step, he was reminded of the beating he'd taken in the explosion. He caught her arm before she could lead him on a 10K power walk.

"Hey." He dragged her to a stop. "Have mercy, Keren. I'm about all in. Unless we need to go farther for whatever it is you want."

Keren's black pantsuit was rumpled. Her white blouse was untucked. Her hair was making a break for it. "Sorry, even with the stitches, I forget you're hurt. It's been a mean few days for you, hasn't it?"

"It's okay, the walk was just getting to me after the stairs." Paul resisted holding on to his aching ribs. "What made you come charging in on me this morning?"

"O'Shea and I decided the guy knew too much about you. How'd he pick Juanita and LaToya to hurt? He obviously knows you well enough to know them. It figures he's been watching you. We wondered just how closely. O'Shea's checking for listening devices."

Paul's breathing slowed until he decided he was going to live. "This is an age where mothers plant bugs and hide cameras so they can monitor their babysitters."

"That's right, so bugs and miniature cameras are easy to buy and install. The bugs can be tucked into couch cushions, slipped under a loose flap of wallpaper, hidden inside electrical appliances, air ducts—even sewn into the lining of clothing."

Paul looked down at the sweatpants he'd slept in and his white T-shirt with the mission logo. "You think they could be in these clothes?"

"Do you just have one outfit you wear day and night?" Keren studied his clothes.

Paul knew it looked a lot like the one he'd worn yesterday. "No, I have several."

"That are all the same?" A smile quirked Keren's lips. "Although your sweatpants yesterday were black and these are dark gray. Sorry, I didn't notice."

Considering the situation, Paul was real glad she was amused. "I don't know where anyone could hide a bug in my clothes."

"A bug or a tracking device." All the amusement faded from her expression. "We're checking everything."

"Tracking device?"

"Well, you said he told you he was watching then sent you running. And he obviously knew when you got to the house, because he blew it up."

Paul looked up at the buildings that surrounded him. "He could be renting one of a thousand apartments right here. I just figured he meant he'd be able to see me part of the time. That I wouldn't know when he was there and when not."

"We'll be thorough." With a confident jerk of her chin, Keren said, "If there's a listening or tracking device anywhere, including in your clothes, we'll find it."

"It never occurred to me he might be tracing me electronically. I guess I've succeeded in my goal to stop thinking like a cop." Paul grimaced. "Which is good. I did a lot of damage when I was on the force."

"I saw your arrest record, your caseload, your solve rate, and your commendations." Keren dragged her hair tie out and twisted her escaping corkscrew curls tight then anchored it again, all with such automatic movements she didn't seem aware of it. "You did a lot of good."

"Yeah, I was a good cop. A great cop. I took every ounce of credit that was due me, and I grabbed a bunch I didn't deserve.

And while I was so busy being a great cop, my wife kicked me out of the house. It was the second time we'd been separated because I spent all my time working, and when I was home, I took all my anger out on her."

"Are you divorced? You mentioned a wife yesterday, but it's pretty obvious she isn't living in that apartment with you."

"My wife and my only daughter were killed just before I quit the force."

"Oh, Paul." Her voice softened. "I'm sorry. I didn't know. We've been going over your cases, but I haven't done any checking into your personal background yet."

Paul thought she sounded more than sorry. She sounded like she felt guilty about something. Just another mystery surrounding Keren's attitude toward him. "My daughter, Hannah, was four. Trish and I were separated. She accused me of having an affair, but it wasn't true. The cheating I did was with work. That was my first priority. I was supposed to be with them that night at a preschool program. I was hoping it would be the first step to a reconciliation." Paul paused for a long time. "Anyway, a case blew up in my face. You know, life and death. Vitally important."

"I know," Keren said.

"They got to the program without me. Heaven knows Trish had learned to do everything without me. On their way home, her car broke down; her cell phone must have been dead. They were walking along a deserted stretch of highway when they were killed. The man who hit them, he called the ambulance. He did more for them than I did." Paul didn't see any reason to spare himself from the hard truth. "I was awful to him in the hospital. Months later, after I'd become a Christian, I went looking for him, to apologize. But he was dead. I couldn't ask him to forgive me any more than I could ask Trish and my little Hannah." Keren snagged his arm and led him on down the cracked sidewalk in one of the toughest neighborhoods in Chicago. She moved at a pace Paul could handle.

"I spent the night after the funeral sitting alone in my empty house, staring at my .38."

Keren gasped and held his arm tighter.

"I thought about pulling the trigger," Paul said. He fell silent. At last he said, "It was the most awful feeling of hopelessness. The guilt, the anger. I had so many regrets. I was a pathetic excuse for a human being at that time in my life. In the depths of the darkest night of my life, I asked God why a jerk like me deserved to live."

Paul looked over at Keren and smiled. "And He answered me, Keren. Not out loud, but clearly, from inside myself. It was unmistakable. It was the purest, most beautiful moment of my life." He ran his hands through his hair.

"It was so clear and strong that it always anchors me. God told me that if I didn't want the life He'd given me, then give it away. Give it to someone who needed it. The call God gave me to the ministry was a miracle. Jesus Christ saved my soul that night along with my life. I went to Bible college and ended up being led by God to quit after a couple of years. The old man who'd run the Lighthouse Mission died and it was going to close. Pastor Bob. There were some shoes that were hard to fill." Paul stopped and looked back at the old building.

"I really believe I've done some good here. I've found peace and, most of the time, I forgive myself for who I used to be."

Paul saw some of Keren's antagonism ebb away.

"I know how tough it is to be a cop and have a home life at the same time," she said.

"But you're a Christian, Keren. I wasn't when I got married. If you married another Christian and the two of you made sincere vows before God, you'd keep those vows. You wouldn't end up with a broken home."

"I've seen it happen too many times. God needs good people battling evil the same as He needs good people doing mission work. I thought at first I could have it all. I was wrong." She quirked a smile. "It's been surprisingly easy to avoid. Not that many guys want a woman who can beat them up."

Paul smiled. Then, as he thought about what she'd said, his smile faded. "But you're so beautiful. I don't believe you don't have men chasing you."

Keren looked at him, and, for just an instant, he could see her entirely. See the peace in her soul and the burning quest for justice in her heart. It was a glorious sight. He reached up and laid his hand on her cheek and marveled at her flawless skin. He let those light blue-gray eyes that flashed humor and temper in almost equal parts wash over him.

"You seem so familiar. I must have met you when we were both detectives." He caressed a curl that had made a prison break. "You don't remember—"

A door slammed behind him. "Pastor P, you gonna be around for services t'night?"

Paul guiltily dropped his hand.

Rosita bounced toward them, her long black hair dangling over her shoulder in a smooth shining braid, her black eyes flashing humor and youth. In her tight, faded blue jeans and Lighthouse Mission T-shirt, she made Paul feel old and awkward, touching Keren's hair like some flirting, addle-headed teenager.

Rosita almost blinded them with her perky smile. "Murray's doin' okay, but it's not as good as when you're there. He's got Buddy and Louie helping him, and I've got a few women picking up the slack in the kitchen, but we need you to come and order us around."

He thought of LaToya. How could he have wasted a second on anything else? He wheeled away from Keren, grateful for the interruption. "Murray's going to have to keep doing it for a while. If you run into trouble, call Father Estrada. He'll take up the slack. Rosita, come here and meet Detective Collins. She's helping us look for the man who kidnapped LaToya."

Rosita's eyes lost their sparkle as she looked at Keren. "It's the same one that killed Juanita, isn't it?"

"We're afraid it is," Keren said. "And, Rosita, we don't think he's done yet. You and all the other women in this neighborhood need to be extremely careful. You mustn't ever be out alone, day or night. We've increased police patrols in the area, and if you ever need a ride, you call a cop. In fact"—Keren pulled a card out of her purse—"call *me* if you can't get anyone else to help you."

"I live in the mission," Rosita said, taking the card.

"And you never, ever go out alone?" Keren asked.

"Well, almost never." Rosita glanced at Keren and away. "Sometimes I got things to do, you know."

"Rosita," Keren said with stern caution, "we have reason to believe these killings may be connected to Pastor P or this mission, since both women who died came from here."

"But they were gone. It's not the same as me livin' inside."

"Rosita, promise me you'll be careful."

Rosita shrugged. "Sure."

"Paul, say something." Keren glared at him.

For some reason that made him want to smile. "Rosita," Paul said, "promise me." He didn't add anything else.

Rosita gave him a mutinous look, then, with a huff of displeasure, she said, "I have a date with Manny tonight. I need to walk a few blocks to catch a bus."

"What time?" Paul asked.

"It's a six-o'clock bus."

"I'll be here at five thirty to walk with you, and you make Manny meet you at the other end and ride back with you and walk you every step of the way back to the mission."

Rosita bloomed with pleasure. "You'd do that for me, Pastor P? Just so I can keep my date?"

"Manny's a good boy, Rosie. I don't blame you for wanting to spend time with him."

Rosita smiled and deep dimples appeared in her cheeks.

"I said he's a good boy, but he's still a boy. Remember what I said, Rosita, about getting too close too fast."

"It's not like I'm exactly a virgin, Pastor P. You of all people know that."

Keren's body jerked just a little. Paul looked at her, but he couldn't read her expression.

Rosita apparently had no trouble. "That's not what I meant." She rested a hand on Keren's arm. "There's nothin' like that between the pastor and me. Never has been."

Paul looked closer. Keren had that detached cop expression on her face.

"I was hooking for crack when I met Pastor P. That's how he knows. He pulled me off the street. He saved me."

"I didn't save you, Rosita. Only God can save you. Now don't change the subject. You watch Manny," Paul scolded.

"Manny cares about me."

"If he doesn't care enough about you to wait for marriage, then he doesn't care enough about you."

"I guess that makes sense," Rosita said with a pout. Then her grin escaped, and Paul knew she was teasing him. "Manny behaves himself, I see to it."

"Good girl. If you explain things to him, he'll insist on bringing you home." Paul reached into his pocket and pulled a ten-dollar bill out. He pressed it into her hand. "Now, no excuses. This will cover the bus ride for both of you."

Rosita clutched the ten dollars to her chest. "Thank you, Pastor P." With a bright smile, she whirled toward the mission.

The two of them watched her run. Keren said dryly, "Can you remember ever being that young?"

"I had a paper route from the time I was nine. I worked nights all through high school. I entered the police academy when I turned eighteen and went to night school to get a degree. I don't think I was ever young."

Keren took a deep breath. "We've got to get back to your apartment. The FBI is sending someone over to inspect the place better than we can, and if they find bugs, they'll try to trace them. They're bringing in a profiler from DC. We'll break this case. We'll get this lunatic."

Paul shoved his hands in his pockets so he wouldn't do something stupid like touch Keren again. "In time to save LaToya?"

They headed back to the building. Keren said, "Hey, how come she can call you Pastor P and I can't call you Rev?"

"It's all in the inflection."

Keren smiled and something passed between them. A moment of uncomplicated peace.

His phone rang.

CHAPTER SEVEN

Pravus leaned close with his fine brush. Details, he loved the tiny details. He imagined how the monks had labored over their translation of the Bible. They'd written it in Latin of course, God's language.

Opening a vein was like breathing life into dust and making a living being. Pravus could feel it, that he was godlike in his creation, and in his power over life and death. The white dress, virginal covering for the foul sinners he chose. It made the perfect backdrop for his art. To protect his work he'd used brown ink for Juanita, since his plans included getting her very wet. But for the rest of them, he'd paint with his victim's blood.

A tremor of excitement shook his hand and he pulled away quickly, terrified he'd ruined it. He hadn't. There was a bit of a waver in the line he'd made, but it was right. It was beautiful. He looked at what he'd done, and he smiled. Pharaoh was a fool. Powerful, but so sure he ruled his little world that he didn't even know the end was coming.

Paul Morris was such a man. Thought he was powerful. Wouldn't let the people go. Ran his little kingdom just like he'd run the police department.

Once his hand stilled, Pravus found again that center of peace and power he'd learned at his father's knee. He'd been taught with the end of a belt to sit still and create.

Father would be so proud.

A few more details. A flourish on the words that made his heart sing. LaToya's veins provided the life in this work of genius. He stepped back.

"It is good." His elation was so great he strode to the window to throw it open and shout. He didn't, of course. He wouldn't waste his words on a world too ignorant to understand him. Then he looked down to where he always watched and almost laughed aloud.

There was someone who'd want to share the news. The reverend. Standing there with the lady detective. He'd seen her at the site of the explosion and listened, then studied her carefully. Everything was at a man's fingertips on the Internet these days. Pravus had already done some searching to find out just who she was, and he now had plans to include her.

Reaching for the phone, he wished he could make LaToya scream. That made the pastor do exactly as he was told. But LaToya lay silently on the table. Her arms tied, spread straight out at her sides, her legs secured. He'd cut deep, but it was necessary. He'd let her sin flow out and used it for something beautiful.

By the time he was done, he would save her.

Paul scrambled to grab his new cell phone out of his pocket. He hadn't let it out of his possession since O'Shea had given it to him. He reached to flip it open.

Keren grabbed his arm. "Don't!"

"This is my chance. LaToya's kidnapper is going to give me some order. This is my chance to do it right and get her back." His phone kept ringing.

Keren's grip was like iron. "Give me a second." She pulled her own phone out. With a press of one button she reached O'Shea.

Paul almost pulled away from Keren, but she held him too tightly. "What if Pravus isn't in the mood to be patient? What if he's watching us right now?"

"He's getting a call," Keren said into her phone. "Are you set?"

She hit a series of buttons on her cell. "Okay, I can listen in, and O'Shea is set to record. Is there a number on your display?"

"I wasn't told anything about my phone being tapped." Paul's phone rang again.

Keren snagged it away from him and quickly recited the number to O'Shea.

"It's not tapped, not really, we just keyed our phones into the same frequency and muted the speakerphones in ours so he can't hear us. And we're recording it, so okay, yeah, I guess it is tapped." Keren glanced up at him. "You don't mind, right?"

"Right." Paul tried to take the phone away from her.

"Cell phones are fast and easy to trace; we need maybe fifteen seconds unless he's got something special going with it. The FBI should be in place by morning with all their space-age equipment. But we've got what we need to track him right now." Keren shoved the phone into his hands. "Answer it."

Paul's finger trembled until he nearly hit the wrong button and accidentally hung up. Then he got it right and pulled the phone to his ear.

"What took you so long, Reverend?"

Paul closed his eyes. Keren's hand settled solidly on his shoulder. He looked at her, and she gave him an encouraging nod.

"Is this Pravus?" Paul wondered at the name. He'd heard it somewhere. Part of his seminary studies maybe, but that had been awhile ago.

"You know I've got little LaToya, and yet you make me sit here with the phone ringing and ringing." The soft, cultured voice cut like a cold knife. "Almost like you don't care. Almost like you understand that she needs to die."

Paul said, as calmly as his terror would let him, "Pravus, you want to rid the world of evil, but you haven't looked closely enough at LaToya. You picked the wrong woman." What was he doing, trying to convince him to let LaToya go and kidnap someone less worthy?

Paul began to pray in his heart. *Lord, give me the words. If there are any words that will reach this man, let me say them.*

"You told me the same thing about Juanita," Pravus crooned. "You are weak, Reverend. Twice you've begged for the lives of sinners."

"Let her go, Pravus. Please, let her go. The way to cleanse the world of evil is to change hearts. To bring people to Jesus Christ with love. Killing people just spreads hate. You don't want the evil to spread, do you?" Paul hesitated over the next words, but they felt right. And when you're dealing with a madman, maybe it's all useless anyway, so he spoke as he felt led. "I'll help you face the demon that's keeping you away from God."

Keren gasped when he said it. She gave him a strangely intent look.

The soft, rhythmic voice broke, and Pravus snarled, "Don't speak such foul words to me! I'm not evil. *They* are evil. *They* are the ones who won't let my people go."

Paul was suddenly aware of O'Shea behind him. O'Shea held up a note that said, "Ask about your police days."

Paul nodded. "I'm sorry for what I did to you back then, Pravus. I did a lot of sinful things. I have asked God to forgive me; now I ask you."

"I'll never forgive you. *Never!* And I'm glad they're dead. It was my first act of rebellion against the pharaohs who tried to keep my genius enslaved, and you were too stupid to even know it. Oh, and tell the pretty detective she certainly is one of the fairest in the land."

A *click* ended the call. "Did you get it?" Keren asked O'Shea.

"Give me a second." O'Shea hit a button on his phone and waited. "I think they could at least narrow it down in that amount of time."

"He knows I'm working with the police." Paul hung up. "He knows there's a woman detective. He's watching me somehow."

O'Shea held out two small metal disks. "We found these bugs. Nothing fancy. But he's watching you closely."

"Listening devices in my apartment? I wonder how long those have been there." It made Paul sick to think of it, though honestly, his apartment was close to the most boring place on earth. He didn't spend much time there, and he certainly never brought anyone home. His life was strictly solo, except for work, since his wife's death.

"We'll track his number." Keren's jaw tensed as she looked at the bugs. "Maybe we'll get lucky and get a name and address."

"He's not that stupid, Collins," O'Shea cautioned.

"Maybe he is," Keren protested. "Your real bright people don't usually go into crime for a living."

"Yeah, the fact that criminals are stupid really makes our job easier," O'Shea conceded.

Keren turned to Paul. "You handled that really well. Good job." Then she and O'Shea began discussing what they gleaned from the conversation.

Before they forgot him entirely, Paul said, "While Pravus was talking, I remembered something else."

Both of them looked up excitedly. They looked almost happy, almost like they were enjoying themselves. Paul's fists clenched in a sudden flash of fury. He wasn't being fair, he knew. They were excited that they might be able to stop Pravus. But he still thanked God he was no longer a cop.

"What?" Keren demanded. "Did you recognize the voice? Do you know who it is?"

"No, I remember I've heard the word *pravus* before."

Keren stepped closer to him. "What? What does it mean?"

"Evil. *Pravus* is the Latin word for 'evil.' *Pravus spiritu* is 'evil spirit.'"

"Like a demon?" The color faded from Keren's face.

For a moment Paul thought she might faint, but he didn't really believe it. He knew he was dealing with one tough cookie. "Does that mean something to you?"

Keren shook her head. Finally, she said, "No, but it confirms something I have known. . .or. . .uh guessed all along."

Paul nodded.

O'Shea sighed, and nodded, too.

They were dealing with a demon. A demon straight from hell.

Keren clapped the magnetic police light to the roof of her car as she drove back to the station.

"Isn't that overkill, Collins?" O'Shea asked.

"I'm going to speed anyway." She shrugged and added wryly, "This will save some uniform the bother of pulling me over and having me rage at him until he lets me go on my lawbreaking way."

"You could just try obeying the law," Paul said from the backseat.

Keren looked sideways at O'Shea.

"You heard the citizen, kid," O'Shea said. "The minute we get back to the station, I'm going to borrow a pad of tickets from a patrol officer and write you up." He heaved his bulk around so he could look at Paul. "How's a citizen's arrest sound to you, Pastor P?"

"It suits me, Mick. I'm in the mood."

O'Shea grinned at Keren, and she slowed down with a glowering look. She reached up and pulled the light back in. "Okay, fine. I'll slow down."

"What'd he mean with that 'fairest in the land' crack?" O'Shea wondered.

"I know what he meant." Keren tried to think of a way to change the subject. "It was just his way of letting us know he's keeping close track. He'll probably say something about you next, O'Shea."

"Yeah, but how did 'fairest in the land' mean he knew you? I don't get it."

"Me neither," Paul said.

Keren squirmed. It was no big deal, really. It was just personal. On the other hand, it meant Pravus had done a pretty thorough background check on her. "I'll explain later. Every time I get to talking I start speeding, so shut up and let me drive."

After a few more minutes of blissful silence, Paul cleared his throat. Keren glanced down and saw that her speed had built back to fifteen miles over the speed limit. She forced herself to slow.

"It's just that I'm so anxious to get back and examine your old case files." She glanced into his eyes using the rearview mirror. "It's almost noon now. If we push hard, we can get through them tonight."

"Don't forget, I promised Rosie an escort to the bus station."

"I'll send a squad car for her. They can see her to the bus station or drive her wherever she needs to go." Keren waved his reminder away. "We don't have time to let you go help ladies cross the street."

"If I'd have told Rosie I was going to do that, I would agree. But I made a promise to a very special young woman. One who has done me the huge honor of trusting me when she never trusts anybody. I've got to go."

"Call her, Paul," Keren suggested. "She'll understand."

"The people in that neighborhood aren't comfortable with the police. If I send a policeman to take her anywhere, she might just react by ducking out the back door and hustling to the bus stop on her own."

Keren tried to burn through his overblown sense of duty by banking a blazing look off the mirror. He merely settled more stubbornly into his seat.

"If you go, at least one of us has to go with you," O'Shea pointed out.

"I'll be fine for an hour on my own. I can take care of myself."

"Not if Pravus phones. Having us there when you got the earlier call helped, even if you don't want to admit it." Keren could have easily gone back to sparring with him. "All of us thinking together helped come up with the right questions for him."

"Fine then." Paul crossed his arms. "You'll have to come. We can bring case files along and work while we drive. Figure something out, because I'm going."

O'Shea shook his head in disgust. "I'm going to play the tape again. Listen for specifics. Maybe we can narrow our search."

The odd voice of Pravus-the-demon haunted them as they drove. It did nothing to improve Keren's mood. She could tell they were all edgy by the time they'd heard it through three times. Keren pulled into an empty spot near the precinct and threw her car into PARK with more force than necessary. "Let's get to work."

They hurried into the station, all of them nearly frantic to cull the files for information.

"Pravus said, 'I'm glad they're dead. It was my first act of rebellion against the pharaoh, and you were too stupid to even know it,'" O'Shea said as they settled around Keren's desk in the squad room.

"I'm glad *they're* dead. They. More than one person," Keren said.

O'Shea nodded. "We look for a case with more than one death. You do the search, Keren. This machine likes you more than it does me."

Keren turned to her computer. "Great, we'll want the paper files later, but right now let's eliminate a bunch of them."

By the time the computer was done sorting, they had narrowed the cases to eighty-three. "I've left all the supposed accidents and suicides, as well as any case where there was more than one death."

"Did you get rid of all the first-degree murders? He said I was too stupid to figure it out. So I must have charged him with something less than deliberate first-degree murder."

Keren went back to the computer. "Okay, not a lot of people go down for first degree, thanks to plea bargaining. I'm down to forty-six cases."

O'Shea said, "Have you taken out the women perps?"

Keren nodded. "I did that first."

"And all the ones who are still in lockup?"

"Done."

O'Shea looked at the vastly reduced number of files listed on Keren's computer screen. "There're still a lot of 'em."

Paul glanced at his watch. "We don't have much time before we have to go back to the mission. Let's move it."

"I'll print out the names of the cases remaining." Keren did so and handed them each a copy of the file numbers and names. "We can pull them from the files and start reading."

"Let's see how many are known to be in the area," O'Shea said.

Keren added, "Some of them may be dead, too. That wouldn't be in the computer. We may be able to narrow this list pretty quickly."

They were only into their first few cases when Paul's phone rang. All three of them froze.

Paul said, "Do you need time to get ready?"

Keren and O'Shea sat poised, their phones already to their ears. They both shook their heads. Paul answered, holding his breath.

"I just wanted to tell you, Reverend, you should remain at home tomorrow morning. You're expecting a package." Hysterical laughter broke through the carefully modulated voice. Then the call ended.

All three of them looked at the stack of files. Paul glanced anxiously at his watch. "It's almost six. I've got to go."

"Paul," Keren said impatiently, "we've only got tonight. You know what to expect tomorrow morning."

Paul stood from his chair. "Do you think I need to be reminded?"

He turned away with an effort Keren could read in every line of his body. She said, "O'Shea, give me the recorder phone. Chances are the wacko is done calling for the night anyway. I'll go. You stay here and work."

She stormed after Paul. "This time I'm using code three, and you're not going to guilt me into stopping. I think this warrants lights and sirens."

"As long as you turn them off well before we get to the mission."

"Deal." When she agreed, he finally quit arguing. Nice change.

⁓

With a giggling Rosita delivered on the first step of her date with Manny, Paul and Keren returned to work. O'Shea pounced on them when they returned to the precinct house. He had the report on the cause of the blast at the gang hangout. "Pure low tech. Just like those listening devices. This guy is no electronics genius."

Keren asked, "What'd he use, dynamite? C-4?"

"Gasoline." O'Shea flipped open the report. "Like I said, low tech. He soaked the basement with gasoline and had containers of gas duct-taped to every creaky support beam in the basement of that building. The bomb squad figures at least ten bombs."

"It's a condemned building overrun by a gang. How'd he get in carrying gallons of gasoline?"

"It wouldn't take that much. A couple of gallons to splash around and another gallon or so to make a bunch of Molotov cocktails, waiting for a spark to set them off," O'Shea said. "According to the few gang members who would talk to us, they never went down to the basement. It was full of junk and the foundation was crumbling. Pravus could have brought the gasoline in early in the morning. He could disguise himself like a homeless man and no one would look at him twice, especially since the people who live in the house are stoned most of the time. No one is prowling around much—not in the morning. Two gallons at a time under a big coat. He could have done it in a couple of trips."

"How'd he detonate it?" Keren reached for the report.

"They're not sure yet, because everything was blown to smithereens." O'Shea didn't hand it over, evidently in the mood to be the center of attention.

"He might not use the same trick again," Paul said as he

tried to picture the bomb. Tried to figure out what he'd do if he saw one.

"Let's hope we get him before we find out." O'Shea looked the report over as he talked.

"We've got an ID on the cell phone. The couple who lost it only realized it was gone when a detective came to their house to ask about it. They keep it in the car for emergencies."

"Are you sure?" Paul leaned forward. "How closely were these people questioned? Some serial killers work as a team."

"We're checking their backgrounds, but they're in their late seventies," O'Shea said. "They live in an assisted-living apartment complex on the North Side. She's a retired social worker, he was an accountant for thirty-five years. They have six kids and seventeen grandkids. They pay their taxes, don't get speeding tickets, and they host a Bible study in their home every Wednesday night. It's just not them, Paul. No amount of stretching will make it fit. They've even got an alibi for the morning of the explosion. They'd gone with a group from their church on a boat ride out on Lake Michigan. We're canvassing the area, hoping we can find someone who saw their car burglarized, but so far, nothing. They don't have a clue how long their phone has been missing. We checked their call records, and the last time they made a call was two weeks ago to one of their daughters."

On that note they all turned back to the files.

It was midnight and no one suggested leaving. They culled the stack to two dozen people in the area who were still among the living. Keren ran them through the computer, looking for current addresses.

She arched her back in her creaking desk chair. She tried to force her spine to bend into a straight line. "If the FBI were here, their profiler could maybe pare this list down further."

She reached for a slice of cold pizza. One of the other detectives had taken pity on them and had one delivered.

O'Shea rubbed both hands over his eyes. "They'll do that in the morning."

"Morning is going to be too late for LaToya," Paul reminded them darkly. He stood from his chair. "More coffee?"

Keren nodded and set the pizza aside. After two bites her appetite was gone.

O'Shea said, "It's better than that syrup I bought yesterday afternoon."

"Yeah," Paul said sarcastically. "But it's still lethal."

"No argument there." O'Shea went back to the files.

Keren said, "Was that just yesterday? It seems like a month ago."

Paul gathered all three cups and went to the coffeemaker. The dregs in the pot were burned black. His stomach was boiling with the acid from the coffee and the tension of the night. He threw out what was in the glass carafe and started a new pot then went back to the chair he'd pulled up to the side of Keren's desk.

When the sun began lighting an east window in the squad room, Paul rubbed his burning eyes. "I've got to go. That first package came early. And I want to be there to question the delivery guy. The one before had a uniform on but no company marking. He could have been hired privately, which means his company wouldn't have a record of who ordered the delivery."

"We've been through nearly all the files." Keren closed the folder she was studying with a soft *clap*. "I'm going to send someone out to follow up on the possibles. The FBI will want to hit the ground running."

She opened her desk drawer and produced two phones. "I've got a borrowed cell—besides the one I've got linked to your number. The FBI can call me if their profiler comes up with anything that might help. And here's a spare one for you, Paul. Now we can stay in communication without messing up an incoming call from Pravus."

Paul's heart lurched as he tucked the little phone in his pocket with a trembling hand. "He's going to do it again. Kill LaToya and do who knows what other act of terror."

"We've staked out possible locations for this strike," O'Shea said. "LaToya used to run with a gang. They don't have such a well-known hangout as Carlo's bunch. Pravus talked about her drug dealing. We are tailing some of her better-known clients and a couple of suppliers that might have been involved with her. LaToya had a record that gives us a lot of places to cover."

"She was real hard core when I found her," Paul said. He paused over the fond memory of LaToya and how far she'd come.

"I looked at her record." Keren got up from her chair and stretched her back. "You worked a miracle to turn that girl around."

"Not me. Pastor P doesn't do miracles. Those are the sole dominion of God."

"I agree. You should have gotten a few hours of sleep last night." Keren took his arm and urged him to his feet.

"I couldn't sleep, knowing that this morning I'd—"

"I know. That's why I didn't even suggest it. But, Paul, he wasn't exactly careful with you last time. You barely survived that explosion. He's glad to play with you, but he doesn't seem to care all that much if you get killed in his chaos. You need to be on top of your game today."

"No, I don't. I just need to give my life over to God. That's how I'll survive. Or how I'll die, serving Jesus Christ."

"Good answer." Keren patted him on the shoulder then jerked her head at the exit door. "Now get the lead out, Rev. We've got a murderer to catch and, just as I predicted, you're a wimp who is slowing me down."

That at least got his attention. He grinned. "Thanks, I needed that." He started moving without her dragging him. By the time he hit the stairs he was jogging.

He was going into the mission alone. They'd agreed Keren couldn't go with him. He had her spare cell phone to notify her if Pravus called. Paul would send her a text message of the location he was to deliver the expected sign to. Keren would then send CPD to the location to evacuate it.

Paul glanced back at her. She gave him a tiny, solemn wave, praying for LaToya, for himself, and for whoever would be the focus of Pravus's wrath today.

CHAPTER EIGHT

Pravus looked through his telescope and saw the pretty detective drive the reverend up and let him out a block from the mission.

The reverend was here. He'd obeyed. The sense of power was intoxicating. The reverend was a puppet dancing on the end of Pravus's strings.

With his telescope he studied the Fairest in the Land as she sat in her car. She wanted to be part of this.

Fine.

The beast felt intense pleasure to think of the pretty detective at his mercy.

LaToya lay motionless on the table. He didn't know if she was sleeping or unconscious. He began another part of his creation. She woke up and struggled like a bug pinned to a board.

Pravus had never been so uncontrolled. He'd never cut himself this many times.

Father had taught him better than to show such a lack of restraint.

In the end, when Father died, Pravus had been in strict control the whole time.

⤙

He'd gotten here at six a.m. Stupid. No delivery was going to come that early.

He could have kept studying files. Paul kept the phone at hand as he took a quick shower and put on a clean sweat suit and gym shoes, getting ready to run. He thought of the last morning he'd taken a jog and dreaded what this day might bring.

There were a few people up and at work in the kitchen. Street people weren't exactly early risers, but a few would stagger in all through the morning—Rosita, then Myrna, an older lady who never spoke a word but had a cooking style suited to a five-star restaurant. Of course, she didn't exactly have the supplies to produce that kind of meal. She created magic with beans and hamburger, though.

Murray and Louie were both at work in the kitchen.

They did little more than grunt hello, though Murray waved with the spoon he was using to stir oatmeal and Rosita had her usual smile.

"I'm tied up again today. Sorry. Thanks for keeping things going." Paul watched the bustle of the kitchen and wanted to be part of it. He wanted his life back.

He wasn't getting it, at least not today.

The front apartment in this building was a quiet room where Paul could watch the neighborhood and spend time in prayer—where he had sessions with individuals, urging street people to sign up for the detox program. Now he went there to keep an eye out for the messenger who'd bring that package to the front door, right past this front window. Usually Rosita, or whoever was on duty, took anything that arrived and, if it was for Paul, tracked him down.

He settled in and turned to his Savior for strength. He let the peace of God ease into his mind and his muscles and his soul. He felt that ambitious, hard-driving, selfish part of himself loosen its grip.

There was every chance he might die today.

There was every chance LaToya might not survive.

By the time he was done praying, he knew God was in control.

He opened his Bible and read with a renewed spirit. He was still reading an hour later. He closed the Bible and asked God what next. Shortly after he asked, he hit a wall. Like a distance runner who'd gone too far, he ran out of steam. He didn't consciously choose sleep. God chose it for him. He simply leaned forward and rested his head on the table, his Bible a pillow, and slept. His last waking thought was of Keren's face. Had he seen her before?

The ringing phone jerked him awake. A thrill of fear jagged through him as he fumbled for it. He managed to drop it twice before he opened it. He made a note of the number on the liquid quartz display. It was the same one as yesterday.

"Just like old times, Reverend," Pravus oozed. "I'm coming to enjoy our little visits."

Paul began praying, trying to forget his fear and center himself on God. There was nothing else to do. The police were doing their best. The FBI would do their best. Paul was going to do his best. But in the end they were in God's hands, the same as every other day. "Pravus, are you going to let me come and get LaToya? Are you going to let my people go?"

"Have you looked at the package?"

Paul hadn't even thought of that. He'd been asleep. He glanced around and saw a package on the table next to where his head had rested. His name and address front and center. Written in blood. Someone, maybe Rosita, had quietly left it. He wondered how many precious seconds had been lost. If the address was inside the package, he could have had the police en route minutes ago.

"I know about your spare cell phone, Reverend. I don't just have microphones in your apartment, you know. I have eyes and ears everywhere. How is the pretty detective, anyway? Is she happy, do you think, chasing down criminals for a living? Is that any way for a decent woman to spend her life? She pretends to be good, but I wonder. Is she one of those who won't let my people go?"

Paul's throat clogged with fear as he thought of Pravus turning his attention to Keren. Only holding God close to his heart prevented him from raging at this lunatic. "I won't use the spare phone, Pravus. I'm opening the package now."

With no regard for possible fingerprints, since he knew full well there wouldn't be any, Paul tore the manila envelope open and the wooden sign slid free. He read aloud, "Pestis ex Rana. Plague of frogs." Paul scrambled for the pictures, terrified to look at them but desperate to find his assignment. "LaToya." The anguished whisper escaped past all his self-control.

"You've seen the photograph?" Pravus nearly sang the question, his voice was so smooth. "Good. I wonder how many people she killed with her drugs. How many more did she enslave by making them addicts? Her death will make the world a cleaner place. The fact that you associated with her and her kind makes your ministry a failure. It makes you a failure, Reverend."

"No, Pravus, that's not true. Jesus went to the sinners. How do you help them if you won't reach out to them? You think you can solve the problems of the world by destroying sinners, but that isn't Jesus' way."

"It was Moses' way. And it was God's way. How many died because of the plagues?"

"But God sent Jesus. He always planned to send His Son. Even in Moses' time God gave Pharaoh chance after chance. LaToya is a part of the kingdom of God now. Even people who haven't repented are loved by God. It's not for you to decide if they're worthy of life."

"You plead eloquently for the people who foul your mission. Jesus was a new way, and now there is a new way yet again. Me. Do you need me to make pretty little LaToya cry and beg so you'll believe she's here? I'd be glad to do it. It would be my pleasure, really. My chisel is newly sharpened."

"No, don't hurt her anymore," Paul shouted. He looked at the picture and saw the absolute terror on LaToya's face. Duct tape over her mouth and around her wrists. LaToya, who had so recently adopted a lifestyle of chastity and modesty, stripped bare and displayed in a photo for her minister. She was cut. Red blood gleamed against her black skin. Beside her lay the dress; it would be her burial shroud. In the picture, Paul could see clearly Pharaoh, Moses, and Aaron painted on the dress just as they were on the dress Juanita wore. Around Pharaoh's feet, frogs, blood red, not green. But Pravus had rendered them with a fine, gifted hand so they were unmistakable.

"Do you see the address?"

It was scrawled in dried blood across one of the photos. "Yes, I'm going. This time I won't fail, Pravus. I'll tell them exactly what you want. Do you have any other words for me to say? Do you want me to preach to them? Should I arrest them? Tell me exactly what you want me to do so I can obey you. I want to do whatever you need so LaToya can be spared." Paul hated the sound of his begging. He wondered if he shouldn't deal with Pravus from a position of strength. Right now he didn't have it in him.

"Go to the house. It's within running distance. Remember, I'm watching you. You're by the front door of the mission this time, rather than in your rooms."

It chilled Paul to realize how closely he was being watched.

"Come out the front door, without contacting the police, and head straight for that address. I'm not going to give you as much time as before, Reverend. I remember a time when you weren't the least bit patient with me."

The phone clicked. Paul read the address, knew exactly where he was going and why, dropped the photo on the table, and ran.

Rosita crept into the entry area of the mission, staying close to the wall. She slipped up to the table and snatched up the picture. She clapped her hand over her mouth at the ugly sight, then she produced yet another cell phone, the one that nice lady detective had slipped her last night. She called with the address.

With another fearful look at the picture, she gathered the pictures into the envelope Paul had left behind and took it into the kitchen with her. She prayed fervently as she carefully slid it behind a cupboard for safekeeping as Detective Collins had instructed her. With a faint heart because of what she knew her friend LaToya was going through, but a soul rock steady in the Lord Jesus Christ, who had pulled her out of a living hell, she went back to preparing breakfast.

Pravus watched the pastor run, then he turned back to the mission for one last glance. Through the front window he saw little Rosita, so happy, so helpful, so terribly soiled, take his package.

He'd planned to involve her eventually, but he was pleased she'd volunteered.

Then he swung his binoculars back toward the pastor. He couldn't see Pastor P every second, but he'd picked this place to live because his view was so ideal. Rather than try to pick out the running man, he just watched the doorway of the house where the good pastor was destined. Maybe this time he'd meet his end.

If so, Pravus would savor it. If not, there were many more people who needed to be shrouded with purity. And many more pictures for Pravus to paint.

⤺

Keren grimly took the message and phoned every car in the vicinity, and there were plenty of them. The fact that it wasn't Paul who called made her angry. What did the man plan to do on his own?

Pravus had no doubt come up with some very creative threats. Even though she'd expected it, planned for it, Keren was furious. She was a lot more comfortable with fury than with being scared to death.

The crack house Pravus had chosen to hit wasn't far, and Paul would no doubt beat them there. Keren went in quiet, no sirens. Nothing to draw attention to herself.

A demon was watching. She knew with God on her side, no one could stand against her.

⤺

Paul set some kind of land speed record running to Ahmad's house.

His ribs were punishing him for it, but they didn't even slow him down. He was up against big trouble with this destination.

There would be no one trying to kill him in this place. In this house they'd all be sleeping off a night of drugging. He wasn't going to be able to get them out in time. He had to stop the explosion. Racing against time, he prayed with every step. He only hoped Pravus had used the same method to vent his rage. Paul had given some thought to defusing a bunch of gasoline bombs. But if Pravus chose another, more elaborate explosive, Paul was going to die along with a house full of people.

He hesitated for one second before he simply set the sign on the ground against the house; then he went in and began opening doors, looking for a way to the basement. Unlike Carlo's place, this was a house, not an apartment building. It was part of a row of ancient, decrepit houses that lined this block. Paul knew if this house went, the whole row would go. But it wasn't a very large house. It didn't take him long to find the way downstairs.

The smell of gasoline hit him the second he opened the door. He ran down the stairs and froze in horror. Every support post in the murky cellar had a gallon glass jar taped to it. A couple of inches of yellow gasoline showed in each jar, all of which had been plugged with red rags. Wires, stripped of their insulation, with two ends frayed and bent just sparking distance apart, ran into every jug and dangled inches above the gas. The wires ran to every light socket in the basement, waiting for a spark to ignite the tightly enclosed fumes. The walls glistened from being soaked with gas.

Paul looked desperately for a fuse box and saw nothing. He ran for the first light sockets. There were no bulbs in them. Instead a converter had turned the socket into an outlet with four plug-ins. Pravus had plugged in a bomb. Paul jerked the plugs out of the first socket, careful not to strike a spark in his hurry. He got all four of them out and ran on to the next converted socket. When he grabbed it, the light fixture pulled out of the ceiling. Its corroded wires nearly broke off in Paul's hand. Paul forced himself to slow down. If he broke a wire he might set the bomb off without any help from a murderer. He gently disconnected the bomb wires from the power source.

Gas fumes thickened the air. He went to the next socket and the next and the next. He pulled the last plug free just as his cell phone rang.

"How dare you toss my sign on the ground like so much trash, Reverend? For that alone I'll declare this effort of yours a failure."

Paul looked around, trying to see anything he missed in the room. The only light filtered through dirt-encrusted windows. At that second Keren came running down the stairs. Paul wanted to shout at her to get out. Get away. But he was starting to know Keren well enough to not waste his time. He pointed at the light fixtures, hit the Mute button on the phone, and said, "Look for any other plug-ins. Look for a fuse box. I don't know what else he might've hooked up wires to."

Keren began checking corners and behind rubbish.

"Your time is up," the voice sang.

Paul unmuted the phone. "No, Pravus, they've agreed. They're going to let your people go, just as you asked."

Keren glanced over at him with her brow furrowed. Paul shrugged helplessly.

Keren went on with her search. Paul walked the edges of the basement, checking every socket, every outlet.

"No, Reverend, scum like that never learn. They never change."

Keren pulled the electric wires out of the jugs, then she looked behind a rusted-out furnace and a pile of toppled boxes and gasped with shock.

She hissed at Paul, "Keep him talking; there's another socket behind this junk. I've disconnected it from the bomb, but I've got to unplug the cord. Even a spark could set this whole place off."

Paul followed her to the dusky corner. All the while he kept talking, trying to buy her the time she needed as she scrambled over the debris. "They believed you, Pravus, and they fear you. I told them your people have been enslaved long enough. Come in here, Pravus, come and see how you've humbled them. Your message reached Pharaoh, just as Moses' message did. It worked.

They're going to let your people go."

Keren slipped out of sight. Paul had to clench his jaw to keep from yelling at her to get out—save herself and let the building blow. Instead, he stood and listened to Pravus like a useless bystander.

"Do you think I'm a fool, Reverend? I don't like to be treated as if I'm a fool."

Paul leaned back and saw Keren wrestling with the plugs. The crackle of sand crumbling off the cement walls told Paul just how quickly and utterly this place would collapse if Keren didn't get that connection broken in time.

"The trash in that house will die. LaToya will die. This time you will die along with them."

Pravus hung up.

Keren pulled out the last stubborn plug. A snapping erupted from every outlet in the basement. But no sparks. Paul held his breath. The fumes didn't ignite.

"He did it. That murderous lunatic pushed the button," Paul said bitterly.

"We knew he would." Keren sagged against the wall. "You held him off for long enough."

Paul lifted the phone and quickly punched in the number he'd seen on his LCD screen. He was almost surprised when Pravus answered.

"What happened?" Pravus demanded. "What have you done?"

Keren quickly pulled out her phone and set it to record. Then she carefully picked her way out of the corner she'd gotten into.

Paul wanted to scream at Pravus, threaten him with lightning bolts and the wrath of God. He held a tight rein on his temper because of LaToya. "The bomb didn't go off. Don't you see, Pravus? God knew these people weren't ready to die. It is God's to give life and death."

Keren hurried over to him, listening intently on her phone.

"I do the will of a greater God than yours," Pravus shouted.

"There is no greater God than mine, Pravus. There is no *other* God than mine. And this destruction is not His will. He still has plans for these people. When your bomb didn't go off, it was God telling you to stop. He was telling you to let LaToya go without further harm. You *must* accept God's will."

O'Shea appeared at the top of the staircase, and two uniformed officers were right behind him.

Stepping away from Paul, Keren spoke quietly to O'Shea. "Pravus is on the phone, be quiet. This basement is full of gas fumes. It's a ticking bomb. If one of the crackheads so much as drops his pipe and strikes a spark, the whole place could still blow."

O'Shea turned to give murmured instructions to the police gathering behind him.

"I'm doing His will! I'm trying to drive the evil out of the world!"

Paul felt sick at the violent fury in Pravus's voice and what it meant for LaToya. *God, please, tell me what to do.*

All he felt was his own fury. The power of it was too strong to let the voice of God in. He continued to try to soothe a madman. "I'm the one you're angry at, Pravus. Aren't I the one who hurt you?"

"Yes! Yes, you hurt me," Pravus screamed. "But you were such a fool. I saw them, the dancer and her mother. But you never knew."

"Yes, I knew. I knew what you did to them." Paul fumbled around, trying to make sense of Pravus's ranting.

Laughter crackled through the phone line, the rapid shift from fury to humor to pure madness. "No, you never knew. No one did. From the first, I was too smart for this world."

"Let LaToya go. Prove you're strong. If you're angry at me, come for me and leave her out of it."

"I'll come for you when it's the plague of the firstborn. That's your time. Until then, I'll prove my strength one plague at a time." Pravus's voice rose until it was a scream.

"If LaToya dies, you'll never prove it to me."

"I'll prove it! I'll prove it for all the world to see." A hollow *click*, and Pravus was gone. And LaToya was alone with a lunatic.

CHAPTER NINE

Paul hit the REDIAL button, but this time there was no answer on the other end.

"We've got to get back to the files," O'Shea said as soon as Paul gave up on his phone.

"Whatever this is about is rooted in your work as a policeman." Keren took Paul's arm and urged him toward the stairs. "He made another reference to your past as a cop. Somewhere you brushed up against a serial killer who was just getting started. You must have stopped him somehow but not nailed him for what he really did."

Paul nodded. He flipped open the phone again and reached for the REDIAL button. Keren wrestled the phone away from him. "Not now, Paul. Let him cool off a little."

"He killed Juanita after his last call to me," he said in a voice so weak and frightened Keren wouldn't have recognized it as his if he hadn't been standing right in front of her.

Keren glanced up at O'Shea. She saw her partner's face twist into a look of compassion. O'Shea shook his head and left to finish rousting the people from the house.

"No, Paul." Keren grabbed Paul's arm. "That's not right. The ME said Juanita was killed hours after the explosion. And if he killed her at that fountain—or even just before he took her there—we have a chance of anticipating where he'll go. We have to keep pushing." She shook him, hoping to shake some courage to him. "We go on the assumption we have time to save her."

"But we didn't thwart his explosion before. You heard him, he was so furious he was raving. He's killing her right now." Paul faltered, and Keren worried that he might collapse. "I can't get to her. She trusted me, maybe the first person she's ever trusted in her life, and now she's dying because of it."

Keren knew she ought to yell at him, goad him, and harass him to bring out the cop in him. When he was being his old, logical self he was more useful; unfortunately, she couldn't stand him when he acted that way. She was drawn to the gentle pastor, but he felt everything so deeply he couldn't function. Not in the face of this insanity.

She'd seen the pictures of LaToya on the wall in her apartment, and she'd seen pictures of her from old arrest records. The change in the young woman was enough to prove to anyone there was a God. It was possible that a sweet, redeemed woman was dying horribly right this moment, and Keren couldn't play tough with Paul right now, even if it might help solve the case.

So she hugged him instead.

In the midst of the gas fumes and dinginess and thwarted destruction, he grabbed her and clung until she couldn't draw a breath. She hung on, knowing she was only feeling a fraction of his despair.

When Keren trusted her voice, she said, "We've got to keep trying." She lifted her head off Paul's chest and put her hands on his shoulders. He straightened away from her, and she looked him square in the eye. "Our only other option is to do nothing."

Paul held her gaze for a long time. She could feel him gathering his strength. He knew they didn't have any choice.

"All right." His voice broke. He cleared his throat and tried again. "Let's get to work on those files."

Keren nodded silently and led him upstairs and toward the back of the house, where she'd left her car. The inhabitants of the crack house were emerging from their rooms, grousing and threatening the cops. She turned back to these people who were alive because a man had risked his life for them. They were throwing their lives away, with no notion of what a precious gift they'd been given.

"Bust every one of them," she snapped. "Lock 'em up and keep 'em there. We don't have to charge them for forty-eight hours, so stall the bond hearing. Maybe the idiots will sober up enough to realize they're lucky to be alive."

"It's for their own protection," O'Shea added. "There's a demon after them."

"Does browbeating these poor, sleeping people make you two feel better?" Paul asked.

O'Shea tipped his head and shrugged and nodded. "Yeah."

"A little." Keren hauled him out the back door.

The FBI was at the station when they got back.

They'd commandeered a small office, and when they called Keren, Paul, and O'Shea in, they made a tight fit. Keren had met several of the local agents over the years and usually worked fairly well with them.

"I'm Special Agent Lance Higgins." A tall man with golden eyes so predatory, Keren had a feeling those eyes would be the last thing a lot of bad guys would see when Higgins pounced. He had black hair swept off his forehead like a mane. He was leaning against the wall behind the gray metal desk in the office, and he uncoiled and stepped forward with leonine grace. He offered Keren his hand.

Keren couldn't help responding to the man's powerful strength. She shook his hand just a second too long before he pulled away. Higgins turned to Paul and O'Shea and gave them the same greeting. He was wearing the standard FBI black suit, but on him it looked great. Two other black-suited men Keren knew were from the Illinois FBI office were standing against the wall on Keren's right.

Higgins gestured to the left. "This is our profiler, Agent Mark Dyson."

With one glance, Keren decided Dyson must be extremely good at what he did or the FBI would never put up with him. Agent Dyson towered over all of them, six foot six and beanpole thin. His long hair was bleached white. He had manic curls almost as wild as hers, pulled back into a ponytail. He wore wire-rimmed glasses so thick they magnified his light-blue eyes, hole-riddled jeans, and a green button-down shirt with the sleeves turned up to his elbows. The shirt was a mass of wrinkles, and it hung, untucked, most of the way to Dyson's knees. He clasped her hand in both of his, and Keren had the weird feeling that the guy could profile her just from the way she shook hands. His magnified eyes seemed to penetrate her mind rather than look at her face.

"I've been combing the Pravus file for over an hour," he murmured. "I have questions."

He waved them into three folding chairs. The FBI agents all stayed on their feet. "You're sure it's a man?"

"Yes. The voice is soft, but it's definitely male," Keren answered.

Dyson periodically glanced at Paul or O'Shea. Keren felt like the guy was boring into everyone's brain, reading every changed expression. But he aimed all his questions at Keren. She felt like she was connected to a human lie detector and fought down a mild resentment. Surely Paul was the one who ought to be questioned.

"The first murder victim is Hispanic, the second black." Dyson tried to drill into her brain with his eyes. Keren could feel the bore holes.

"There's only one murder victim," Paul snapped. "The second is still a kidnapping. We hope that she can be rescued."

"We should be going through Pastor Morris's case files," O'Shea said impatiently. "You don't need to talk to all of us at once."

"Most serial killers pick victims of their own race." Dyson ignored Paul and O'Shea to focus on Keren. "Usually they're acting out rage against an abusive childhood, and they're trying to punish their mother or father or some significant person in their lives."

"Obviously that's not the case here, Agent Dyson," Keren said with some sting, "since he's already picked girls of different races."

"Don't jump to conclusions, Detective Collins. Maybe his mother was biracial, or maybe his mother was one race and his father another. Those are the kinds of details that could identify him for us."

"Great." O'Shea rubbed his hands together as if preparing to dig into a great meal. "If you can guarantee he's biracial, we can throw out all the files except those."

No one missed his sarcasm.

Agent Higgins said, "Not helpful, Detective."

O'Shea rolled his eyes.

The interrogation went on and on. It took Keren about five minutes to realize every question Dyson asked was already answered in the file he'd been studying. Keren saw Paul grow fidgety and begin glancing at his wristwatch.

An hour had crept by when Paul lunged out of his chair. "We

can't sit here anymore. You've got enough. Pravus could be out there right now killing LaToya. I have to do something besides talk!"

"If our profiler can narrow this down, we could go straight to the person responsible for this." Higgins glared at Paul.

Paul grabbed the doorknob. Keren could see him trying to force himself to stay in the room. He said through clenched teeth, "Agent Higgins, you're right to an extent. Agent Dyson can help. We know how profiling works. But this is a pure waste of our time. There is nothing we've said that isn't in our report."

"That may not be true." Higgins stood and went to the door to stand close to Paul. "Sometimes people have impressions that they haven't put in their report. You may not even be aware of them, but they can come out under questioning."

"Yes, I know that, but we're trained policemen." Paul stopped talking for a long minute, then he went on. "I mean *they* are trained policemen and I *used* to be one. We know how instincts work and how to pinpoint minor clues from tone of voice and background noise. Your methods are very useful with civilians, but they are a waste of our time."

"You've been a minister for five years, Reverend Morris. You haven't used those instincts for a long time."

"Oh, but they're still there." Paul stood away from the door and crossed his arms, his head hung down until his chin nearly rested on his chest. "Despite my best efforts to rid myself of them, all my old habits are right there, dying to spring to life."

Dyson seemed to have ignored the whole exchange between Paul and Higgins. "I want to listen to the recorded messages again. I heard the ones from last night, but the one you brought in this morning is new."

"Fine." Keren rose from her seat. "Listen to the tapes while we get to work."

"Sit down, Detective." Higgins wasn't making a suggestion.

Keren didn't answer to the FBI. Despite the strong first impression of Higgins's competence, she longed to shove his orders down his throat. But she did want to hear this morning's tape, so she sat.

The first two tapes had nothing new. Paul said, "You hear where he talks about what I did to him? We think—"

Dyson waved his hand abruptly at Paul as if he were an annoying bug. Paul fell silent and stood by the door with his jaw clenched so tight Keren thought he might break some teeth.

The last tape, when Paul called Pravus back in the basement of the crack house, held all their attention. Paul sounded steady and strong as he tried to reason with Pravus. Keren thought of how he fell apart afterward.

He was a courageous man with the power of God in his voice. She suddenly decided she'd find time to sit in on one of Paul's sermons, even if she had to steal a shopping cart and live on the street for a few days to qualify for admittance. She knew he'd be riveting when he spoke of his faith. God was using him powerfully, or he could never have led two girls as lost as LaToya and Juanita to the Lord.

Pravus's voice pulled her attention back to the tape. "I saw them, the dancer and her mother. But you never knew."

Keren had forgotten he'd made that statement.

"What does that mean, the dancer and her mother?" Keren hit the PAUSE button. "Can you remember a case involving a dancer, either as the victim or the perp?"

Paul shook his head. "It doesn't ring a bell."

"That would be the two people," O'Shea said. "A dancer and her mother. Were there any mother and child murders in those files?"

Dyson said, "You're assuming the dancer is a child. Why is that?"

"Good point." Keren nodded. "We could be reaching. The dancer could be a boy or a man, or an adult woman. Adults have mothers."

"I don't remember a mother and daughter murder," Paul said, "but there were a couple of child murders. Let's look more closely at them."

"He might mean something else," Higgins cautioned. "Narrow your search for now, but don't get married to this theory."

"We won't," Keren said. "It's just a starting place."

Keren glanced at Higgins. "Are you done with us?"

"For now." Higgins waved at the door.

They left the office, but Keren could still feel Dyson's probing eyes hunting around in her brain.

⤺

O'Shea stood and went to the coffeepot. "It's been nearly twelve hours since his last contact. Why don't you try the phone again, Paul?"

"I've tried every hour on the hour and a dozen more times when I couldn't control myself." Paul was dialing before O'Shea quit talking. "He's got it shut off. He'll leave it shut off until he has something to say to me."

"Don't drink that coffee, O'Shea. You've got to go home and get some sleep." Keren pressed the heels of her hands to her burning eyes. "I'm losing my ability to read the English language, let alone Latin. I haven't slept since about three yesterday morning. We've got our people and the FBI going twenty-four hours a day."

"And chances are," Paul said in a bleak voice, "we're going to wake up tomorrow with the discovery of LaToya's body."

"It was two days before we found Juanita, Paul. We might get tomorrow still. And our synapses are going to french fry the rest of our brains if we don't sleep."

"You go ahead," Paul said. "I can find Higgins and see if he needs help. I got a couple of hours of sleep this morning while I was waiting for Pravus at the mission."

"You got two hours of sleep?" Keren was almost violent with jealousy.

Paul tried to smile. She could tell he really tried. He said, "I won't sleep tonight. Impossible."

"You're asleep in that chair. We're not getting anywhere."

"Did I ever tell you I have a wife?" O'Shea asked.

Paul shook his head. "No, you've never mentioned that."

"I forget it myself sometimes." O'Shea glanced at his watch. "She's way nicer about this job than I deserve. It's ten o'clock now. She'll still be awake if I hurry. I'm going to go see if she recognizes me. See you in the morning." He stood and began pulling on his suit coat. "If you don't want to take the time to go home, Keren will show you where the bunk beds are. A few hours' sleep will help clear the cobwebs."

O'Shea didn't hang around to see if they took his advice.

Paul sagged back in his chair. "I'm afraid if I fall asleep I'll wake up to the news that LaToya's body has been found floating in a frog pond somewhere."

Keren stood so quickly her chair rolled back and smacked into the desk behind her. "Why not? Why not a frog pond somewhere? Where would this nut go to find frogs?"

Paul eyes jerked wide open, all sleepiness gone. "A pet store?"

"Good, where else?"

"Is there a park in Chicago that has frogs? Some kind of reptile garden or a zoo?"

Keren snapped her fingers. "How about a petting zoo? There's one in the park where Juanita was found. Pravus has been working solely in the area around the mission."

"I think there is some kind of pond at that petting zoo," Paul said. "Let's go take a look. If we could stake it out and Pravus came—maybe he won't kill her until he gets there. Maybe we can—"

"Paul, chances are he won't do anything tonight. It wasn't until two days later that Juanita showed up."

"But he might move faster this time. Last time, maybe he was enjoying the destruction he caused. This time there was no show. His need to kill might move the schedule up."

Keren gave him a long look.

"I know I'm reaching," Paul said with quiet desperation in his voice. "But I can't go lie down on some cot and rest while there's a chance she's still alive out there. Working on these files is driving me crazy. I'd rather be interrogated by Dyson again. I need to do something."

"I know. Every time I close my eyes I see those cuts on Juanita's body and the pictures of LaToya and that death shroud he painted. Let's go. Even if we don't find anything, we can scope the place out and decide where to set up a stakeout for tomorrow night. Maybe the fresh air will wake us up."

Keren drove through the quiet streets.

Paul suddenly sat up straighter. "I'm supposed to preach a sermon tomorrow morning."

Keren looked sideways. "I'd forgotten it was Saturday night."

"Police work isn't exactly nine to five, is it?"

"You'd know that as well as anyone."

Paul nodded. Keren pulled into a little park and the two of them got out. There was a well-secured area that held the larger animals—miniature goats, a Shetland pony, a baby calf. Keren had done patrol in this park when she was in uniform. "There's a pond over there. Listen, you can hear frogs croaking."

Paul broke into a run. He was sprinting across the uneven ground by the time he got to the pond. In the dim streetlights that barely reached this corner of the park they could see the pond. Its surface was unbroken. LaToya wasn't there.

"Thank You, God. Please, God, be with her. She's so new in her faith. She's turned to You so completely in the last year. Help her to endure in her faith through this test. Let me. . ." Paul's voice faded away.

Keren stood beside him and let the soft lapping of the water and the breeze that stirred through the surrounding trees become a chapel. She added her own silent prayers to Paul's, turning her mind away from the question of why LaToya had to suffer this when she'd so recently turned her life over to God. It was a question that had no answer. An answer wouldn't do any good anyway. It had happened. They had to go on from here.

Time passed and finally, in the peace of the night, Keren found herself talking. "I know what he meant when he said I was one of the fairest in the land."

Paul opened his eyes. "What?"

"In the phone call, he said I was one of the fairest in the land," Keren reminded him.

"It's from the book of Job," Paul said. "Job's daughters were the fairest in the land. It was probably just his way of saying he was watching. He could see how pretty you are, and he wanted us to know he had actually seen you."

"Pretty?" Keren broke off a short laugh and combed her fingers through her ratty hair. She was lucky to get her hand back. "Yeah right. Anyway, the reason he said that—"

"You don't think you're pretty? Oh come on. Your eyes are beautiful. Your hair is like—"

"You made a crack like that before. You said men had to be chasing me. Wrong. It's a nice thought, Paul. Thanks. Now, as I was saying—"

Paul caught Keren by the shoulders and pulled her around to face him. "Don't change the subject just yet. I say you're pretty."

Keren gave him a gentle smile. "Okay, well, near as I can figure out, you're one of the few."

"Well, who else matters, huh?" Paul leaned down and kissed her. The kiss, soft as a breeze, was over before it began. Paul pulled away just an inch and their eyes met.

"We should have never stopped fighting," Keren whispered.

They moved toward each other at the same moment and their lips met. Paul's arms went around her and pulled her close, as close as they'd been this morning after he'd listened to a madman tell him about the impending death of his friend. Keren's arms circled his neck.

"I've been dying to touch your hair." He sank one hand deeply into it. It was as soft and thick as he'd imagined. He tugged on the heavy leather barrette, and as it came loose, her hair tangled in his fingers like living silk. It felt so perfect it shook him back to sanity.

"We have to stop." He pulled away.

Keren took a second to understand the kiss was over. Then she nodded. "Yes, this is wrong. This isn't going to happen."

"Absolutely not," Paul said with fierce sincerity. "It's a terrible mistake."

Then he kissed her again.

CHAPTER TEN

A bush rustled just behind Keren in a little stand of scraggly trees and shrubs. She jerked out of Paul's arms and whirled to face the sound. Paul's old cop instincts sprang to life. He grabbed for the gun he always wore in a shoulder holster.

It wasn't there.

He dropped into a crouch and grabbed for Keren to shield her from danger.

She wasn't there.

He heard her charging toward the noise and he went after her. Suddenly there was more rustling and Keren emerged from the dense undergrowth tucking a gun into the small of her back.

"It was nothing." She was washed blue and black in the streetlights. Her hair danced free around her face, and Paul's hand closed on her barrette.

The adrenaline that had surged through Paul's veins and thrown him into action had no outlet, so it converted itself to anger. He marched toward her and grabbed her upper arm.

"What do you think you're doing, dashing into the woods like that?" He shook her hard. "You didn't even think." He pulled her up to his face. "You just disappeared." His nose almost touched hers. "He could have been there. Pravus could have been waiting!"

Keren laid her hand on Paul's mouth. He fumed behind her hand. "I'm sorry. You're right. I think—" She shrugged and smiled sheepishly at him. "I think I might have been running away from you as much as running to check on that noise."

Paul growled under her fingers, and she uncovered his mouth. He lowered his lips to hers. She stepped away so quickly she almost did a dance step. "No, don't. We lost our heads there for a minute; there's no reason it should happen again."

Paul advanced.

Keren moved away. "If you back me into that frog pond I won't be responsible for the damage I do to your. . .uh. . .ego."

Paul stopped. He crossed his arms firmly to keep from reaching for her. "You're an aggravating woman, Keren."

She held her hands up as if to surrender. "I know. Believe me, I've heard it before. Let's go. I'll call in this location and have patrols stepped up overnight, then tomorrow I'll put it under constant surveillance."

"Not good enough," Paul said, shaking his head.

"It's the best I can do. Arranging full-time surveillance takes time."

He thought he might be pouting. It was humiliating. Still, he refused to budge. "Just go. I'm staying here." He shoved her barrette into her hands.

"What about tomorrow?" She clenched her fist around the hair tie.

"What *about* tomorrow?" Paul asked.

"Sunday? You're a reverend? Don't you have somewhere you need to be?"

At her teasing, he felt the worst of his turmoil ease. How had he ended up kissing her anyway? "You know I haven't kissed a woman since my wife died five years ago."

Keren's eyes widened. "Really? Five years?"

"Yup. And I didn't do much of it then, 'cuz my wife wasn't overly fond of me. I wasn't overly fond of her, either. I wonder what it means."

"That you weren't fond of your wife?"

"No, that I abandoned five years of peace and quiet to risk kissing a woman."

"It means you should have waited a little longer. I'm not a candidate to break your fast, buddy."

"Tell me about it," Paul said. "Now go home. I've got this covered, and I have someone preaching for me tomorrow."

"Ah, yes, I remember. Murray, the fire-and-brimstone specialist. Rosie wasn't thrilled." Keren latched onto Paul's arm and hauled him toward the car.

"Murray does okay." Paul didn't tell her, but he was just escorting her. He was going to plant himself by this pond until he got his hands on Pravus or somebody came up with a better idea. "And there are others almost as good, although Murray's the only one who does any preaching. Buddy is a good guy when he takes his medication, and Lou does okay. And we've got a Catholic priest who pitches in a lot, though there's a Catholic mission he's mainly involved with."

Keren opened her car door.

Paul said lightly, "I'm staying."

Keren narrowed her eyes at him. If they hadn't been so close to a streetlight Paul might not have known how much danger he was in. An extended silence grew between them. Paul suspected she was trying to assess her chances of beating him into submission.

She must have thought her chances were poor because she pulled her keys out of her pocket and held them out to him. "Get in."

He took the keys. "What are these for?"

"I figured you wouldn't get in if you didn't have them."

"Because kidnapping me is so obvious?"

"Right." She dropped onto the seat behind the wheel. "I'll

call around and get someone over here as soon as possible. In the meantime I'll wait with you."

"No, you don't have to."

"Of course I don't have to, moron." Keren snorted. "If you ordered me to do it, I'd be out of here like a shot, but since I thought of it myself, I'll stay." She slammed the door in his face.

Paul thought about arguing with her. Instead, he went around the car and got in. "Thanks, it's kinda spooky out here."

Keren laughed then looked across the front seat at him. Paul looked at her. He managed to get his thoughts together enough to keep from reaching for her. . .again. "So, you were trying to say something back there, back before"—Paul waved in the general vicinity of the pond—"whatever madness that was. I'll listen. Fairest in the land?"

"Oh yeah, right. It's my name." She looked forward again and twisted her hair into a coil with such ease Paul knew she'd done it a thousand times before.

"Keren?"

"Yeah. Keren, with an *e* instead of an *a*. Only that's not all of it. My whole first name is Kerenhappuch. My parents named me after one of Job's daughters." She anchored her hair with the bulky contraption she used as a barrette.

Paul sat up and turned to face her, "Do you have sisters named Kezia and Jemima?"

"Not that many people know the names of Job's daughters. Well done. Nope, I've got two younger brothers."

"Named Kezia and Jemima?"

Keren laughed. "Wrong again. Anyway, I never use it, the Happuch part. Out of respect for my parents, who really are terrific people—the evidence of my name to the contrary—I haven't changed it. I've signed everything for years 'Keren H.

Collins.' There was a time when having Happuch as part of my name was almost too much to bear."

"When you were twelve, I'd bet." Paul settled back into the seat and stared out at the night with a smile.

"And thirteen and fourteen and fifteen. We moved the year I turned fifteen. We lived in a small town where everybody knew my name was Kerenhappuch, to the big anonymous city of Chicago. I insisted my folks enroll me in school as Keren, and no one was ever the wiser. I actually have a little affection for the whole name now. Anyway, when Pravus said, 'Fairest in the land,' I came to the conclusion that he knew what my real name was, which means he's dug pretty deep. It's not on any records that don't absolutely demand a full name. And those are usually private documents."

Paul quit relaxing. He remembered the ominous way Pravus had spoken of Keren, wondering if she was one of those who wouldn't let his people go. "Why didn't you say something? Keren, he's probably already looking for his next victim. He's picking people I know."

"I hope he comes after me," Keren said with grim satisfaction. "I'd like to see what he'd do with a woman who was expecting him. No, I don't think he'll pick me. He's a coward. He'd avoid me."

"Except he's crazy as a loon. There's really no way to predict what he'll do next."

"I'm being careful. I haven't gone home except to change clothes since this started, and I'll be doubly careful now. He'll have trouble catching up with me. If we really begin to think he might target me, we can set my apartment up and lure him in."

"Keren, have you seen the pictures of LaToya and Juanita? I promise you, if you even think about doing such a dangerous thing, I'll parade up and down in front of your building shouting, 'Run, Pravus, it's a trap!'"

Keren laughed. "Well then, let's hope it doesn't come to that, because I'd hate to have to arrest you, and I'd do it in a heartbeat if you got in my way."

Paul relaxed again. "Tough talk."

"You bet. And it's not just talk." Keren reached for her radio. "Let me get someone out here to watch this pond so you can get some sleep and preach your sermon in the morning. Rosita didn't sound that excited about Murray. I've been sleeping in the precinct, and I think I'll do it again tonight. Pravus was definitely trying to sound threatening toward me, like he was targeting me. If he decides to turn his attention my way, I don't want him to find me before I'm ready."

Paul sat quietly while Keren called for backup. "It's going to be at least a half hour before anyone can get loose from what they're doing."

When she spoke, her voice woke Paul. He said, "Talk to me, Kerenhappuch. This stakeout isn't worth much if I'm napping."

"Okay." She was quiet for so long that Paul wondered if she hadn't dozed off. The only reason he doubted it was because he could feel tension coming off her in waves, even with two feet of car seat between them. "You believe in spiritual gifts, don't you, Paul?"

"Yes. Of course I do. I've been given the gifts of preaching and teaching." He hesitated, because despite her casual question, he could tell this was important to her. "What made you mention that?"

"Well. . .I've got a gift, too. I. . .I don't talk about it much. I learned to keep quiet when I was very young, after a couple of dreadful experiences. Then later on, when I finally did talk about it. . .to. . .someone, it ended up underscoring my decision to keep it quiet."

Paul knew when something was sitting heavy on someone's heart. "What gift?"

"I know. . .well, what I mean is, I know when. . . The gifts of the Spirit are pretty well known for the most part. Teaching, preaching, wisdom, even the more miraculous gifts like healing, speaking in tongues, and interpretation of tongues are ones people talk about. But mine is. . .well, it's. . ." She fell silent again.

Paul didn't rush her. Finally, when it looked like she wasn't going to say any more, he asked, "When was the last time you talked about this?"

Keren let her head drop back on the headrest. "With the exception of my parents. . .and one other time. . .I haven't talked about it since fourth grade. I made a really public announcement in school about someone. . ." She looked sideways at him.

"Go on."

"A boy was pushing a smaller kid around in the lunchroom, and I announced to the whole room, 'He can't help himself. He's possessed by a demon.'"

Keren rubbed her hands over her face. Paul could well imagine the fallout from such an announcement. "So did you get beaten up?"

She came out from behind her hands. "If only I had. Unfortunately, the principal came in at that moment."

"Unfortunately?"

"Yeah. Instead of getting punched, which might have been the end of it, I got hauled into the principal's office, and he called my parents. Then he called the boy's parents. He thought I was being a little hard on the kid, I guess. It turned into a circus, because the bully's parents demanded I apologize. So, right in front of his big, nasty father, I said with perfect sincerity to this big, nasty kid, 'I'm sorry you are possessed by a demon.'"

Paul couldn't stop himself from laughing.

"You can imagine how well that went over."

Finally, he said, "You were pretty harsh."

"I wasn't trying to be. It was true. I thought they'd want to know. I'd never even said such a thing to my parents. Maybe the gift hadn't come to me yet or maybe I'd never been near someone possessed by a demon before, but the whole thing was really unexpected by everyone. Me included."

"Were your parents. . .how did they handle it?"

"They had a long talk with me and they supported me, believed what I'd said. And they got out the Bible and read 1 Corinthians 12 to me and talked about their own gifts. We had plenty of time for all this because I got suspended from school for three days. They helped me to appreciate my gift, but we decided I should maybe be a little more discreet about it. Then I got back to school and, well, let's just say kids can be cruel. I've never. . .well almost never. . .talked about it again."

"So you just ignore what you see?"

"No, but now I know better than to blurt something like that out in front of everyone. I've learned the art of thinking before I speak."

"Some people never learn it."

"Well, I did—the hard way." Keren glanced at him as if she expected him to haul her up to his office and call her parents. "So anyway, that's my gift. I discern spirits. I can tell when a demon has taken up residence in someone's soul."

"Every time?"

Keren seemed to give his question considerable thought. "I guess I don't know if I can do it every time. I only know sometimes

I can. I assume God lets me see it because He wants me to know, either to help or to be careful."

"That's a beautiful gift, Keren. I've talked to a few people who believe they have such a gift, but it's more subtle with them. They talk about being repelled by certain people, and they think that's a sign that they have an evil spirit of some kind. But I've learned that people can be really bad without a demon being involved. Or at least God doesn't always reveal a demon when I'm tangling with criminals. It's not a well-understood gift."

"I've never talked to anyone who claimed to have it." Keren ran one hand back and forth over the steering wheel and seemed to be looking into the distance. "But then, I've never asked because I never talk about it."

"You said you did one other time, outside your parents and that fourth grader. And it was bad. Tell me about that."

Keren scowled at him. "You listen like you're some kind of. . . of. . ."

"Pastor?" Paul smiled at her.

"Yeah." She slumped in her car seat. "Just like a pastor."

"Occupational hazard." Then silence stretched, and Paul quietly prayed for her to feel safe with him, safe enough to tell what was obviously a very difficult story. And for himself to have some wisdom to offer. Wisdom didn't seem to be one of his gifts when it came to Keren.

Apparently the silent treatment worked. Keren inhaled slowly and said, "I was engaged once."

That caused a very basic, very unpleasant reaction.

Jealousy.

Paul was shocked at the strength of it. Now he was afraid to talk for fear of saying something stupid.

"What happened?" There, that sounded neutral enough.

"I had a lifetime of secrecy behind me, but I knew I really needed to be open with the man I wanted to marry. I kept putting it off more out of habit than anything." Keren sounded guilty, like she blamed herself for the end of her relationship. "In fact, I put it off until the night he proposed. But he was a strong Christian. He was a decent man, someone I really thought God had chosen for me. It seemed so right."

"It was obviously wrong." Paul didn't think he quite managed neutrality with that comment.

"Obviously." Keren nodded. "I really didn't think he'd be put off by it. He produced the ring and I said yes."

Paul could hear the bewilderment and hurt in her voice.

"We spent hours that night talking about the future. He owned a house, but he offered to sell it, and we'd buy one together. We talked about me being a cop, and he wasn't real thrilled with it, but I'd told him it was a calling and I expected to make a career of it and he seemed okay with it. We talked a lot about our faith and wanting to raise our children the way we'd been raised, and somehow we worked our way around to that story I just told you."

"Fourth grade."

Nodding, Keren said, "He was really taken aback by it. He started asking a lot of questions, really detailed stuff, because by then I'd already confronted a lot of people in trouble. The questions took a turn that was weird, accusatory. Honestly, it reminded me a little of that mess in fourth grade, and I kept expecting him to call the principal and my parents."

"I wonder why he reacted so strongly. It seems strange that he would."

"He changed the subject back to my work, and suddenly we were having a fight. The first real fight we'd ever had. We were so compatible. The whole thing was shocking. By the time the date came to an end, the engagement was over."

"How long had you been dating?"

"Close to a year."

"And that was it? You couldn't work things out?"

"I couldn't even get him to talk to me. I phoned a few times and he wouldn't answer. I still thought it was about being a cop at that point. After a couple of weeks of him ducking me, I went to his house and waited for him one night, and when he came home, he had another woman with him."

"In two weeks he'd found someone else?"

"When they walked up to me, the woman he was with said, 'Is this the exorcist cop?'"

Paul flinched.

"He asked me if I was going to add stalking to everything else."

"You dated him for a year and never saw this side of him?"

"Not helping, Paul."

"Sorry."

"It was a betrayal like nothing I've ever felt before. Not just that he was so...repulsed. But that he'd obviously told this woman. Made a joke out of it." She shook her head silently for a while. "I felt like God gave me a choice right there and then to serve Him or to have a man in my life. Well, I couldn't believe it was right not to serve Him. So I decided marriage just wasn't for me. Not in God's plan for me. If I was called to be a police officer and given a gift that was so hard to understand, God's will must be for me to remain alone. And that was it. I walked away. I haven't dated. I certainly haven't kissed a man since. And I've never talked about my gift to anyone again."

"I'm glad you walked away. What did he want you to do? Ignore a gift that could help so many people?"

"No, I think he just wanted me to get away from him and stay away." She pulled herself out of her dark mood enough to glare at Paul. "And there's no *could* about it. I do help people."

"Sorry." Paul was glad to hear her temper, much better than the hurt. "I didn't mean you didn't. I'm honored that you felt like you could talk about it with me."

"You should be."

"I'd like you to come over to the mission. If I knew there was something more than simple human weakness involved with some of my people, maybe I could help them more."

"There's more."

Paul said cautiously, "More gifts?"

"No. . .well, sort of. My gift is discerning spirits—that's not only demons. I can also discern when the Holy Spirit is flowing strongly in someone."

Paul looked at her for a long time. "That would be such a wonderful thing to see."

"It is. I sensed the Holy Spirit in you the first time I saw you lying there all beat up in that hospital. You have a spirit of courage and joy that is so strong."

"Was that before or after you started yelling at me?"

Keren was silent for a few seconds. Sheepishly, she said, "Before."

Paul looked at her.

She gave him a quick glance then went back to staring out the windshield. "Your spirit, your love for the people who come to your mission, it has an unusually powerful effect on me, Paul. I'm afraid I'm letting it confuse me."

She rested her elbow on the open window and propped her head up with her fist. "That kiss—it shouldn't have happened, but there's something. . ." Keren shrugged.

"Let's deal with the kiss later."

Keren gave him a dry look, like she knew he didn't want to deal with it at all, and she agreed; but they were still going to have to deal with it.

"So if you saw the Holy Spirit in me, why did you get so angry?"

Keren gave him a disgruntled look. "You really don't remember me, do you?"

Paul sat straighter in his seat. With all the other revelations tonight, he had a feeling this was the one she wanted to talk about least, and therefore was the one that he needed to hear most. "I asked you if we met. We did. I knew it. But I can't remember when."

Keren shook her head and crossed her arms. She said in a disgusted voice, "We didn't exactly meet. But you didn't like the way I handled a case and tried to have me busted out of the police force. All I can guess is you must have done it so much that one little incident doesn't carry much weight."

"I did what?"

"You heard me."

"When? What happened?"

"Let's leave it for now," Keren said. "I'm sorry I brought it up. You tried to paint me as an incompetent little girl who was too softhearted to arrest the bad guys, and I was tough enough to survive the suspension, plus the harassment from every cop who knew what happened."

"You can't make a statement like that and then let it drop."

"You dropped the kiss. Now it's my turn to drop something."

"Keren," Paul said, doing his best to sound threatening. He'd been good at threatening at one time. She gave him a *You-don't-scare-me* look.

Finally, Paul said, "All right, fine. But I'm going to find out what it is. I'm a cop—"

"You *were* a cop," Keren corrected him.

"I'll track it down. Or maybe I'll just pry it out of you."

"Why don't you just reread some of your old press clippings? You had enough of those."

Paul heard the venom in her voice and wondered how they'd gotten from a kiss to this. He studied her mulish profile and tapped his foot on the floorboard irritably, then he decided to change the subject. For now. "You reacted so strongly when I told you *Pravus* was Latin for 'demon' because you sensed this about him?"

"It's bad." Keren nodded. "Evil is permeating every aspect of this case. Nothing bothers O'Shea, but the crime scene, the blood. . .it really shook him. And I've never seen Dr. Schaefer lose her cool. They don't know it, but they're sensing the demon in this, too."

Paul thought of the ME's unsteady voice during the autopsy.

"I've never had an experience like this," Keren said. "Where I could feel the demonic presence even when the person hosting the demon isn't around. I felt it at the explosion, at the fountain where we found Juanita, at the autopsy, in LaToya's apartment. . ."

"Do you think you could sense him if he were near?"

"I don't know. Whatever is inside of him is incredibly powerful. If I could focus on him with some internal radar, it would be the first time I ever have."

"Are you sure?"

"Sure? What do you mean?"

"Maybe you aren't aware of it. Have you ever been pursuing a criminal and you picked the right alley to go up or the right door to look behind? You told me once that O'Shea says you have great instincts. Maybe, without you being aware of it, you've been able to track down evil better because of your gift."

"I've never considered such a thing. You know, not every criminal I arrest has a demon. You'd think they would. Sometimes I see demons in the strangest places. I've seen the struggle in some people, and, if they are open to it, I've helped them."

"Can you cast demons out?" Paul's heart started pounding.

"I don't cast them out the way Jesus did. The people I've helped have done it themselves. I've encouraged them and prayed for them, but I've never found an ability to just tell the demon to come out and it works. Remember the demon that the disciples couldn't cast out?"

"Yes, the story is in Matthew and Mark. I'm always particularly interested in the seemingly small stories that occur in more than one book. They must have left a strong impression. And I think God wants us to understand that they have special meaning."

"Well, in Matthew, Jesus is pretty hard on His disciples, saying they don't have enough faith. But in Mark He says this kind of demon only comes out with prayer and fasting. That's the way I approach demons. I begin praying. I only speak in the kindest way to the person who is possessed. I pray every second I'm with them. I can tell if they are interested in my help or not."

"And if they are?" Paul prompted.

"Then we pray together."

"And it works?" Paul was fascinated.

"It works. It works a surprising amount of the time, because part of my discernment seems to be. . .well, usually. . .I think I can discern a spirit in someone who is open to being free of it. Because I usually help them, so it stands to reason, right? God gave me that type of understanding as the true purpose of my gift. Leading them to Jesus Christ always has to be part of it. I'm afraid I'll leave them empty and more demons will come and take up residence."

"That's from Luke." Paul was impressed. "You've really done your homework on Biblical demons."

"Can you blame me? It's a huge part of my life. It's why I became a police officer."

"To chase demons?"

"No, because sensing them and seeing the damage they do, both to the ones they possess and those around them, gave me a special heart for the people who struggle with them. I've found my gift very useful as a cop."

There was a lull while Paul considered the strange conversation. "And our killer's demon is bad news?"

"The worst news imaginable," Keren replied.

"So, Juanita was killed by a demon, and now he has LaToya at his mercy."

"God is holding LaToya in the palm of His hand, Paul. And Juanita is being bathed in His love. No demon really has any power over God, you know that. Good is stronger than evil."

"I do know that." But Paul was glad she'd reminded him. "And I know that to live is Christ, and to die is gain. I tell Rosita that every morning when she scolds me for jogging through the neighborhood."

"I like Rosita." Keren grinned at him.

"I like her, too, but she's a nag." His eyes had adjusted to the dark until he could see every nuance of her face, the moonlight casting her skin in blue, her eyes a glowing, ghostly gray.

"So we do our best, and we leave the rest to God." Keren shifted in her seat as if it made her impatient to accept that. "I'd lose my mind at work if I couldn't."

"I never could leave anything to anyone, least of all God, when

I was a cop. I let the job consume me until it almost ate my heart out." Paul snorted. "What almost? It did eat my heart out. I lost my wife. I lost my daughter. What were they if not my heart?"

Paul paused then whispered, "I was a bad father."

"Hush." Keren reached for him then pulled her hand back. "You know better than to waste time with regret. Your faith won't allow that kind of wallowing. Turn to face God and the challenges of today, and let the past go."

"Sounds easy."

"Not easy, simple. There's a difference." Keren ran her hands into her hair and fiddled with her hair tie.

She was self-conscious now because he'd done something so stupid as kiss her. "Simple to say but not so simple to do."

"Like I said, simple, not easy."

She was going to quit touching him, and only now was he aware that almost no one ever touched him. He often rested a hand on the shoulder of the homeless people he served, but they didn't touch him back. He suddenly missed the touch of a human hand desperately. And he knew exactly who he wanted to touch him.

He turned to face her. "Maybe it's time we talked about that kiss." He closed the distance between them.

A patrol car pulled up to Keren's door. Paul threw himself across the car seat, away from Keren. He saw her gun come up to just below the window. She was on edge, even though the car was marked and both men in it wore uniforms. One of them got out and came up to her window.

"Are you Detective Collins?" He was young and eager. It saddened Paul to think how soon those eyes would become cynical.

"Yes." Keren flashed her badge at him. "Let me see your badge, officer."

Keren kept her gun out of sight.

The man tapped his chest where it was clearly pinned.

Keren studied it for a long minute before she slipped her gun into its holster without the young officer even knowing she'd had it ready. The kid wasn't nearly scared enough.

"Were you informed of why you were needed here?"

"You suspect that the man who blew up that building downtown might use that pond over there as a dump site for his latest vic."

Paul realized Keren had gotten used to saying LaToya. She glanced at him. He'd wanted them to be less detached when they talked about Juanita and LaToya. Keren had told him no, but somewhere along the way he'd converted her, and now this officer's language chilled him.

"That's right. This guy is a stone-cold killer." Keren jabbed her finger in the cop's face. "Don't either one of you sleep. Don't daydream. Don't let your guard down for a second. Don't let someone drive up to you or walk up to you. Assume everyone's got a gun and will open fire as soon as they're in range."

The cop straightened and his face looked pale in the streetlight.

Keren continued. "He definitely studied the other dump site and waited until he was alone to leave the body. He'll be watching, waiting for you to make a mistake."

"Yes ma'am." The cop stood at attention.

"And when you make a mistake with this maniac, you'll end up dead." She slashed one finger at him like she was slitting his throat.

The officer took a half step back. "Yes ma'am!"

"I'll radio to have someone take over for you when your shift ends." Keren pulled out of the parking lot.

"You went overboard a little scaring that kid, don't you think?" Paul asked.

"I sure tried."

Paul slumped down in his seat. "Good girl."

CHAPTER ELEVEN

P, reach your sermon tomorrow like you're supposed to," Keren ordered Paul as she pulled up at the shabby back door of the old brick mission. "It'll remind you of who you are."

Paul leaned over and kissed her good-bye, as if he'd done it a thousand times before and it was his right. He pulled back and his eyes ran over her face.

"What's that thing you've got in your hair?"

Keren, flustered, reached up for her leather tie. "It's the only thing that works."

"Works? What does that mean?"

"Keeps my wild mop of hair under control." She pulled the odd contraption free and her hair spread in a riot of curls all around her head.

Paul took the hair ornament. "Beads, ties, weird." He looked up at her. "You ought to let your hair loose. I love it down."

Reaching out he caressed it and closed in again.

It took Keren way too long to put a stop to that. She waited until he was inside then drove back to the precinct to sleep.

There was a light burning in the room where they'd met with the FBI, and Keren went to see what was going on. Higgins sat at the desk, Dyson on a folding chair. Both were poring over stacks of paper.

"You're working late, gentlemen." Keren wished she'd just walked straight to the room with the cots.

Higgins gave her that I'm-a-predator-and-you're-lunch look, and Dyson did his odd impression of a mind reader.

"Can you give us a minute, Detective?" Higgins had a way of making requests that sounded like orders. "We've got some things we'd like to go over with you."

Feeling every ounce of the weight of her long hours without sleep. . .and the poor quality of the sleep when she did get it, Keren said, "Sure."

"The mayor has asked us to be part of a task force to deal with this."

"I've been expecting that. The bizarre murder, the explosion combined with the second abduction—"

"We want Pastor Morris to be part of it." Higgins was so alert, Keren couldn't shake the sense that he was always on the hunt.

"I'm sure he'll be agreeable to that." Privately, Keren suspected they'd have more than they could handle if they tried to keep him out.

"Have you made any headway on the profiling?" She sat down on a folding chair next to Dyson. Higgins faced them from across the desk.

Higgins looked at Dyson and Dyson turned his spooky blue eyes on her.

"We've come to the conclusion that Pravus has too much inside knowledge of the mission to have done research on it from the outside."

A chill raced up Keren's spine. "You mean he comes and goes in that building all the time."

Higgins nodded. "It's possible it could be a deliveryman or someone with a reason to be in the mission, but it's more likely—"

"It's one of the street people." Keren hated the thought of it.

"No, it's someone who's *masquerading* as a street person."

Keren considered her impression of evil. She needed to go in the mission when the inhabitants were around. But there was no way to explain that to these men.

"What is it, Detective Collins?" Dyson asked. He was watching her like a hawk. . .or maybe a vulture.

"There's a church service in the morning, during breakfast," Keren said reluctantly. "Someone should attend and get a closer look at those people."

"We need a list of everyone who is associated with the mission."

Keren hated the thought of using Paul's mission service in her police work. It seemed like such a betrayal of people who might be making a fragile step in faith. "It's a very transient group."

"It figures this guy hasn't gone anywhere," Higgins said sarcastically.

"And they're not going to cooperate." Keren was getting tired of Higgins, and all the while he sparred with her Dyson stared, trying to pick up nuances. When he asked questions it was like her every word, gesture, and expression was being watched under a microscope. He was sitting beside her, so if she focused forward she could ignore him, but she could feel his creepy gaze boring into her brain. He was probably a real bust at parties.

"Not cooperating is almost a defining characteristic of street people." She wished she'd never mentioned Paul's church. She should have let it come from the FBI. "A lot of them probably don't even go by their real names."

"I'll bet every one of them has a rap sheet and a mug shot." Higgins slumped back in his chair, but the sense of his utter alertness never eased.

"You know, Higgins, the people at the mission are really going through a tough time."

"They're bums."

"They're mostly mentally ill, with no family to care for them."

"They're drug addicts and alcoholics who did so much damage their families finally washed their hands of them and dumped their problem on the streets."

"A little compassion wouldn't be out of place here." Keren's jaw tightened. She should drop this. She should get some sleep. "A lot of them are bipolar and they drink and drug to silence the voices in their heads. And a lot of families just can't deal with it. A lot of them have tried and tried until they've given up to save what's left of their own lives. That mission is trying to do more than just feed them. Paul is trying to lead them to a Christian faith that will give them hope, help them find a purpose for living and a reason to reclaim their sanity."

" 'Paul'?" Dyson asked. "Is he more to you than a witness to a crime?"

Suppressing a flash of irritation, Keren kept quiet. She preferred talking things through, bouncing ideas off O'Shea. The two of them worked well that way. But Higgins just seemed to delight in pointing out the obvious when she'd only meant to run through her thoughts aloud. And Dyson, with his eternal search for the key to everyone's thoughts, was about halfway to a mental patient himself.

Higgins made a soft scoffing sound. "Figures a mission would force hungry people to sit through a sermon in order to get food."

Keren's impression of Higgins dropped through the floor.

"You're a believer?" Dyson was still watching her. Still reading her mind.

"Why don't you"—Keren turned and met Dyson's spooky blue eyes directly—"use whatever ability you have to profile Pravus instead of trying to pick up messages from every tiny expression that flicks across my face? Or is reading minds some trick you do to win bets in a bar?"

Dyson kept staring.

Higgins sat watching, too. Keren decided she'd had enough of it.

"Maybe if I wasn't running on little to no sleep for the last few days I could enjoy being stared at. I'd enjoy having my faith sneered at. I'd enjoy listening to you mock a man who has committed his life to helping people in need." Keren rose from her chair. "Yes, he preaches a sermon. He's trying to give them more than a meal that will last a few hours. But no one is denied food if they refuse to stay. If you don't have anything to say about the case, then I'm going to try to get some sleep."

"One more thing before you go, Keren." Higgins spoke mildly again, but he might as well have shouted at her to stop.

"What is that?" Keren turned to face him.

"We've listened to the tapes. You have to know Pravus has you in his crosshairs. It's very possible he sees you as one of his potential victims."

"Wow, *Lance*. Did you figure that out all by yourself? Or did you fly a whole bunch more people in from DC to help you?"

"We expect cooperation from local law enforcement agencies, Detective."

"And you sometimes don't get it, is that your point?"

"I'm not talking about sometimes. I'm talking about now, and I'm not seeing much of it from you." Higgins's golden eyes had seemed so attractive and contained such strength when she'd met him earlier. Now they repelled her. Between his rudeness and his crude remark about the mission's outreach and the contempt he held for the homeless, she was fed up.

"And why do you think I'd hesitate to work with you? What possible reason could I have? I'll bet you don't even need Dyson reading my mind to get the answer to that. Unless you're both idiots, you should get it loud and clear."

Dyson stared. Higgins stood as if he needed to be on the prowl. Neither of them answered.

"Good night, gentlemen. If I have any spare time tomorrow, maybe I can stop in again to be insulted for things that have nothing to do with this case. I'm sure it never gets old. . .for you." Keren left the room, closing the door behind her with a firm *click*.

The lousy bed made it easy to get up early.

She ran home to shower and change. As she entered her apartment, a chill went up her spine. She'd known Pravus was possibly going to target her, even hoped for it so they could get him. But now Higgins's voice haunted her. It made her furious that her own home spooked her. Stepping into the main room, she suddenly saw all that was wrong about her apartment. She was savvy about personal safety, but she lived in a decent neighborhood and hadn't ever worried much.

The building had a secure entrance. But she was on the ground floor. It wouldn't exactly take a CIA agent with cat burglar skills and high-tech electronics to get in. Access could be gained with a hammer slammed through her patio window, for heaven's sake. And there were bushes and shade trees on the side where her glass patio doors were. There was a stylish streetlamp back there, but it was more for show than illumination. The shrubs and trees shrouded the area in darkness.

Now, in full daylight, she stood for a moment, looking out in that pretty little green space. She'd always loved it. It had helped sell her on this apartment. Now it scared her and she hated that. Hated knowing she was vulnerable and that, along with her own danger, she might bring danger to her neighbors.

She'd already known she might be a target, but she didn't think it was her time yet. Not while Pravus was busy pouring out his madness on poor LaToya.

Rushing through getting dressed—to get out of an apartment she'd enjoyed for the last few years, she didn't put on church clothes. They'd be badly out of place at the mission. Only now, several days too late, did she realize that she should have been hanging around the mission from the first, trying to sense that demonic presence. It irritated her a little that Higgins and Dyson had helped her realize that. She wanted to believe their presence was a waste of taxpayer dollars.

So, though she'd already decided she wanted to listen to Paul preach, now she was going for another, less honorable reason—a cop reason. She hoped Paul didn't realize it. Or if he did, he didn't blow a gasket.

She wore khaki slacks, a polo shirt, and her best shoes. Nikes. One of the rules she lived by was that she never put anything on her feet that wouldn't allow her to chase a fleeing criminal or run for her life.

She got to the Lighthouse Mission in time for breakfast. Paul was on the business side of a counter covered with steaming stainless steel pans.

"Hi, come to help?" He saluted her with a spatula.

"I'm counting on it." Keren ferreted out a huge apron and asked Rosita if she could use a break from dishing up eggs. Rosita gladly gave up her spot in the serving line.

Standing next to Paul, Keren checked to see if he was as exhausted as she was.

He had red veins running through his eyes and dark circles under them, but he smiled, and for one split second he focused on her lips. She thought he might just kiss her again right here in front of everyone.

"Get to work." He jabbed his spatula at her pan of eggs and grinned.

Keren ignored a stab of regret that he hadn't followed through and kissed her. "Right away, sir."

A line filed past and she scooped eggs onto the trays of shuffling homeless men and women. She ignored the smell of unwashed bodies and mass-produced food and watched the men as they came through, mindful of the way people treated the homeless. She said hello to each of them. This was her precinct, and she knew a few by name because they were regulars in the neighborhood. Some of them recognized her as a cop and gave her doubtful looks, but they must have been hungry, because they took their food and moved on.

Paul was in his element. He talked to each man and woman. He asked about personal matters and apologized for being gone so much that week. LaToya's name came up several times, as did Juanita's. It was an insular community in many ways. They knew what was going on around them, even if they chose not to get involved with it.

When the line finally dwindled, Paul said, "I really appreciate your help this morning, Keren. Some of my most regular helpers are missing today. Murray didn't even show up to preach. This is about half the crowd we usually have. I think they blame the mission for the trouble in the neighborhood."

"What else can I do?"

"Fill those white thermal pitchers with coffee from the big pots and pour." Paul smiled and arched his brows in a conspiratorial way then whispered, "If they take a second cup, they usually settle in and stay for services."

Glad for a chance to move through the crowd, Keren filled a pot and circulated through the room. She laid her hand on many shoulders and occasionally stopped to talk.

She was surprised how much she enjoyed this act of service. Paul came up behind her to trade her nearly empty coffeepot for a full one.

"Jesus reached out over and over to people who were outcasts," he murmured in her ear. "He calls us to do the same. The act of serving is one of the purest forms of Christianity, and it invariably returns more to us than we ever give."

"But if we're doing it for the blessings we receive, then is it a true act of service?" Keren asked.

"Ah, philosophy," Paul said with a grin. "I suppose that depends on what's in your heart. Is this a pure act of service, Keren, or are you here trying to earn God's blessings?"

Before Keren could respond, Paul leaned closer. "Or maybe you're trying to catch the interest of a certain preacher."

She pulled away and gave him her best squinty gunslinger look.

"That cranky look's not scaring me off. I'm definitely interested." He left to refill his pot, and it was only with the greatest effort that Keren managed to close her mouth.

She turned back to the men she was serving. *I'm not here for that, Lord.*

No reassuring answer.

Am I?

She got to a man who had gone through the line before she'd arrived, and, as simply as that, she sensed the demon. Not Pravus—the impression was nowhere near that powerful—but there was no denying her discernment.

The man looked and smelled like the rest. His clothing was

hanging in tatters. He was probably mid- to late-forties, but the street added years to a face. He could be younger. He had on a ragged sweatshirt that might have at one time been red. One of the shirt's wrists was ripped away, the other hung by a thread. His pants were army fatigues, and his hair and beard looked like they hadn't been washed or combed for years, or cut for a decade.

There was an empty place beside him; in fact, there were only two others sitting at the utilitarian table with him, and they were seated as far from him as possible. Keren wondered if the other transients could sense that he was different, more awash in evil than the rest of them. She eased herself into the chair beside him. She glanced up and saw Paul shake his head at her. So even Paul was careful of this man. She nodded once to let him know she got the message but she didn't move. She was praying silently, asking for Jesus' intervention, asking for leading. She laid a hand on the man's arm and he turned to her with a sudden jerk. He snarled under his breath like a cornered wild animal.

Keren didn't flinch. She looked at the man, trying to see past the surface, trying to see if there was someone here who would be open to her. Their eyes locked. She saw the struggle in him, the bitter unhappiness, the total defeat.

At last she said, "I know a way out of the darkness."

"There is no way." He moved as if he would get up and leave, but something kept him in his seat.

She gripped his shoulder and spoke softly. "Accept my prayers. I can help you get free from what's inside of you."

The man's eyes cleared and Keren saw his longing. "What's your name?" she asked.

"R–Roger." Keren wondered how long it had been since he'd spoken his name out loud. His eyes lost focus, and she saw the effort he made to hang on to himself. "My name used to be Roger Prewitt."

"Your name is *still* Roger Prewitt." She leaned close. "I'm going to pray for you, Roger. The demon inside of you can be cast out. He'll stay out if you turn your life over to Jesus. You can get out of the misery that controls your life."

"There's no way out." Roger shook his head. Lice crawled along his hairline. His voice was guttural, as if he hadn't used it in a long time. "This has been with me since I was in a car accident. I made a deal and I thought it was worth it to survive. But it's *not* worth it. I'd rather have died that night than live like this. But at the time, burning alive was too much to face."

Keren saw twisted, damaged skin on the back of his hand. She reached for the sleeve with the wrist cuff torn away and carefully pushed the shirt up. She uncovered deep, ugly scars.

"You must have been in terrible pain and you were weak."

"How can you know that?" Roger's voice grew loud and agitated.

"There's no great miracle in my knowing fire is terribly painful. There's only what's obvious when I feel the demon in you and know a moment of weakness let it in. God sent me to help you."

"He didn't help me that night. He left me to die. Satan was there. He spared me and now he claims my soul as payment."

"You're wrong." Keren laid her hand over his scarred hand and didn't try to conceal the grief she felt for Roger's suffering. "Life and death isn't a deal Satan can make. God alone can give life and death. *God* saved you that night. But Satan can stand by and whisper lies in your ear. He's the prince of lies."

"So I gave up my soul for nothing?" Roger's head began to sag as if it weighed too much to hold it up.

Keren let his sleeve fall back over the brutal scars and firmly raised his chin. "You didn't give up your soul. The soul God gave you is alive in you, longing desperately to be returned to its proper place in God's kingdom."

"I made my choice." He said it as if it were a matter of honor to him that he keep his bargain. "There's no way out for me. I'll live out my life on these streets. Then I'll die. Life and death are both hell, it makes no difference."

Keren forced him with sheer willpower to hold her gaze. "It doesn't have to be that way. We can cast out the demon. God can restore joy and peace to your life."

"Peace?" the man said with aching sadness. "I haven't known a moment's peace in twenty years."

"You could rest in the Lord. Think of finally being at rest with your Savior. Aren't you tired?"

"I'm tired," he whispered. "I've been *so* tired for *so* long."

"Pray with me."

She began praying, softly enough no one around them could hear, but loudly enough to include Roger. She felt the war between good and evil being waged. She prayed, and then she felt a hand rest on her shoulder. She looked up at Paul. His other hand was on Roger's back. Roger's eyes popped open.

"Let me add my prayers to yours," Paul said.

Roger nodded confidently, as if Paul's presence made him stronger. Suddenly Roger began to pray along with her and Paul. Tears sprang to Keren's eyes. Her voice broke, but she continued to pray. She felt Paul's hand settle on her back, and his words, different than hers, different than Roger's, blended with theirs and became a harmony of pleas to God for freedom for one man.

Keren could feel the darkness begin to lose its battle. A high-pitched shriek, one she knew from experience only she could hear, built until it cut her eardrums. The demon battled until Roger's body began to tremble. Roger's hands shook and Keren grabbed them and held them tight.

With a quick, loud *crack*—again audible only to her—and one last hideous scream of fury, the demon was gone. Keren opened her eyes and looked into the face of a changed man. Wonder filled Roger right before her eyes.

"Pastor P is going to preach a sermon today, Roger." She kept his hands gripped firmly in hers. "You're going to hear it with new ears. You need to replace the despair that's inside you with love. You need to nurture the peace you've been given."

"How did you do this?" Roger asked in awe.

"Not me," Keren said. "Don't ever think it was me. God revealed your sorrow to me and used me to pray with you. God removed that demon from you. All you've ever needed to do was turn to Him and simply ask for freedom."

"That's all I needed to do? But why did He wait so long? Why did He let me waste all these years?"

"He didn't wait." Keren shook her head. "I can promise you He's tried many times before. He's sent people before, but you weren't ready to listen until now."

"How can you know things about me like that?"

"I don't know things about you. But I know God. I know He's always trying to bring His children home."

Roger's eyes seemed to look back over the years, and Keren hoped he was remembering times when God had tried to bring him back.

"You're right." He nodded. "I know you are."

Keren cradled Roger's grimy hands with their claw-like nails, caked with dirt. "God loves you, Roger. He has never left you, not during all these years you've lived such a hopeless life. He has never quit calling to you. God asks us only to believe in Him, to believe in Jesus."

"I do believe. How could I live through what just happened

and not believe." His hands turned in her grip and clasped Keren's. "I've done so much evil in my life. I abandoned my wife and children. I've wasted my life hating the whole world."

Roger looked sideways at Paul. "Can you help me. . . ." He looked down at himself. "I want to be clean and decent. I have two children. I need to find them."

"You know I'll help you, Roger. I've been praying you'd let me help you for a long time."

"Why would you pray for me, Pastor? There's so much more hope with a lot of these men. Why would you pick me?"

"I didn't pick you over them, Roger. I pray for all of you. Every one of you, every day, by name."

Roger's eyes filled with tears.

Paul's hand on Roger's back shifted. Keren knew it was an offer of comfort.

"Are all of these men like me?" Roger asked Keren. "Is a demon living in all of them?"

"I can't answer that. God told me there was a demon in you. He may only tell me of those who are ready to listen."

"So we can't know for sure." He looked around the dingy room with its dozens of grizzle-faced, raggedly dressed men and the handful of equally suffering women. "I wonder—" He looked at Paul. "Would you accept my help? If God can find me here, then He can find these other men."

"I think God is speaking to your heart right now." Keren patted his hand. "He's telling you of a way to grow in your faith by helping others."

"I would welcome your help," Paul said. "You could speak to the homeless with so much wisdom because you've experienced it. You know the struggle."

Keren, Paul, and Roger talked quietly until Paul stepped to the front of the room.

CHAPTER TWELVE

Paul talked about Juanita and led them in a prayer for LaToya. The crowd seemed to nearly vibrate with the attention they paid him once the women were mentioned. Paul knew God was using this nightmare for good. After he finished his prayer, he preached a simple sermon of salvation. When he was finished, his eyes rested on Keren. She sat next to Roger, still holding his hand.

Paul felt such profound respect for her. She never shrank from Roger because of his smell or the wild look that always lurked in his eyes. She had shown the kind of compassion and courage that Jesus Christ had shown in touching the leper and eating with the tax collector.

Though Paul had reached out to Roger many times, the truth was, Paul had never held much hope. Roger seemed further gone than even the average transient.

Keren had seen the demon in him.

Even more, she'd seen a way to deliver him, and she'd seen Roger's longing for deliverance. Now she sat at Roger's side, and everyone who'd come in for breakfast stayed for a change, to listen to Paul's sermon.

Paul didn't know what Keren made him feel. He only knew she made him feel *something* for the first time in a long time. He didn't like getting entangled with the police. He remembered last night when those bushes rustled. He'd reached for his gun. It had been a reflex. Thinking about it now sickened him.

He couldn't deal with the things she awakened—the cop things, the man things—so he left it up to God and walked out among his congregation. He spent time talking with each of them. He saw Roger, now standing clear eyed, talking rationally, ministering to those who gave any indication of being interested.

Roger came up to him. "Can I stay here and help you? I'll cook or clean or whatever you need."

"Of course you can stay. We'll find you some clean clothes and get you a bath and a good haircut, and then I'll help you find your family."

The joy that flooded Roger's expression was almost more than Paul could take. He pulled Roger close and hugged him.

Roger tried to back away. "I'm so filthy, Pastor. Let me get cleaned up before you touch me."

Paul smiled. "No. I'm not hugging you to be nice, I'm just so happy. I'm so glad you've found God's love. I've been dirty a few times in my life, so I'm not afraid."

Roger let Paul hug him again.

They talked about Roger's future for a bit, then Roger thanked Paul for speaking of LaToya and Juanita. "You know, I overheard someone in the breakfast line talking about all that gasoline being hauled into LaToya's old hangout. I think whoever did it dressed up like he's homeless. He just walked right in with a baggy coat." Roger looked over at the knot of men and women.

"Do you remember who said it?" Paul asked, studying the crowd.

"No, I never look left or right. Least I never did before. It was just talking. But no one left today like some days. You could ask around."

"I will. Thank you. Maybe someone here is a witness."

Rosita came up and asked Roger if he was ready to get settled.

"Where's Murray today, Rosie? I thought he was going to preach."

"I don't know, Pastor P. But I'm glad you came. I wasn't in the mood for him. And Louie was supposed to show up. He hasn't gotten his hours in this week. If his parole officer calls, he could be in trouble. This place doesn't run as well when you're not around."

"What about Buddy?"

"He's been comin' and goin' a lot lately." Rosita was suddenly very earnest. "You know he likes the roof over his head and the food in his belly, but he's never really come all the way with us, Pastor. I'm afraid we're going to lose him back to the streets."

"I don't want to judge him, Rosita. We can't know what's in his heart." Frowning, Paul said, "We just have to keep praying for him."

Roger went with Rosita to find some clean clothes in the mission storeroom.

The crowd was slower to disperse than most days. They talked quietly on one side of the room, and Paul and Keren had a chance to visit alone.

"You spoke so beautifully, Paul. It almost broke my heart to listen to you comfort these folks. They're all concerned for LaToya and saddened by Juanita's death. It was a wonderful choice to talk about them."

"I didn't choose it. It's not what I planned to say this morning. I was thinking about Roger and trying to get him to see how God can come to anyone anywhere."

"That's the message he needed to hear exactly. It's the message everyone needed, including me."

"Roger just told me there was talk in the crowd today about the bombs. We need to see if anyone here knows about it."

"Okay, we can—" Keren stopped talking and whirled to

face the group of people near the door. She froze only for a moment, then she charged toward the crowd. She began moving quickly through the tight bunch. Paul was a little slow to react, but then he was right after her. He didn't know what she was doing, but he knew it was important.

"Did someone just come in?" Keren asked. "Did another man come through that door?"

The homeless folks looked around. Paul could see they wanted to help her. But none of them had noticed if their number had grown by one.

Keren seemed to draw into herself, concentrating on something. Then she pushed on through the crowd and went outside. When Paul got to her, she was looking up and down the sidewalk.

"He was here." Keren turned in a circle, totally focused on the area around her.

"Who?" Paul looked for anyone slipping down an alley or crouching behind cover.

"Pravus."

"Pravus was here?" Paul turned to her. "How do you know? Did you recognize his voice?"

"No, I felt him."

Paul stared in astonishment at Keren. "Are you sure?"

Keren turned to him and snapped, "Of course I'm sure. Why would I say such a thing if it wasn't true?"

Paul nearly shouted. "But that's great. If you can sense the demonic presence, then maybe you can find him from a distance. Concentrate. Maybe we can figure out which way he went."

Keren slammed her fists onto her hips and glared at him. "Don't you think I'm trying?"

Paul fell silent. She was right. He was only distracting her. He waited and watched and prayed.

Finally, Keren shook her head in disgust. "Nothing." With a sudden burst of impatience she growled, "Why did God give me that moment of recognition if He wasn't going to let me catch him? What's the point?"

Paul turned to her and smiled right into her fire-breathing face. "Don't you dare question the ways of God, missy."

"Missy?" Keren said with a dangerous gleam in her eyes.

Paul laughed. "I saw what you did in there for Roger. Whatever God just revealed to you must be exactly what you need."

Keren relaxed and took a deep breath. "Yeah, okay sure. You're right. I know it. But it doesn't make any *sense*."

Paul knew Pravus was out there, watching. No sense letting the lunatic know Keren mattered personally to Paul. But his eyes locked with Keren's and she quit talking. So what he was feeling, the thrill of what he'd seen her do for Roger, must have shown in his face.

"Let's go back in the mission and find out who might have seen a homeless man around that crack house. Maybe we can get a description."

"The mayor has called for a task force and there's a meeting today. Then we need to finish looking at the files."

Paul's heart sped up. "Maybe we're going about the files all wrong. Maybe you could sense evil in a file."

"I've never been able to do such a thing before," Keren said.

"Yeah, but this guy is broadcasting on a real powerful frequency. It could work. Let's swing by the frog pond while we're on our way. And I had another idea. Let's see if we can get surveillance, just for tonight, since tonight is when he's most likely to strike, on as many ponds and reptile houses as possible. How about the Lincoln Park Zoo?"

"That's a little far north. He seems to be working in this area."

"Yeah, but his stunt with that bloody pond was a cry for attention. And you managed to tone it down so the press didn't even mention it. He might go outside the area if he thought it would get him the spotlight he craves."

"I can ask about Lincoln Park."

Paul began shepherding her back into the mission. "I know Chicago PD, they're all dying to stop this nut before he makes a career out of attacking this city. We could probably get a boatload of officers to volunteer—maybe they'd even forego overtime."

"Okay, we can try."

CHAPTER THIRTEEN

The frogs died in the houses, in the courtyards and in the fields.
They were piled into heaps, and the land reeked of them.

Pravus packed them carefully, almost sad to say good-bye to his second plague. He dressed LaToya in the shroud with care, took a long, loving look at the painting he'd created, then he hoisted her still form into his car trunk and waited for darkness.

She hadn't moved for hours now. He had been boiling with rage when his explosion didn't happen and the reverend wasn't able to get them to let his people go. The beast within him drove him to his most exquisite creation yet and he'd needed everything LaToya could give to make it perfect.

He had an odd moment of wondering when the beast had first come—when the voice had first spoken and given him strength. At first, the beast had the voice of his father. But it was different now. It had become a snarling, wolfish howl.

The noise only quieted when Pravus was under complete control of himself, and that came when he created. He turned his attention to LaToya for a moment.

She slept.

He was always frustrated when his sculpture wouldn't be still, but her motionlessness was boring. Perhaps he'd taken too much, perhaps his rage had reigned over the artist this time, which meant a lack of control. But he looked at the gown and he knew he'd done something wonderful. He couldn't regret it.

All in all, it was high time to be finished with this one.

⌒

Keren believed firmly in a day of rest, but she wasn't getting one this Sunday. Not with LaToya still missing and a meeting of the mayor's task force. She and Paul headed into the precinct soon after the mission church service with no new information about anyone carrying gasoline into the crack house.

"We've got a bigger meeting room." O'Shea was at his desk when Keren got there.

"Good, we need it. Let's go." Keren led the way, with Paul and O'Shea right behind her. When she entered the room, she saw the same four FBI agents as yesterday, plus two other detectives and Dr. Schaefer.

Keren nodded a greeting to Dee, surprised to see her there. The department really was pulling out all the stops.

Then the front of the room drew Keren's eye. A bulletin board stretched nearly the whole length of the room, covered with pictures. Her eyes were drawn immediately to Roger, his photo snapped as he entered the mission.

"Pastor Morris, good. You're here." Higgins stood at the front of the room, clearly in charge. "We have pictures of everyone who entered the mission this morning."

Keren glanced at Paul and saw his distress. These people weren't cold statistics. He knew their stories, knew that each one of them had come to the lowest place on earth in his own way. And each needed help as individuals. Now their faces were on a wall, their photos taken without permission. Their privacy about to be deeply violated.

"With the profile we've created, we're working on the theory that one of the people who hangs around the mission is our perp. We're cross-checking everyone for priors, especially a history of violence. And we've got our eyes open for fanatical religious beliefs, since this loon is quoting the Bible constantly."

Keren's jaw tensed, and she felt Paul go rigid beside her. Rosita was up on that bulletin board.

"You stood outside my mission today snapping photographs?" Paul spoke through gritted teeth. "How many of my people did you scare off? We had about half the usual crowd this morning."

"We were discreet, Morris," Higgins said. "We didn't want to tip off the bums that we were suspicious. What we need to know from you is who's missing. We need you to study this group and add any names you can think of. We want your impressions of them and any background information you might have. And we want you to think hard about who might be pretending to be homeless, since obviously our perp takes his vics somewhere."

Keren flinched at the cop talk. Why hadn't it bothered her before?

She felt the subtle shift in Paul's temper, his fight to control himself. This did need to be done, but Keren hated it, hated the cynicism, hated the intrusion and disregard for the street people.

"And what do you have to report, Collins?" Higgins asked. "You told me you'd go there this morning to get a closer look at the suspects."

"I never said I'd—"

Higgins cut her off. "We saw you go in and stay a long time. What have you learned?"

"What?" Paul turned to look at Keren. "Higgins sent you there this morning?"

Her face heated up, and Keren knew she was blushing. "Paul, it's not—"

"Last night Detective Collins and I agreed," Higgins interjected, "that she should learn the identities of the crowd that hangs around down there. Going in the guise of a volunteer was good thinking."

Higgins was acting like Keren had followed FBI orders to go to the mission this morning. She did a little profiling herself. Higgins wanted to cause trouble between her and Paul. She wasn't sure why. Her gut reaction was that he was irritated at her for walking out on him last night and petty enough to get a little payback. But she'd like to think the FBI had better men working for it than that.

"Did you get any impressions? Let's start with your report." Higgins looked at Keren and waited.

The silence was almost too much for her. She couldn't report that the demon they were hunting for wasn't there. But she could go up to that bulletin board and jerk about a dozen of the twenty pictures they had up there down, just because she trusted herself. It would save the task force hours and hours of hard labor.

Of course, no court in the land would accept that, and no cop or FBI agent worth his salt would trust her judgment. She wouldn't have believed it herself if she wasn't living it.

In the end she could only relate facts. "I didn't get any impression among the people there that one was *masquerading* as homeless."

She glanced at Paul. He had no expression. The cop was back. His eyes piercing. His jaw tight. Detached and cynical. Everything Pastor P wasn't, and everything she'd detested about Detective Morris.

He seemed to accept what amounted to her lying and betraying him and his people for the job. In fact, he understood about putting the job before anything else.

He probably believed she'd set him up. She didn't think he'd doubt what had happened with Roger, but she'd done her best to learn names and make contact with everyone. And now that just added to the image of her being at the mission under false pretenses.

"I saw you come charging out of that building just before you left," Dyson weighed in. "You moved like you were running after someone, and you looked in all directions and appeared extremely frustrated."

Keren tried to relate what she'd felt in words these folks would understand. "There was talk, a rumor about someone knowing about the bomb in the crack house. One of the homeless people told me that. He wasn't sure who'd said it. When he—" Keren couldn't lie and she couldn't tell the truth. "Look, I'm a cop. I thought someone across the room reacted. . .strangely. I couldn't see who it was, just movement, a response by someone in the crowd. I moved fast, trying to see who it was. I didn't see anyone. I can't describe anyone. I know you can't do it on my say-so, but if you'd trust me, I'd pull a lot of pictures down off that board, eliminate them as suspects. It would save us time."

Dyson narrowed his eyes. The jerk.

"I feel certain that—" Keren saw something. Studying the pictures, she said, "Paul, some of these people weren't there this morning. I don't recognize them, at least."

Keren went up front and pointed to several photos. "Who are these men? There are five or six I don't remember." She looked over her shoulder at him. He'd followed her and was watching where she pointed.

"They weren't there." Paul looked up at Higgins. "Where'd you get these five pictures?"

"They came up shortly before Detective Collins came out.

Identify them, Morris." Higgins, giving orders again.

"That's Murray." Paul pointed.

"Who was supposed to preach, right?" Keren asked.

"That's right." Paul jabbed each photo as he named them. "That's Buddy. Louie. Casey-Ray. McGwire."

"I don't remember seeing any of them."

"They drove up right at the end. The driver let four passengers out," Higgins said. "These pictures are pinned up here in the order the pictures were taken."

He jabbed a finger at Murray's picture showing him behind the wheel of a car. "The others went inside and returned almost immediately. Based on the way this one stayed behind, double parked—the others only needed to run inside briefly. They exited the building, got in the car, and drove off. Only a few seconds later you came out. They must be the disturbance that drew your attention. Since it's clear they never planned to stay, you probably misread the situation."

Paul's eyes, still fully shielded as he became the cop, shifted to hers and away. Keren thought of Dyson and Higgins and their watchfulness and didn't react, but she knew exactly what Paul was thinking. One of those men was almost certainly the killer. She'd felt him. They could narrow their suspect list to five right now. And here, in a room full of law enforcement officers, she had no way of explaining that without claiming a revelation from God.

Which these people wouldn't believe.

But they were under so much pressure to hurry, Keren had to focus the search. She did her best to come up with a reason these people would understand.

"We need to look closer at these men. I don't expect you to take my word for it with no solid evidence, but my gut tells me this is where we should look first." She pointed at Murray then swung her finger down the line of photos.

"We can try to nail down where these men have crossed your path when you were a cop, Morris," Higgins said. "We don't count the others out, but we've got limited time with a missing woman to find."

"Is it possible"—Keren turned to Dyson—"that something happened after Paul left the force? These men know him *now*. Have you worked on the theory that this could be rooted in Paul's life as a pastor rather than a cop? I'm trying to remember exactly what Pravus said. Did we jump to some conclusions?"

"I'll listen to the tapes again and see."

Keren turned back to the pictures, satisfied that she'd given one of the FBI agents what amounted to an order.

Then she turned to Paul. "Let's go look at your files again with these men in mind. Do any of them have known addresses? Or are they truly homeless?"

Paul stared at the picture of Murray. Keren had heard him talk about the man as a friend. "I've got addresses on Murray and Buddy. Louie lives in the mission. Casey-Ray and McGwire live on the streets. They sleep in the mission on cold nights. So did Buddy and Murray for that matter, until they cleaned up their act."

"And Louie?" Dyson asked.

"On parole."

"For what?"

Paul's jaw was so tense Keren wasn't sure he'd be able to move it to answer.

"He murdered his wife."

⏎

Paul tried not to turn into a cop. He really did.

But he'd gone right ahead and turned.

Hearing that Keren had been assigned to come to the mission this morning made him sad. Hurt. More than a little confused. Cynicism was much more comfortable.

She was a cop. She had a job to do. So did he. Being a pastor investigating the people with the biggest trust issues in the world could very likely destroy years of work. Betraying his congregation, even for the best reasons, was painful, and he preferred to not deal with that pain.

His blood cooled. His feelings faded. He could do this—but only as a cop.

"We need known addresses on the two men you say have one." Higgins moved to the center of the room. "And do you have full names? Background information will speed things up."

Paul told them what he knew. "Except for Louie Pike, I only know what these men have told me. Murray is Leo Murray. He volunteers at the mission. I don't file income tax forms or pay him a salary, so I don't have a social security number for him. Buddy is the same and I don't even know what his real name is. I asked him. 'Buddy' is all I've ever gotten. Casey-Ray is a former boxer, or so he says."

"He coulda been a contender instead of a bum?" Higgins asked.

Higgins's sneering attitude should have annoyed him but Paul didn't let it. Not when he was thinking like a police detective. The black humor had always helped him cope with the tough stuff.

"McGwire—that's not his real name. He rarely talks. He wears an old St. Louis Cardinals number twenty-five Mark McGwire jersey. I've never seen him without it, and I've known him for at least two years now. So that's why we call him McGwire, because that name's written on his back. He follows Casey-Ray around, but he's not exactly sane, I'm sure. I can't imagine he's the one who phoned me. Pravus's voice didn't sound familiar, and I've heard all these men talk, even McGwire on a few rare occasions." Paul stopped and tried to connect Pravus's voice to one of those five men. He couldn't.

But Keren believed Pravus had been in that room. And he trusted her. He couldn't think of what she'd done for Roger and doubt her. But he could doubt what had brought her there. He'd been stupid enough to think it was at least partly because of him.

He gave the FBI all the information he had on the five men and added names of several others missing from the morning service.

After telling them Murray's and Louie's addresses and the alley that was home to Casey-Ray and McGwire, Paul said, "I want to go with you to talk to these men, Higgins."

"No. Maybe we'll bring you in on the two homeless men if they're not where you said they'd be. You can help us hunt, but we want to question them without you being involved. We don't want a pastor there making it easy for them."

"If I'm there, you've got a lot better chance of gaining their cooperation. They're all hostile to the police. You'll be lucky if they don't hide from you."

"We'll be watching close. They won't get away." Higgins was so sure, Paul dropped it against his better judgment. That's what a cop would do.

"Buddy and Murray could be in their apartments right now. Sunday afternoon is really quiet at the mission." Paul narrowed his eyes and looked at the picture of Murray behind the steering wheel. "And as far as I know, none of those men owns or drives a car. So I don't know where that one came from."

The whole group turned to the picture.

"Did we get the plate number?" Higgins asked.

"I've got a photo of it pulling up. I'll get the make and model from the picture and run it," one of the agents said.

"Good." Higgins turned his grim expression on Paul. "We want to know everyone pictured here. Do I dare to hope you know all of them as well as you know these five?"

"I probably know less about most of them."

Higgins groaned. "Great. Give us what you've got. We'll run it down, put the pictures through our face recognition program. It'll take awhile."

"Look, I don't run background checks or take prints from the homeless people who come in to get a meal."

"Well maybe you ought to start." Higgins turned away. "Now what have we got from forensics?"

Paul was real tempted to keep arguing with Higgins. But he kept his mouth shut by sheer force.

"No DNA evidence." Dr. Schaefer shoved a stack of file folders onto the desk near the front of the room. "Everything I've got is here and I made a copy for each of you. The short version is, there was no DNA on the victim's body. Not surprising, considering the fountain.

"I've got the specifics of the wounds and cause of death in a file for each of you, so you can run the details through NCIC for a similar MO. As far as searching the apartments, where it appears the girls were taken, there are so many stray hairs in both LaToya's and Juanita's homes, we can't begin to identify them all. Apparently these ladies had wide circles of friends, and we've found a dozen or more people for both of them who admit to being in their house. Sorting through all of that would take months and not put us one bit closer to the killers."

"And we don't have months." Paul glanced at his watch.

"Detective Collins and I have theorized the frogs. We informed you of that, right?" Higgins nodded. "I've got ten teams who are staking out every park, fountain, and mud hole within a mile of the mission. We can't know if Pravus will stay close when he dumps the body, but Dyson thinks it's a probability."

"You think he brought Juanita alive to that fountain, don't you, Dr. Schaefer?" Paul asked the ME.

"Yes. She hadn't been dead long when she went in the water. It's my considered opinion that he killed her there."

"So he's not 'dumping a body.'" Paul couldn't be cool while Higgins callously discussed the mission and LaToya. "He's bringing *LaToya*, who is at this point still a *kidnap victim*, to the place he plans to kill her. If we cover every possible place, we have a chance to save her."

"I know." Higgins's hazel eyes flashed with irritation. "Everyone who's standing guard knows."

"Just make sure they do." Paul had led a lot of cases. He knew how to run an investigation every bit as well as Higgins. "If you get sloppy, then LaToya dies, Higgins."

"I don't get sloppy." Higgins bristled and squared off against Paul.

"I think you do. I think talking about a body being dumped is you being sloppy enough to get someone killed."

Everyone in the room froze. Even Paul was shocked at the command in his voice. He remembered this. The ability to take charge. The sweet taste of power.

"Get it straight, all of you." His eyes swept the room. "We go out tonight with a plan to save this young woman. If any of you can't remember your job, I'll be glad to replace you with someone who knows what they're doing."

Higgins's brows arched nearly to his stupid, stylish black hair.

Paul knew when he said it he had no clout to get anyone replaced. But then maybe he did. He could go to the press. He knew how to get his hands on a TV camera and a microphone. It was a skill he'd developed to an art form back in the day.

"Are we done here?" Keren asked.

Was she on his side? Or was she still taking orders from Higgins? Paul trusted her as a cop, but suddenly he didn't trust her at all as a woman. A woman who had kissed him pretty enthusiastically a few times. Would Keren flirt with him or kiss him to stay close to the mission?

When Paul was a cop, he'd never done that, but the opportunity had never come up. He'd been ruthless when it came to solving a case. Would he have stooped low enough to feign an attraction to a woman if it would have added to his solve rate? He knew he would, even as a married man.

"Stay here and tell me what you know about the rest of these people, Morris." Higgins jerked his head toward the door. "The rest of you can get to work."

It didn't take long. Higgins seemed to respect Paul more when he acted like an arrogant jerk. So they worked well together, getting what Paul knew about the men on the bulletin board.

"We'll let you know if we have trouble finding those men." Higgins nodded to the door, clearly telling Paul to get out.

Paul was glad to oblige.

Keren was poring over the police files of the suspects they couldn't eliminate, looking for a face that matched one of those five men in the car Murray was driving. It had to be one of those men. Or did it? Had someone else come in, maybe from the back? Wondering about it was driving her crazy, so she went with what she knew and tried to mentally add years and facial hair and maybe a disguise to the pictures, maybe even plastic surgery.

Paul came in and started sorting through files without talking to her or O'Shea, who was working beside her. She thought Paul believed her about why she was at the mission, but she didn't ask, settling for the quiet rather than start something. They'd deal with it later.

Dyson came and asked Paul a few questions about how the Lighthouse Mission operated. "Where does its funding come from? Who does the books? Who has keys?"

"We may have culled too deep on these files," O'Shea muttered. "I'm going to look at a few we eliminated." He left, probably to return very soon with a lot more work.

Once they were alone, Paul said, "You're sure it's one of those five?"

"I'm sure that Pravus was in the mission after the services. The timing is right. Someone could have come in from the back maybe, or—or—"

"Maybe came down from upstairs, the sleeping quarters."

"Of the five, Louie is the one with a murder rap. He murdered his wife?"

"Yes, Louis Pike went down for voluntary manslaughter. His other crimes were just thug stuff. Bar fights. A couple of B and Es. He'd done time in juvie. Been in foster care most of his life. He was drug involved. He did five years, and his parole includes community service, which is how I got him."

"Does he seem capable of this?"

Paul shook his head. "He's young. He'd have been in his late teens when I was on the force. He's a known quantity. Not with a missing past like most of the men at the mission. I don't see how I could have done him damage and now not remember him."

Paul looked up. "He's always been Louie Pike, if you know what I mean. He's accounted for. No name change, no gaps in his history. His face looks the same now as it did in his teens. I'd recognize him if I'd run across him before. Plenty of paper on Louis Pike. So if I hurt him or arrested him, he'd be in here, listed by name."

"And he's not."

Paul shook his head.

"It almost seems more likely it's someone like McGwire," Keren said. "All that silence. The way he dresses and looks, that full beard. Even the way he keeps his head down, it'd be a good disguise."

Paul stared into the distance. Keren was sure he was thinking of the interactions he'd had with all these men. "If he's faking then he's never missed a note. He's a great actor."

"Listen, while we've got a second. . ." Keren didn't want to mess up this moment when they were trying to solve this crime and save a life, but she had to say something. "I didn't come down there on Higgins's order."

Paul turned his eyes on her. Cop eyes. Detached, analytical. Rude. "It's the job, I get that."

"Higgins suggested it, but I'd already decided I wanted to hear you preach."

"So showing up had nothing to do with solving this crime."

Keren narrowed her eyes at him. "Every breath I take involves solving this crime, Paul. And it had occurred to me that I might be able to sense Pravus if he was down there. But I would have come anyway."

The coldness wavered. Keren thought she caught just a glimpse of hurt.

Before he could mask his feelings, she added, "You saw what happened with Roger."

Paul's expression relaxed. He nodded. "I saw."

"You can't believe that was part of being a cop. Yes, I was hoping I could pick Pravus out of the crowd, but—"

"The FBI wants you to carry this phone, Morris. It's more easily traceable than the one you have." A uniformed officer held out a cell phone to Paul.

"I can't figure out how to run this dumb thing," Paul grumbled as the young officer walked away. He sounded like a pastor again.

The tension eased and Keren managed a smile. "You'll be fine."

Paul tapped away at the buttons with his brow furrowed. "Have you tried simply concentrating on each file?"

"I can't get a sense of anything from them. I've tried."

"You've never even told O'Shea about this, have you?"

She shrugged. "No, and it's embarrassing to sit and try to vibe out a demon while I'm holding paper in my hand like it's some kind of Ouija board. But I've tried."

"Tried what?" O'Shea returned.

"Tried nothing." Keren had to stifle a groan at the stack of files her partner carried. "Good grief, you want us to go back to considering all those?" Keren turned to glare at Paul. "What were you, the Energizer Bunny of cops?"

They got back to work. As soon as it could possibly be declared night, Paul was ready for the stakeout.

"It's five o'clock." Keren held him off. "We can't even conceal ourselves until dark. No way is Pravus going to strike in full daylight."

"I'm going to the same frog pond we staked out last night." Paul went back to combing through files.

Keren could see Paul was pinning everything on being there to intervene when Pravus surfaced with LaToya. A small army of cops was going to sit a vigil on every green space and body of water near the Lighthouse Mission.

When the sun was finally low enough in the sky, O'Shea stood up and pulled on his suit coat. "I've got my own water hole to stake out. I'm making the freak do some real police work for a change."

"Freak?" Keren asked, though she had a pretty good idea.

"Dyson. I can't decide if he's psychic or psycho. I bet he lives in his mama's basement—alone."

By tacit agreement Paul and Keren teamed up, and, at nine o'clock, they gathered some supplies before they abandoned the musty halls of the precinct station and headed for the park in Keren's car.

"Paul, you know we're just guessing about this location." Keren badly wanted to lower his expectations. He had a battle-weary cop's view of reality and the redeemed heart of a Christian. The combination ought to make him the toughest man walking the planet. Even with all that, he was going to be devastated if LaToya turned up dead.

"Even if we get him, she might already be dead," Keren reminded him gently. "Dr. Schaefer said Juanita was killed very close to the time her body was dumped. But the findings could be off, especially since she was in the water so long. She could have been killed wherever Pravus was hiding then brought directly to the fountain."

"You don't have to tell me it's a long shot." Paul settled lower in the seat with a pigheaded look on his face, as if he expected her to hit an ejector button to get rid of him.

"We need to leave the car off a ways and slip in close." Keren pulled into a parking structure a couple of blocks from the park. "We have to figure Pravus will be very careful about dumping her."

"How about we hunker down in those bushes you ran into last night?"

Keren glanced at him, grateful he didn't add, *To get away from kissing me.* "Sounds good. I brought a thermos of coffee, a couple of waterproof sheets, and two blankets."

"I hope it's good," Paul said. "Strong coffee like we make at the Lighthouse Mission, not that wimpy stuff you and O'Shea like to drink."

With an inelegant snort, Keren gathered her blankets from the backseat. "Like you've never had coffee at a police station. We drink it burned and black. I can't believe there's a cop in the city with any stomach lining left."

They quit talking as they neared the park. The gang problem had abated some in recent years. The park was still a known hangout for them, but the trouble usually started later at night. In the settling dusk, it was deserted.

Keren felt foolish climbing into the twenty-foot-square thicket of stunted trees. If anyone was around, they were busted, because the park was very open.

They studied the area around the pond. The park swept away in three directions. Keren looked down a grassy slope that didn't often see a mower. The setting sun was forgiving to the sparse grass and the litter. The green expanse was broken occasionally by rusty playground equipment and decorative plantings that had been hardy enough to survive the neglect that so often plagued the South Side. The city was close at hand on the side they'd come in on.

Paul whispered, "Do you have a good range of vision?"

"Yes, I just hope Pravus doesn't decide he wants to hide in the bushes. These are the only ones, and it will get real crowded in here with the three of us."

"If he does climb in, he'll be within grabbing distance."

"If he's coming to this pond, he'll probably come in from the street. There's no place to park nearby. Let's sit back-to-back so we can see in all directions."

Keren laid her ground sheet down and they settled in to wait among the prickly branches. They didn't dare talk above a whisper. As night fell, the land around them began to move. Keren marveled at the life in the little park. It seemed like a place of neglect and danger that would probably be best plowed up and cemented, but there was life here. Squirrels, creatures Keren would have said lived on nuts, began eating in the mounds of refuse scattered around the park.

"They're hardy little things, aren't they?" she whispered.

"What?" Paul turned around.

Keren said, "Look at 'em all."

"In the middle of all this concrete and traffic, who'd think there was so much wildlife."

While they watched, pigeons came down in hordes from the buildings around the park and settled into their night's feasting. Rabbits hopped boldly around the open area, belying their reputation for being skittish.

"Oh yuck, look." Keren pointed at several rats that scuttled out of the alley.

"Big deal," Paul murmured, too close to her ear for comfort. "They're a link in the food chain. Anyway, what's a pigeon except a rat that can fly in your window? What's a squirrel except a rat with a more socially acceptable tail? What's a rabbit—"

"All right. I get your point. They're a big, fat, ugly, disease-bearing part of the circle of life. I still hate 'em." They fell silent and watched.

After a time, Paul said, "Look at the way they're eating the grass."

"What?" Keren focused more analytically on the animals.

"They're spread out all around that knoll over there." Paul pointed to the top of a rise at the far end of the park. "I wouldn't have thought they would graze. Maybe the rabbits. . ."

Her spine chilled. "It isn't normal. They're all over."

Keren felt, more than saw, Paul shrug. "I suppose the animals that adapt to urban life are the ones that learn to eat what grows in urban areas."

The animals' presence distracted Keren from thinking about the futility of the night. The unlikelihood of Pravus showing up here was demoralizing. Sitting in a bush all night was a waste of time. But Paul needed to do something, and if being in a thicket like a two-hundred-pound jackrabbit helped him, she'd stay. The minutes ticked by, and the weight of Pravus's threats pressed on her like a physical thing.

"Let's switch sides," Paul whispered. "I'm starting to be hypnotized by all this grass. If I could watch the traffic it might keep me alert."

"Okay." Keren glanced at her watch. She was trying not to watch the minute hand creep around. The slowness was maddening.

They settled in again, and Keren was just fighting off the urge to look at her watch again to see if it'd been two hours or two minutes when they heard the first rumble of thunder. Keren groaned. "Rain. That'll make this real pleasant."

Paul didn't respond. The wind came first with a few light gusts, then it began whipping up. Lightning danced across the sky. Keren pulled a blanket around herself and handed Paul one.

A bolt of lightning lit up the park. Thunder rolled and the storm drew closer.

While they shifted around, Paul asked, "Do you suppose these bushes are the tallest things around?"

Keren growled at him, "Thanks. I hadn't considered being struck by lightning."

"Worrying about it oughta keep you awake anyway." Paul laughed softly, and, as if to reward his teasing, the lightning became wilder, the thunder exploded around them, and the wind cut through, even with the small copse of trees and bushes to protect them.

Keren was no longer so concerned with their voices carrying thanks to the pounding thunder. "You know, if he were coming, this weather might change his mind." She watched all the night animals desert the park to seek shelter. Because she was watching them so closely, she was completely focused when, at the top of the rise at the far end of the park, lightning flared and silhouetted a man against the buildings. A man carrying something that looked very much like a body in a loose-fitting white dress.

"That's him!" She threw off the blanket. "C'mon." She ran. The lightning flashed again and she saw him. He was setting the bundle down gently, almost reverently. He fell to his knees beside the body as if to pray before the world went dark again. Keren did her best to set a world speed record.

Paul came alongside her. She hissed, "Do you see him?"

"Yes!" Paul passed her.

The thunder and lightning were coming at the same time now. Another bolt of lightning showed the man with his arm reaching high in the air over the body. Until now Keren and Paul had been running silently, hoping to close the distance between them and the killer.

But they were out of time. Paul shouted, "No!"

Keren reached for her gun. She'd have to shoot uphill and run at the same time. And if her bullet went wild, who knew where her shot might land.

The man held his hand high. He looked toward the sound, maybe unsure if he'd heard a voice in the crashing thunder. He saw them, and, when his eyes landed on them, Keren knew it was Pravus. The demonic evil in him washed over her until she wanted to cry out with fear. Instead, she ran straight into the face of evil, prepared to fire if she had to.

The man held his hand aloft. When the next bolt of lightning brandished, Keren felt the palpable cruelty as Pravus laughed over the wicked thunder. LaToya was clearly illuminated, lying motionless at the top of the slope. Pravus looked at them, as if to be sure they were watching, then he slashed his weapon down with brutal force.

Keren cried out, even as she knew it was too late. "No! Please, no! No! No! God!" She fired her weapon, aiming for the ground just off to the side of her target.

As his arm descended, Keren's shot diverted Pravus's attention for a split second. Or maybe it was her prayer.

LaToya, who a moment before had seemed as still as death, wrenched herself sideways, and Pravus's killing blow missed.

Paul shouted, "She's alive!"

Pravus screamed and grabbed at LaToya. She threw herself sideways until she rolled down the hill from him.

Paul and Keren were closing the distance fast. Pravus screamed in frustration and leaped to his feet. He threw the weapon at LaToya, in one last desperate attempt to be granted the victory of killing her. Keren fired again and Pravus turned and fled. Paul got to LaToya's side first. Keren slid to her knees beside them. LaToya lay unmoving on her side; a sculptor's chisel protruded from the center of her back. Blood flowed from the wound. Keren shouted over the storm, "Call an ambulance!"

As she knelt there, scrambling to find a pulse, she felt the ground turn to life under her. LaToya's body crawled with something living. Keren realized something squirmed under her. The sky lit up and she saw frogs—hundreds of little frogs crawling and hopping over every inch of the ground.

Paul shouted, "I've got a heartbeat!"

Their eyes met over LaToya's battered body. Paul snarled, "Give me your gun."

"My job, Rev. Call for backup and get an ambulance out here." Keren jumped to her feet and ran after Pravus.

"Keren!"

Keren shouted over her shoulder, "Don't let her move. That chisel might have hit her spine." She ran in the direction Pravus had gone. She could feel him. She knew unerringly which way to go. She shouldn't go after him alone. It was completely against procedure, but she couldn't stand to let him go without pursuit. Stopping him was too important.

The park ended in a rundown neighborhood that led to Paul's mission.

Keren dashed up an alley that vibrated with Pravus's presence. Normally she would have slowed down and gone into the pitch-black alley carefully, but she heard pounding footsteps ahead, still running. She came out the other end of the alley, ran across a deserted street, and disappeared into another alley. She thought she caught sight of movement ahead of her. She picked up her pace. As she came out of the dark bowels of the back alley, she heard a car roar to life through the next alley. She ran across the street and dived back into the darkness, putting every ounce of strength she had into getting there, getting her hands on him, getting off a shot, at least getting a look or a license plate. She barreled out of the alley, and twin headlights bore down on her.

Unable to stop her forward motion, she hurled herself up. The car hit her feet. She landed with a bone-cracking *thud* on top of the car. She rolled, bounced on the trunk, and slammed onto the unforgiving pavement. With a sickening *snap* her skull hit concrete. Tumbling, she clung to her gun until she stopped.

With pure willpower, she rolled onto her belly, focused on the disappearing car, and fired at the rapidly disappearing vehicle. No light shined on the license plate. She heard glass break and a taillight went blank. She unloaded her weapon at the car, then it skidded around a corner, and in the streetlight she made out the shape of the lights and the silhouette of the car, a sedan. Dark. Four doors.

They'd said the car Murray was driving was a dark-green Malibu. Keren thought this might be it.

It sped around a corner, and Keren shoved against the pavement, to go after him.

She made it as far as her knees before her head began to spin. She stared at blood dripping onto her hands and had a vague idea that it wasn't a good sign.

She was only distantly aware of the lightning and thunder as the storm broke and rained down on her collapsing form.

Paul couldn't leave LaToya's side. He gave the 911 operator directions with his cell in one hand while he tried to stem the gushing wound in her back and hold her still with the other. An ambulance siren sounded in the distance.

"Hurry," Paul prayed as he carefully avoided touching the chisel, afraid he'd make it worse. How could it be worse? He laughed harshly. It wasn't a sound he'd heard come from himself for five years. But he recognized that cynical cop laughter well.

He felt something crawling inside his shirt but he didn't have a hand to spare for himself. The creeping feeling of the trapped frog seeped into his guts and filled him with loathing.

The blinding lights of the ambulance swept across the park. Following Paul's careful directions, it drove straight out onto the grass and sped toward them.

LaToya's pulse was weakening. Her breathing was so shallow he had to lean right next to her mouth to hear it. The rescue squad skidded to a stop. Paramedics raced toward him. He thanked God for the rapid response. They pushed him aside. He yelled instructions about the chisel.

"I'm here with a police detective. She went after him," Paul shouted at the first responding paramedic. "You have to keep it quiet that she's alive." He grabbed her arm and shook the poor woman until she threatened to belt him. Then, knowing he had her attention, he said, "The man who tried to kill her is the serial killer who blew up that building last week. He'll come after her if he knows she's alive."

With soothing tones that Paul knew she practiced, the woman said, "We can put out the word she died. I know the guy you're talking about."

"What is this crawling all over her?" one of the paramedics asked, his voice strangled with horror.

"Frogs," Paul said hoarsely. "Last week it was a plague of blood. This week is a plague of frogs."

The paramedic who asked made an inarticulate sound of disgust.

"Where are you taking her? What hospital?"

"We'll go straight to Cook County," the woman medic said.

Paul said, "I'm here with a police officer. She chased the man out the south side of the park. I'm going after her!"

The sound of gunfire froze everyone in their tracks. Paul whirled to face the direction of the sound. The direction Keren had run.

"Wait for the police, sir! They're equipped to handle this!"

"Just don't let anyone know she survived. Please. Send the police after me." Paul turned and raced in the direction Keren had gone. The sky opened up and poured.

Paul sprinted toward the shots, sick at heart from what he might find. He heard a car roaring away and tore down one alley after another. He almost tripped over Keren, lying unconscious on the pavement. He had his cell phone out for the second time in minutes, calling for help.

Blood coursed down the side of Keren's face. The rain pelted her and turned the trail of blood into a red river. Paul fumbled at her wrist for a heartbeat and, when he found a strong, steady pulse, he relaxed for just a second. Her breathing was even and deep. He started checking her for gunshot wounds. It was so dark that he had to wait for lightning to flash for him to see. She had her gun still clutched in her hand, and he pried it free and checked the load. He'd counted the shots. He knew her gun's capacity and that she'd keep it fully loaded. It was empty now.

All the shots had come from her gun.

The bleeding on her head must be from a nasty scrape, not a bullet. A welt the size of an egg was swelling up from under the scrape. He pulled a handkerchief out of his pocket and held it out to the rain to wet it then pressed it against her head to staunch the bleeding.

Paul ran his free hand over her inert form and found no more blood, except on her hands, which were grated raw. He did his best to check for broken bones, and when he found none, he gently held out her hands to the rain to rinse away the worst of the dirt and gravel.

He noticed movement in the alley across from them. All they needed to end this dreadful night was to be mugged. He glared at the alley, hoping he would finally have the chance to do more than just call for help. He had a visceral need to fight back.

Keren distracted him when she moaned softly. It was the most beautiful sound he'd ever heard.

"Keren? Keren, did he shoot you?" He knew the answer but couldn't stop the panicked question.

"No," she groaned, trying to sit up. "I shot *him*!"

"Don't move. An ambulance is on the way. You're bleeding, honey. You've got to lie still." Paul held her down with little trouble, because she was still semiconscious. Trust Keren to fight the world standing on her own two feet, even when she was battered and bleeding.

She said in a husky voice, "I'm drowning."

Paul realized the now-pouring rain was hitting her right in the face. He leaned over her to shelter her with his body. "Did you really shoot him?"

"No!" she snarled, then she tried to sit up again. "I didn't do anything! I didn't see anything! I shot at him and I got a couple rounds into the car, but I didn't even slow him down. They might as well get me a Seeing Eye dog!"

Paul held her down. Then he thought of something that might help. A little. "LaToya's alive. The paramedics are taking her to Cook County Hospital." A gust of wind blew the rain sideways so Keren got hit in the face. Paul leaned closer.

The distant sound of an ambulance told Paul help was on the way.

"Is she going to make it?" She sounded like knowing LaToya was alive really had made her feel better.

"I don't know. But she's got a chance. Thank God, she's got a chance."

"Will you pray with me, Paul?" Keren asked. "Pray for LaToya?"

"I'd love to pray with you." Paul began speaking to the Lord. "Dear God—"

"Wait a minute," Keren interrupted. "Something is crawling around inside my clothes." She reached under her shirt.

Paul realized he had a few wiggly spots, too. "Frogs."

Keren shuddered. "Gross." She tossed one frog out and went back after another.

Paul said doubtfully, "Maybe we'd better keep them. They might be a clue."

"Can you store them in your shirt?" Keren groaned. "I've had about all I can take for one night."

"Yeah. Sure. I don't mind amphibians in my clothes." Paul thought gloomily that this was what chivalry had come to. He caught the frogs as she extracted them. She found two, he found five on himself. He gently bundled them up in the front of his sweatshirt.

As the ambulance pulled up, Keren groused, "Did I hear you call me 'honey'?"

"It must be the head injury," Paul said.

"It had better be."

CHAPTER FOURTEEN

Pravus, in his fury, brought down a nightmare on Melody Fredericks.

He didn't play out the ritual like he'd planned, but the satisfaction was surprisingly intense.

Terror such as he'd never known followed him home. He could feel the eyes on him. Surely someone had seen what happened.

Pravus prepared quickly for his artwork. He'd listen and be ready to run, but he couldn't move yet. The beast was like a starving wolf licking its jaws. He had to paint. He had to create.

Because she'd fallen into his hands, he had no time to prepare, so that would come now. There was an address in her purse, so he could find her house. The reverend wouldn't even feel pain over this. So why involve him?

Pravus quickly carved the sign for this plague. It wasn't his best work, but Melody Fredericks wasn't worthy, so it hardly mattered.

Finishing the plaque in quick time, he slipped up to her home. A pretty house in a nice neighborhood, not the isolated, dreary apartment he was used to. He quietly hung the plaque in place and went back to his creation.

Only to find she wouldn't supply him with paint. Dead women don't bleed. He looked from his latest creation to the empty white gown and fumed.

There was no help for it. The only one available to bleed was himself. Pravus raised the chisel to his own arm. The pain was pleasure and the beast was content.

✎

Paul spent the night between Keren's cubicle—where she seemed determined to make every doctor and nurse who came in contact with her reconsider their occupation—and the waiting area nearest LaToya's operating room. When O'Shea came barreling into the hospital, Paul turned the tiny frogs over to him.

O'Shea, befuddled, stuck them in a plastic evidence bag as if they might contain fingerprints. They stared, wriggling pathetically, through the bag. O'Shea muttered, "Airholes." He poked a few before he gently lowered the bag into the pocket of his brown suit.

Then Agent Higgins came.

Paul felt like a criminal under interrogation.

Keren heard them talking and demanded loudly, from behind the curtain, to be included.

"It'll probably kill her," the doctor said sarcastically. "But the nurses are pooling their money to hire a hit man anyway, so what the heck. Go on in."

She was sitting up, so Paul didn't take the doctor's dark warnings of death very seriously. The hit man? Maybe.

Paul had to go through it again, with Keren adding details.

"You got the make and model of his car at night, on a dimly lit street, after you'd been run down?" Paul asked incredulously.

Keren rolled her eyes. "Some of us do this for a living, Rev."

O'Shea said, "I'll put an ATL on a dark-green Malibu with a broken taillight and bullet holes."

"An Attempt to Locate for possible connection to a homicide." Keren nodded. "It's got to be the same car we saw those men driving outside the mission."

"But when he was questioned, Murray had already reported it stolen." Paul shook his head. "The cops remember him because he was so upset. He'd just bought the car. The first car he'd owned in his life. That's why he was giving everybody a ride. It was stolen before he'd owned it two days. I can't believe it's him."

He saw Keren and O'Shea exchange a glance of pity and didn't even have the gumption to snarl at them.

"A stolen car is really convenient," Keren said. "If he's got a place to hide it, he can use it once in a while and it'll all be blamed on someone else as long as he's not caught."

Paul ducked away while they grilled Keren. No one else was there for LaToya but him. The paramedics had already "slipped" and told a reporter she was dead. The police were in full agreement that it was best she be declared dead for now. It made Paul sick when he overheard a spokesman for the hospital say the words. It was far too close to the truth.

There was a nurse in the operating room who spoke to him every time she came out. "They're bringing in a plastic surgeon to try to fix the cuts in her arms with the least scarring possible. We've taken pictures from every angle, as the police requested. We've already handed the white dress over to the detective."

The next time the nurse came out, she said, "She's sedated, but the EEG shows she's in a deep coma. The final stab wound was the only potentially fatal wound, but the cumulative effect of all that trauma and blood loss is extensive. It's the doctor's feeling that she's probably been in a coma for the last twenty-four hours."

Paul ran his hands through his dark hair and felt it standing on end. "I saw her move just an hour ago. I saw the man who did the cutting on her strike the last blow. She rolled away from him. She saved herself."

The nurse shook her head. "That's not possible. The doctor

is estimating how long she's been out, so it could be less than twenty-four hours, but it's definitely longer than one. There's no way she could have made any defensive movements so recently."

"But I saw her," Paul insisted.

"Maybe she rolled because the hillside was steep and the man leaned against her wrong. Whatever caused her to move saved her life."

Paul quit protesting. He didn't need to find out more. Whether LaToya had done the impossible and awakened or Pravus had shifted his weight and knocked her aside or God had simply sent her rolling away from that chisel, the end result was the same.

Paul had witnessed a miracle.

His heart filled with the blessing of it. LaToya would live. God had directly intervened to save her. It wasn't yet her time. In that dimly lit, lonely waiting room, he shook off the cop and found the pastor and praised God to the highest reaches of heaven.

It was only after he'd spent time in praise and regained a modicum of his peace that he remembered the moment he'd demanded Keren hand over her gun.

"Give me your gun!"

If he could have wrestled it away from her, he'd have gone after Pravus and. . .

God, forgive me. Paul sat with his legs spread, hands clasped between his knees. His head hung in shame. *I'd have killed him.*

Paul began again, his earlier closeness to God lost. He prayed for forgiveness, and as he prayed, he knew that it wasn't God who was going to be the problem. God was there pouring love and forgiveness down on him in abundance. It was himself. This side of himself—the violent, cynical side that had been such a neat fit for the way he'd acted when he was a cop. Now, with Pravus to fight and the police at hand constantly, he was being pulled back into that life.

God, please, I don't want that to be me. Give me a peaceful and contrite heart. Give me humility. Paul buried his face in his hands as he prayed. *Make the longings of my heart be love and joy and sacrifice. Take away this willingness I have to fight and hate. Please, Lord, forgive me for wanting to kill that man.*

Paul wasn't fighting for his soul. His belief in his own salvation was rock solid. It was his own nature that he fought. In the end, he didn't find the satisfaction he hoped for. Even as he prayed, he felt the hunger to close his hand over that gun and hunt down Pravus personally. Paul felt like he'd lost five years of spiritual growth in a single week.

Keren was part of the problem. She'd pulled that gun with lightning speed. She went running headlong toward danger. She did what a cop was supposed to do. Paul was afraid that if he became involved with Keren—which he wanted to do very badly—the life she led, or more exactly, the lure of it, would swallow him whole.

The nurse appeared again with another update and the news that it would be hours before LaToya was out of surgery. The chisel had pierced a lung and severed muscles. And she had deep cuts that needed sutures. Paul remembered the police questioning Keren and went back to the room where she was corralled.

He went behind her curtains, expecting to find her in a hospital gown. She was almost dressed, just tucking in her shirt.

"Hey!" She glared at him. "Knock next time."

"It's a curtain. How do I knock on a curtain? What are you doing with your clothes on?"

"Not a question a reverend should be asking," she replied smartly. She sat in a chair and reached for her socks.

Paul said, "Get back in that bed! I heard the doctor say he wanted to observe you overnight because you have a concussion."

Keren began pulling on her socks. "Says the man who checked himself out of the hospital without his doctor's approval."

She flinched when she leaned over to grab her shoe. He pushed her hands aside and knelt in front of her and lifted her foot to rest on his knee. "They needed the room because of the explosion. That was an emergency. They've got plenty of room for you."

Keren didn't wrestle him for her shoe. She straightened gingerly in the hard chair and Paul heard her squelch a sigh of relief. That tiny show of weakness must have made her mad. "Didn't you take that cervical collar off a week before the doctor said you could? And quit wearing your sling the minute his back was turned?"

Paul lifted her other foot and slid the black Nike on gently, thinking of all her bumps and bruises. "I was fine. Doctors have to be overcautious, because they'll get sued otherwise."

"Amen." Keren stood. "I'm out of here. I promise not to sue."

Paul steadied her when she wobbled. "You're not supposed to sleep for twelve hours because of the concussion." Paul knew he was right, but he didn't kid himself he'd ever convince Keren.

"No problem. I'm going back to work, so I'll be up."

O'Shea called from outside the room, "Her head's a hard one, Pastor P. She'll probably be all right."

Higgins was out there, too, and he laughed.

Paul pulled the curtain aside and let Keren step out ahead of him. "I can't leave. I've got to stay and see how LaToya does."

"I'll stay with you." Keren seemed to forget her plans to begin tracking down Pravus.

"If you're staying in the hospital anyway," Paul growled at her, "why don't you just lay back down there?"

Keren narrowed her light-colored eyes at him. The blue had turned to a gunmetal gray that looked like she wanted war. "How about this for a compromise? I'll do exactly as I want, and you shut up."

"That's the deal she always gives me." O'Shea laughed and slapped Paul on the shoulder. "Take it, kid. It's all you're going to get."

It had been so long since someone had called him "kid," Paul almost liked it. "At least when you keel over and I have to call 911 for the third time tonight, it won't take the paramedics long to get here."

"Sounds like a plan." Keren turned to the FBI agent, still in his black suit even in the middle of the night. "Are you done grilling me, Higgins?"

Higgins said, "For now."

He and O'Shea turned to leave. Keren and Paul headed for the surgical floor.

"I'll be right back, Higgins." O'Shea's voice turned Paul and Keren back.

O'Shea came up close and spoke in a whisper to Keren. "There are going to be questions about tonight, so get ready for them."

"What questions?" Keren asked.

"You discharged your weapon."

"At a fleeing felon."

Paul noticed Higgins reach the exit door then stop and look back, one brow arched on his movie-star handsome face.

"Anytime you fire your weapon, you answer for it—that's routine. You'll need to file an incident report."

"I know that." Keren sounded cranky, but Paul suspected she was just in pain and taking it out on the world.

"You fired at a moving vehicle, in the dark."

"He ran me down." Keren ran one hand into her hair and fiddled with her weird barrette. She took a quick look at Higgins.

Higgins started back toward their secretive little group.

"You ran out of an alley into his path. You could have run into the path of any oncoming car. You didn't know who was driving it."

"I did. It was him and you know it." Keren scowled.

"I do know it. But you made a real fast judgment call, and I've yet to hear you say you saw the guy's face, saw him get into that car, kept your eye on him the whole time. You need to get your story straight. I understand how you could be sure it was him, but IA isn't going to trust you like I do."

Paul felt his blood chill as he thought of the headaches of an internal affairs investigation. Keren could end up suspended, even fired. And he needed her on this case.

"I appreciate you mentioning it. I've got nothing to hide."

"Good." O'Shea turned just as Higgins came up.

"Why do I feel like I'm not invited to this party?" Higgins's hazel eyes looked at all of them like they were a herd of gazelles and he was the king of the jungle. And speaking of animals, Paul thought of that weird gathering of critters in the park tonight. He'd meant to ask about that.

"Just cop stuff. We're done here." O'Shea turned and left.

"Being suspicious is how I make my living." Higgins smiled then turned to follow O'Shea.

Paul thought the smile was a little too warm and aimed very particularly at Keren. But then Paul was so tired he was sucking fumes, and he might be making stuff up.

Keren started down the hall toward the OR. "Now, tell me how LaToya is holding up."

Paul caught up with her and repeated everything the nurse had said to him.

"You felt that guy, didn't you?"

Keren sat in one of the chairs in the waiting room, with her forearms resting on her knees, her hands clasped between her legs, her head drooping. Paul sank down in a chair next to her, so tired he could barely see straight, and he hadn't been run down by a Malibu.

Of course he'd had a building fall on him recently.

"Yeah." Keren turned to look at him. "I never even thought of it until Mick said that. I knew he was in that car. There's no doubt it was him."

"But you didn't really see him, did you? And if you hadn't had that sense of him, you'd have hesitated before you fired. You'd have considered it might have been an accident when he hit you."

Keren's eyes seemed to look into the past, as if she were reliving that race she'd run, chasing a serial killer.

"I've almost never talked about this gift I have and now I can't shut up about it."

"I'm honored." And he was, deeply.

She spoke carefully, as if putting words to a story that unfolded in her memory. "I heard him running. I was following the sound of his footsteps, but the presence of him guided me."

"Sounds like you've got a Spidey sense or something."

Keren slugged him in the leg and managed a smile. "Great image. Maybe I oughta get a red ski mask to wear for work. It'd at least control my hair."

Paul reached over and pulled her hair tie loose.

"Hey, stop that."

"It was hanging by about ten hairs. Just relax."

Keren did, probably because she was so beat up. "I'm not

going to lie, I refuse to. But no one will understand the concept of a spiritual gift leading me anywhere. After the guy hit me..." She ran both hands deep into her coiled explosion hair and sat silently. At last she said, "I heard the car door slam. I heard the engine. The driver gunned it. Took off. Aimed straight for me. I think I can honestly say it was an unbroken trail that I followed from the crime scene. I heard it all."

"And if they hammer on it long enough and don't accept that?" Paul reached over and caught her right wrist. It couldn't be too badly hurt; she'd fired her gun real efficiently with it.

"I'll give them my story and they can do with it what they want. I'm a good cop with a good record. All but—" Her blue-gray eyes came up and nearly burned a hole in his hide.

"All but the bad mark you've got because of me." He held on to her hand, and she let him, so that was a good sign.

"Let's just drop it for now. I need some time to think it through, get it straight in my head."

"I need some time to pray for LaToya." Paul let her go before she made him.

"That, too." Keren managed a smile. The two of them sat quietly in the waiting room and prayed.

The window in the lobby began to lighten, and they received word that LaToya was through the surgery and out of recovery. Her coma had deepened. She was now in a room where Paul was allowed in to see her for a few minutes.

She lay motionless, hooked up to every monitor imaginable. But she was alive. Paul's most heartfelt prayers had been answered.

Higgins impatiently appeared, hoping to question LaToya.

It woke up the prowling cop inside Paul, the one he'd spent the night lulling to sleep. Higgins was just doing his job. Paul still wanted to slug the guy.

When the sunlight began to give them hope that they had a better day ahead, O'Shea came into the waiting room. "Well, I've got good news and bad news. And the bad news is so bad that we'll never get to the good news if I tell you the bad first."

With a jerked move of his hand that accentuated his distress, he tossed a copy of the Monday morning *Chicago Tribune* on the coffee table in front of Paul. A picture of LaToya appeared at the top right corner. The headline read, "Second Murder in South Side Park."

"That's great," Keren said, pleased. "Did the paper agree to cooperate?"

"No," O'Shea said with disgust. "They just got the red herring we tossed out and ran with it."

"They're going to be mad when we tell them the truth," Keren predicted. "I can hear them now, 'Police Lying to the Press,' 'Citywide Cover-up,' 'What Did the Mayor Know and When Did He Know It?'"

O'Shea said, "So what else is new? They got enough of the sensational details about LaToya to make a front-page story, but they haven't found out about the carving or the frogs, and they also don't know LaToya is connected to Juanita. Once the serial killer connection comes out, we won't be able to take a step without a reporter's camera flashing in our faces."

"So what's the bad news?" Paul looked at the picture of LaToya. It was one of the pictures that hung by her front door. She smiled so beautifully.

"We have another missing person. A woman. And there's a carving."

"Who?" Paul's stomach skidded. He thought of several women he'd helped over the years. Which one was it? Then he thought of Rosita. Had she gone out last night to meet Manny? He should have double-checked. He should have talked to Manny himself and made sure the young man understood the seriousness of the situation.

O'Shea cut into his panic. "Her name is Melody Fredericks."

Paul thought for a long minute. "That name doesn't ring a bell."

"She's from outside your neighborhood," O'Shea said. "The preliminary report on her doesn't fit the profile of the other vics. She's the co-owner of an upscale Hyde Park restaurant who never got home from work Sunday night. Her husband called the police to check for accident information when she was only two hours late. Outwardly at least, he seems frantic. She's the mother of two. A couple of unpaid parking tickets are her only brushes with the law."

"Is it possible it's a copycat?" Keren asked. "Maybe her husband saw a way to save some money on a divorce settlement."

"I don't know yet. My report says the husband is frantic and has an alibi that, at first glance, looks fairly solid, home with the kids. Ten and six, old enough to know what time Daddy tucked them in at night. But they were asleep at the time the wife went missing, so he could have slipped out. But there's definitely a carving, and it looks like Pravus's work."

"What does it say?" Paul was sure he already knew.

"Pestis ex Culex."

"Plague of gnats." Paul shuddered. "The other two were taken from apartments."

"Like I said, it doesn't fit. She's a well-known, successful businesswoman, with no ties to the mission we can find. She certainly isn't someone who used to live on the streets and got her life back through the mission."

"The press isn't talking serial killer yet. Maybe Pravus picked a higher-profile victim because he wants people to notice." Keren noticed her barrette lying on a coffee table and picked it up. She groaned in pain when she bent over but went about corralling her hair.

"I'm heading over to her place now. I'd like you to come along, Paul. Maybe you'll recognize her. We need your help to figure out why she was taken."

Paul looked at the door to LaToya's room. "I don't think I should leave. What if LaToya wakes up? I don't want her to be alone."

"Can you give us a minute?" Keren asked O'Shea.

"Sure." O'Shea walked out of the waiting room.

Keren stood and reached for him. Paul hesitated then took her hand. When she tried to pull him up, he cooperated. Keren's body was battered, and since she seemed inclined to manhandle him, he made it easy.

When he stood, she went into his arms so simply and beautifully Paul didn't give a second thought to his concern about being too involved with the police in general or her in particular. He just held her.

They stood that way for a long time, comforting each other, sharing their badly taxed strength. She'd done the same for him in that basement, after she'd defused a bomb and he'd enraged a murderer.

Paul liked her style.

Finally, she pulled back. He bent to kiss her.

Before he could, she said, "Call the mission. Have someone bring Rosita over here."

"Who? The regulars at the mission are all suspects."

"How about I go get Rosita and bring her back here then catch up with you. She can call you if there's any change. We can be back here in a few minutes if she wakes up." She added, "You know we've got to go."

"This is what I remember about being a cop." Paul stepped out of Keren's arms when he thought about the life he had left behind. "All the times I *had* to go. All the important things I missed because I was needed somewhere."

"Yeah, that's the way it is," Keren said with calm acceptance.

"And I was so self-centered. I always thought what I needed to do was more important than anything else. . .more important than my wife. . .more important than my daughter. . . ."

"You were needed, Paul. That's the life of a cop." Solemnly Keren added, "That's why you got out. That's a big part of why I've stayed single. For far too many of us it's not a family kind of life."

They stared at each other for a long minute. Paul still wanted to close that distance. But he couldn't do it. Their kisses had always been spontaneous, but now, somehow, it was as if Keren was asking him to stay away, because only hurt lay in pretending it could be different. He had to wonder if it wasn't at least in part because she was using him, using her connection to the mission to search for a killer. Being a cop first and a woman second.

With a wrench that felt as if it broke something inside him, Paul turned away from her. "You get Rosie. I'll go with O'Shea to see what nightmare I've brought down on poor Melody Fredericks."

CHAPTER FIFTEEN

Gnats came on men and animals.

When Pravus used his own blood to provide for his creation, the sweet, vicious agony of it actually kept the beast quiet. But as soon as he was done painting, the hunger grew again.

He studied the white gown she'd wear and fumed because he didn't have time and he couldn't bleed fast enough. He did what he could, but it was infuriating because he was denied her screams, denied her pleas for mercy.

The beast inside him prowled, hungry, prodding Pravus to do this right. Mocking him.

He hadn't taken the right woman in Melody, and the end for LaToya hadn't been right.

Pravus should never have run. What lived in him was powerful and dangerous. He should have turned it loose on the reverend and the detective. The beast had urged him to stay, fight, even to the death. But cowardice had won, and Pravus had abandoned his prize.

A quick glance at the newspaper told him the girl had died, and that had given him some shred of peace, but it had been haphazard, sloppy. And it warned him that the park was not a safe place to leave his creations. He was surprised that the police had been there waiting.

That was shrewd. But he was more shrewd.

Looking at the white gown, he saw that instead of the delicate precision of his usual painting style, he'd rushed this, he'd skimped. His child wasn't perfect. He didn't care for Melody Fredericks. He didn't see how hurting her would hurt the reverend, and that was the point.

The hunger to inflict pain on the reverend rose and battered him. Then he had an inspiration and smiled. The risk was high, but it would be worth it.

A high-pitched sound reached Pravus's ears. For a moment he thought the poor battered Mrs. Fredericks was laughing at him, mocking him, and Pravus turned to strike. But she wasn't making a sound. That's when he realized it was his own laughter. Or maybe the laughter of the beast.

Because it was so brilliant. He couldn't contain his glee when he thought of how hard this would be on the reverend.

Delighted with his inventiveness, savoring the strength he'd honed his muscles to for just this purpose, Pravus waited, bided his time, picked his moment, and disposed of Melody.

When he was finished and back home, the satisfaction faded more quickly than it had before. Though he'd enjoyed it, the beast was starving. He looked around at what he'd created—his children, his people—and wanted them to be free. The reverend had stood in the way of their freedom and now he had to suffer.

He'd loitered at the mission and knew word was spreading that people connected to the Lighthouse were being targeted. And he could see the results of the warnings. No one walked alone except the mindless street people, and they weren't who he wanted.

But neither was Melody Fredericks. Even though it had been brief, he'd gotten surcease from the appetite of the beast.

So he wasn't going to be allowed to stalk and wait and choose with the care he preferred. That was a pity, because of them all, this was his favorite so far. The steady killing he'd done in the park. He'd spent days preparing for the plague of beasts. This gave him many chances to kill.

Accepting that wasn't easy, but it was necessary. Even God had to compromise to achieve freedom for His people. Pravus compromised now because he needed someone new.

He needed someone *now*.

~

Paul spent so many hours being grilled, he almost turned into a T-bone.

He had never heard of Melody Fredericks. He'd never met her. He'd never seen her. He'd never eaten at her restaurant. The mission had never gotten a contribution from her.

Nothing.

When he wasn't being questioned, he was poring over his old cases.

Keren filed her incident report and had a long talk with her lieutenant. She came out quiet, her blue-gray eyes more ghostly than usual.

"How'd it go?"

She sat down at her desk. "Later. I want to go over these files again."

His interrogation, her interrogation, endless paperwork to comb, and through it all he kept thinking, *Pestis ex culex. Plague of gnats.* Then, *Pestis ex rana. Plague of frogs.* He could still feel those frogs crawling around inside his shirt.

He kept in touch with the hospital by phone. Every time he called he felt more detached from LaToya and his work as a pastor and more attached and comfortable as a cop. The drive to solve this crime and save Melody Fredericks overcame any need he felt to sit with LaToya. She was unconscious. She needed *someone* there, maybe. The doctors said talking to her might help. But why him? He'd forgotten how important police work was. All those years since his wife and daughter had died, he'd battered himself about how he'd put his job first. But back then he'd had a child who needed him. Now he had no one except the people he could save by catching a killer.

Anyone could sit at the bedside of an unconscious woman. Only he knew his cases and his people from the mission well enough to cross-reference the two groups and find the killer.

He didn't get back to the hospital all day and it didn't matter, because LaToya didn't wake up. They returned to the ICU waiting area at ten o'clock that night. Paul glanced at Keren walking beside him. She must think she was doing guard duty. As she strode along, even her walk screamed cop—impressive, considering the argument she lost just last night with a sedan. Purposeful, fast, long strides, going somewhere. Paul was walking just like her.

Rosita was waiting in the intensive care lounge.

"How many hours have you spent here today?" Paul settled into a utilitarian gray chair in the waiting room and caught himself fidgeting, impatient with the long, wasted night ahead. Giving himself a mental shake, he groped around for peace, and it proved elusive.

"I didn't count." Rosita rose from the chair where she'd sat reading.

His conscience pinged. "I didn't mean for you to end up sitting here all day."

"It don't matter." Rosita frowned. "LaToya is still unconscious."

Paul leaned forward in the chair beside Rosita. "I'm not

worrying about LaToya—well, that's not true, I am—but I'm talking about you. I don't want you to feel like you're being taken advantage of."

Rosita waved a book in the air. "C'mon, Pastor P, I been sittin' readin' all day. Closest I ever come to a vacation. It was great."

Paul relaxed. "I really appreciate it. I just don't want her to wake up and be all alone."

"I know how it is to be alone. I'm glad to do it." Rosita stood and began to pull on a jacket that lay in a chair nearby.

"You're not going home alone, are you?" Paul stood, ready to hold her there by force if necessary.

"She's not if that's Manny." Keren pointed toward the exit.

Rosita looked down the long hospital hallway and lit up when she saw a man standing at the end. "Manny said he'd come and sit with me when he got done with work today."

Paul waved at the silhouette, and Rosita hurried off with a wide grin on her face.

"You're a nice man, Pastor P." Keren settled into a chair beside him.

Paul sank back and tried to let go of the driving need to be doing something. "I don't feel very nice lately." He looked sideways at Keren. "I wanted that gun from you last night."

Keren shrugged.

"I wanted to hurt that guy. Kill him." Paul wanted Keren to admit she was shocked and disappointed in him.

"There's always a tug-of-war inside a person." Keren shrugged her brown suit jacket off and began rolling up the sleeves of her yellow button-down shirt.

Paul noticed her scraped-up hands and saw her move her aching joints gingerly. He still wanted some time alone with Pravus.

Wanting to catch Pravus is the right instinct. Your human ⌐ide also wants revenge. That's perfectly normal. The part of you that is ruled by God actually goes against human nature. So, yes, you wanted my gun. Yes, you saw yourself making Pravus pay for the harm he'd done, but God has a nice firm grip on you. You'd have done the right thing in the end."

Paul eyed the nasty bruise on her forehead, almost covered by the hair that had escaped her barrette, and felt himself sink deeper into cop mode. "How'd it go with the investigation into the discharged weapon?"

"I told my story, told the truth." Keren exhaled slowly, maybe with relief. Maybe her ribs hurt. "But I didn't tell all of it. I can't decide if I feel right about it. Am I denying God when I deny this gift?"

Paul tried to shift into pastor gear. This would be an excellent time for that. All he could do was remember how badly he'd wanted that gun. "You did right. They wouldn't have understood if you'd talked about discerning spirits."

"But there's no *law* that allows me to shoot at a person I can't see, can't identify, but 'know' in some spiritual way is the right man."

"Tell that to Spiderman."

She slugged him but there was no force behind it. There was an extended silence before she added, "They seemed to accept my story and be okay with it. They didn't take me off the case, so that's a good sign. But it's by no means settled."

"If I were still on the force I'd probably be making an example of you right now."

Keren scowled at him, and he smiled right into her bared teeth. She couldn't sustain any true anger, but Paul suspected that was mainly because she was tired.

"You know, that's the first time I've ever pulled the trigger on my gun outside a shooting range."

Keren ran her hands through the wild curls that rioted, trying to escape the bun on her head. She rescued her barrette and replaced it with graceful efficiency.

Paul wanted to offer to help. Having his hands in her hair was very tempting.

"Part of me feels like a failure because I didn't stop him. But then, the other part of me is horrified that I could have killed a human being. The part of me that's horrified seems like the Christian part, but I'm not sure it is. We have to stop this guy. I may have no choice except to kill him before this is over." She had her hair back under control long before Paul had himself under control. She leaned forward, forearms on her knees, and turned to look at him.

"I shot a man while I was a cop." Paul remembered the price he'd paid.

"Killed him?" Keren asked, watching him closely, like a good little investigator.

Paul matched her pose and noticed his face was really close to hers. Well within kissing distance. Talking about killing someone put a damper on his wayward thoughts, though. "It was my third year on patrol. I don't think, even now, that I had a choice. He was out of control, unloading his gun in every direction. He'd already hit a couple of bystanders. He put a bullet into me before he was done." Paul rubbed his shoulder and felt the old scar under his T-shirt. "Of course, I acted like it was nothing. I was at my very macho best. I never admitted to anyone how torn up I was inside. I'd only been married about a year when it happened. I didn't talk to my wife without biting her head off for six months. I got drunk every Friday night for a year. That was the first time she left me."

"Didn't you go to the department shrink?"

"Yeah, they required it. I went and didn't tell the poor woman anything. I was too tough to even admit to myself how scarring it was to take a life."

"You're talking about it now," Keren said.

"Yeah, I am." Paul leaned toward her slightly, just to see if she'd stay put or move away. "I like talking to you, Detective Collins."

"I like talking to you, too, Pastor P." She didn't move much, but a little, and definitely in the right direction.

Before Paul could close the last few inches, a nurse came out of the IC unit. "I can let one of you go in for five minutes this half hour and the other go in next half hour. You can do that all night if you want to. Like I told the other lady who was here, don't ask her questions about the attack. Even in the coma it could be upsetting to her, but go ahead and talk to her. It definitely helps our patients to hear a familiar voice."

Keren never took her turn—since Paul's was the only familiar voice—but she stayed. He never suggested she go home. She might not be safe at home. She never suggested abandoning him. Instead, she stretched out on a hard vinyl sofa and slept.

Keren woke in the first light of dawn as Paul came back from sitting with LaToya. His hair was curling and messy. His clothes looked slept in. He had dark circles under his eyes and he was cradling his arm to his chest, reminding Keren that a building had fallen on him just recently.

"How is she?" Keren sat up on the vinyl couch, aching in every joint from the car wreck and the uncomfortable bed.

"No change. Still in a deep coma. But the nurse said her vitals are strong. They're really hopeful she'll wake up and be okay." Paul's smile was weak, but it was there.

Keren ran her hands into her hair and realized her barrette was gone. She looked around.

"This what you're after?" Paul dangled it from two fingers. "It fell out in the night."

"My barrette never falls out. That's why I love it." She stood, suppressed a groan of pain, and snatched it away from him. Her eyes narrowed suspiciously. "How'd you get it?"

"You really don't like your hair?"

"Of course not."

"Because it's about the most beautiful hair I've ever seen." Paul's eyes flashed as he studied her corkscrew curls, made more awful by a terrible night's sleep.

"You have really bad taste." She began finger-combing her hair into a ponytail. "You probably get all bothered by clown wigs on Halloween."

Paul laughed. It was a great sound.

Higgins came striding into the waiting room. "Is she awake yet?"

"No, sorry." Keren looked at Higgins, immaculate as ever. A few nights sitting up with one of his vics might do him a world of good. Might help him remain a human being. "What have you discovered about the people you had up on the wall yesterday?"

"I left a report in triplicate on your desk," Higgins said.

"Why don't you just phone next time?" Keren asked. "Save yourself the drive over."

"It was on my way, and I wanted to make sure Pastor Morris came in early. I've got a long list of questions about the people we're investigating. A few minutes talking with you, Pastor, might save us hours." Higgins gave the door to the intensive care unit a disgruntled look, like the room was committing a crime by keeping LaToya from him.

"We're taking a lot of heat over Melody Fredericks. Any second now, the press is going to connect these killings and go ballistic."

"I'm coming in as soon as someone comes to sit with LaToya. I expect her any minute."

Higgins glared as if he was tempted to arrest Paul and drag him into the station house. But finally he left, alone.

Keren pulled on her blazer and checked her gun, tucked in a holster at the small of her back. It hadn't helped with her night's sleep, and the hospital wasn't real happy about her wandering around armed, but she wasn't going anywhere without it.

O'Shea arrived with Rosita. They'd convinced her to wait for O'Shea, rather than take the bus or the El.

"Buddy's back," she announced cheerfully. "Louie showed up for his shift just as I was leaving and Murray was already at work on breakfast. They'll keep things running at the mission so I'm free to be at the hospital."

"I'm going to get some coffee in the lounge. Anyone else want a cup?" O'Shea rubbed his face, looking like he'd slept about as well as Keren and Paul.

"Is hospital coffee as good as mission coffee?" Rosita asked.

O'Shea shrugged. "Probably about the same."

Rosie shuddered. "I'll take a cup."

Keren and Paul passed. O'Shea wandered off in search of caffeine.

"You haven't told anyone what you're doing, have you, Rosita?" Keren asked.

"No. Not too many of them remember LaToya—she's been off the street for a while. So it's not like they'd want to take a turn sitting with her. I told them a friend of mine is in the hospital, and that's not a lie."

Paul smiled at this former crack whore, who now worried about telling a lie. "Thanks. We've got to keep working on catching this maniac."

"I'm rooting for you, Pastor P. I'm glad to do anything that will get this nut off the streets."

They walked toward the exit door. Keren said, "I should go to the mission. I'd probably be able to eliminate Murray and Buddy just by meeting them."

Paul nodded. "And I need to go over those pictures again with Higgins and see what he's come up with."

O'Shea came down the hall, handed Rosita her coffee, and headed after Keren and Paul. "Any change in the vic?"

Paul shook his head.

"She's shown no signs of regaining consciousness." Keren shoved her hands in the pockets of her slacks. "Paul's going to go with you and get to work. I'll be right behind you. I've got to run an errand first."

"You're not going home, are you?" Paul asked. "You know Pravus is paying attention to you now."

"I'm sure I'd be fine. Pravus works in the dark. But no, I'm not going home."

"Keep in touch and don't take too long," O'Shea said. He and Paul went one way, Keren another.

It was a wasted trip. There must have been some morning break, because there was almost no one at the mission, except a woman in the kitchen who wouldn't speak to Keren or make eye contact. But she was baking bread that smelled like heaven. Hunting in the back rooms of the mission, Keren found a group of ladies from a local church who were stuffing envelopes.

"Where is everybody?" Keren asked the group of gray-haired worker bees.

One of them smiled at her from behind her trifocals. "It's the first of the month."

"What's that have to do with anything?"

"Welfare checks, social security checks, disability checks all come out today. Most of the people here will have money for the next few days. It gets pretty quiet."

Frustrated, Keren headed for the station.

When she got there, O'Shea had more details. "We've narrowed the type of chisel down to a very specific artist's tool." He started talking before she had a chance to stick her purse in her desk drawer. "Only a half-dozen stores in the metro area handle them. The one Pravus threw was old, but we're hoping he might be compulsive enough to need one exactly like it, so we're monitoring the stores and any mail-order businesses that sell them."

"Sounds good," Keren said as she settled in. "What about the frogs?"

"The frogs were really interesting."

Keren exchanged a look with Paul. He shrugged. "I thought they were pretty interesting when I was picking them out of my clothes."

Keren shuddered, remembering. "How so?"

"Well, they're not a usual kind of frog. They're a really small tree frog, native to the southern part of the United States, mainly Louisiana. They can also be purchased in pet stores, but no stores would carry that many. The medics estimated there were over a hundred frogs crawling on LaToya and scads of them were hopping away in all directions. They got twenty in the ambulance with them because they seemed to kind of cling."

"Tell me about it." Paul rubbed at his stomach as if he could still feel the little wrigglers inside his shirt. "I'm going to go home for the night. I hope a shower helps me forget just what special little frogs they were."

⤺

Paul nearly staggered as he climbed the stairs to his apartment that night. He would have gone back to the hospital directly from the station house, except he hadn't showered or changed clothes since Sunday morning—two days ago. He was starting to disgust himself. A shower, a change of clothes, and right back to LaToya.

He opened his apartment door, jogging straight for the shower. The apartment smelled stale, like it had been closed up for too long, which it had. He felt like a jerk, leaving LaToya all day. As her pastor and her friend, not to mention the catalyst of this mess, it was his duty to be at her side. He rushed through his shower and pulled on a pair of blue jeans, a sweatshirt, and running shoes; then he ran to his tiny spare bedroom to snag his jacket.

He pushed the door open and the air hit him in the face. It was thick. It was alive. His mouth filled with choking dust that crawled down his throat.

Then the smell hit him.

Choking and covering his mouth, he fumbled for the light switch on the wall. The bare bulb was almost snuffed out by the swarms of gnats.

He could just make out the body on the floor. Covering his mouth and nose with one hand, he knelt and virtually pushed aside a solid wall of bugs. He felt for a pulse. There was none. The body was stone cold. She was long dead. But the smell of death had told him that before he'd touched her.

Gnats covered her body. They clustered on the hideous rust-brown painting on her death shroud. Paul lurched to his feet, suddenly remembering he was invading a crime scene. He backed out of the room and slammed the door shut behind him. He ran into his bathroom and spit gnats out of his mouth, clawed at his face to wipe them away, then pulled out his cell phone and called Keren as he rushed out into the hall.

O'Shea beat Keren there. Paul was leaning against the wall outside his door, posting himself as guard. He'd been thinking like a cop. Call it in. Preserve the crime scene.

"Where is she?" O'Shea pulled out a handkerchief and reached for the doorknob.

"No." Paul moved to block O'Shea from going in. He wasn't sure if it was to protect the crime scene or O'Shea. "It's bad."

"Melody Fredericks?" O'Shea didn't protest.

"Yeah, well, I'm sure it's her, but I couldn't see her really."

"Why not?"

There was an extended silence. Finally, Paul said, "Gnats."

Keren emerged at the top of the stairs as Paul spoke. She grimaced.

Paul repeated his orders to stay out. The three of them stood waiting.

When Higgins got there, Paul said, "Wait a minute."

"I'm allowed in." Higgins reached for the door.

Paul grabbed his arm. "You're going to run into a million gnats when you get in there. Cover your mouth."

"I'm not afraid of a few bugs." Higgins looked at them like they were wimps.

Paul almost let him go in without further warning. "You'll need to cover your mouth to breathe. There's a small bedroom on the right, beside the kitchen. The body is in there."

Higgins looked at Paul for a long second and pulled a handkerchief out of his pocket. Then he went in. He was back out in thirty seconds, with his mouth and nose covered.

"She's been dead at least twenty-four hours." Higgins swatted at the bugs all over him. He muttered, "Crazy freak. Where did he get all these gnats? When were you last in there?"

"I left here Sunday morning after church and I haven't been back. I've been at the hospital." Paul could hear himself talking like a cop, reporting the facts in a brisk, no-nonsense voice. "She may have been here since then."

Higgins looked up and down the hall. "We'll need to question the staff. Aren't there offices on this floor?"

"Yes," Paul said in the clipped tone he couldn't shake. "But they're closed today. It's always quiet around here on the first. Welfare checks."

"With this case, I didn't expect it to be easy," Higgins said sardonically. "I opened a window to thin out the gnats. I don't think we need to keep them *all* as evidence."

"You'll need to get face masks before you can go in there and get her out," Paul said through his tensed jaw.

Higgins didn't even debate it. He placed the call and settled in to wait with the rest of them.

Paul's phone rang.

He flipped his phone open without a second thought.

"No," Higgins hissed, "wait for the trace."

Paul wasn't thinking about anything else, except who would be calling him. He knew.

"Are you expecting a package to arrive momentarily, Reverend?" the silky smooth voice asked.

Paul waved at them to pay attention. O'Shea immediately started recording. Higgins gave Paul a disgusted look and began the process of having the call traced.

"You ruined things for me last time," Pravus crooned. "This time I don't think I'll give you a chance to spread my message. But

203

you will find a carving in the room with pretty Melody."

"I didn't ruin things," Paul said. "I gave them your message and they heard. That's why the bomb didn't go off. They listened to me. They let your people go."

Pravus hesitated. "No one as evil as they are would accept the message I sent. You're lying."

Paul *was* lying, and he had the strange idea that he shouldn't be. In fact, he decided in a split second that he wasn't acting at all the way he should be. Whether that was God's inspiration or his own temper, he couldn't be sure. "All right, Pravus, you want the truth? The truth is no one is going to listen to your message because they know the message is being sent by a coward."

Keren's hand clamped on his forearm in warning.

Paul ignored her. "Everybody knows you're a fool who *says* he speaks for God but really only speaks for himself. I'm sick of your threats. I'm sick of listening to a weak little piece of slime who thinks his pathetic imitation of God's miracles makes him equal to God. Read the book of Exodus, Pravus. Over and over Pharaoh's magicians do their little tricks to try to copy the plagues. They're trying to prove Moses is just doing tricks, too, but they can't prove it, because Moses is doing the work of God. Well that's all you're doing, Pravus. A bunch of sneaky, little tricks. You say you hate me, but you're too much of a crawling worm to face me and take out your anger where it belongs. So instead you hurt innocent women.

"You're the fool, Pravus. You're so weak that you have to use women to act out your hatred for me. What did I do to you when I was a cop, anyway? I'll bet whatever it was, you deserved it."

"I killed the dancer and her mother. They beheaded the voice in the wilderness. And you were too blind to see it. I was too smart for you then, and I'm too smart for you now. Why do you think I picked her? Why do you think I put pretty Melody right under your nose? So that this time, even someone as stupid as you could see my creative brilliance. I'll make sure the whole world knows they should have let my people go."

"Pravus—" A sharp *click* told Paul the call was over. He looked up at Higgins.

Higgins shook his head in frustration.

"Why isn't the sign out here in the hall?" O'Shea asked. "And where's the threat against some larger group?"

"He's changed his pattern. It doesn't make any sense." Higgins stared at the cell phone number on the caller ID. "It's a new number. We'll track down the number, but it'll be another stolen cell phone."

"Don't serial killers usually follow rituals?" Paul crossed his arms, stared at his closed apartment door, and realized he wanted to go in and examine the body more closely. The thought didn't scare him a bit.

Mark Dyson spoke from behind them, "Only some of them."

They all wheeled around, surprised to see him. Paul thought the guy was spooky. Now he was moving like a spook, too.

Dyson stuck his hands deep in the pockets of his blue jean jacket. "Some serial killers are incredibly hard to find, simply because they *don't* follow rituals. There is speculation that only about thirty percent of serial killers ever get caught. The rest of them travel around, kill one or two people, and move on. They change their method of killing. They don't keep souvenirs. They choose street people and runaways who won't be missed. They're very smart and they learn about police procedure so they can be careful not to leave evidence or, even better, they plant misleading evidence that manipulates a crime scene.

"That's the second time he's said, 'The dancer and her mother.'

I wonder what it means to him," Dyson said.

Keren started pacing. "Pravus said, 'They beheaded the voice in the wilderness.' John the Baptist was the voice of one crying in the wilderness."

Paul was suddenly excited. "Yes, and Herod had him beheaded."

"Herod ordered it, but do you remember why?" Keren said with growing excitement.

"Sure, Herod's wife had her daughter. . .dance!"

"That's right." Keren lengthened her stride as she walked back and forth in front of Paul's door. "The dancer and her mother. They are regarded as particularly evil, especially the mother. Even Herod, who was a nasty guy, wanted to spare John the Baptist, but his wife wanted him dead."

"So how can that have anything to do with Pravus's grudge against me?"

"He thinks everyone is evil but him," O'Shea said. "So we don't need to necessarily try to find some mother-and-daughter team in your case files who did something shady."

"Like ask for someone's head on a platter?" Paul asked cynically.

"Especially if he was first starting out," Higgins said. "He said they were his first, and you missed it."

"We've been over those files a dozen times now." Keren slapped her hand on the dingy walls of the hallway. "There is no mother-daughter murder in any of them."

"Not even an older woman and younger woman. I don't see what he's getting at. The only mother and daughter deaths I can think of are. . ." Paul quit talking suddenly. It was odd. He was being a cop again and liking it. He'd been good at it. Then, because he was thinking like a cop, his logic drew him to a conclusion that knocked him back into a pastor. His vision narrowed and sound faded. He took an unsteady step back and stumbled against the wall.

"Who? You thought of someone, Paul? What mother and daughter?" Then Keren knew, too. She whispered, "Oh no. It can't be."

CHAPTER SIXTEEN

If you do not let my people go, I will send swarms of flies on you and your officials, on your people and into your houses. The houses of the Egyptians will be full of flies; even the ground will be covered with them.

Pravus blinked his eyes to stop the burning, then he swiped one hand across his forehead. Sweat burned his eyes. It was passion. It was suffering for his art.

He looked from his new creation to the tainted woman who needed him so much. It was a shame he'd had to stop the screaming, because he had a sense that the screams let the evil out. And naturally, no one could hear her. Pravus was too smart for that.

But the noise had violated the art, stopped its flow.

Now she lay there in silence and Pravus loved her. She needed him. Poor thing. Needed him to purify her, create something beautiful out of her ugliness.

Turning back to the gown, he remembered the substandard dress he'd made for Melody. But the paint. Dead women don't bleed. What other choice did he have?

Looking down, he saw the slits in his own arms. He'd given. He'd done his best without Melody to help. Now, this new woman was generous.

The last one he'd hurried. It hadn't satisfied him for long, hadn't quieted the beast for long, but while he was creating, there had been peace and pleasure sufficient to be worth it. Especially after he'd thought of leaving her at the reverend's home. That was a second type of brilliance. A different type of art.

The brush trembled. His hand shook worse. The beast prowled inside him and told him it was because the reverend hadn't suffered enough. Because he hadn't known Melody.

This one would be better. Not perfect, but the reverend would know.

He watched his hand shake and heard the beast pacing and growling and saw no reason not to be painstaking with this gown.

Laughing, he looked at the woman who'd fallen so easily into his hands. He'd done her a favor, using her to create. But the dress, it wasn't his best work.

Father would be furious.

But this victim wasn't worthy of his art, so why bother?

Then he knew how to make even this meager creation one of his worthy people.

His laughter rose higher until it echoed off the walls.

Time for Kerenhappuch to get involved.

The tough cop who'd been waiting in the hallway crumbled into a gentle, wounded pastor.

"It wasn't murder." Paul covered his face with one hand. "It's not even in my case files, because I didn't handle the case."

She'd talked to a few people who remembered Paul Morris from his days at Chicago PD. The main word they used to describe him was *tough*. As cold-blooded as any cop you ever met. Not violent, not if he could avoid it, but when he couldn't avoid it, he was as ruthless and unfeeling as a robot. Most of this was said with a fair amount of respect and even some affection.

"What? Tell us what this is about!" Agent Higgins demanded.

Dyson's eyes seemed to glow.

She'd also heard from a few people who weren't fans. One guy told her the most dangerous place in Illinois was standing between Paul Morris and a television camera. That Paul was the one who'd done a good impression of a jackbooted thug when he dealt with her years back, and he was the one who'd been standing in front of his door when she got here. That side was a good cop. Having him working this case, in his cop mode, greatly improved their chances of bringing Pravus to justice.

The trouble was, she couldn't stand that man.

The cool, analytical police detective seemed to have nothing to do with Pastor P, who felt everything so deeply, he carried the weight on his shoulders from every sin, real or imagined, he'd ever committed. Paul's wife and daughter had been killed accidentally, and it had brought him to the brink of suicide and ultimately to a faith in God. But now, knowing it was no accident, Keren prayed silently he could handle it.

Paul leaned forward as if he was losing consciousness. He braced his hands on his knees, his head hanging down. All his tough-cop demeanor faded and he was himself again. Or was the cop the real man and Pastor P only a facade?

"His wife." Paul wasn't going to be able to answer Higgins, so she did it for him. "His wife and daughter were killed, hit on the road by a man driving by. The man called the ambulance. He went with them to the hospital and showed only concern and regret. And now he must be talking about them, claiming them as his first. The dancer and her mother," Keren mused. "Herodias telling her daughter to ask for John the Baptist's head on a platter."

"The preschool program had a little dance number in it." Paul spoke to the floor. His shoulders rose and fell as if breathing was all he could manage. "My daughter dressed up like a ballerina for it. She loved that stiff little skirt and she wouldn't take it off. Or so Trish said. I wasn't around much."

His voice broke and even Higgins had the sense to keep quiet while Paul got ahold of himself. "Hannah was wearing it when she died."

Paul's legs seemed to give out, and he sank until he was sitting on the floor, his knees drawn up. Keren went to him and rested a hand on his bowed shoulders. "I'm so sorry."

"I saw her broken body, in that tiny skirt."

"Pravus knew." Keren kept her hand on him, trying to share some of her strength. It was hard when she wanted to curl up and cry with him. "Pravus must have stalked them. But why did he choose them?"

"It could have been random. A simple act of madness," O'Shea said.

"All your wife or daughter would have needed to do was cross paths with him." Keren rubbed Paul's shoulders as she thought.

"Pravus calls himself an artist, right?" Paul kept his head down, but his shoulders squared and he sat more erectly, as if he were trying to pull himself together. "My wife worked in an art gallery. Maybe she came in contact with Pravus at work and somehow drew his attention."

"It doesn't matter about that." Higgins clapped his hands together. "We've got him!"

Keren rounded on Higgins. "It doesn't matter?"

Dyson sharpened his gaze, but Higgins didn't answer her. He was too busy dialing his phone. "We can track him down. What was his name, Reverend?"

"Francis." Paul's head came up, and with a single lithe move, he stood, swiped the back of his hand across his eyes, and spoke with a steady voice. "I'll remember his name until the day I die. Francis Caldwell. He cried. He stood in that hospital waiting room and cried because he felt so bad." Paul's eyes narrowed. They still glistened with tears, but he had it under control now.

Keren was shocked at how cold he sounded. He'd gone back to cop. Maybe it was all too much for him to stand without turning off his emotions. It was almost too much for Keren, and they weren't talking about her family.

"I knew at the time he was an amateur artist, but no connection between him and my wife was ever found. Why would it be found? No one looked. Not even me. He was so kind." Paul slammed a closed fist against the wall behind him. His sudden fury made Keren jump.

"That little murderous demon *cried* and begged me to forgive him. I was insane with guilt and grief and rage. I jumped on him, and the EMTs had to pull me off. I—I think I'd have killed him with my bare hands, but I never once believed it was *deliberate*. Caldwell quoted scripture to me. He asked for forgiveness. He prayed out loud, almost rambling. He seemed so distraught, he was on his knees part of the time. It seemed a little extreme, but he'd just killed two people."

"Extremely religious is a long way from a demon," Keren said.

"Demon?" Dyson's head came up and he looked at her hard.

"Demon," Keren repeated, "or evil. Latin for Pravus, the name he calls himself."

"Pravus, is that like depravity? Depraved?" Dyson asked.

Keren exhaled slowly. "Maybe. Latin root words aren't exactly part of my skill set. We can look it up. It fits, doesn't it?"

"Satan himself masquerades as an angel of light." Paul quoted scripture, and it gave Keren hope that the pastor was still in there somewhere. But Paul's voice was so cold she was frightened for him. "I came down hard on Caldwell. He had a couple of minor charges—one was reckless driving. He had an assault charge he'd pled down to a misdemeanor. I put it in the worst light possible to make it look like he was a repeat offender, pulled strings, called in favors. He got a couple of years."

Higgins got off his phone. "We'll throw everything we have into locating Francis Caldwell. I've already started the wheels turning. Maybe we can get to him before he hurts anyone else."

Paul's jaw tightened, and he didn't respond.

"We'll go through the records and find Caldwell's current address. And if he's hanging around the mission, we should be able to find an up-to-date picture and pick him up."

"Wait a minute." Paul's eyes sharpened. "I know what Caldwell looks like. I'd have recognized him if he was hanging around the mission."

"A disguise," Higgins said. "Maybe even plastic surgery. Maybe lifts in his shoes. A full beard like so many homeless men wear. He could have changed his appearance radically."

"That must be it." Paul stared sightlessly. Probably running faces through his mind, searching for the one that could be Francis Caldwell.

The ME team got there. Keren felt sorry for them as they entered the swarming apartment.

Keren and Paul got back to the station house just in time to be informed that another woman was missing, Katrina Hardcastle.

⌒

Francis Caldwell had vanished off the face of the earth.

He'd taken all his money—a sizable amount—out of the

bank, in tidy, nine-thousand-dollar chunks so he wouldn't alert any officials. He hadn't filed a tax return, registered a car, or used his social security number since the death of Paul's family. There was no record of his existence for the last two years. Keren spent another day tracking down the men who lived near the mission. She stopped in at the mission near mealtimes when she could manage it and got no further sense of Caldwell being near.

But the word was out on the street about the danger circling Paul and the mission, and many of the regulars were missing.

She and Paul spent another night in the hospital with LaToya. And as they worked, they waited for a phone call or another plaque.

She'd gotten copies of all the pictures Higgins had, plus the ones Paul had added of those who hung around the mission, and she and Paul eliminated all the ones Keren was sure she'd been close to.

There were still too many. But Keren kept coming back to those five men who'd driven away together in Murray's car Sunday morning. It had to be one of them. It had to.

Dawn broke over the hospital ward after another lousy night's sleep.

Keren said, "I've used up all the clothes I had at the precinct. I've got to go home. I've been showering at work, living out of my locker, but it's crunch time for human hygiene."

"You're not going to your place alone." Paul looked as if he was prepared to be very stubborn.

"Good, I can use a bodyguard."

A smile bloomed on his face. One of the few she'd seen since they'd realized what had happened to his wife and little girl. Then it faded.

"I know what you're up to."

"What?"

"You think that if you let me play bodyguard for you, then I'll be a good sport about it when you reciprocate."

With a quick tilt of her head, Keren said, "Maybe. But I still want you to come with me."

Rosita arrived at the hospital and they left her to sit with LaToya.

"Do you really want me as a bodyguard?" Paul asked. "Are you scared?"

Keren studied his face. It was cool, the cop, and it irked her.

"He was at your place, not mine." They rode the El while Paul flipped through the pictures for what had to be the one hundredth time.

"You're driving yourself crazy with that." It was too early for rush hour, so Paul could spread the pictures out. The steady roar of the El was such an everyday sound, Keren barely heard it as they rushed along.

"Why can't I recognize Caldwell?" Paul flipped to the most recent photo they could find of Francis Caldwell. It was over five years old. A skinny little man. Short, weak chin, eyeglasses, painfully short dishwater-blonde hair.

Caldwell would be in his thirties by now. He'd gotten a few paintings carried in a smaller art store before he'd killed Trish and Hannah Morris. The photo was a publicity shot, and Keren had to assume it was the best picture the little weasel could get of himself.

The few paintings he'd gotten listed in the stores were either sold or disposed of. There was no record of where they'd gone. Keren wondered if those paintings would be bloody, ugly things.

"He's not a man who would attract attention." Keren stared at the picture, trying to add years, weight, a beard, madness. "But I'd be able to recognize him if I saw him. And so would you."

"So we're wrong about him hanging around my mission."

"We're not," Keren insisted. "I know he was there, and we know he's got inside knowledge."

"Which means he's a regular." Paul nodded. "And he was there as recently as Sunday, and he's most likely one of these five men."

Paul lifted up the five pictures they'd chosen to focus on as the El's brakes gave their high-pitched squeal and the train slowed. Keren caught the handrail.

"But we can't be certain. If I were dead certain, I'd do whatever it took to point the FBI and all our police resources on these five." Keren stuffed the pictures back in her file folder and shoved it in her oversized purse as they exited the train.

"The FBI is going to do some work on that photo of Caldwell. Age it. Try a few possible alterations in case he had plastic surgery. Give him a beard, lose the glasses."

Keren marched down the hall to her apartment, wishing she had picked one on a higher floor. It ate at her just how accessible her home was to a lunatic. She tugged the barrette out of her hair as she walked and let the heavy mass of it fall down her neck. "I'll never get a comb through this."

"Don't tell me you're going to be hours getting dolled up."

Keren whirled around. Paul grinned at her.

Another smile.

Rolling her eyes, she decided to let him live. For now. She moved faster, ignoring her protesting muscles. Her feet echoed in her building's hallway.

"You won't have to wait long." With a smug smile she added, "And I was just patronizing you before, about the bodyguard thing, so you'd let me take care of you. I'm fine without a watchdog."

"Well, you're getting one anyway. And if you don't quit

complaining about it, I'm telling everyone at the station your real name."

Keren glared at him over her shoulder. "You wouldn't dare!"

"Try me," Paul said lightly.

"I'm being blackmailed by a missionary." Keren trudged when she wanted to jog. Her ribs reminded her of the little argument she'd lost with a Malibu grill. She probably had cracked ribs. One of her knees was determined to make her sorry for every step.

She wondered how Paul was holding up. "We've been at the hospital three nights now. I'm thinking of putting it on my next Christmas card: 'Cook County: my home away from home.'"

"I'm getting close to liking the chairs in the hospital, now that my spine has been bent out of alignment enough to match them." Paul wasn't even breathing hard, the big jerk. "And I don't know when they'll let me back into my place."

There was a stretch of silence, then Paul asked, "Do you think she's going to wake up?"

Keren stopped and turned to face Paul. "Of course she's going to wake up. Why would God have saved her the way He did in that park, if He didn't have further plans for her?"

Paul nodded but without a lot of assurance. "She's been out so long."

"Three days isn't that long when your injuries are as traumatic as LaToya's. She needs to heal, then she'll wake up." Keren laid her hand on his arm. "I know she will."

"And what about the two since then?" Paul covered her hand with his. "Melody Fredericks dead, Katrina Hardcastle missing. He's escalating, Keren. You know he is. He's on a rampage, and we're not any closer to finding him than we were that first day."

"Of course we're closer. We've got his face sent out to every cop in town. The FBI has it entered on their database. And we're tracking down those Internet bug sites. If he ordered from them, he had to give a mailing address. We'll get him."

"How could I have not thought of my wife and daughter right away? I actually knew the loon. Why didn't I think of him?" Paul's fist clenched. "We could have saved LaToya what she's going through, and the other two women wouldn't have even been hurt."

"He already had LaToya by the time the dust settled from that first explosion. Figuring it out instantly wouldn't have stopped that."

"But the other two. If we'd have gotten his picture out—"

"Stop!" Keren cut him off. "You know better than to play this guilt game. Stop whining and pull yourself together."

The General George Patton school of psychological counseling. Maybe she ought to slap the poor guy, too.

There was a visible battle inside of Paul and finally the kindhearted, worried pastor faded away, replaced by the police detective, eyes sharp, head nodding. "You're right. Sorry. Wasting time. As soon as you're ready to go back to work, we can sit in on Melody's autopsy."

Keren looked at him for a long time. She didn't know quite what to make of his seesawing manner. As soon as she had some spare time, maybe she'd talk to him about his Pastor Jekyll and Detective Hyde personalities. For now, she just headed down the long hall again.

"Why doesn't he call?" Paul groused. "We found the body at my place yesterday. Another woman disappeared the same day. Where has he stashed the latest vic?"

Vic? Keren glanced over her shoulder, but he was staring angrily at his phone, as if he could glare it into ringing.

"It's flies this time, isn't it?" Keren asked.

"Yeah, the fourth plague is flies. He can have a ball with that."

They reached Keren's apartment. The door swung open when she touched the knob. She immediately snatched her hand back. She heard a high-pitched whine. Then she smelled death.

Paul pulled out his handkerchief and gingerly pulled the door shut before more than a handful of flies could escape.

"I think we found Katrina Hardcastle."

They backed away from the door. It was only after they were across the hall that they spotted the sign hanging over the door.

"*Pestis ex Musca*," Keren read aloud, thinking, *Caldwell knows where I live.*

Paul translated: "The plague of flies."

Keren swallowed hard then forced herself to lean against the wall across from her door, and called O'Shea.

A glance at Paul showed he was in pure cop mode. Keren thought this was more the time for the kindly pastor.

Keren left the autopsy with a headache she decided to blame on the chemicals in the lab. Dr. Schaefer escorted them out to make a few final points, complete with eight-by-ten glossies.

"This one is definitely different than the others," Dr. Schaefer said with a considerable amount of gallows enthusiasm. "Her wounds are postmortem and they're minimal, no bleeding. I suspect the blood on the shroud is his. We're doing DNA testing."

"We know who did this now." Paul picked up one of Dr. Schaefer's gruesome snapshots with no apparent emotion. "The test doesn't help us find him."

"DNA testing will be useful in court," O'Shea reminded him.

"She had a skull fracture and a broken neck. Her right arm is crushed. There is a compound fracture of the tibia and femur, and massive trauma, particularly down the whole right side of her body. I'd say she either fell a long way, or, more likely, she was hit. Hard."

Dr. Schaefer was making Keren sick, but there was no escape from the report. "There's shattered glass imbedded in her skin. I'll bet it proves to be the kind of glass used for headlights. She died instantly."

"He ran her down?" O'Shea asked.

The ME looked up and nodded. "That's what it looks like, Mick. I can pinpoint the time of death on her more exactly than on Juanita, too. She never spent time in a pool of an indeterminate temperature." Dr. Schaefer considered carefully. "I'd say, judging by the rigor and the extent of decomposition, she died Sunday night."

"Sunday night?" Keren asked. "That's when he was trying to kill LaToya."

"That's when he ran scared from a crime scene." Paul looked as calm as if he were figuring a math problem in his head. "He hit you with his car, Keren. Maybe he hit someone else, too."

O'Shea said, "Makes sense. That would explain why you don't know her, Paul. It was strictly chance. That may be why he killed her in such a different way."

"And he made up for neglecting you," Keren added, "by dumping Melody at your house."

"Maybe it was different, but satisfying just the same," O'Shea speculated. "So he decides to play the next one the same way. Pick a victim at random—you don't know Katrina Hardcastle either—and make his point with the dump site."

"So will the next one come to your place, O'Shea?" Keren asked. "Now that Paul and I are both out of a place to live."

"Not me," Paul said. "For now I live at the hospital, and as soon as LaToya wakes up, I'm going to bunk in the homeless shelter."

"Which, being a homeless shelter," Keren said, "is exactly the same as being out of a place to live, which I just said."

"When I get time, I'll convert part of the office into living quarters." He sounded lighthearted, but then his voice cooled until he showed no emotion at all. "I don't think I'm going to be able to sleep in my place for a while."

Keren heard him earlier referring to Melody as the vic. Caldwell was doing more damage than he knew by pushing Paul away from his peaceful life of faith.

Then she thought of her apartment. "I don't know if I'm going to be able to sleep in my place ever again."

"Caldwell is losing it. Look at the painting." O'Shea held up photos of the dress that had been found on Melody. "Remember how carefully he painted Juanita's shroud? And the work on the first two signs was meticulous." O'Shea held up the sign from Keren's apartment. "This one that arrived with Hardcastle is sloppy."

"It looks like he carved it out in a few minutes. He didn't bother to sand or varnish the wood," Paul noticed.

"I'd say our killer is spinning out of control." Keren ran her hand over the splintered wood.

"Which should make him careless and easier to catch," Dr. Schaefer added. "I've got to get back to work."

"You can see the deterioration of his mental state in this work." O'Shea gestured with the eight-by-ten picture of the dress. "The drawing of Pharaoh isn't nearly as realistic. I wouldn't even think it was a pharaoh, if I hadn't seen the earlier paintings."

Jabbing a blunt finger at the dots at the bottom of the picture, he added, "And these aren't identifiable as gnats. I mean, I don't know how he'd do that, but he managed to depict exactly what he wanted with the other paintings."

Paul said, "Pestis ex culex. The plagues must have some special meaning to him. Why hasn't the profiler come up with something?"

"I think they've quit involving Dyson since they got a name."

"Well then, why don't they send him back to DC?" Paul muttered. "That guy is weird."

"Caldwell is falling apart." Keren stepped back from the table.

"I'll do the Hardcastle autopsy first thing in the morning," Dr. Schaefer informed them. "But my preliminary examination tells me victim number four died more like Juanita. He took her alive. My staff has done a species examination of the frogs, gnats, and flies. They've come up with supply houses and websites that sell things like these in quantity. Here's a copy of the suppliers."

"Great, we can get a court order and have a look at their customer lists." O'Shea nodded with satisfaction.

Keren glanced at Paul. "What's the next one?"

He didn't miss a beat. *"Pestis ex bestia."*

O'Shea snagged the list of Internet sites that dealt in bugs and frogs. "I can't keep track. What is *bestia*?"

"Beasts or animals." Paul reached for the exit door and stopped. "The plague of animals."

"So he's going to turn loose a herd of sheep in O'Shea's house?" Keren asked scathingly.

O'Shea's face turned ice cold. "I need to call my wife." He opened his phone and walked a few steps away.

Keren tried to think of anyone else who would need to be warned. Her family wasn't around Chicago.

"She's going to stay with her sister in St. Louis for a while." O'Shea's voice was impassive, but he clicked his phone shut with undue force. "Now what about the plague of beasts?"

Keren wanted to tell O'Shea how sorry she was for the whole

mess, even though it wasn't her fault. But O'Shea's expression didn't invite comment.

Paul must have gotten that, too, because he went on. "Actually, the plague of beasts was a little different. Up until then, all the plagues had been some sort of blight. Blood made the water undrinkable. Frogs covered the land, and they crawled into beds and into the food. The gnats and flies made the air impossible to breathe. But the plague of beasts was about hurting the animals. Of course, that hurt the Egyptians by extension. But Caldwell might not be setting loose a herd of sheep so much as killing a bunch of animals, and his next victim along with them."

"Where do you find a flock of sheep in Chicago?" Keren wondered.

"Or any animals." O'Shea handed the pictures to Keren and she took them, annoyed that because of her purse she ended up being a pack mule. *There* was a kind of animal.

"Mounted police, maybe?" Keren tried to think of different kinds of animals that might be in danger. "Horses? A stable?"

"Could he be planning some kind of attack on a zoo?" O'Shea wondered.

"Zoos are sewn up pretty tight," Keren said. "So far, he hasn't done any high-tech breaking and entering."

"He got into your apartment," Paul reminded her.

"Yeah, but it looks like he used a sledgehammer on my patio door."

"That's low tech," O'Shea agreed.

"He got into your apartment, too, Paul," Keren pointed out. "And the lock wasn't broken."

"Yeah, but the mission is wide open. I don't lock my door."

"You don't lock your doors?" O'Shea exploded. "What kind of dumb thing is that to do?"

"I've got nothing anybody wants." Paul shrugged. "My furniture comes from donations. If someone needs my old couch enough to steal it from the fourth floor, then they're welcome to it. I'll just get another one from our used-furniture storehouse."

"What about stealing your life? You've got enemies," Keren warned. "Even before this nightmare, Carlo and a host of others weren't overly fond of you."

" 'The Lord is my light and my salvation—whom shall I fear?' " Paul quoted.

" 'Don't help a good boy go bad,' " O'Shea tossed back, quoting from an old television commercial.

"Mine's from the Bible, yours is from TV."

"There's truth in it, Paul," Keren said. "You might be tempting someone if you make an attack on you too easy."

"Maybe." Paul shrugged. "Maybe you're right. I don't think the lock to my apartment door works, and I have no idea where the key might be. I'll check into it."

"I'd appreciate it," Keren muttered. "Thanks for your help, Dee."

Dr. Schaefer nodded then squared her shoulders and turned to get back to her ghastly work.

"Now." Keren reached for the door. "Where do we look for beasts?"

They were considering the possibilities when they stepped out into the late afternoon sunlight. A herd stampeded toward them and surrounded them. But these animals shouted questions.

"Is it true, Pastor Morris, that you are friends with four women who have been killed in the last two weeks?"

"Where did they come from?" O'Shea growled.

"No comment." Paul began shoving relentlessly through the throng of reporters.

"And Detective Collins, a dead body was found in your apartment? A body covered with insects?"

"No comment." Keren kept moving. She had ignoring reporters down to an art.

"Are you and Pastor Morris both involved with these women, Detective?"

Keren was going to be seeing spots for a month from the flashing cameras. She waded toward her car. Someone caught her arm and tried to drag her to a halt. She recognized a woman reporter for the crime beat of a local television station and saw a video camera right behind her. Keren pulled free, trying not to be rough enough to provide good footage.

"Is the killer someone who wants revenge on both of you?"

Paul reached the front passenger-side door. O'Shea provided an escort for Keren around to the driver's side.

"Is it true you and the pastor worked together when you were both on the force?"

"The Chicago Police Department gives a daily briefing at headquarters, as you all know," O'Shea announced over the din. "All your questions will be answered then."

"Even the question of whether Detective Collins and Pastor Morris are having an affair?"

Keren jerked to a stop and turned to see who had asked that. She saw a man smirking at her from one of the sleazier local tabloids. She glared at him, and it was like pouring blood in shark-infested waters. The snapping cameras went crazy.

"C'mon, Detective Collins, admit it." The man tipped back his hat and sneered. "That's why the killer is focusing on the two of you. The pastor is kicking up his heels with a lady cop, and this nut is offended."

Paul had already gotten in the car. Keren prayed desperately that he hadn't heard the insinuations. She tamped down hard on her temper and began moving again. O'Shea helped wrestle her door open. She slid in and slammed her door shut, hoping she'd catch a few fingers in it.

She glanced at Paul. His eyes flashed fire and his jaw was tensed into a firm line.

O'Shea climbed in the back. "Guess the press finally put all these cases together. Took 'em long enough."

Keren took another look at Paul. "I'm sorry. I don't know where they got an idea like that."

"They're going to print that." Paul reached for the door handle. Keren grabbed his shoulder and sank her fingernails into his sweatshirt hard enough that he turned on her.

He jerked against her grip.

"Get ahold of yourself, Paul." Keren saw the photographers leaning against the windows, recording everything.

Fuming, Paul asked, "Do you know how many kids I've counseled about abstinence? Do you know the battle I fight every day against the single-mother culture that guarantees a life of poverty to so many women and children in my neighborhood? If they print something like that, it will undo years of work in a single day."

He caught Keren's hand to pull it loose.

"Don't you dare open that door." Keren let go of him and started the car. "If you go out there, I promise you I'll leave you to those wolves."

She backed out of the parking stall.

Paul didn't get out.

Keren could see that it cost him.

He stared at his white-knuckled hands. "I don't know who I am anymore. I'm so angry at Caldwell and so angry at these reporters. I haven't had time to pray or read my Bible, and all of a sudden it's like I'm losing my faith. Am I so weak that if I'm deprived of quiet time for prayer and daily exposure to God's Word that I just forget what I believe?"

Keren heard a satisfying *thunk* as she backed into a particularly foolish reporter, who thought she'd stop rather than run a man down.

Paul turned around. "Keren, you hit him!"

Keren glanced at Paul and smiled. "I've got too much respect for a man's innate sense of self-preservation to stop."

"It won't hurt to thin the herd a little anyway," O'Shea said. "Survival of the fittest. Darwin would be proud."

Keren looked at Paul. There was a war inside him. She needed the cop, but she liked the pastor. She had been meaning to talk to him about it, but now wasn't a good time. Despite herself, she asked, "Why do you think getting angry has anything to do with being a Christian?"

"Because it does," Paul said vehemently. "It does for me. My anger has always been Satan's greatest hold over me. When I first gave my life over to God, I had to fight the rage in myself constantly."

Paul looked behind them. Keren glanced in her rearview mirror and saw the reporters racing toward their cars.

Paul turned forward again. "I can hear the devil whispering anger into my ear. Anger is what ruined my marriage, it was what drove me to work eighteen hours a day. It was what made me turn my back on my daughter."

Paul took a deep breath and Keren saw his clenched fists open. "It took me years to get a handle on it, even after I was saved. Now it's like all that time spent training myself to control my temper and respond to people with love is just gone."

O'Shea said, "Only a moron wouldn't get angry over a maniac like Caldwell."

"Yeah," Keren agreed. "And those reporters spend time in college learning how to annoy stories out of people. They're masters at getting under your skin so you'll react without thinking. I wanted to deck them myself."

"Anger is a sin," Paul said firmly. "Anger is rooted in hate and that's the opposite of love. I try so hard to love the people I come in contact with at the mission. They've all been arrested and assaulted and ignored. Love is the only thing that has any hope of working with them."

Keren was free of the mob of reporters now and she drove out of the parking lot, picking up speed to head back to the precinct. She saw several cars fall in line behind them. "Anger in itself isn't a sin, Paul. Jesus got angry. Don't forget about Him knocking over tables and driving the people selling doves out of the temple. I've got Him pictured as furious."

"Jesus had one or two episodes of purely righteous anger."

"What are you talking about?" Keren asked. "You went to Bible college, didn't you?"

"Yes, I went to Bible college." Paul gave her an annoyed look, like he was tired of her interfering when he was busy beating himself up.

"So was that just a name, or did you actually study the Bible?" Paul turned on her. She smiled.

"Yes, we studied the Bible," he growled.

Keren pulled up to a red light. "So, I remember Jesus spending half His time getting in someone's face—always someone powerful—and telling them they were blind guides, hypocrites, fools. He got angry all the time."

Paul gestured in front of them. "I, on the other hand, want to throw a fit every ten minutes, because I have to wait in traffic."

"That hasn't been my experience with you," Keren said. "When you get angry, you've always had provocation."

"Big-time," O'Shea said.

Keren started the car moving again. "You've handled all this with incredible grace and Christianity."

"Yeah," O'Shea added. "And besides, there's a big difference between wanting to punch some mouthy newshound in the face and actually doing it."

Keren sensed Paul's anger ebbing away as she opened up some space between themselves and the reporters and that ugly autopsy.

He breathed slowly and seemed to relax. Finally, he said, "Thanks. I appreciate the support. But you don't know what churns around inside me. The anger I'm fighting is sin. I can't let it get the best of me, and you shouldn't encourage me to let it loose."

Keren opened her mouth to talk about her own anger and the struggle she, and most likely every human being, had.

O'Shea butted in. "Okay, feel guilty all you want." He reached between Keren and Paul and offered them the list of Internet companies. "But do it in your spare time. We'll track these down online, then we'll go kick some doors in. They mostly sound like suppliers for laboratories, although one of them might supply fish bait."

Paul looked at the list. "Lab experiments?"

"Sure, everything from medical research to insecticide testing to high school biology class," O'Shea said, as if he'd known it all along.

Keren said dryly, "You don't think a biology teacher had to personally go out and catch those frogs we had to dissect, do you?"

As if she'd known it all along.

Paul tightened his grip on the list. "I hadn't thought of that. But it shouldn't take long to track him down. How many orders can there be?"

CHAPTER SEVENTEEN

There were thousands.

Most of the orders were massive and had shipped to well-known companies, so they could be eliminated immediately. But Keren was relieved to find there weren't that many suppliers. Four in the Chicago area. Far more if the lunatic Caldwell had them shipped in from out of town.

"We're going to have to go into these places with a court order." Keren hung up from talking to the second bug mail-order house. "We ought to be able to get to all of them this afternoon. I guess they have more than their share of trouble with animal rights activists. They're very careful with their customer lists."

"Animal rights extend to gnats now?" Paul asked incredulously.

"Apparently." Keren called and set the wheels in motion for four search warrants.

When she got off the phone, Paul said, "I'll bet you anything a gnat lands on someone from PETA, they swat the itchy little pest just like everyone else."

"Who'd have thought you could order a case of gnats." Keren shook her head in wonder. "This really is a great country, isn't it?"

"Let's get the paperwork in order and start tracking this down. It's possible he's ordering from out of town, so we'd better find out quick if we need to expand our search."

"O'Shea's out trying to narrow down the exact location where Melody Fredericks got hit. He's hoping to find a witness. It's up to us to check out the labs." Keren grabbed her last clean blazer off the back of her chair. She had to go shopping, and she wasn't spending money on good clothes ever again. "Let's head for the first one. The search warrants will be waiting for us by the time we get down to the front desk. I'm getting unbelievable cooperation on this case."

She shoved her arms into her blazer. Paul helped her slip it on, then he lifted her hair out of the collar. She had put it in its usual messy bun this morning, but she had a nagging headache after breathing formaldehyde all through the autopsy. She'd let it loose, hoping that would help. It hadn't.

But finding out this company might have an address on their perp did. She glanced over her shoulder. "Thanks. I get used to being treated like one of the guys."

Paul rested his hands on her shoulders. "We're due a break in this case. Maybe this is it."

They picked up the search warrants and headed to the police parking garage. Paul's phone rang. They both froze. It was the first call they'd gotten from Caldwell since they'd found Melody Fredericks's body.

"Let me call Higgins." Keren had the agent on speed dial. "Maybe we can get a trace on this loon."

Paul backed against a cement block wall while his phone rang and Keren talked.

"Do you have the recorder ready?"

She took a glance at Paul when she heard the detached tone in his voice. He was in full cop mode. Keren finished talking to Higgins and pressed the required buttons on her phone.

Paul stared at his LCD panel. "Caller ID says he's using a new number. Why don't people keep better track of their phones?"

She remembered the last time he'd talked to Caldwell in this mood and dreaded what she was going to hear. "Higgins said to try to keep him talking. Tracking a cell phone doesn't take long." She took a deep breath and said, "Okay, answer it."

Paul flipped the phone open. "Morris."

Keren listened on her own phone and stepped closer to Paul, as if she could protect him from the oily voice that was taunting him.

"You have been a very bad boy, Francis." Paul didn't sound like he needed protection.

Keren gave him a frantic shake of her head. Of course, it was too late.

There was an extended silence on the phone. Finally, when Caldwell spoke, it wasn't with his usual cultured tone. His voice had the snarl of an angry beast. "So you finally figured it out, did you? I suppose it was inevitable. But you proved to be so stupid before, I really doubted if you'd ever identify me.

"There you were, ranting and raving about my careless driving." Caldwell's voice lightened as he reminisced. "What a pathetic excuse you were for a policeman."

A laugh erupted from the phone so shrill Keren jerked the phone away from her ear.

"The truth is, I planned for your wife and child to die months before I finally killed them. I thought of every detail. I savored watching them and learning about them. Your wife was very careless about closing her curtains, you know. You could train her to be more modest, if she were still alive. I even arranged for you to be living away from home. I planted the evidence your wife found that made her throw you out of the house. You got angry when she accused you of being unfaithful, but you never asked yourself where she got that idea. I watched the two of you fight. A few times I watched. . .when you *didn't* fight."

Paul's eyes were neutral, cool. He didn't react to this sick invasion of privacy.

"I'm surprised you could stand to touch her, Reverend," Caldwell went on. "Your wife was not a nice woman. She deserved everything that happened to her. I created the whole thing. . .the car trouble, the battery failing on her cell phone. I slipped in behind her at the dance recital, got her purse from under her folding chair, took her battery out, and returned everything. No one saw me in the dark auditorium. I even took pains to keep you away from that school program, so you wouldn't be there to help. Having her husband be a policeman made it all the sweeter. Even then, I was controlling you like a god."

"Why them?" Paul sounded angry now, but it was a cold kind of anger, all the more frightening for the depth and control he exerted over it. "Why kill my wife and daughter?"

"Your wife worked at the art gallery where I wanted to display my work. She humiliated me, when she should have been kissing my feet for doing her the honor of choosing her."

"You mean she thought your artwork was lousy, and you killed her for it," Paul taunted.

"Your wife was the first one. I saw the evil in her. The evil needed to be destroyed so my art could be let go into the world."

"And my daughter? What had she done?"

"Your daughter needed to die so your wife would understand what she'd done. I enjoyed making her witness her daughter's death. Your wife was still alive after I hit her the first time. So I went back and made sure she was dead. Your wife deserved to die, and your daughter would have been another one just like her."

"And did your mother stand by and watch you be hurt, Francis?"

"She only wanted me to be free. She wanted what was best

for me," Caldwell raged.

"Were you bad, Francis?" Paul jeered.

"Yes, I was bad," Caldwell seethed. "But my father helped me learn discipline and control. And my mother understood and supported me in my art."

"If you turned yourself in, it would go easier for you."

"Easier?" Caldwell laughed. "How much easier? Life in prison instead of a lethal injection? That's not a very tempting offer."

"There's more than prison for you if you come in, Francis. There's help. You need help." Paul fell silent.

There was an extended pause, then Caldwell returned to the chanting voice he'd used at first. "Did you enjoy finding you had company when you got home last night, my pretty Keren?"

Keren glanced up at Paul, then the two of them scanned the area in all directions.

"Yes, I know you're listening. And I know all about you carrying on with the reverend. You don't think that reporter came up with the idea on his own, do you? You're a part of this now, just like the good reverend is. That's why I sent you your own little gift. If you set out to catch me, then you have to accept that you've become part of what is between me and the reverend."

Anger flushed Paul's face. Keren glanced at her watch and decided to talk to Caldwell to keep him on the phone.

Before she could speak, Caldwell said, "I wonder who will get my next present. There are so many who are worthy to be honored. I've already got her, you know. But I'm not sure what door you carve your message on when a woman is homeless. I guess I'll just carve it in her back."

"Francis, you can't do this. Let me help you," Paul said fiercely.

"I didn't really choose her, Reverend. You did, that first day. I warned you not to talk to anyone on your way to the building."

"I didn't talk to anyone," Paul insisted.

Then Keren heard screaming through the phone line and Caldwell's high-pitched laughter.

"Pastor P, help me!"

Paul's eyes flared in recognition. "I ran into her, knocked her shopping cart over. She doesn't know anything about this."

The phone clicked off.

Paul pressed the phone against his forehead. "He's got Wilma."

↩

Keren called Higgins to report Wilma's kidnapping. Higgins cut her off before she could tell him.

"We got a location on him," the FBI agent said exuberantly. "We're moving on the place now!"

"The call gives you probable cause," Keren said.

"We don't need to wait for any paperwork. We can kick the door in." Higgins rattled off the address.

"We're already in the parking garage." Keren headed for her car at a fast clip.

Paul was right with her. He shoved her toward the passenger side. "I'll drive, you talk."

Keren didn't like the take-charge attitude, but they didn't have time to haggle. She said to Higgins, "We're on our way."

"You'll be ahead of us by a couple of minutes." Keren could hear Higgins breathing hard. Even now he was charging toward his car. Paul started hers and squealed the tires as he backed out of the space. He was roaring for the exit before she got her seat belt fastened.

"We're going in quiet, Collins," Higgins shouted into the phone. "I'm sending the SWAT team so we can secure the entire building. I don't want him to have any warning. Don't you two go in alone."

"We won't. We're going to do this right." Keren clicked the phone.

"He's been right across the street from the mission?" Paul asked in shock. "No wonder he knew everything about me." Paul went in quiet, but he went in fast.

"He's probably been studying you for weeks." Keren got another call from Higgins and learned more.

"Longer if he knows about Juanita and LaToya. Why didn't we search those buildings?" Paul clutched the steering wheel as he skidded around a corner.

"It's impossible." Keren twisted her hair and refastened her barrette to hold some of the escaping tendrils. "The mission is surrounded by buildings—thousands of apartments. We'd spend months going door-to-door."

"He probably picked all ten girls before he hit Melody Fredericks by accident."

"Then he figured out a new way to torment you." Keren heard about ten thousand miles' worth of tread being burned off her tires and only wished Paul would drive faster. "It wasn't necessary to kill your friends, which was getting harder with all the warnings we've been putting out. There were other ways to make it personal."

"What else did Higgins tell you? Does he have more information on the guy?"

"They ran the building occupants as soon as they got an address. One person rents the whole top floor."

"Name?" Paul looked away from the traffic as he ran a stale yellow light. Horns honked but he floored it and raced on.

"He didn't have that yet. Even in a run-down tenement, how

can anyone afford to rent a whole floor?"

"He had money," Paul remembered. "We checked his bank accounts that he'd emptied."

"This is close enough." Keren unhooked her seat belt before they came to a complete stop, prepared to hog-tie Paul to keep him from going in before SWAT arrived.

"He's hurting her. Right now, he's in there torturing Wilma." Paul pulled up well away from the building and stared at it as if he could bore a hole in the wall with his eyes and see where Wilma was.

Keren wondered how long she could keep him in the car. She wondered how long she could keep herself in the car.

"So a rich man lives on the fifth floor of that wreck of a building," Keren said, craning her neck to see to the top. "He's got a clear view of two sides of the mission, and it's tall enough he can see most of what's going on, on the other sides."

"And with a telescope set up in the right place, he could watch most of what he's sent me to do. He saw me plow into Wilma that first morning he contacted me. Wilma." Paul fell silent.

"Is she a friend?" Keren laid her hand on Paul's shoulder.

Paul shrugged. He rested his elbow on the open window and ran his hand over his face. "Kind of. I tried to be a friend. She had. . .has. . .mental problems, and she solves them by guzzling a bottle or two of mouthwash every day."

"Mouthwash? She drinks Listerine?"

"Not Listerine. It costs too much. She buys generic. You can get a two-quart bottle for a dollar. It's about 75 percent alcohol. They all drink that or plain-label cough syrup. Some even drink rubbing alcohol. It'll all give you a buzz. They buy it at a discount store a couple of blocks over. I asked the store manager to quit stocking it, but he refused. He said they'd just walk until they found it. And I know he's right."

"So Wilma is really one of the hard-core homeless," Keren said thoughtfully. "Not the type he's been going after at all."

"Do you think we could get some tracking devices and put them on some of the homeless people without their knowledge?" His knee started bouncing up and down. Keren could see his patience running out. "We could see if Caldwell grabs them and get to them before he hurts them."

"We're going to get him, Paul. We won't have to track anyone." Paul grabbed for the door handle.

Keren clutched his collar.

Higgins pulled up beside them and rolled down his driver's-side window. "I've got cars in place on all four sides of the building. We'll secure the exits, double-check the basement for one of his bombs, then go in."

A radio crackled in Higgins's car. He lifted the handset and talked quietly; then he hung it up and said, "SWAT's here. We've got to wait for the all clear before we can go in."

A parade of black-clothed, heavily-armed SWAT team members stormed the building.

Keren thought she'd explode from the maddening wait. Finally Higgins got the go-ahead.

Higgins talked rapidly on his radio. "SWAT reported that the basement was clear of explosives. Let's go." Higgins reached the door, swung it open, and went in ahead of a dozen other men. Paul and Keren were left for last.

"I should have asked Higgins for a gun," Paul said through his clenched teeth.

"Get a grip." Keren didn't like bringing up the rear either. But this was Higgins's show. "He'd never give you one. And you don't need it."

"He might have." Paul glanced at Keren. His eyes were as cold as his voice. "I can be pretty persuasive."

They ran quickly and quietly up the five flights of stairs. The whole building was a slum. More apartments empty than lived in. Graffiti on the walls, broken light fixtures, and shattered glass littering the hallways. They got to Caldwell's floor and it was no better, except the doors were all hung and closed.

Higgins went up to the first one and tried it. He whispered, "Locked."

He turned to the dozen men who had accompanied him. "I want every door kicked open at the same time. Don't go charging in without backup."

"Ready?" There were five doors on both sides of the hallway. Two men stood at each door. Keren and Paul stood back, out of the way, near the door Higgins had chosen.

"Go!" Higgins's voice exploded. Ten doors crashed open.

"FBI," Higgins shouted. The same shout echoed down the hall. Higgins disappeared. Keren and Paul went in right behind him.

"This is it," Paul said to Keren. "We've got him."

CHAPTER EIGHTEEN

They missed him.

Every room was wide open. There was no place to hide. There was no killer.

"He was here," Higgins raged. He touched a coffee cup sitting on a counter. "It's still warm. He can't have been gone long." He called into the hall, "Fan out. We've got the exits blocked. Check every apartment in this building."

But Paul knew it was a waste of time. They all did. One clue said it all. A wooden sign, set neatly beside a shiny new telephone, that said, WELCOME, REVEREND.

"The hand of the Lord will bring
a terrible plague on your livestock."
EXODUS 9:3

Pravus was wise to the ways of police. They were right this minute kicking down the doors of that old building.

For one long beautiful moment, he imagined them finding his people. He imagined the awe. He'd done them a great honor to let them be the first to see his work. Would they be wise enough to cherish what he'd given them? Would they finally set his people free?

With a smile, he acknowledged that they probably would not.

He was as far above them as Michelangelo was from kindergarten finger painting. He hated to give up the little paradise he'd created, but it didn't matter. He had a spare paradise.

Looking backward was a waste. He looked forward. He'd already done such powerful work here that what was left behind easily faded. But then he'd always had the skill of separating himself from little hurts.

When his father would enforce Francis's studies with his hard hands, the poor little boy had needed escape and Pravus had taken him away, far away. Then the two of them would watch that pathetic Francis take the punishment while they'd sit back and laugh at the boy's fears and tears and his father's futile lessons.

As if Father's blundering training could make Pravus's genius better. It was already so staggering, it was nearly painful.

The beast offered to come inside him and protect him. Francis had jumped at the chance, thrilled with the offer of power.

And the two of them had set out to watch Francis, and laugh, and create.

The day had come finally when they'd tired of Father's cruelty and put an end to it. And Pravus had finally known freedom. And the next person to harm him had earned wrath that couldn't be satisfied through art. She had sneered at his work.

Oh she'd used polite words, but she'd been too blind to accept the blessing he tried to bestow upon her. And then the reverend had brought the law down on Pravus. The reverend had sealed his own fate.

From that moment, Pravus had plotted revenge. Pravus visited a plague on the reverend and anyone who got in his way. The whole city would suffer, too.

He turned back to Wilma. . .unworthy of his gift, but good enough because it hurt the reverend. Good enough.

The police were too stupid to find him. Simple call forwarding led them to his other building to discover the gifts he'd left. Television stations would send camera crews. Art galleries would take notice, and the power of the plagues would only enhance the stunning gift.

Pravus laughed to think the real shame was that the police would use force and ruin the only working doors in that tenement.

He went back to making Wilma into a creation of beauty.

Pestis ex bestia.

The plague of beasts.

This one he really liked.

⌐

"I thought I'd seen the worst that men could do on this job. But this tops it all." Keren checked every room. He had covered the walls with paintings, carvings. Ten rooms, ten themes, ten plagues.

The room Higgins hit first was Francis's tribute to the plague of blood. Red. Everywhere. The walls painted red, the paintings on the walls brutal works in red and black, the photos of Juanita enlarged to the size of posters. PESTIS EX SANGUIS was carved over the door, right into the woodwork.

Three other rooms were the same, except for the theme. All of them were decorated. And the ones where Caldwell had already carried out his plague included pictures of his victims and the plague Caldwell had visited on her. In the last room were posters of Wilma wearing her white dress.

Keren walked up to the huge picture. "How'd he make the picture so big? Where did he buy the equipment?"

"We found a room where Caldwell must have slept. He had his own photo enlargement equipment." Higgins's cell phone rang and he checked the number and turned his back to talk.

"Nothing painted on Wilma's dress is even identifiable. He's getting so sloppy." Keren leaned close. "You can tell from the lines on this one that his hands are shaking. I can't believe he can walk around in the open and not be noticed." Keren looked at Paul. "He probably isn't. We probably couldn't pick him up at the mission anymore. I doubt he's even coming in."

"I can't tell." Paul studied the crime scene with cynical eyes, assessing, searching for clues. "So many of the people are gone, it doesn't shorten our list much."

They all went in the room that was a tribute to the plague of beasts. Keren said, "There's no sign that Wilma's ever been in here."

"He's taken less time with each room," Higgins observed. "The setup, the larger paintings, were obviously done before he took the first vic, before he started to deteriorate. The things he added after each kidnapping get progressively sloppier." Higgins pointed at the pictures showing awful bleeding cuts on Wilma's arms. "The display of photos is rushed. Each gown shows he's getting more and more out of control."

Paul stared at the oversized pictures of Wilma. From where Keren stood, she couldn't tell whether he was the cop or the pastor. He seemed to be frozen somewhere in the middle. Finally, he visibly relaxed and Keren knew, for the moment, he was letting the cop take charge.

"This is the latest vic." Paul pointed at the walls.

"You know her?" Higgins asked.

"First one I've been able to ID since LaToya," Paul said. "I wonder if Caldwell is back to his original plan of taking women I know, or was Wilma just handy? Get forensics in here. The DNA won't really help catch him, since we already know who we're hunting for, but when we get our hands on him, there will be plenty in these rooms that'll help put him away."

Paul and Keren finally had a chance to brief Higgins and Dyson fully on Wilma.

"She doesn't fit at all." Dyson almost foamed at the mouth, he was so furious. "Elderly, alcoholic, lives on the streets."

"Fredericks and Hardcastle didn't fit either."

Dyson spun around, his fists clenched, and glared at Paul. "Don't you think I know that?" He stormed off.

Paul could hear him ranting for long minutes after the man left the apartment. Dyson acted like Paul and Keren had deliberately set out to thwart him.

Higgins said, "We'll keep our focus on tracking Caldwell. I don't care if he's living in a bunker under a nondescript building, I'll find him. You two go check the rest of the laboratory supply stores. He still needs a shipment of locusts. And it's a cinch he won't have them shipped *here* now."

When they came out of the tenement house, they ran into reporters.

They fought their way through the crowd and got onto the street, only to have cars staked out to follow them.

"They know my car," Keren said quietly, her voice carrying below the racket of shouted questions. "Do you have one?"

"Nope. Let me drive yours again." He held out his hand for the keys. "I'd forgotten how much I like it."

"Do you have a license?" They got through the throng of reporters and set a fast pace toward Keren's car.

Paul shrugged. "I don't think it's lapsed."

Keren gave him a long look. "But do you have it with you?"

"I've got forty-eight hours to produce it if I get ticketed for driving without it. You know that." Paul held out his hand again.

"But driving without it is still illegal, *Pastor* P. A couple of days ago you were hassling me for speeding."

"What's your point?" Paul wiggled his fingers impatiently.

Keren glared at him, but she could see inaction right now would drive him right to the limit of his self-control. She handed him the keys.

The reporters gave chase, and a little parade formed in the passenger's side mirror. "Head for the expressway so you've got room to maneuver."

"Way ahead of you." Paul gave her a *No-backseat-driving* look.

"How do you survive without a car?"

Paul pulled onto the expressway and moved across three lanes of traffic to the fast lane. "I take the El. A car is an albatross around my neck in this city." He swerved in front of a car in the slower lane then cut sharply onto an off-ramp and left the few remaining reporters in the dust. He turned around and backtracked, changing directions until he was sure he'd shaken any tail.

"They're going to make it hard to do our job." Keren glanced at her watch. "I had hopes of getting to all these places today, but we won't make it now."

They went to the first address on the list.

An hour later, as they left the second supply store, Keren said, "I can't believe how many people wanted this strange combination of bugs. What are the chances that a dozen companies in Chicago were in desperate need of gnats, flies, and frogs all at the same time?" She stared at her notes, but they stayed the same.

Paul had taken his own notes but didn't check them because he was driving again, trying to get to the next place before it locked down for the night. "But these orders were all for other things, too. And there is no order for locusts. And what about the beasts? What in the world will he do for that?"

"I can't stand to think of it."

"And boils, and good grief, hail. How's he going to produce a plague of hail?"

"He's an artist," Keren said dryly. "I'm sure he's very creative."

"He may have ordered other things to throw us off." Paul tapped the steering wheel as if he were listening to music. "We may have to track down every name we've been given, but a lot of these orders add up to serious money. And most of these ordered test tubes and microscope slides and a variety of chemical solutions worth thousands of dollars."

He veered across two lanes of traffic and swerved onto a side street. He wasn't dodging reporters now, so he was just driving like a lunatic for the fun of it. Keren vowed to take her keys back as soon as he stopped.

"The orders are mostly connected to schools or medical labs." Paul took a corner so fast the tires whined. "We won't track down any of these large purchases unless we have to. Let's hope we find an order that matches what we need."

"What do we stake out for beasts? Is it possible he'll go back to the park? Or back to someone's apartment that he wants to torment?" Keren grabbed the armrest on the door beside her to keep from tipping over toward Paul. "We found LaToya because we anticipated his hunt for frogs."

"We found LaToya because we got lucky." Paul straightened the car out and floored it. "Caldwell brought his own frogs, and we just happened to be close at hand."

"We found LaToya," Keren said, "because God wanted her found."

Paul glanced sharply at her and seemed to lose his focus on their conversation for a minute. He looked back at the street and tightened his hands on the steering wheel and slowed down a bit.

"So beasts, does that mean sheep, cattle?" Keren didn't know whether to pursue the conversation about God or not. They were almost to their destination.

"In the Bible it says plague of beasts or livestock or animals, depending on which version you read." Paul seemed to shift mental gears as he spoke of the Bible. Keren hoped it lasted. "If Caldwell wanted to be true to the meaning of the Bible, he'd go to the nearest cattle ranch or stockyards and leave Wilma there."

Keren's stomach twisted to think of what might be coming. "But he wants to stay close to the mission. That's been the only thing he hasn't deviated from. Even my apartment isn't that far."

"So where do you find animals?" Paul pulled up to the lab supply store.

"There is a petting zoo at that same park. But he hasn't been back there since LaToya." Keren was relieved to have arrived alive.

"We can stake it out."

They got out and got to the front door just as it was closing for the day. Keren used her badge and Paul let them assume he had one, too. He did a lot of bullying to get the manager to stay around and let them check the recent orders. Keren called the last lab supply store, but there was no answer. "We'll have to try that one tomorrow."

They left the building. Paul went to the driver's side as if it were his right. "Let's track down the name of the guy who runs that last store and get him to let us in."

"It's too late, Paul. We took forever in that last place, and I thought the manager was going to wring our necks. It's almost sundown. We're going to have to wait until tomorrow."

Keren would have wrestled him for the keys but decided he needed to bolster his spirits, so she let him drive like a lunatic for a while longer. He seemed to enjoy that. "We're closing in on him. We'll find him through the place we check tomorrow, or we'll find him in the lists we already have."

"Maybe, unless he went out of town for this stuff." Paul's foot tapped, and he stared unseeing into the lowering sun but he remained in the parking space.

"Let's go see how LaToya's doing." Keren waited.

Finally Paul started the car. "If there was any change I'd have heard," he said, as if going to see her was unnecessary. With a shrug of his shoulders he added, "We might as well go there and sleep on the couches. We're both as good as homeless."

As he drove, Keren wondered if she shouldn't give him a pep talk about not being such a cynical jerk. She remembered very vividly now why she'd been left with such a bad impression of Detective Paul Morris.

~

They drove through a fast-food joint and ate in the car on the way to the hospital. Paul wondered if he could call this a date. He nearly smiled at the thought.

Since Keren paid for both of them. . .since Paul had no money. . .it was a real modern kind of date.

The cop was in full control of him after the day he'd spent, and he decided he liked it, at least for now. He even toyed with the idea of giving the press a few words next time they rushed him. He could work it to raise money for the mission. They might be able to help with the search for Caldwell. He hesitated when he remembered how casually he was dressed. He needed to get a haircut. Maybe buy a suit.

His thoughts seemed to shove the pastor out of the forefront of his thoughts. How had he survived in the Lighthouse Mission? He hadn't done anything for himself in years. He never ate anywhere else, had no friends outside the mission. He'd lost all perspective.

The doctor was with LaToya when they got to the hospital and a nurse said he'd be awhile so they should settle in. She also told them LaToya hadn't shown any signs of regaining consciousness.

"We're wasting our time sleeping here." Paul looked around the pretty waiting room. The hospital did its best to make it a nice place to wait through a bad time.

But it was still a hospital waiting room.

"I think I'll go back to the mission to sleep."

Keren glared at him.

"What?"

"You've been Detective Morris all day. Can you give it a rest?"

Paul smiled. "Give what a rest? What's that mean?"

Scowling, Keren said, "I'm going to go in first to see her."

"Why should you go? You don't even know her."

"Then I'm going to sleep the whole rest of the night on that stupid couch and you can go in once an hour and hopefully spend some time trying to regain your sanity."

"Hey, I'm sane."

Keren arched a brow at him.

"I just need some sleep so I can do my best to solve this crime."

"Good, shut up then, and get some sleep." She jabbed her finger at the torture chamber that was almost his home. "Right there. You're going to need it."

She stomped off, and Paul caught himself watching the way she moved. Not one single appropriate thought in his head.

While he tried to get comfortable, Paul seriously considered leaving and sleeping at the mission. Even those beds were better than this lousy couch. He'd decide after he saw LaToya, but it felt right. Leaving, resting, was the best thing he could do to stop that lunatic Pravus.

⌐⌐

The next thing he knew, he was waking up.

He ran his hand over his bristly face. He felt grungy and shabby and he was sick of it. "I've got to get a shave."

Instead of going to the mission, he decided he'd swing by the station house for a shave and shower. He could get the latest on the investigation. Maybe call the task force together to bat ideas around. He looked down at his ratty clothes and wondered how to get something clean and sharp. The press might be around. He could speed up this investigation if he slipped Caldwell's name to the press.

"I'm checking into a hotel for a few days just to get some decent sleep." He spoke aloud just as he fully heard the bustle of the hospital around him and realized with a shock that it was morning. It brought him to his feet. He'd slept through the night. He hadn't gone in to see LaToya once.

The door to LaToya's room swung open. Keren came out, tucking her cell phone in the pocket of her blazer. "You're awake, good. Rosita just called. She's on the way over. Manny's escorting her. We can get into that lab supply store by eight."

He was embarrassed to have missed his turn visiting and let that twist around to annoyance. Keren could have awakened him. "We don't need to wait for Rosita. What are the chances LaToya will wake up in the next few minutes?"

Keren stared at him. "But Paul, you've been so insistent that she not be left alone."

Paul ran his hand over his face again and wondered what he looked like. She seemed to be looking at something she didn't like.

"The best thing we can do for LaToya is catch the man who

did this." He felt the cop in him talking. He fought it but couldn't seem to quite get his head clear of that analytical coolness. "She won't really be alone; there are doctors and nurses around. Let's go." Paul took a step toward the exit.

"Just one stinking minute!"

He turned back to her. "What? Let's get going."

She stood militantly in front of LaToya's door, with her hands planted firmly on her hips. Boy she was a feisty little thing. Cute, too.

"We're not leaving her here alone."

"Why don't we see if we can get a police officer on her door?"

"Because we're trying to keep her low profile. We don't want the fact that she lived to get out. Besides, *you're* the one who didn't want to leave your friend's side."

"I've got a good feeling about today. I want to get going." He pulled the keys out of his pocket and tossed them in the air. "We can get this guy before he does somebody else."

"Before he *does* somebody else?" Keren walked toward him with narrowed eyes. "That's all you've got to say about this nut carving on a friend of yours? What is *wrong* with you? I'm standing here tied up in knots, expecting to hear word on Wilma any minute, and you're tossing my car keys in the air as if you're enjoying yourself."

Feeling wildly out of control and enjoying it, Paul tossed the keys again just to watch her fume. Keren didn't disappoint him. She snatched them in midair. He took a half a step toward her and caught her hand. He pulled her closed fist up between them.

"I'm driving, Keren." He smirked as he pried her fingers open.

Keren clamped her hand tightly closed. Paul pulled her closer until their tussling hands were the only thing keeping their bodies apart.

He looked up from their impromptu wrestling match and noticed how rumpled and sleepy-eyed she was. "You know, you're really cute when you're mad."

Controlling all her fire would be a delicious pleasure. It churned him up inside until he hooked one hand around her waist, yanked her hard against him, and lowered his head to taste all that temper and spirit.

She slammed her fist, complete with car keys, into his gut.

With a grunt of pain, Paul stumbled backward. "Why'd you do that?"

"Here's a newsflash. I'm not *cute* when I'm mad. I'm *mad* when I'm mad!"

"Pastor P, what's going on?" Paul whirled around to see Rosita standing right behind him. Manny, who'd become her bodyguard the last few days, was at her side.

Paul couldn't gather his thoughts for a minute. He saw something in Manny's eyes, a look of understanding. So he'd caught exactly what Paul had been thinking of when he'd leaned toward Keren.

Manny arched a brow at Paul and gave him a smile of brotherhood. "Different rules for you and the lady cop than for me and Rosita, hey, Pastor P?"

"LaToya still hasn't come out of her coma." Keren ignored Manny's comment, all business. "We need to go. Thanks, both of you, for helping."

Paul thought Keren was walking out, but when she got to Manny, she stopped and stuck her face into his. "Pastor P is having a bad day, so, for a second, he forgot the rules. *Forgetting* the rules isn't the same as them being *different*. I'm going to spend the next hour or so *reminding* him of the rules, because I *never* forget them and *Rosita's* not going to, either. Then, when I'm done!" She stepped closer.

"Reminding him!" She lifted her chin.

"If he's still alive!" Her nose almost touched Manny's and Manny took a step back—smart man.

"He'll come back here and apologize for acting like a *pig*, when he's supposed to be a *pastor*."

Manny held her gaze. . .he was a little braver from three steps away.

Keren said through clenched teeth, "Anything about that you don't understand, Manny?"

Manny shrugged and said sheepishly, "Sorry, I was out of line."

Keren turned to Paul. "In the car! Now!" She stormed out of the hospital.

Keren's temper tantrum shocked Paul out of the strange mood he'd been in pretty much nonstop for the last two days. He couldn't believe he'd grabbed her like that. He ran his hand over his face, through his hair, and brushed the lines of recently removed stitches. Then he started after her. He was so embarrassed at what Rosita had witnessed, that he knew he had to stop and take whatever humiliation was due him.

He looked, and she only seemed concerned, which was almost worse than if she'd been disgusted. He could lead someone into sin with his behavior.

"I'm sorry, Rosita. This whole mess. . ." He waved his hand at LaToya's room and looked at Rosita. Suddenly he realized that she had lived harder and seen more in her life than the most seasoned cop. "Rosie, do you ever relapse? Does it ever get hard to remember you're a person of faith?"

"It happens, Pastor P," Rosita said kindly.

"I've got to get out of this." He looked in the direction Keren had gone. "I can't deal with police work. It brings something out in me that I can't seem to control. It's a feeling of. . .of power, and I love it. It's like a drug, and I'm high on it right now. I feel smarter than anyone else. I get smug and arrogant. Cocky. I think I'm a better cop than the real cops. I am better. I'm really good at this. But—" He shook his head, trying to clear it. "I need to get back to the Lighthouse."

"You can't seal yourself in the mission and hide from the rest of the world," Rosita said with a gentle smile.

"Can living in a mission be hiding? I would have thought that was life at its toughest."

"It doesn't count as tough unless it's tough for you," Rosie said simply. "It was like giving up letting guys slap me around. For me that was harder than kicking the crack. Weird, isn't it?"

All of Paul's pastoral concern for Rosie flared to life. He watched her closely when he said, "But you did it. No man has slapped you since you found the Lord, has he?" He glanced at Manny.

Manny raised his hands in surrender. "Don't look at me, man. I'm afraid of her."

Rosie flashed her thousand-watt smile at Manny. She turned back to Paul. "Manny's good to me. It's what I grew up with, watching men knock my mother around. They came after me, too, and so did Mama. It feels like love to me, how sick is that?"

Manny rested a hand on the back of her neck. "It's not love. You know that, right?"

Nodding, Rosita leaned closer to Manny, and his hand dropped until his arm circled her waist.

Paul wondered if there might be a wedding and they might let him perform it. The idea helped him get a better grip on the humble, faithful side of himself.

"Maybe giving up the power of being a cop wasn't so easy for you," Rosita said. "Maybe you're some kind of adrenaline junky. You just didn't know it because you cut yourself off from it. And now this case—it's like falling off the wagon."

"So what do I do?" Paul really hoped Rosita could tell him.

She took on a glow. "I think it's the same as drugs and booze, Pastor P. One day at a time. There's no way out of this mess until it's over." Her glow faded and she looked at LaToya's door. "So you don't have any choice but to deal with it the best you can. You know, God is letting this unfold, with you in the middle, for a reason. Maybe it's time you faced your old life."

Paul thought of how he'd grabbed Keren and the disrespectful way he'd treated her. She'd gone to her car and he knew she'd be waiting for him. . .waiting to take him apart.

"And facing forward takes you straight into the angry clutches of Detective Collins," Rosita said. "And by the way, anything she does to you. . .you deserve."

"Good luck, *amigo*," Manny called after him.

Keren kept both hands on the wheel to keep them off Paul's throat as he slipped into the car beside her.

"So, Stupidville just took a vote and you're the new mayor?" Keren slammed her foot on the gas before he got the door closed.

"It was a landslide." Paul grappled for his seat belt, as if he suspected she had violent plans for his side of the car.

"What's the point of having a head if you're not going to use it?" Keren left rubber behind on the pavement as she pulled out into the traffic.

"I promise I'll sit here quietly while you let me have it, even if it takes all day. I deserve every word of it."

"Don't think you're going to get out of this by being sorry and nice," Keren snarled. "It won't save you."

Paul sighed. "I'd hoped it would."

"I know this is hard for you."

"Please don't start sounding like you feel sorry for me." Paul waved her politeness away. "I woke up just as you came in, and it was like I—I sort of time traveled back to the days I was a cop. I'm awake now. I deserve scorn, contempt, rage, compound fractures. But I don't deserve sympathy, and if you start being nice instead of crushing my out-of-control ego, I promise I'll maul you again just to get your angry juices flowing."

She glanced over at that last bit, and his eyes weren't really back to normal—there was still heat when he said he'd maul her. And plenty of cynicism. She did need to abuse him. It was the right thing to do.

"I don't know where to start."

Paul said, "Why don't you start by telling me what I did to you that made you so mad at me in the first place. It wasn't something like that was it?"

Keren slammed her palm on the steering wheel. "Was there a time when you did things like that? You were *married* when you were on the force. Please don't tell me you were that big of a slime. I don't know if I could forgive you, even if God is up to it."

"No, I never cheated on my wife. But I sometimes. . .well, I didn't always treat women with. . .well. . .respect. The thing is, there might be a few women who'd tell you I was kind of a. . .a. . ."

"Jerk?" Keren supplied.

"Well—"

"Pig?" Keren wheeled around a corner.

"Some of them might—"

"Letch?" The back end of the car fishtailed.

"I don't think letch is—"

"Scumball?" She straightened out and floored it.

"Now, Keren, scumball seems a little—"

"All of the above? You want to supply your own words?"

"You're doing fine. You don't need my help." Paul shrugged. "Anyway, I wasn't unfaithful. Disrespect to women, yes, but I disrespected men, too. Nothing sexist about it. I was an equal opportunity, arrogant jerk. All my trouble with my wife was about how important my work was and how unimportant my family was." Paul slid lower in the seat and she caught him taking a quick look at her.

She clamped her mouth shut, trying to figure out whether to commiserate or go after him with her nightstick.

"Aren't you going to yell at me? Please don't tell me you're done, because I really can't stand the guilt if you let me off the hook this easily."

"Okay, no problem."

Flinching, Paul said, "That was reverse psychology."

She narrowed her eyes. "Tough luck. I guess the only reason I'd stop yelling at you would be because I decided you were hopeless. And I really don't want to think that."

"Don't give up on me."

"Now you're being the kindhearted pastor again. Turn back into the cop so I can yell at him."

"I'm not brave enough to do that."

"This weird morphing thing you've been doing, into the cop you used to be, has to be an aberration." Keren glanced at him, but mostly she watched the road. "Maybe tearing a strip off your hide will help you get a handle on it."

Paul squared his shoulders as if he were prepared to wave farewell to his hide.

"How do you reconcile manhandling me, insulting me— 'You're pretty when you're mad.'" Her voice was pitched low, whiny, pure mockery of a man's voice. "How do you go from urging O'Shea and me to call Juanita by her name, to referring to Wilma as a vic? What's happening to you?"

"I told you, anger is a sin I struggle with," Paul said. "The last few days, I've been letting my anger rule me. And as my sin ruled my temper, it began to rule my life."

"That stunt this morning wasn't anger, you moron! It was pure ego. Pure disrespect for me. Blaming it on your temper is a cop-out, and I'm sick of hearing you make excuses!" Keren wheeled them around a corner and two wheels left the pavement. Paul didn't suggest she slow down. She hoped it was because he was too scared.

"Take some responsibility for your actions! You may need to come to terms with your temper. But I don't think the battle you're waging is with anger. There can be Christian strength in anger if you control it and express it justly."

"Not for me," Paul insisted.

Keren looked sideways at him and wondered how she could penetrate that thick skull. She wasn't even sure she wanted to. This morning brought back all the hostile feelings she had for him. Even now, when he was more his normal self, she distrusted him. "That just sounds like stubbornness to me. I'm telling you, your anger isn't the problem. You're making excuses."

"It's a doorway into sin." Paul sat straighter in his seat.

Keren slammed her fist against the steering wheel. "Not if you control it!"

Paul turned on her and roared, "I can't control it!"

Keren slammed her foot on the brake and pulled the car into a parking space.

"We don't have time to stop the car and argue this out," Paul growled. "We've got a murderer to catch."

"We're there." Keren shoved her car into PARK. She very deliberately took the keys out of the ignition and put them in her pocket.

Paul looked at the building they were beside. "Oh. I thought you were stopping so you could concentrate on yelling at me."

"I don't need to concentrate very hard to find stuff to yell at you about. I can drive at the same time."

Paul shrugged. "I've been making it easy for you."

"Amen to that." Keren reached for the door.

Paul grabbed her arm. The look Keren gave his hand left burn marks. He let her go. "I am sorry. I am. Really. I was so completely out of line that I can't think of the words to express how much I regret what I did. And it wasn't just disrespecting you. It was leaving you to watch LaToya. It was wanting Higgins to give me a sidearm last night. It was calling Wilma. . ." Paul dropped his face into his hands. "I actually said, 'We can get this guy before he does somebody else.' That makes me sick."

"Me, too." Keren was surprised how much she meant it. "C'mon, we're not going to solve *you* now. Let's go check out Bugs R Us."

CHAPTER NINETEEN

All the livestock of the Egyptians died.

Did they really think they could stop him?

Pravus went through his daily routine just as he always had, but his eyes were always open, always hunting. He saw several that would have done. He'd watch them go in and out of the mission, and it was like they called to him, *Stop me*, in voices that only he could hear. *Stop me, please, before I do more harm to the world.*

They cried out to him as always, but today the only ones who were alone were the bag ladies. The beast inside him growled and paced, demanding to be let out. Pravus knew the bag ladies wouldn't be enough, not for long, but he felt as if the beast would start eating him, chewing his insides until he was consumed, if he didn't feed this need to kill.

He washed dishes because it kept his hands in the water and no one could see them shaking. He couldn't shave, because his hands trembled until he thought he might cut his throat. The result was his false, full beard didn't stick as well to his face. He worried constantly that it might slip. His own beard wasn't gray and it was so thin it didn't disguise his appearance at all. Even with the plastic surgery and tinted contacts and lifts in his shoes, he was afraid the reverend might recognize him.

He was spending less and less time here. He didn't want to

look the reverend or the pretty detective in the eye—afraid he wouldn't be able to conceal his triumph. So he ducked out when he could and was careful to make sure neither of them was around when he came back.

Normally he helped with the cooking, but he kept feeling the beast erupt. The thrill, the pleasure, the power of being out of control with a butcher knife in his hand was enough to make him avoid food preparation. He washed dishes and listened. He'd overheard several of the women working out a schedule to never go out alone, even discussing moving in together temporarily. The urge to kill grew in him like volcanic pressure.

He saw a woman leave alone and it drew him out of his rage. She didn't suit him. She was the wrong type to sate his hunger. But he couldn't wait any longer. He felt like he'd explode into a killing rampage in front of everyone if he didn't put a stop to the evil around him. And if he exploded, well, he was too smart to be caught, but he'd have to give up this masquerade that kept him close enough to watch the reverend.

The plague of boils was next. He had it all arranged. Not as much killing as the plague of beasts, but he'd inflict plenty of pain. And all the while he'd imagine it was his father.

Pravus caught himself. He hadn't meant that. He'd meant the reverend. He'd imagine it was the reverend he was killing.

The beast snarled at him for making that slip. They both owed everything to his father.

Impatience finally goaded him into going after her. He'd still be hungry when he'd taken her, but she'd be an appetizer. He'd be done with the plague of beasts after tonight. He couldn't resist getting someone new. She'd do for now, but the feast was yet to come.

He followed her out.

Paul was afraid to lead the way on anything for a while, mainly because he was afraid to turn his back on Keren. So he let Keren go in first. The laboratory was as clean and sterile as any doctor's office.

Clean and sterile was where the resemblance to anything normal ended. The young woman who greeted them fit with the disturbing supplies this place sold.

"Hi, I'm Frodo." She spoke around a wad of gum. And it was the name printed on her name tag. Frodo Baggins. Paul wondered if she'd had it legally changed, her mother had actually named her that, or the name tag was whimsical.

"I'm an intern." She had enough rings pierced into her eyebrows to hang a shower curtain.

"We need a look at your shipping files." Keren tapped the badge on her belt, right next to her gun.

Frodo looked at the paper Keren produced and couldn't have been more cooperative.

In fact, she was so eager to help, Paul wondered if she had a rap sheet. He decided to run her name on NCIC when he got back to the station. With a stab of dismay, he realized he was thinking like a cop—again. He should have been inviting her to church, not wondering if he could bust her on outstanding warrants.

Frodo let them come around to look at her computer screen while she called up the shipping files. She scrolled down while they read.

"Stop!" Keren grabbed Frodo's hand.

"Pravus Spiritu." Keren looked at Paul.

"We've got all his orders shipped." Frodo pointed to the address.

"Let me see what all he's getting." Keren leaned closer. "Flies, gnats, frogs, and a whole lotta locusts."

"He planned for us to find him. He deliberately used his name." Keren jabbed at the screen. "Do you have a manager, or are you running this place single-handedly?" She did her best to intimidate the young woman.

It worked.

"Yes ma'am. Howie, uh…that is, Mr. Guthrie, is in back taking a break. I'll get him right out here." She disappeared through a door.

Keren said, "Dilated pupils."

"I smelled weed." Paul looked at the shipping address. It was the building where they'd found Caldwell's paintings. "Pravus Spiritu."

"You used both those words earlier when you told me what *pravus* meant," Keren remembered. "*Spiritu*, 'spirit. Evil spirit.'"

"The guy is nothing if not honest."

Howard Guthrie, early thirties, prematurely bald, wearing dress pants and a tie under his buttoned-up lab coat, looked a lot more like a scientist than Frodo did. Keren greeted him with a firm handshake and asked for his cooperation. He seemed to get the point instantly that his cooperation was only a formality. They were going through his files. Period.

Paul said, "We need a printout of his file—everything you've got."

Frodo leaned her body fully against Howie to watch the monitor while he typed. "I'm the one who talked to him. He's a pretty weird dude."

Paul wondered if this kid was a good judge of *weird*.

"Weird how?" Keren asked.

"Oh, just the way he fussed about the orders, like the bugs

were gonna be house pets or something. And he was very specific about the address and the time of delivery. He made me read it back to him twice to make sure I'd gotten them right. I got the idea he was just obsessive in general, and it didn't have that much to do with these shipments."

"What's going on?" Guthrie asked.

Paul arched an eyebrow at Keren. He'd let her decide how much to tell.

"Have you read the paper?" Keren asked. "About the serial killer and the plagues he's acting out? Frogs, flies, gnats? None of this rings a bell?"

"I heard about it, yes." Guthrie's brows arched in alarm. "You mean those flies and gnats and frogs were ours? That's what he used them for?"

"Yes, and the locusts are coming up."

"Whoa, creepy," the intern said.

Paul got the impression the punkette thought this was all real cool, and it took a wrestling match to keep his temper under control. He leaned toward Frodo. Keren stepped between him and the girl. She probably thought he was going to go ballistic. She was probably right.

"We'll be sending someone around to talk with you. We'll put a trace on your phone in case he calls back. You've talked to this guy. We have a profiler who will want to interrogate you."

"Hey, I don't know nothin' about him."

"You know he's fussy. You've heard his voice. You're one of the few people we've found who's had actual contact with him who's still alive."

"I'm not talking to the police. You can't make me." Frodo crossed her arms.

"We *can* make you." Paul took a step around Keren. "If you

don't, that makes you an accessory to *murder*."

"Hey, I didn't know anything about any murder." She backed away until she could duck behind Guthrie.

"You do now." Paul's voice was cold, pure cop. "To withhold information that could lead to his arrest makes you an accessory—an accessory after the fact to murder. You could do serious jail time for that, understand?"

"I'll see to it that I'm in charge of all phone orders until this is over," Mr. Guthrie said. "And we'll *both* cooperate with the police any way you ask."

"Howie, what's the deal?" The intern slid her hand up Howie's arm.

Mr. Guthrie patted the hand. "We'll be fine."

Keren and Paul exchanged a long look, then Keren nodded her head. "We'd appreciate it. He's kidnapped another woman."

"And she's going to be found dead," Paul added. "Killed by this maniac."

"And covered with my locusts?" Mr. Guthrie swallowed hard.

"No, he's not up to that yet. Right now he's reenacting the plague of beasts," Paul said brusquely.

The two "scientists" looked suitably sickened.

CHAPTER TWENTY

O'Shea was on the radio when they got back to the car. He sounded exhausted and about fifteen years older than he had before this case started. "We found the next vic. She's in the same park where he dumped LaToya."

Keren started driving. "How bad?"

There was a long silence. "Bad."

She thought he wasn't going to say anymore. "You have to see it for yourself. I'd say he brought a plague on the beasts."

"Did he get in the petting zoo? We had extra security on it."

"No, he isn't interested in a frontal assault. He was more creative than that."

"We'll be there in ten minutes."

"Use the siren. We're not holding this site a second longer than we have to. The press is all over us and there's a crowd gathering."

"On my way." Keren clapped the light on her roof and hit the siren.

"Wilma." Paul buried his face in his hands. "God, I'm sorry for what I said. Forgive me."

He lapsed into silence and Keren looked at him. When she saw his lips moving, she knew he was still praying, and she thanked God for that. It was exactly what he needed.

It was what she needed, too.

⌒

"Plague of beasts," Paul said. "He managed it."

"Well, he's an artist after all. He's bound to have a good imagination," Keren said, resorting to a cop's black humor.

Wilma lay on her back near the spot Caldwell had left LaToya. Keren couldn't see her, though. She was covered with dead birds and squirrels and rabbits. Caldwell had sprinkled poison birdseed and pellets on her, and little animals had been feasting themselves to death all night. They had piled up on her and were scattered across the park in all directions.

The police had established a perimeter, and Keren had to gather her courage before she could duck under the yellow tape.

Paul laid his hand on her back, and she looked at him. She saw his vulnerability.

He couldn't hold her gaze, so he looked away before he admitted, "I've got to get out of this, Keren. When you're done with me here, I'm going back to the mission. I'll help any way you need, but I'm not going to ride along with you, investigate with you anymore. I can't bear this."

Keren nodded. She agreed he needed to go back to his own life.

They walked toward Wilma. Some of the animals were still alive, fluttering and twitching from the poison. Keren said to O'Shea, who stood near the vic, "What killed them? Could we save the ones still alive?"

O'Shea shook his head. "It's arsenic. We had a vet called to the scene immediately. He said the effects are irreversible once they've eaten the poison." O'Shea pointed to the area, surrounded by cops. "We're having a terrible time keeping some of the bolder animals, like squirrels, from running out here and grabbing the poison. We have to get the crime scene work finished so we can get it cleaned up."

Keren tread carefully as she got near Wilma. The ground was so covered with dead animals that she had to nudge them aside to step on the ground. She shuddered when cold fur and feathers brushed her ankles. She slipped her foot under a squirrel and pushed it gently aside and was surprised at the lack of rigor mortis. She looked at the medical examiner crouching over the body.

"Have you examined these animals?" she asked.

The ME looked up, and Keren was taken aback. Through clenched teeth, Dr. Schaefer growled, "I'm busy, if you don't mind, Detective."

Keren came up beside Dee and, careful of the little creatures that had fallen before this sick cruelty, knelt beside her friend. "I'm not trying to tell you how to do your job, Dee. This is getting to me, too."

Dr. Schaefer's head dropped for a second, then she seemed to find something deep inside herself to draw from. Her shoulders squared, and she looked Keren in the eye. "Sorry. That wasn't meant for you."

"No problem. I dish it out as often as I take it. I know how it is."

They worked in silence, gathering evidence.

A crowd was building around the park. A press corps shouted questions to anyone who got too close, and they had to bring in extra police to hold back the crowd.

The process of working the crime scene was tedious, and the sun had begun to lower in the sky when they had everything they needed.

Dr. Schaefer seemed to relax with a long, slow breath. "What were you saying about the animals?"

Keren said, "It's just that I moved one and it's soft. Shouldn't it be stiff? It was killed hours ago. Would they be soft again after only one night?"

Dr. Schaefer turned to move her gloved hands over several of the poor animals within reach. "You're right. Some of them have been dead longer than others. Some may have been dead long enough that rigor has relaxed." She shrugged and said, "He's probably been killing them for a while and collecting them, just so his plague of beasts would really make an impression."

Keren recalled the night she and Paul saw the animals feeding together in the park, and she knew Dee was right. "Nothing in that revelation was important enough to interrupt you from your examination," Keren said. "I know you're trying to get her out of here."

Keren heard movement beside her and glanced up to see Paul coming close. She looked back at Wilma. He'd been hanging back all this time, and Keren couldn't blame him.

"The painting on her gown is the same as on the others," Paul said.

"It's done by the same hand," Dr. Schaefer added, "but the deterioration is getting worse. I can read the words because I know what I'm looking for. "Pestis ex bestia" written on the white dress across her abdomen. "Eamus Meus Natio Meare" across her shoulders. 'Let my people go.' I don't know if they would be legible if I were coming into this case cold."

"He's running amok now." Keren studied the crude painting.

O'Shea stood several feet away, where his weary cop's eyes never quit surveying the area. "Everyone in the neighborhood has gotten really cautious," he said. "The press reports have been so sensational that women aren't taking a single step outside their apartments alone. A lot of them aren't even staying alone, because the newspapers and television made a huge point of the first two being taken from their apartments. Even the pimps are staying close to their girls."

"So he's down to street people," Paul said. "Like Wilma."

"They're all he's going to be able to find easily. And he's in too big a hurry to plot and plan like he did with Juanita. There was no sign of forced entry for her or LaToya. He found a quiet way to get inside."

Keren looked at O'Shea then glanced over at Paul. "Or else he knew them."

"We've suspected he poses as a homeless man to move easily around the area." O'Shea looked at the throng of gawkers, gathered around the crime scene perimeter.

Like being hit by lightning, Keren was jolted by the feeling of evil. She leaped to her feet then froze, afraid a direct search might scare their quarry away. "He's here," she hissed.

O'Shea looked up sharply then turned his well-trained eyes on the crowd, hundreds of people gathered, gawking. "We can't corral all of them."

"We have to." Keren itched to turn on the crowd of onlookers and try to pick out their killer. Trying to be casual, she turned, wishing the feeling she had was more exact.

"How?" O'Shea studied the gathering. It lifted Keren's heart to know he trusted her even when it made no sense that she would know this. "There are more coming, others leaving all the time."

"He's not leaving."

"Keren, they're standing in doorways and alleyways. Half of them would vanish if we even approached them, and you can bet our boy would be one who'd vanish."

"Is there someone here with a video camera?" Keren asked under her breath.

"Sure," Dr. Schaefer said, watching Keren closely. "Forensics always videotapes the crowd that gathers around a scene like this. Sometimes we find our perp standing, rubbernecking with everybody else."

"Have you done it yet?"

Dr. Schaefer asked, "How can you know he's here? What's going on?"

Keren snapped, "Have you done it yet?"

"Yes, once."

"Get them to do it again—quietly and thoroughly. I didn't feel him before, so he may have just joined the crowd. We can look at the tapes and compare who came in just now."

Dr. Schaefer gave her the look that she might normally have reserved for a mold slide under a microscope, but she turned to the closest assistant. "Norm, have Tommy take another video of the people gathered around."

Her helper was unfolding a body bag a few feet away. "He's done already, Doc."

"Norm!"

The young man, apparently not very brave, said with wide, worried eyes, "What, ma'am?"

"I wasn't making a suggestion. I was giving an order. Tell him to be casual about it, but I want everyone who is gathered around here on tape. Everyone! If he sees someone ducking behind someone else, or walking away, get them. Understand?"

"Yes ma'am." The young man dropped the body bag and turned away.

"Casual, Norm," Dr. Schaefer demanded.

Norm did as he was told.

"Whoa, you'd make a great mom." Keren thought Norm's acting was a little stiff, but, after all, he'd studied pathology, not theater.

Dr. Schaefer turned back to the body. "You're going to tell me what this is about sometime, right, Keren?"

Keren still felt the evil. She knew Pravus was within her reach. "You're a trained investigator, Dee. Figure it out yourself."

"I will," Dr. Schaefer said.

Norm was back in a couple of minutes. With some help, Dr. Schaefer wrapped Wilma in the body bag then said to Norm, "Back the meat wagon in here."

Paul flinched.

"Pansy," Dr. Schaefer said dryly.

Very carefully, Keren eased away from Wilma's body. While the forensic team worked, she slowly moved toward the crowd. When she got close enough to the mob, the press attacked, which eliminated any chance she had of moving around incognito. She pushed through the press and the onlookers. The crowd kept stirring, coming and going. There were gang members, homeless people, businessmen, people of every description.

There was nothing about any she got near that told her this was the one. Knowing that lifted a weight off her shoulders about the shooting she'd done at the car. She really had followed faint running footsteps. She really had pulled the trigger because of more than just this feeling of evil. She walked through the crowd several times, praying God would open her eyes.

Looking particularly for homeless people, she made a point of touching them when she could, but most of them slinked away when the press identified her as a police detective.

Anyway, not all the people who worked at the mission were homeless. She hunted for those five men who'd been in that car out in front of the mission, photographed by Higgins, but she couldn't pick them out of this mob.

Wilma was loaded and the coroner's wagon drove slowly

across the expanse of green.

Higgins stepped toward the reporters. "I'll make a statement now."

The press abandoned Keren without a backward glance.

Pulling Keren aside, Paul asked, "If you can feel the demon, why can't you cast it out?"

"It's not like that."

"Well, what is it like?"

"It's not something I can *do*. My gift is to discern spirits. I can't cast them out like some exorcist."

"Are you *sure*?"

"The person with the demon has to do it. Like with Roger, I can help them believe such a thing is possible, but the choice to be free has to come from the one who's possessed. That's the only way I know."

Keren watched the video camera being swept across the crowd. Keren turned to Paul but only for a second. She couldn't stop moving through the crowd, searching, praying. "You're done here."

He nodded. "I think I'll walk back to the mission now."

"I'm not letting you go alone." As casually as possible, she pressed on shoulders, eased past people, making sure to brush against them. Paul kept pace. "We both know that one of these times this"—she turned to hiss at him—"this maniac is going to turn his attention on you."

"I don't think so," Paul said. "He's after women. He may be blaming me for this, but his hatred is for women."

"Maybe so, but you seem to be his real target. Maybe he only plans to torment you, but I wouldn't count it as an established fact that it's some mommy dearest situation." Keren felt the demonic presence ease and wanted to scream. Who was it? There were people walking away in all directions. She checked her watch. The video would be time stamped. She'd see who walked away at just this time.

"The profiler is researching his background since we know his name now." Keren kept studying the crowd, trying to fine-tune her sense of evil. "He's hoping, if we look into his past, it'll help us predict the future."

"You don't have to escort me home. I see Roger over there." Paul pointed at Roger, standing alone.

"Okay. But don't go alone with him."

"You don't trust Roger?" Paul looked alarmed.

"Yes. No. Look, it's not him, but just. . .just make sure there are several of you." Keren studied the people near Roger, but none of them were the killer. The killer was gone. But maybe she could eliminate a few suspects. "Are any of the men still here that were riding with Murray that morning?"

"I don't see them." Paul studied the crowd.

Frustrated, Keren dragged her cell phone out of her pocket. "Let us know if anyone calls so we can start a trace." She pushed a couple of buttons. "That's how you record. Don't forget it, even if he calls in the middle of the night."

"I don't like you going without a cell." Paul accepted the phone only when she jammed it into his hand. "He may have his eye on you, too."

"I can get another one from the station. And I'll ride back with O'Shea. I'm not going anywhere alone either, Rev."

They stood and watched Higgins finish his little press conference then approach them across the killing field of the park.

As soon as he left the press, his expression turned grim. His perfect hair even seemed a little flat. "We have another woman missing."

The top of Keren's head almost blew off. "And you told the press before you told me?"

"No." Higgins's eyes glittered gold and icy.

"So you lied to the press?"

"Sure."

"We really try not to tell blatant lies to the press here. They don't forget."

"Doesn't matter to me. I'm going back to DC when this is over." Higgins shrugged, not the tiniest speck of concern for Chicago cops and their relationship with a skeptical press. "She's homeless, but someone saw her being taken, and when they went up to the spot she'd been dragged away from, they found a sign that said this." He held up a scrap of paper that said, "*Pestis ex ulcus.*"

"I can't take any more of this." Paul ran one hand into his hair.

Keren grabbed his arm. "Tell us what it means first, Paul. I've got them all written down back in the car and at the office, but I can't remember them."

Paul said, "I can barely remember my name."

"Morris," Higgins said sharply.

Paul reached for the paper but pulled his hand back at the last minute as if touching it would bring the plague on himself. "Plague of boils."

"Boils?" Higgins grimaced. "What does that mean?"

Paul said, "This one might be the worst yet. He could go a lot of different ways with boils. He could infect someone with anthrax or smallpox."

"If he had access to such a thing," Higgins said doubtfully.

"Boils are nasty blisters. A plague of them, they'd cover your body." Paul stared at the paper in Higgins's hand, then he said under his breath, "I've got to get out of here."

"Go," Keren said. "We've got nothing left, except to get the dead animals tagged and bagged." She wanted Paul away from there. She wished she could order him out of the city.

"We'll handle it," she said.

Paul watched the coroner's team start picking up dead animals, sacrificed to a madman along with poor, harmless Wilma. Then he jerked his head as if he had to force himself to look away and stalked off toward his friend from the mission.

"What's the matter with him?" Higgins asked.

Keren watched Paul walk away, then she turned to Higgins. "He's just trying to remember who he is."

"That's something I never waste time doing." Higgins turned his tawny eyes on her. She wondered if he'd ever tried to hypnotize the truth out of perps.

"Why not?" Keren asked.

"Because I'm afraid if I figure it out, I won't like what I find."

Keren frowned. "I think, right now, Paul's afraid of exactly the same thing."

She went back to work gathering evidence. They found hundreds of poisoned pellets still scattered around.

Keren stayed alongside city crews, working into the night, so the plague of beasts could come to an end.

CHAPTER TWENTY-ONE

"Festering boils will break out on
men and animals throughout the land."

Pravus raised the red-hot andiron out of the fireplace and turned to the woman. Her eyes widened in terror as he approached. She struggled against her bonds.

This was an experiment. He didn't know quite how to raise satisfactory boils on a body. It wasn't an art form he'd worked with before. But a true creator had to try new things. Finally, when he felt that his work was worthy to be one of his people, he turned his attention to the gown. This he understood. But it was almost impossible to paint. He felt like his blood raced faster. He felt like maybe he'd finally found his true calling. Torture as art.

The boils painted on the gown were hard to recognize.

Laughing, Pravus thought of how angry his father would be. How frightened his mother would be while she begged him to behave and make Father happy.

But neither one of them was here to stifle his power. The ability to create only possessed by a god.

He'd silenced those ugly, critical voices years ago. Shortly after the first glimpse of the beast had come and helped him, saved him.

Now, to do a poor, fast job of the gown suited Pravus and

suited the beast. He was a genius. He wouldn't be confined by anyone else's vision of art. It didn't matter if anyone else could see. The vision was his.

He got lonely for the sound of screaming again, but he didn't have to live without it.

Smiling, he found another object and heated it, not quite so red hot this time.

⌐

Coming back to the mission was an act of cowardice.

Paul needed to stay on the job. He needed to keep tracking down leads, however slim. He thought of Wilma, poor, muddled Wilma, who never hurt anyone except herself. He thought of the slaughter of animals, so senseless. A madman's idea of a joke. Right now he couldn't stay with the police. Not even Keren. Especially not Keren, not after the way he'd treated her this morning.

Paul got back in time to serve supper. He worked with his flock, talking to them, loving them, but he didn't find what he was looking for.

The mission always had empty beds in the summer. The homeless people preferred to sleep outside, but they came in to eat. Paul scooped up creamed corn alongside Murray and Roger. They'd taken up the slack in the kitchen.

He should call Keren. Get her down here to see if Murray was their killer.

Roger had proved to be invaluable with Rosita gone so much to be with her "sick friend." After the food was dished up, Murray, who had rediscovered a love for music since he'd found God and sobriety, returned with his guitar and played quietly in the spot where Paul delivered his sermons.

Paul couldn't stand the thought that Murray was the killer.

But who? Was it really one of these men here tonight?

When everyone, even the cooks and servers, were eating, Paul had a moment to himself behind the counter. He studied the room and tried to find the peace God had given him so abundantly since he had turned in his badge and gun and picked up a Bible.

It wasn't there.

He despaired of the turmoil in his soul. "I've lost it, Lord. I've lost the tranquillity that has sustained me through good times and bad here at the mission." He looked from face to face.

O'Shea's words echoed in his head. *"Caldwell is someone you know."*

Keren had said, *"It may be someone staying at the mission."*

Buddy came wandering in and grabbed a tray and served himself.

Paul hated that he was looking for suspects among the men he was supposed to help, but he kept looking. He'd studied the pictures of Caldwell. No one here resembled him; but Francis Caldwell had been a meticulously neat man, well dressed, obviously well-to-do. That polished man could very easily disappear under ragged clothes, a beard, and a layer of dirt.

Paul didn't know if the thought came from God or himself, but he looked closer. He had been a cop. Describing people was, at one time, his vocation. He knew Francis had a rather prominent Roman nose and a weak chin, but he had enough money to have plastic surgery if he wanted to disguise himself more thoroughly.

Louie came in just then with McGwire and Casey-Ray. All five were here. He reached for his phone again just as Roger got up. Roger had turned into someone Paul couldn't recognize. With the demon thrown out, he was a new man. Roger went to talk with Buddy and the two of them left.

Paul used the analytical side of himself, the cop side, to note that Roger was about the same height as Francis Caldwell. For that matter, Murray and Buddy were, too. An inch or so taller, but that could be explained with thick soles on their shoes. And Roger had definitely had a demon.

Paul suddenly wondered if Keren could have sensed the demon in Roger, even cast it out, but, like Legion, there had been more. Maybe Satan even manipulated Keren. Yes, she'd felt the devil leave Roger, and Paul had seen the change in him, but later Keren had again sensed the demon.

Keren had felt Pravus at the kill site today and Roger had been there. Paul clenched his jaw. *Kill site!* That was something a cop would think, not a pastor. "Forgive me, Lord."

Paul tried to reclaim the joy in Roger's transformation, but— as they had since he'd come back to the mission—peace, joy, and love all evaded him.

Paul could just be reacting to all the tragedy he'd lived through in the last few days. He wished Keren were there to help him. He pulled his cell phone out of his pocket to call her, then he shoved it back in. *No! Not tonight! I'm not going to let the world come and drag me out of here tonight!*

Instead, he listened while Murray sang of faithfulness and redemption. Buddy came back inside and offered to help Paul wash dishes. Paul was ashamed of himself for suspecting any of them.

Paul looked at this quiet man. Rosita had doubts about Buddy's faith. And Paul didn't have assurance that Buddy had truly given his heart over to the Lord. Buddy, a painfully thin man, with a perpetual baseball cap to cover his balding head and a full beard salted with gray, asked Paul what was happening with the police about Juanita's and LaToya's deaths.

Paul heard the sorrow in Buddy's voice and was tempted to

tell him that LaToya was still alive, but he caught himself. "We could spend some time in prayer later, if it would help you come to terms with the loss of our friends."

As he expected, Buddy made sounds of interest, but, in the end, found an excuse not to pray.

When Buddy left the mission for the night, Paul phoned the hospital and got put through to Rosita. He told her he'd be over to sit with LaToya in a few minutes.

"Pastor P, just let me stay here, hokay? If you're back at the mission for the night, then stay there and get some rest. I'm half asleep here already, and I'd rather just sack out on the waiting room couch than come all the way back there."

"I don't want you staying there alone. Is Manny with you?"

Rosita laughed. "You're the man who says to live is Christ and to die is gain. How's come you're so afraid for my safety?"

Paul was unable to come up with a logical response. Finally he said, "I'm not going to be able to sleep tonight if I think you're in danger. You don't want to be responsible for me lying awake, do you?"

Rosita laughed out loud. "Good one, Pastor P. I'll use that the next time I'm telling you not to go jogging in the neighborhood." In an artificially nervous voice she said, "But Pastor P, I'm losing sleep with worry over you."

"Rosie," Paul growled in warning.

"I won't budge from the hospital," she promised. "I'm probably safer here, away from the mission."

"You may be right." Paul sighed. "Promise me you'll keep the necklace on I gave you. And don't head over here alone in the morning. We'll manage breakfast. I really do want you to be safe, Rosie."

"I promise." Then she added, "Speaking of safe, it sounds like you survived the angry lady cop this morning. I knew you could talk your way out of it. Or did she put the bruises somewhere no one can see?"

"Good night, Rosita!"

He was listening to her infectious giggle when he hung up on her.

Paul spent awhile going from table to table pouring coffee. He spoke to everyone, called them by name, asked about their lives. He was particularly careful to speak to the women, reminding them of Wilma's death and the danger they faced on the streets. He urged them all to sleep in the mission that night. They ignored his warnings.

O'Shea had said another woman was taken. Paul couldn't pinpoint anyone who was missing—or rather, he noticed several regulars gone and guessed that most of them had just found food elsewhere and slept in their alleys. As he talked to these people who dwelled in so lowly a place in this world, he was more aware than ever of the way they looked and smelled and the terrible waste of their potential.

He had loved trying to reach them, and now he didn't know why he bothered. His apathy frightened him. If he lost his zeal for the Lighthouse and couldn't reconcile his Christianity with life as a cop, where did that leave him? Paul didn't know who he was or what he was supposed to do with his life. He kept talking and serving and wondering how to restore his love for his calling.

After everyone had cleared out for the night, Paul went upstairs. He stood in front of his door, dreading the thought of re-entering his apartment for the first time since they'd found Melody Fredericks. The police had given him the green light to use the place again. After a long struggle, he forced himself to go in. He was met by a much-reduced swarm of gnats.

Moving quickly, he showered then found a pair of gym shorts and a T-shirt. He looked around his shabby little apartment. The Chicago summer had made the un-air-conditioned space stifling. The smell of death lingered. "How have I been able to stand living here for the last five years?"

Several gnats tickled his face. As he watched them lazily circle, he could feel the gnats he'd inhaled the morning he'd found Melody. He could taste the ones he'd swallowed.

He couldn't bear the thought of sleeping here. "I could go to the shelter," he said to the empty room, but he knew he couldn't do it. Not tonight. He went to his bedroom, picked up the top mattress from his twin bed, and carried it—sheets, blankets, and all—out of his apartment and into his business office across the hall. He tossed it on the floor and dropped down on it.

The office was simply another converted apartment. A dim streetlight cast a shadowy light through the window. He lay there and stared sightlessly at the ceiling in the dark room. He couldn't relax and he finally figured out why. He hadn't locked the door. The office, with its old computer and its petty cash, was one of the few doors that was routinely locked.

"The one who is in you is greater than the one who is in the world." *"To live is Christ and to die is gain."* He waited for God's peace to settle on him. *"If God is for us, who can be against."*

He believed it. He believed wholeheartedly in God. But he still had to admit defeat and get up and throw the dead bolt. While he was up he doubled-checked the windows. Then he touched his cell phone and the spare Keren had left.

He said to the empty room, "Where are you, Pravus?"

The silence of the room mocked him.

In despair, he whispered, "Who are you killing tonight?"

CHAPTER TWENTY-TWO

So they took soot from a furnace and stood before Pharaoh.
Moses tossed it into the air, and festering boils
broke out on people and animals.

P. ravus closed his father's special Bible, the slim one still written in the ancient Latin. Pravus couldn't read the words, but his father had told him what it said. He remembered everything.

He went to the woman, taped securely to the high table. Pravus looked at the gown hanging beside her. Eamus meus natio meare. Pestis ex ulcus.

Then he looked at her.

Boils.

He'd used burns. It was close enough. The reverend said he was like the magicians copying Moses' tricks. He'd used that cold, hard policeman voice, and Pravus nearly choked on hate.

Pravus wanted fear.

The reverend had become less afraid in the last few days. The beast whispered that it was because Pravus had abandoned his path of choosing victims to maximize the reverend's pain.

He'd have to fix that. He'd gotten so involved with the pleasure of the kill and the hunger for more, he'd forgotten his search for freedom for his people.

Pravus waited for full dark, then he left his plague of boils to be found later. It was getting more difficult to dump the bodies.

The police were out in force in the area around the mission. The park was staked out around the clock. He knew from police questioning that the car had been identified, and unless it was an emergency, he kept it out of sight in the underground parking lot beneath a condemned building.

Everyone was watchful. Pravus thrilled at the challenge.

When he had relieved himself of the burden, he wandered about with his typical aimless stroll, walking like he was a weakling, which covered the corded strength he'd gained by hours of exercise. He needed the strength to carry his victims so he could present the plagues to the reverend.

He went into his building determined to change and emerge a new man. Clean and well dressed. The beard that so completely changed the shape of his face, unglued and left behind.

It didn't happen, though. He couldn't shave. His hand shook too badly. And the beast pushed him, prodded, prowled, and gnawed.

He needed a new cell phone. But he didn't have the patience to follow an older couple or search a car in a parking lot or an unlocked garage.

Instead he went to a store and bought one of those phones you could buy minutes with. There was no record of who bought those—the number wasn't connected to his name, since he paid cash. Untraceable, Pravus was sure.

When he had it ready, he had a few more things to do, then he'd get back to his true purpose—his need to punish the reverend.

$\sim$

"So what's the deal with you and the preacher?" O'Shea settled his ample backside in his desk chair and talked around a mouthful of meatball sub.

Keren kept her head down by sheer force of will. She was seeing double from hours of going over Caldwell's phone records—the phone records of the six cell phones he'd stolen so far—his bank records before he cleaned out his accounts, and the videos taken of the crowds at the park. She knew the exact time she'd felt the demon there and she checked her time against the videos. But all the suspects were there and they all walked away together right at that time. It made her even more certain it was one of them, but there was no way to eliminate anybody.

The task force had met again. They'd traced the car to Murray...who had reported it stolen. Fingerprints of three of the men—the ones they could catch up with—had turned up nothing interesting. Dyson had come up with a new profile, but the man seemed real cranky about the generalizations. They'd heard every detail of what Higgins had found about Francis Caldwell's childhood. Which wasn't much. His parents were both deceased. Nothing about either death had raised red flags at the time, but now Keren had to wonder.

She made herself very busy fussing with a stain on the report in front of her. It needed to be cleaned up immediately.

She rose from her seat. "I'd better get a damp cloth. We don't—"

"Sit," O'Shea barked.

Keren didn't sit. "You don't give me orders, Mick." They'd received a sketchy report that couldn't be confirmed of a homeless woman, known on the street as Lupe, being snatched. Paul hadn't been in. There was no report of a phone call. No threat to blow something up. Keren missed talking the case over with him, but she couldn't stand dragging him back into the investigation.

"Sure I do." O'Shea smirked. "I'm senior officer around here, and you're just a little baby girl cop."

The waiting was driving her crazy. She didn't need to look up and see double of O'Shea. And she sure wasn't going to answer his snoopy questions.

Keren resisted the urge to slug him. O'Shea was trying to distract her with his obnoxiousness so she'd quit watching her mouth. "You're not senior when it comes to asking me questions like that."

O'Shea took another huge bite of his sandwich and chewed. Way before all the food was swallowed, he asked, "You know what I think?"

"Don't know. Don't care." Keren enjoyed the tiny flash of caution in O'Shea's eyes. He'd heard that sweet tone before. He knew his potential for becoming a victim of assault and battery was high and increasing by the moment.

Unfortunately, he wasn't quite scared enough. "I think you're hot for each other."

"Mick!"

"What?"

"Don't talk like that. Hot? He's a man of the cloth for heaven's sake! And what about me? You know I don't. . .I mean no man's gonna. . .I mean. . .oh, *you know what I mean.*"

"Yeah, yeah, I know." O'Shea held up both hands to defend himself, one clutching the half-eaten sandwich. "Okay, pick another word."

"Well, I'd say we're. . ." Keren caught herself. She'd spent plenty of time with O'Shea in the interrogation room, and she knew how good he was. He could make people admit to crimes they'd just thought about committing. Sometimes the lawyers, who were sitting in on the questioning, broke down and confessed to crimes they'd committed, unrelated to the case at hand. He didn't usually use his talents on her, though.

She switched to attack mode just to even the playing field. "What'za matter, Mick, your pathetic life so boring you have to entertain yourself by making stuff up about me?"

O'Shea nodded, studying her like she was a menu at Burger King. "Good girl, I almost got you, but you recovered. So. . ." He returned to his sandwich and the beginning. "What's the deal with you and the preacher?"

Keren rolled her eyes. She decided the statute of limitations was up on O'Shea's order to sit, so she plopped back into her chair. "There's no deal."

"C'mon, honey, give. This is your old buddy Mick talking. I've seen the way you look at each other when you think no one is watching."

"How does he look at me?" Keren caught herself again. Man, he was good. "I mean, not that you're right, but tell me, just so I know what you're imagining."

O'Shea laughed.

Keren's cheeks heated up.

O'Shea had, in many ways, stepped in and become a father to her since her own parents had started going to Fort Lauderdale for the winter and traveling extensively in a Winnebago year-round—except she'd have never talked so rudely to her father.

"Is there any chance you might choke to death on a meatball?"

"You don't have that kind of luck."

Finally, just to shut him up, she said, "Have you noticed that the preacher man is turning back into a cop?"

"Yeah, and it's driving him nuts." O'Shea nodded. "He falls into the lingo, changes his tone of voice and the way he holds himself. His whole attitude changes. Then he freezes up when he says something particularly cold blooded, and I can see the guilt. The poor guy's struggling."

"He asked me for a gun the night LaToya was dumped."

"That was enough to make anyone fighting mad," O'Shea said grimly.

"He asked for the gun in the heat of the moment, and he regretted it afterward," Keren continued. "Then, only days later, when we went into Caldwell's apartment building, he asked again. And this time he meant it. It wouldn't surprise me if he shows up with a piece at the next dump site."

"Does he have a license?" O'Shea, ever the cop, asked.

Keren shrugged. "They usually let former cops have one. I don't know about concealed carry. That's a little tougher."

"They'd give him one," O'Shea said with certainty. "Wanting to blow someone away has gotta be tearing him up inside. The day we first met him, in the hospital, I got the idea he was kind of meek. Strong in his convictions, but no dynamo, if you get what I mean."

"Well, you were wrong—as usual." Keren waited for O'Shea to turn red. He obliged her, then she laughed in his face. "He's a tough cookie, even in preacher mode. But now he's losing it. He's a decent guy who left the hassles of law enforcement behind, and now it's like he's being taken over by it."

"Is that admiration I hear?"

"Of course I admire him. He's. . ." Keren caught herself again and fell silent.

"He could rejoin the force," O'Shea said. "I've asked around. He was a good cop. As good as it gets."

Keren shook her head. "I'd hate to see him do that. He has such peace in his life at that mission."

"'I did not come to bring peace, but a sword,'" O'Shea said.

Keren was always startled when O'Shea came up with something Christian. She knew he was a man of faith, and she'd especially liked him because he respected her own strong beliefs, but he didn't wear it on his sleeve.

"And we're the sword, is that what you're saying?" She was

used to the idea that she battled evil, but she'd never heard it put quite that way before.

O'Shea hunched one shoulder. "On this case, with Caldwell, I'd say for sure we're the sword. Somebody's gotta be the sword, 'cuz this guy needs a sword taken to him—bad."

Keren nodded and stared into space, thinking about how desperately they needed to stop Caldwell.

Finally, O'Shea broke the silence. "So what's the deal with you and the preacher?"

Keren threw her coffee cup at him. She wished it was stoneware full of boiling hot coffee instead of Styrofoam and empty.

～

Keren crawled out of the lousy cot in the police lounge the next morning around five. "I want my apartment back," she growled to no one, because no one else was stupid enough to sleep here.

Except she didn't want her apartment back. No way did she want to sleep in that room with her memory of Katrina Hardcastle and all those flies.

She showered at the station house. She'd brought half her wardrobe in by now, and when she got out to her desk, O'Shea was waiting for her like the specter of death.

"Another one?" Keren should have saved her breath. The answer was obvious.

"I just got the word that a body was dumped. I don't have any details, just an address." O'Shea headed for the door. "A half a block from the mission."

"We've got cops all over that area! How is he getting in?"

O'Shea shrugged and kept moving.

Keren fell into step alongside him. "Why do you suppose he writes in Latin?"

O'Shea said, "Oh, I don't know, maybe when we get him, we'll find a connection in his twisted brain to explain it. Maybe, in the end, he's just a loon."

"Boils this time," Keren remembered. "Pestus ex ulcus, isn't that right? The plague of boils?"

O'Shea didn't answer her, and she didn't want him to.

"Should I call Morris?" O'Shea had his phone out of his pocket.

"Leave him for now." Keren started jogging down the stairs. "It's so early you might wake him up. If he's sleeping for once, let him get another hour or two. There's no rush. We can just walk over and talk to him from the dump site. There's nothing he can do anyway."

"Identify her."

Keren sighed. She was all too sure Paul would be able to identify her.

Keren moved faster, but what she wanted to do was run away.

CHAPTER TWENTY-THREE

*Throughout Egypt hail struck everything in the fields—
both people and animals; it beat down everything
growing in the fields and stripped every tree.*

P. ravus crooned to the woman in front of him, "I've got the perfect place for you. It's going to be cold, but you won't care for long."

He was finding his work to be more of a chore. Eluding the police was heady, but the beast told him his victims were unworthy.

He didn't even bother to call the preacher this time. Pravus hated to admit it, but he was becoming bored with his creations and living now only for the kill. He worked away, but he couldn't put the love he needed into his art.

And then, like any true artist, he was inspired. He needed to pick a moment when the reverend was distracted, and he knew just how to do that—how to listen in on his room. Strike while the reverend slept.

He went to the window to look down on the mission, and the final piece of the next child he'd create came to him instantly, when he saw pretty little Rosita.

❧

In spite of all the nickel-sized burn marks on her, Paul easily identified the schizophrenic Hispanic woman who came and went from the mission.

He had to fight back his rage when he stood over her, thrown away like garbage in an alley.

"I should be praying," he said to O'Shea. "Or crying."

O'Shea shrugged.

"If I look in a mirror, will my eyes be as detached and cool as yours?" Paul shoved his hands in his pockets to keep them from hitting something.

O'Shea looked away from the mutilated body. He stared at Paul but didn't say anything.

Paul could feel his own cold-blooded cop personality oozing out of him. "Let's get this over with."

"The FBI just pulled Keren aside to ask her some questions. She'll be back in a minute. She'll want to hear your statement, maybe ask some questions."

"I'm not waiting around." He gave his statement, then he went straight back to the Lighthouse.

He went later to visit LaToya. She lay immobilized in the hospital bed. The beeping monitor was the only thing that proved she was alive.

Caldwell didn't call.

The streets around the mission were so heavily patrolled that the vagrants and gangs were driven inside or underground. By the end of the day, there wasn't a single person in the mission. No one showed up for the evening meal.

Paul ran down a list in his head of every woman he knew who lived on the streets. He tried to figure out a way to track them down and bring them inside for the night. Even thinking about it was a waste of time. He'd never find them, and if, by some fluke he did, they wouldn't come with him unless he used force.

He considered using force—considered it hard. In the end he

stayed inside and prayed.

His prayers seemed futile, and he thought about the gun permit he'd been issued when he left the force. He was tempted to get one. He was sorely tempted to walk a foot patrol up and down the South Side, hunting Caldwell. Make himself an easy target to see if he could draw this maniac out.

⟶

Pounding awakened Paul after only a couple hours of restless, nightmare-plagued sleep.

Coming instantly awake, something he'd learned on the force, he rolled off the mattress, got to his feet, and yanked the door open.

Higgins was in the hall. "We've got another one." He jerked his head toward the stairway. "I'll wait for you downstairs."

"What is going on? Why didn't he call? Why is there no sign delivered to me? Why no threats, no bombs?" Paul took the time to pull on his running shoes and was after Higgins in seconds, wearing the jogging suit he slept in.

Higgins led the way to a seedy bar a block from the mission.

Higgins pushed his way through a crowd, Paul right on his heels, until Paul saw the ghastly contents of the bar's ice machine.

Paul saw the gaping eyes and the cold blue skin. "Talking Bertha."

"One of yours?" Higgins asked.

"One of mine." Paul analyzed the position of the body. The medical examiner, a young black man, fixed plastic bags over the woman's hands, hoping to preserve evidence under her fingernails.

"Anything?"

"Nope, just routine." The ME started loading equipment in a kit.

"Okay if I touch her?"

The ME dragged a pair of plastic gloves out of the kit and tossed them to Paul. "Go ahead. I've got everything I need. We're ready to transport."

"When'd you find her?" Paul glanced over his shoulder at Higgins as he pulled on the gloves.

"The bar has a silent alarm that went off at two a.m. Police response time was three minutes." Higgins rapped out the details as the examiner left.

"So she was probably dead when he brought her in, not like the first two. Juanita was probably killed on-site, and he was planning to kill LaToya the same way." Paul crouched down to pinch a clear plastic encased hand, hanging suspended from the wide door of the ice machine. "Those welts on her body look like burns." Higgins snapped plastic gloves on his hands and ran a finger over the raised welts on Talking Bertha's neck, just above the words EAMUS MEUS NATIO MEARE, painted on the white dress she wore.

"This is the plague of hail, right?" Higgins flipped open his notebook.

"Yeah, these are probably freeze burns. Liquid nitrogen, maybe."

"How does she fit the profile?" Higgins lifted an eyelid over Talking Bertha's slack, lifeless eyes.

"She knows me. What other profile is there?" Paul stood away from the body. His stomach twisted at the casual tone of his voice. He knew it was wrong to work over Bertha's body without praying, without crying, without feeling for her. "I've got to get out of here."

"Go then. We'll send someone over later."

"You don't need a statement. You know everything I know

already." Paul turned on his heel and walked out.

Keren showed up at the mission an hour later.

Paul saw the dark circles under her eyes. Her hair looked like she hadn't done more than run her fingers through it and twist it into her barrette for days. He was tempted to smooth the riotous curls. He wanted to take her in his arms. He wanted to share his strength with her and take some of hers for himself. But was that the cop who wanted that or the preacher?

Because he couldn't be sure, he led her toward the coffeepot.

He got her a cup and one for himself, and, remembering that Caldwell had been watching the mission, Paul dragged her away from the front windows and they sank down at the table closest to the lunch counter.

"He hasn't called?" Keren asked.

"I'd have let you know," Paul said with more bite than he'd intended.

Keren nodded and closed her eyes. She held her coffee cup like her hands were freezing, even though it was seventy-five degrees outside. "Sorry. That just slipped out."

"I know." Paul drank his stout, bitter brew until he'd emptied the cup.

"So are you still spending the nights at the hospital?"

Paul shook his head. "Rosita is pretty much living there. It's safer than her going back and forth."

"You moved back into your apartment?" Keren asked idly.

"No. I don't think I ever will. There's another one on that floor. Not big and not in good repair. But I think I'll move into it permanently." He got up to refill his cup. He got back and noticed hers was empty. He refilled hers, too, without asking.

"Thanks," she said, again gripping the cup.

"What about you?" Paul asked. "Are you going back?"

Keren shook her head. "I'm already hunting for a new place. I'm sleeping at the precinct for now."

"Those cots'll kill your back."

"Tell me about it," Keren muttered. "O'Shea said I could stay at his place when his wife comes back. I know her pretty well. She's a nice lady. It would work for a couple of weeks if I can't find something soon." She shrugged. "Who's got time to apartment hunt?"

Paul didn't respond.

"Are you okay?" Keren looked up from her cup. "Are you getting yourself back a little?"

"I'm trying." Paul took a long drink of the acid coffee. "I don't know how much success I'm having. I know I should be helping more, but I just can't. Not right now."

"I understand. I respect your desire to get away from it."

"Why would you?" Paul slapped his cup onto the table with a sharp *click*. "You can't get away from it. The women who are dead can't get away. But I bail out when it gets tough. I'm not firm enough in my faith to work beside you and still be a Christian."

Keren fell silent. She looked up from her coffee and met his eyes squarely for the first time since she'd come in. She studied him. She opened her mouth once then closed it again. After a few silent moments, she said, "I've decided to give you a break, now that it doesn't matter, and tell you where we met."

Paul was instantly alert. They'd started getting along so well he'd forgotten the little fact that Keren had started out hating his guts. "Okay."

"You never really met me. Everything you did was on paper and on TV."

Paul tried to remember.

"I arrested a man who was wanted for a string of crimes, including one you were working on. It was a B and E, nonviolent. No gun." Keren's eyes lost their focus as if she were looking into the past. "It was the weirdest thing, the way I caught him. It was a pure accident. I was just new to the detective unit, and we were called in, hours after the fact, to this B and E. I was poking around in the alley behind the high-rise, and here comes this boy out of a ground-floor window. We had a decent description of him and I was sure he was our guy. He should have been long gone. There was no reason why he would have still been hanging around. It was like he was delivered into my hands. I yelled, and he just lay down. I never even drew my gun. I slapped the cuffs on him and while I was securing him, I sensed the demon."

"He was possessed," Paul said.

"Yeah. The other cops were all over him so I couldn't do anything right then, but I rode back to lockup with him. I never left his side while he was booked. Then I got a chance to talk to him alone in the interrogation room. I only said a few words to him about the demon. The boy was so ready to turn to God, I'll always believe that somehow he stayed behind, waiting for me. It was all in the hands of God from the minute I responded to that call."

"So you led him to the Lord?" Paul asked, feeling the spurt of pleasure that always lifted him when he heard of someone turning their life around.

"Right there in that dingy room." Keren smiled at the memory. "And he really was changed. I visited him every day in jail. I was afraid for him to be in such a bleak place with his new faith. I spent hours talking to him. I had my pastor go in to see him, and a group from our church that ministers to prisoners virtually adopted him. The poor guy was swamped with Christian support."

Paul said, "And he was one of my cases?"

Keren nodded. "Lucas Vilsack. You probably remember him because he was six foot seven and had bright green hair when he was arrested."

Paul snapped his fingers. "He got out of jail and went to college. He's playing forward for Notre Dame."

"That's the guy."

"I remember him. I tied him to a string of burglaries that went back two years."

"Sixteen months. He started in when he became possessed. Ran away from a really good home, lived on the street."

"So what's the problem?"

"The problem is—"

Paul cut her off as the light dawned. "I came stomping in on that case and found out he was being given probation and community service. He was going to walk."

"Because I had been working my butt off arranging for him to walk. While he was out on bail, he'd met with every one of his victims and arranged to pay them back. He had plans to do community service by speaking to high schools about the mistakes he'd made with his life. He'd already given a couple of speeches and they were wonderful. He could really have reached some kids. And he was back in school and involved in a youth group in my church. I had contacted every jurisdiction where he was wanted. He was making no effort to cover up any offenses, because he admitted to things that hadn't even been connected to him. I'd talked to everyone and urged them to meet him and judge for themselves if his remorse was genuine. And that includes you. I called you and—"

"I wrecked it. I wanted to make an example of him. I couldn't be bothered to meet him, and I was sure he was just conning a rookie detective. I used my influence to make sure he did some real time."

"Five years. He got out in two because he was a model prisoner."

Paul closed his eyes as more details came back. "And I did my best to have you, and every other cop who was letting him off the hook, busted back to a uniform."

"There were four of us. One was older and he took early retirement. The other two ended up walking a beat for a while, but they eventually left the force. They were all three good cops who didn't see a future for themselves once they had bad paper in their jackets from the charges you filed against us."

"But you stayed on."

"I managed to hang on to my detective shield, mainly because I was a woman, which made me furious on the other guys' behalf, but I was too much of a wimp to resign in protest. I spent six months sitting in the evidence locker doing paperwork. The only reason I stuck with it was because I felt police work was where God wanted me. Then I found something in an evidence box that broke open a case O'Shea was working. He got me transferred. We've been partners for two years now."

"And it was my fault."

Keren gave him a squinty-eyed look. For some reason it pleased Paul that she didn't just wave it off and say, "No big deal, what's six months of my life?"

"Yeah, it was your fault. You were so cynical, and the cameras were rolling. You couldn't be bothered to just listen to the kid. You never gave him five minutes of your precious time. Yeah, it was your fault." She fell silent for a moment. "And Lucas is okay, and you're okay, and I'm okay, and none of it matters anymore, except your name is eternally linked in my mind with insufferable arrogance."

"That's all?"

"Yup, that's all."

Paul rested his face in his palms. "Sorry." He peeked out between his fingers. "I'm really sorry."

"Too late," Keren said.

"I promise you I'll call Lucas tomorrow and apologize."

Keren arched an eyebrow at him. "Too late for that, too. He made it, in spite of you."

"I'll find those three cops and apologize personally, and allow the older one to beat on me awhile. The younger ones might hurt me."

"This isn't funny."

"Okay, the young ones can hit me, too."

"I can get you their names and addresses by nightfall."

Paul was afraid she meant it, and if she did, he'd have to do it. He owed them all. He smiled at her. "The only bad part of hiding out here instead of working with you is that I've been worried. When you said I could be your bodyguard so you could be my bodyguard, I meant it. I need to know where you are. I've been imagining you in Caldwell's hands. I've got to do something to make sure you're safe. But I turn into a man I don't like or respect when I'm doing police work. I've got an idea, but it might just be. . .that I'm not so much worried as I just. . . miss you."

"I've missed you, too." Keren set her coffee cup down with a *thud* and covered her mouth. From behind her hands, she said, "Forget I said that."

Paul circled the table and pulled Keren up out of her chair. He looked into her eyes until he felt like he could see all the way to her heart, and he saw himself in her heart. "Uncover your mouth."

Muffled, she said, "No way."

"I really need to stay away from you," he said as he got closer to her.

"Agreed," Keren said between her fingers as she backed away.

Paul advanced. "Stand still and let me kiss you. You're as hard on me as this whole cop mess."

Keren retreated. "I'm hard on you?"

He gave her a wry look then snagged her by the arm and kissed her on the forehead. "Okay, that's enough anyway."

She nodded and stepped away. She tripped over her chair. She flung her arms out. Paul caught her, pulled her close, and kissed her. His mouth missed her forehead this time and landed square on her lips.

And her hands weren't protecting her mouth at all when they wrapped around his neck.

CHAPTER TWENTY-FOUR

Hello, Rosita." Pravus was careful to be his usual polite self as he stepped into the hospital lounge.

Rosita took a quick nervous look at the door to the intensive care unit. He wondered who her sick friend was. She'd certainly been faithful to her this week.

"What brings you here?"

"Pastor P asked me to come over and bring you back to the mission."

"He did?" Rosita relaxed.

"Yes, he even found someone to lend me a car." Pravus had to be very careful not to smile.

"A car? Where'd he find a car in our neighborhood?"

"I don't know." Pravus shrugged.

"Well, whoever lent it to him, I'm grateful."

"Pastor P doesn't want you out alone."

Rosita rolled her eyes. "He won't even let me walk to the bus stop in the daylight."

"Well, good for him." Pravus knew just how thoroughly the reverend had warned everybody. He was sticking his neck way out to come into the hospital, with the plans he had for Rosita. And the hospital had security cameras, so he'd never be able to show his face again. That's okay, it was worth it. Once he had little Rosie, they'd come to him.

"He's right, you know. You have to be careful with this guy

out there killing people."

Rosita rose from the couch. "I know he's right, and I've been doing as he says."

"It makes life more difficult, but it's a good idea to be careful."

"And he said I should come back? Is he coming to take a turn sitting with. . ." Rosita fell silent and looked uncertainly at the ICU again.

Pravus picked up her jacket and helped the gullible little fool slip it on. "Yes, in fact, we may pass him on the way out."

Pravus gestured toward the door politely, his heart thudding with excitement as sweet Rosita walked out of the hospital by his side. He wanted to take her arm, touch her in some way. He controlled himself. There would be time for that soon. Plenty of time. He led her to a dark green car parked near the entrance.

Rosita said, "What happened to this car? It looks like a bullet hole in the back window."

Pravus shrugged. "I'm just borrowing it. It's a tough neighborhood. I suppose that's exactly what happened."

Rosita, despite all the warnings she'd been given, accepted the easy lie. Pravus felt laughter welling up in his throat. He fought it down, his hands sweating until they left wet spots on the steering wheel. He drove away from the hospital.

"I have to make a quick stop on the way back," Pravus said. "Pastor P asked if, since we have the car today, could we pick up some things that have been donated to the mission. Do you mind helping me carry them out?"

Rosita said pleasantly, "I'd be glad to help."

A few minutes later, he pulled into a parking garage. His parking garage. His new home.

"You're really a good driver," Rosita observed. "When have you had a chance to drive in the city?"

Pravus parked the car and got out. As he waited for her, he said, "I drove when I was younger. I guess it's like riding a bike."

"This is a wreck of a building." They walked to the elevator and got in. Pravus pushed the button and they went up. When they got to the top floor, he got off and went to the closest door.

"They're demolishing it. I guess that's why they're giving things away." He produced a key and let himself in.

"Why do you have a key to this apartment?" Rosita said.

Pravus heard her nervousness and his hands itched to grab her, make that tinge of fear bloom into screaming terror. He let the door swing open. "I have the key because the apartment is mine."

A bug ran out of the apartment and Rosita squeaked and jumped back. "What is that? A cockroach?"

"It's a locust."

Rosita looked inside just as Pravus's hand rested on her back. He'd written the words *PESTUS EX LOCUSTA* in giant letters on the far wall so she could see them from here and know.

Once it was too late.

He shoved her inside and kicked the door shut.

⤙

"I will bring locusts into your country tomorrow.
They will cover the face of the ground so that it cannot
be seen. They will devour what little you have left."
EXODUS 10:4–5

Darling Rosita. She had been so surprised to see him at the hospital. Pravus felt like he had rediscovered his reason for living. He was fulfilled and happy and restored to his path.

Rosita lay before him, still untouched. Her deeply tanned

skin, the burnished brown of her people, was nearly the color of fine wood. She would be a delight to create with. Then Pravus thought of the pretty detective's skin. Lighter, but beautiful in its own way.

She would be next. It would suit the beast in him to visit the plague of darkness on the pretty lady detective.

Then the plague of the firstborn. The good reverend was the eldest in his family.

When it came time for the plague of the firstborn, then, finally, Pravus would get the ultimate atonement. He'd told Patricia Morris when she rejected his art that she would regret it. She had the chance to set such a wealth of beauty free. His people. His children. His creations.

He'd heard whispers of the demon for years, and Pravus had always enjoyed the power of the devil. The reverend's wife had treated him as if she were a ruler, a pharaoh, barring his way to the respect, the wealth, the freedom he and his people deserved.

And when he killed her and her child, for a while it had been enough. He might have never struck again if the reverend hadn't wielded his power so corruptly. True, Pravus was a murderer, but the reverend didn't know that. The reverend accepted that it was an accident. But he'd brought his crushing boot down on Pravus's neck out of spite.

While he'd sat in jail, the anger had burned. It ate at him. Grew in him along with the beast. He'd have let the reverend go if it hadn't been for prison. Pravus had spent his time behind bars planning what he'd do when he was free. How he'd free himself and his creations—and use the reverend to do it.

Once Pravus was out and his death had been accepted, he made his preparations to punish the reverend. It was no longer about a woman's foolish decision. It was between the beast and

God, with Pravus fighting on the side of the beast, fighting for power and the right to create. The right to have his people set free and revered by all the world.

Pravus would earn the right to be God.

It was time for the end to unfold for his father. No. Pravus shook his head. The reverend. This was about the reverend.

The last three plagues would rain down so hard the reverend would be grateful for death.

Pravus couldn't wait to begin the end. He should have waited, done his painting, made his carving, but he couldn't wait to share his good news about Rosita. He reached for his new cell phone.

Paul lifted his head. "What am I going to do with you?"

Based on his actions, Keren guessed he'd keep kissing her while he decided. Her arms tightened around his neck so she could be comfortable while he was thinking.

"I've decided I like your hair tie, too." Sinking his hands into her hair, he seemed to play with it, as if he really did like the terrible mess. Smiling against his lips, Keren decided she liked her hair, too.

His phone rang.

He reached for it and almost answered before Keren snatched the phone out of his hands. "Do this right." Her voice was husky, but her thinking was still functional.

Paul shook his head as if to clear it then nodded as he fumbled for his second cell phone. He speed-dialed Higgins. Higgins set up the trace and began to track down the caller ID number. Keren worked on the recorder buttons and was waiting when Paul said, "Higgins is ready to triangulate."

She nodded. "I'm ready, too. Go."

Paul answered his phone.

"Hello, Reverend. Have you missed me?"

Keren's phone beeped. Seeing Higgins's number, she switched to him.

Higgins hissed, "He's not on a cell. It's a landline. We need more time to trace it."

Keren mouthed to Paul, *Keep him talking.* She switched back to Caldwell's call.

Paul's eyes flashed with understanding. "No, I can't say that I have, Francis. I would've preferred it if I never heard your voice again."

"You don't seem to have the correct attitude, Reverend," Caldwell purred. "I've decided that's my fault. I faltered for a time when I chose my victims."

"All of this is your fault."

"Put the pretty detective on, please."

"What are you talking about, Francis? You called me, so you talk to me."

"She's standing right beside you. She's wearing a tacky, ill-fitting brown blazer. Are you listening, Kerenhappuch? Brown really isn't your color. With all that flyaway brown hair, you look like something dirty."

Keren looked up sharply at the mission's front window. She looked at Paul, and they both nodded. Caldwell was watching them, looking in this window.

She touched her hair then pulled her hand away and pushed MUTE OFF on her cell.

Paul grabbed for her phone, shaking his head.

Keren dodged him. "All right, I'm here, Francis. I can't thank you enough for the fashion advice."

"I just wanted to let you know you're next, pretty girl. You're my choice for the plague of darkness."

Keren felt a cold chill crawl up her spine, but she didn't let so much as a breath of it sound when she responded. "You'll never try for me, Caldwell. You pick on defenseless women. You wait until their backs are turned and grab them."

"They come willingly every time, Kerenhappuch."

"I'm sure Melody Fredericks came willingly." Keren's voice dripped with disdain. "And Talking Bertha, a homeless woman who couldn't even be convinced to stay in the mission overnight, came willingly with you. Hah."

"I honor a woman when I choose her, and they all know it by the time I'm done."

Keren remembered that she'd thought the time might come when she'd have to offer herself up as bait to catch Caldwell. That time was now, and she was ready. "Guess what? I think you're a lousy artist, Pravus. And I think you're too much of a coward to ever come for me. I think you're an insect. That's why you're obsessed with acting out this pathetic version of the plagues of Egypt. You see yourself in creepy, crawly things."

"Like locusts?" Caldwell suggested.

Keren looked up at Paul and their eyes met. Keren glanced at her watch.

"Why have you called, Pravus?" Paul asked. "What stupid, cowardly thing have you done this time?"

"This time?"

A high-pitched scream nearly slit Keren's eardrum. She jerked the phone away. The sound was quickly muffled, but they could still hear it. The pain, the terror. Keren felt tears burn her eyes. They had to find him! They had to stop him!

"No screaming, my dear. No one pays attention to such things in this neighborhood, but still, I must ask you to refrain, or I won't let you talk to your precious Pastor P."

The voice returned, and, through broken sobs, they both heard, "Pastor P? He told me you sent him. I believed him. It's—" Her voice was cut off.

"Rosita?" Paul shouted. "Rosita, is that you?"

Color drained from Paul's face, to be replaced with sheer terror. He clutched the phone until Keren was afraid he'd snap it in two.

"Of course it's her. I took someone precious to you. Someone to get you involved again. Perhaps, when the plagues are over, I'll just start at one again. The plague of blood. Oh, but wait, who will I call? You'll be dead, Reverend."

"Let me talk to Rosita. Put her back on."

Rosita continued crying in pain.

Caldwell crooned, "The only reason I'd let her talk is so you could hear her scream. Is that what you want, Reverend? Do you want me to make her scream?"

"No! Stop! Please, don't." In anguish Paul cried out, "Rosita!"

"Pestis ex locusta. Intriguing, isn't it? I think, instead of letting her provide the paint for my work, I'm going to cut her open and fill her belly with them while she's still alive."

The muted screams increased. Paul covered his eyes with the hand that wasn't holding the phone. Keren saw tears seeping out from under his fingers.

"It worked didn't it, Reverend?" Caldwell crooned. "You're involved again."

"It worked, Caldwell," Paul said furiously. "I'm back in."

The phone cut off. It wasn't long enough. Keren slapped her phone shut with a growl of rage.

Her phone rang again. It was Higgins. "We've got him! We got him a minute in."

"How? It wasn't long enough." Keren went to look out the window. Hundreds, maybe thousands of apartments where the front window of the mission could be visible. He was in one of them.

"I've already got cars en route. We had them stationed in the neighborhood."

"Where? Tell me."

Paul's eyes sharpened and he moved close enough to listen to Higgins.

"We didn't need to trace him. Morris had us hide a bug on Rosita to trace her. We've been watching it ever since we identified her on the phone."

"He did?" Keren shot Paul a look. "He didn't tell me he did that."

"I haven't had a chance." Grabbing her phone, Paul said, "Just tell me where she is."

"He's in that brownstone across and one south of the mission. GPS places him on the top floor."

"Of course it's the top," Paul said. "Caldwell likes the penthouse."

"Get over there," Higgins ordered. "Seal off that building as best you can, but don't go in. We're only minutes away."

They both ran. Keren hit the button that dialed O'Shea. He answered on the first ring. "Has the FBI clued you in?"

"Yes, I'm on the way—"

"We're almost there." Keren cut him off. "Right across the street from the mission. One building to the south."

"We should have kicked in every door in that area." O'Shea was running, breathing hard while he talked. "We knew he was close."

"There are ten thousand doors, O'Shea." Keren knew Caldwell

was looking right at them. There was no way he wouldn't see them rushing across the street. He knew. He'd be moving. He'd be killing Rosita.

"I'll be there in five minutes."

"He's got Rosita." Keren picked up her speed.

"The little cook from the mission?"

"We heard her screaming, Mick. And Caldwell was watching us, looking right in the front window. He told me what I'm wearing. We're not waiting until you get here to back us up. We're going in now. We've got to stop him from killing her!"

"Keren, don't! You know he was ready for us last time. You could be running straight into a trap!"

Paul pulled the door to the brownstone open and began sprinting up the stairs. Keren felt the demonic presence the instant she stepped inside. The call from O'Shea dropped in the concrete stairwell, but she couldn't talk and run anyway. Jamming the phone in her pocket, she picked up her speed to stay with Paul. Four flights. Every second they were closing in on him, but he had another stairway to use to get away, besides the fire escapes. Caldwell might evade them, but he'd have a hard time doing it with Rosita tossed over his shoulder.

They charged on until they reached the top. Paul began kicking in doors. Keren said, "Don't waste your time. He's in that one." She ran straight for the door at the far end of the hall. The evil was so thick she had trouble inhaling. The door practically vibrated with the contained demonic power.

Keren pulled her weapon and kicked the door in. Rosita lay in her white death shroud, her arms spread out at her sides, blood and locusts everywhere. "Paul, she's here!"

Paul ran past Keren. He was already on the phone, calling an ambulance. Keren entered the room with her gun held in two hands, extended straight in front of her. A locust landed on her face. She ignored it.

She turned quickly in a circle. He was here, but she couldn't pinpoint the evil. It was everywhere. She turned again, gun ready. There was a door ajar that led to the kitchen. There were four other doors in the apartment, all closed. Closets, bedrooms, bathrooms, Keren studied them, still turning, still trying to cover them all. Her heart pounded until she thought it might explode out of her chest. The evil was choking her. She prayed for strength as she waited, trying to keep Rosita safe until help could get here or they could get out. Releasing one hand from the gun, she pulled out her phone to tell Higgins exactly where they were.

Paul finished shouting directions into his phone. He tugged a knife out of his boot. Keren had known he'd arm himself somehow.

Rosita had been cut, but it didn't look life threatening. Locusts swarmed everywhere and flew thick in the air. Keren hit the speed dial for O'Shea's number then swiped her upper arm across her face to knock the locust away, all without letting go of her gun or stopping her rigid watch on the doors that hid Caldwell.

Paul slit the tape on Rosita's arms and ankles. She flailed as if she were fighting Paul's help. He got to her mouth last and very carefully pulled at the corner of the tape. Rosita grabbed at the tape and ripped it away with a scream of pain.

"Get out," she screamed. "He's here!"

The lights went out.

Keren realized in a split second that the windows in the room were boarded over. The hall door had swung shut whether by accident or design. She'd bet on design.

Suddenly the evil had a direction. Keren heard the slight *squeak* of a door opening. She whirled around to face one of the closed doors.

Rosita shouted, "Pastor P, the killer is..."

A crushing blow to Keren's hands knocked her gun to the floor. Her phone went flying. "Paul!"

The dull *thud* on her head cut off her cry for help.

⤶

*"Stretch out your hand toward the sky so that darkness
will spread over Egypt—darkness that can be felt."*
EXODUS 10:21

Pravus felt it, and he made sure Kerenhappuch felt it, too. At least she'd be able to feel it when she woke. He pulled the rough wool over her head and tossed her over his shoulder. He felt the strain of it. Yes, he'd honed his muscles, but he'd also drained his own blood when he needed to create. It was telling on his strength.

But he managed. He did what he had to do.

He vanished out of the apartment through the passage he'd spent so much time creating. It was the work of seconds to secure her with tape. He dumped her limp body in his trunk, was out of the garage and driving toward the expressway before he heard the first police sirens.

⤶

Paul heard it all.

Over Rosita's shouts, he heard the *squeak* of a door opening. A quick rush of footsteps on a loose floorboard...

Keren yelling his name...

The *whoosh* of something solid swinging through the air... The clatter of a gun hitting the floor... The sickening *thud* that cut off Keren's words...

Then silence.

Darkness. The plague of darkness.

"He's here, Pastor P. He's doing all of this. He killed Juanita." Rosita broke into sobs. "He hurt LaToya."

Paul ran toward the sound Keren made, but there was only darkness. "Keren," he roared. "Keren, answer me."

But she didn't, and he knew that could only mean one thing. She couldn't. Fighting down panic, he groped wildly, trying to latch onto something, anything. Rosita crashed into him, sobbing and crying out the identity of the man who'd taken her.

I've nurtured a viper.

And now he'd taken Keren. A woman he thought he could love. A woman he already *did* love.

Paul held Rosita to support her as he went toward the sound of the door he'd heard squeak. He was so disoriented in the stygian darkness that he wasn't even sure how to get out of the apartment.

When he began to despair of ever escaping the pit created by a demon, a door crashed open and men came running into the room. O'Shea was one of them. There were seconds of confusion and the lights came on, blinding Paul. Then he saw Rosita, wearing the ghastly painted dress, shaking violently as he held her upright.

"Where's Keren?" O'Shea roared. "What happened in here?"

One of the policemen slid an arm around Rosita and said, "Let's get you out of here, miss."

Sobbing, Rosita walked out, well supported by the patrolman.

Two other cops came in, then five more. They fanned out into the apartment, covering the whole thing in seconds.

"Where is she, Paul?" O'Shea grabbed him by the front of his shirt as if he'd beat the answer out of him if Paul didn't start talking.

"Gone," Paul said helplessly, now studying every corner of the room. Locusts flew and crawled everywhere. Paul heard the crunching under the feet of the searching officers. "She's gone."

"Gone where? Did she go after Caldwell alone?" O'Shea shook him again.

"He took her." Paul wrenched away from O'Shea and began slamming open doors, seeking, finding nothing. "The lights went out. I heard Keren yell. And then she was just gone."

"Think! You must have seen something!"

Paul checked every closet feverishly, even though the police were already doing it. "It was dark. Pitch dark. With that door closed, there wasn't a shred of light in this room."

"Then you heard something. You know something. Quit whining and try to think like a cop! Give me a report!" O'Shea's voice cracked like a whip, and Paul felt the sting.

"I never saw Caldwell. I have no idea how he got out of here." Paul gave up. She wasn't here.

O'Shea grabbed Paul with surprising strength and spun him around so they were face-to-face. O'Shea's face burned dark red with fury. His teeth gritted and his fists clenched. Paul thought O'Shea might attack him, and if he did, Paul would take whatever beating was handed out. He deserved it, every second of it.

Wishing O'Shea would hit him so he could be punished for leading Keren into this nightmare, he said, "All I know is what Caldwell said on the phone. We were just off the phone with him when Higgins called us with his address. He was making Rosita scream. We had to come."

"You should have waited for backup," O'Shea roared.

Paul shouted back, "We couldn't wait for backup while he was killing her."

"So you disregarded procedure," O'Shea growled.

Paul shoved O'Shea hard. "And saved Rosita's life." He knew he was asking for a fist right in the face. He knew it was what he wanted—deserved.

O'Shea shoved back but didn't take a swing. "And now Keren's gone, and Caldwell is still on the loose!"

"I know," Paul roared as he clenched his fists and shoved his face right up to O'Shea's. "But we've still got a chance to stop him."

"What chance to stop him? Stop him from doing what?"

Paul's head dropped with the weight of his fear. "On the phone, he said. . .he said. . ."

"What did he say?"

"He insisted on talking to Keren. He said she was next."

"Next? Next for what?" O'Shea demanded. "What did he say?"

"He said Keren is his choice for the plague of darkness."

CHAPTER TWENTY-FIVE

Total darkness covered all Egypt for three days.
No one could see anyone else.

Pravus hummed as he drove. Three days. Darkness had to fall for three days.

He wondered if he could be so patient. The beast was prowling, hungry, but he'd soon be fed. This time they'd make it a long, slow meal.

The pretty Kerenhappuch was so tempting. He'd thought Rosita was his most beautiful treasure so far, but he'd expected more time with her. How had the reverend found him so fast? The phone in the apartment would have been hard to trace. But the reverend had figured out where he was somehow.

He'd be more careful about calling this time.

He focused instead on the beauty of his newest conquest. He thought he heard movement in the trunk. The thrill of the power he had over her was so heady he almost swerved the car. But he had everything under complete control. He went to the third and last building he'd prepared.

He realized then that until now he'd thought it would be enough to bring the plagues down on the reverend and kill him. It would complete his work.

But now he knew it wouldn't be enough.

When he moved on after the reverend's death, he'd have to start over.

More blood.

More bugs.

More darkness.

More power.

He hummed as he thought of it.

⤳

Keren awakened to complete darkness. Her head throbbed. She was disoriented by the vibrations around her and her inability to move...and the dark.

The plague of darkness.

This was it. The nightmare she'd been chasing after all this time had caught her.

Panic rose in her chest, and she fought to move her arms and legs. She screamed, but her mouth was covered and no sound came out. She fought with the violence of a trapped animal for long moments, rolling in the confined space, her bound feet kicking out at anything they touched.

Tears stung her eyes and a low-pitched whine, deep in her throat, accompanied the tears. Sobs, muted behind the gag, wrenched her body.

Think! She had to quit wasting time. She closed her eyes, and, drawing on every ounce of her willpower, she shut out the pain and the discomfort of her contorted joints and began to use her head.

First, prayer. When she had enough control over herself to pray, the rest was easy. God was in control. They had saved Rosita because it wasn't her time. Keren knew she would live or die by God's will, not Caldwell's.

That's when she felt it. The evil. Pravus. She had been feeling him all along; his overwhelming evil had added to her terror.

Now she knew what it was and she could face it.

I am in Your hands, Lord. Let it be according to Your will.

She tested her arms. Tied together. Her feet the same. She lifted her hands, which were bound in front of her, and touched her face. She had some kind of a scratchy hood over her head. There was a smooth cool strip around the hood over her mouth. She recognized the feel of duct tape. She struggled with it. Her fingers were taped together until they couldn't move, but she could rub at the tape, and finally it slipped below her mouth. Now she could talk. Cry out for help. But she couldn't get the hood off, so the darkness remained.

The rev of a motor and the smell of gasoline told her she was in a car. The trunk.

She rubbed her leg against the floor of the trunk. Since they'd been fighting Caldwell, she had begun to wear a hide-out gun strapped to her ankle. It was still there. She curled up and tried to get at the gun with her taped hands.

She thought of all the victims. The autopsy suggested that he'd begun painting with his victim's blood right from the first. Keren's stomach quailed at the thought of Caldwell's brutality and the horrible vulnerability of being in his power. Tears cut like acid across her eyes. She fought for control. She drowned out the fear with prayers for courage and faith no matter what she faced.

The car slowed. She rolled backward and knew she was on an incline. Muted sounds reminded her of her car in the police parking garage. They were parking. Caldwell had reached his destination.

She tugged against her binding one last time, scrabbled at the hood with no effect. When she was sure there was nothing she could do, she accepted it. Then she gathered herself for what was to come. The car stopped. The door opened and closed. The trunk popped open over her head.

"Hello, Kerenhappuch. Welcome to *pestis ex tenebrae*. The plague of darkness."

Keren screamed. Behind the hood she shrieked with every bit of her strength. "Help! Call the police!" A hand clamped over her mouth.

Caldwell leaned close. "You can scream all you want. I'm only shutting you up so you can hear me explain. We're in a completely private place. Now I'll let you go back to your screaming so you'll believe me."

Somehow, whether from the certainty of his voice or an assurance from God, Keren believed him. "I suppose I did enough of it. If there's anyone around to hear, the police will be on their way."

"Yes," Caldwell said in his crooning voice. "And if there's no one to hear, you might as well spare further strain on your throat."

Keren knew that with every passing moment she was being pulled deeper into Caldwell's web. For now, there were no reasons to fight. She simply lay still and waited.

She was lifted out of the car. Her head hit the trunk lid and her legs scraped across rough metal as he struggled to drag her out. Her cop's brain started filing information. He wasn't overly strong. He wasn't a big man. He set her on her feet briefly and steadied her with one hand while he slammed the trunk shut. He leaned close to her while he reached for the lid. He didn't smell like a homeless man. She'd deliberately brushed her hand against his face. He had a short, stubbly beard. She tried to match that description with the pictures Higgins had taken. Murray had no beard. Except she hadn't seen him lately and the picture was over a week old. He could have stubble like this.

Louie. Who'd killed his wife.

Maybe.

Buddy.

She'd seen pictures, read the police description.

Casey-Ray and McGwire had full beards in those pictures. But if they were disguising themselves as homeless, who knew? They could have shaved or worn a fake beard.

His breathing hissed, and she knew from the sound that he was about four inches taller than her. That made him five nine or ten. His hands were uncalloused. He was slender and of a slight build. She refused to believe it was Roger. She'd met him. She knew it wasn't him. And Murray helped with the preaching. Keren would hate it if it was him.

She heard a jet coming in for a landing and she knew exactly where she was. He'd taken her out of the area surrounding the mission. She'd expected him to simply go into another neighborhood building. He'd used two of them already. But he was near an airport, which, with its open surrounding area, might explain why there was no one to hear her scream.

As she figured that out, she also knew O'Shea was not coming. She knew Paul wasn't going to talk to someone from the neighborhood and get the final clue he needed to find this place. Higgins was not going to figure this one out in time. She was completely on her own.

Caldwell hoisted her over his shoulder with a soft "ummph." His feet echoed on the concrete floor, taking her to the plague of darkness.

A still, small voice echoed in her head, and it was so clear and so pure that she smiled. *If I am with you, who can be against you?*

"No one," Keren answered aloud. "No one can stand against God."

"What?" Caldwell asked.

"God just reminded me that He is with me. You can't do anything to me that isn't God's will."

"Remember that while I'm painting my pictures." Caldwell's hands tightened on her.

Then she had an inspiration. It could only have come from God, because it was in complete opposition to everything in her head.

Always before when she could feel a demon, it was so she could help. She'd only thought of sensing Caldwell's demon as a tool for tracking him. But what if she was meant to help him? Could she find it in her heart to try to save this evil, brutal madman? Could that be God's will?

It was always God's will that the lost be found. A soul be saved.

For a moment Keren clamped her mouth shut tight. She didn't want to deliver him from evil. She wanted to get to her gun and blow him away.

She saw Jesus Christ, nailed to the cross, saying, "Father, forgive them, for they do not know what they are doing."

She saw the apostle Paul persecuting Christians, even killing them, and going on to become one of the mightiest disciples in the history of the world.

Yes, God wanted to save Francis's soul. Of course He did.

"I can feel the demon in you, Francis. I can help you be free. Don't you want your life back? Don't you want to be rid of this enemy who has invaded your soul?"

"Shut up!" Caldwell shook her and began walking faster. He was breathing hard from effort and anger.

"I know you think I'm here with you because you kidnapped me. I know you have a plan that you began formulating long ago.

I know you want to hurt Paul."

"I did hurt him. It has been glorious watching him suffer. Killing his wife wasn't enough. I wanted to do worse to her, but she was dead. I didn't make her suffer enough. Then her husband interfered in my life and I found someone else who needed to be punished."

Keren didn't bother arguing with him, she just kept saying what that vision of Christ on the cross led her to say. "But Francis, I'm not here by your will. God sent me here."

"Did He tie you up and take you into darkness?"

"He didn't do it, Francis, but He allowed it."

"My name is Pravus!" He walked faster. His arms were like coiled rattlesnakes ready to strike.

"God did all of that because He wants me to talk to you. He loves you."

Suddenly she swung wildly forward and slammed down on the hard floor. Her skull cracked hard on the cement. Stars danced in her head.

Caldwell leaned over her and snarled, "My father is the only one who loves me. He saved me from the evil that wanted to rule me. He made the evil let me go, just as I'm trying to get evil to let my people go."

There was a violent tug on her head. She wondered if she'd pushed him too far and he intended to kill her right now and be done with it. Then the hood was gone and she could see.

"Buddy!"

Paul had talked about him some, she'd seen his picture on the bulletin board—but she'd never met him. Then she thought of the one time she'd seen him—he'd been with a group from the mission at the park—when they'd found Wilma. When she'd sensed the demon. But she hadn't been able to pinpoint him as the source of that evil.

"My name is Pravus." He slung her over his shoulder and began walking again.

He hadn't replaced the hood. Keren wondered if he had intended to give her this respite from darkness. Somehow she suspected Caldwell's vision of this plague had included her being plunged into darkness and left there until she died in darkness. She wondered how long it would take him to get back on course with his plan.

Silently, she thanked God for letting her see, although there wasn't much to see. She looked around and saw Murray's car, with the bullet hole in the back window. The echoing enclosure must be some sort of parking garage, but it was a shambles. The cement was cracked. The ceiling had caved in at one spot. She heard a jet take off nearby and suddenly knew exactly where she was. There was an old apartment building left standing near the airport. It was remote because all the buildings around it had been demolished already. Not even the homeless would come in here. There was no one here but her and Caldwell.

They entered the building, and Caldwell began carrying her up the stairs. He was unusually strong for his size. Keren felt the corded muscles in his lean arms. But even so, he was testing his limits. Breathing hard, walking slower.

"Your father punished you. He told you he would drive the evil out," Keren said gently, hoping to start him talking again.

"Shut up. I'm not listening to you."

"He hurt you and called you evil until you believed him. But it wasn't true. He was wrong." She felt such compassion for the little boy who had been so warped, that she no longer had to force herself to do God's will. She found it easy to reach out.

"You don't know anything about me. My father saved me!"

Caldwell opened a door and went in. He walked to the middle of the room as Keren studied her surroundings from her upside-down position.

He flipped her off his shoulder and she landed with a *thud* on a hard wooden table. She tried to slide off the table, but Caldwell made such quick work of fastening her feet to a metal hook embedded in the wood that she knew he'd done it many times before. She thought of her gun strapped to her ankle. He didn't notice it, and Keren wondered if God had closed his eyes to it.

She'd never killed a man. She didn't want to do it now. But she would. God forgive her, she'd kill if she had to. She knew it was in her to kill someone to save the lives of innocent victims.

"Francis, God has sent me to you."

"No, He hasn't!" Caldwell lost his cultured voice.

"I am here with you because I have a special gift." Keren looked at him, staring into his eyes, willing him to listen to her. "I have a gift that lets me see the demon inside of you, and that lets me see the sad, hurt little boy who doesn't want to do this bad thing."

Caldwell leaned down until his face was inches from hers. "I'm doing God's will."

She shuddered but quickly controlled herself. "You don't have to let this demon tell you what to do. I can make him leave. All you have to do is want it, Francis. All you have to do is reach out for God."

Caldwell produced a delicate tool from a smaller table beside the one where she lay. She recognized the chisel. It was identical to the one they'd found in LaToya's back.

He used the chisel to slit the duct tape from her hands. For a moment, she hoped she might have reached him and he was setting her free. But he wrenched one hand straight out to her side and deftly wrapped tape around it. She saw that the table was specially made so her arms could be extended straight out at her sides and secured.

Even as he did it, she knew the demon had him firmly in his grip. *Why did You let me feel him, if not to free him from the demon?*

There was no answer. Maybe this wasn't about Caldwell. Maybe this was her test.

He rounded the table. When he reached for her hand, she was ready. She rammed her fist into his face. With a howl of pain, he recoiled from her. He crouched down, mewling like a wounded kitten, until he had nearly curled into a ball on the floor. Keren desperately reached for her gun but her bound arm wouldn't let her get to it. She rolled sideways to loosen it. With a snarl of rage, Caldwell leaped from the floor and lunged for her. She slammed the back of her hand into his jaw and he staggered back. Recovering instantly, he grabbed at her hand and she landed a solid blow on his nose. Blood spurted out. She caught a hank of hair and slammed his head on the wooden table.

With a shriek of pain more animal than human, Caldwell threw his whole weight on her free arm. He pressed it back and she couldn't hold out against his weight. He fumbled for his tape and bound her free arm out at her side. She couldn't move.

She was completely at the mercy of a demon.

The demon found his chisel where he'd dropped it and brought it to the table. His nose was bleeding. When he saw the blood dripping off his chin, he dabbed at it and said, "You drew first blood, Kerenhappuch, but I'll draw last."

He began slitting the arm of her shirt.

↶

Paul was waiting for O'Shea to throw a fist, when Higgins rushed into the room with a half dozen FBI agents.

"Do you have the location on Keren?" Paul strode toward Higgins.

"Location?" O'Shea was right beside him.

"Yes," Paul said. "I bugged her just like I did Rosita."

"You can trace her?" O'Shea asked. "Why didn't you say so?"

"Because I was searching for her in this apartment first." Paul turned to Higgins. "Where's the computer?"

At that moment, one of Higgins's agents pulled a sheet of plywood off a window and climbed out on the apartment's only fire escape. The distressed metal shrieked.

"Did you hear that?" Higgins asked Paul.

"No," Paul said. "No way did he go out that fire escape. Even if he found a way out without letting light in, I'd have heard that racket. He's gone, and he's got Keren. She left her gun and her phone behind, but she's still wearing the tracking device I put in her hair tie."

A man carrying a laptop computer burst into the apartment.

"Check Detective Collins's location." Paul ran to where the man had set up the little computer on the bloody table where Rosita had been tied only minutes before. The computer began a relentless beeping. The screen filled with a map of Chicago, with a little white dot flashing.

"He's stopped," the computer operator said. "The signal just came online and it's stationary."

Higgins bent down to study the screen. "He's by the airport. Several condemned buildings in that area. It's a good bet he's holed up in one of them. I'll have an address by the time the GPS is done working."

Paul grabbed Higgins's arm. "Let's go. They can call you with an address while we drive."

"I'm going to put an end to this right now." Higgins charged out of the room.

Paul glanced at O'Shea, and the two ran after Higgins.

CHAPTER TWENTY-SIX

Keren heard the fabric of her white blouse rip. She willed herself to be calm.

"Francis, take charge of your life. I'm here to give you a chance for redemption."

Caldwell looked up from his cutting. "You're here because I brought you here. I'm in control. I'm enjoying my power over you far more since you struck me."

Keren wondered if she had miscalculated when she attacked him. She saw the fire in his eyes and the blood dripping from his broken nose and couldn't regret defending herself. But, if it was possible, the feeling of evil that oozed out of him was worse.

"Francis, you're *not* in control. A demon is telling you every move to make. If you really want to be in control, you have to get him out. This demon only controls you if you let him. If you pray with me, if you turn to God, you can be free."

Caldwell looked up and for a second, something flickered in his eyes, but it was quickly gone.

This kind of demon only comes out with prayer and fasting.

"God, help me," Keren prayed aloud. "Touch Francis's heart. Give me the words to speak. I know You want him to come home. I know—"

"Shut up." Caldwell lunged so his face was inches from hers. "No one will save you. You're mine."

"the demon that lived among the tombs, when he saw Jesus,

330

cried out, 'What do you want with me, Jesus, Son of the Most High God? In God's name, don't torture me!' Jesus has command over demons." Keren had tried reaching Francis by appealing to his humanity, but now she spoke to the demon. "God is more powerful than you, Pravus. You know that if He willed it, you would be back on the floor, just like you were when I hit you. You'd be curled up, begging for mercy."

Caldwell raised his hand to strike her.

"Do you know you can't even lay a hand on me unless God allows it?" Keren asked. "Good is stronger than evil, Pravus. God is stronger than Satan. You think you are victorious when you kill a woman, but God is in charge. He can slap you down with a single wave of His hand, if He chooses."

"Then why doesn't He? Why will He stand by and let me kill you, like I've killed all the others, if He's so good?"

Keren tried to calm her voice. "That is something I have to deal with every day on my job. I've finally made peace with the simple fact that bad things happen because the earth is the earth. We are human beings with human failings. If we want perfection, we have to go to heaven to find it. God's main work is in our souls. And He's in my soul, Pravus. Even if you batter my body, even if you kill me, I'll still be fine, because I'm a believer in Jesus Christ."

Keren remembered Paul's constant comfort. "To live is Christ and to die is gain."

Caldwell used his chisel to run a slit the length of Keren's other sleeve. The rip of the fabric would soon be replaced with cuts to her flesh. "Then you should thank me, Kerenhappuch."

"Thank you? Why?" Keren felt her sleeve fall open.

"Because you are about to gain."

⤵

"We're doing this one right," Higgins snapped as they raced toward the location the tracking device registered. "If you had waited, Morris, Detective Collins wouldn't be in his hands, and Caldwell would be in custody!"

Paul sat beside Higgins in the dark, government-issue sedan. "We couldn't know that. If you had heard Rosita—"

"Look, you're too emotionally involved to use your brain on this one, that's why you've got to let me take charge. I've got cars en route. Some of them might be there already."

"Then send them in," Paul said with a surge of hope. "Maybe he hasn't hurt her yet."

"They will *not* go in. Not until I order it. We set up a perimeter. We close off any escape routes. We do this right, and Caldwell doesn't slip away to kill again!"

"And how long is Keren at his mercy while you make sure all your Is are dotted?"

"I don't know," Higgins said with vicious sarcasm. "Why don't you tell me? You're the one who let him get his hands on her!"

O'Shea said from the backseat, "It was all a setup from the beginning—the pitch dark, the escape route he used. When we finish tearing that place apart, we'll find he built a secret door somewhere as an escape hatch. If they hadn't gone in when they did, Caldwell would have disappeared with Rosita, and we'd be no better off than we are now."

Paul looked over his shoulder at O'Shea. The man was like a rock in the middle of Higgins's condemnation and Paul's panic. O'Shea, who knew Keren better and had loved her longer than any of them.

"You've got to be crazy to be able to stay so calm," Paul said to the grizzled veteran of countless manhunts.

"Yeah, I guess that could describe me. But the thing that's keeping me from acting like a complete jerk"—he threw a fiery look at Higgins—"is Keren. Keren isn't a woman to be at anyone's mercy."

Paul ran his hands through his hair and tried to get a handle on the careening images in his head. Keren cut. PESTIS EX TENEBRAE painted onto a death shroud. Keren trapped somewhere in the spirit-sapping dark, as he had been for those few minutes with Rosita.

Keren.

Paul remembered who he was dealing with. He looked over his shoulder and, unbelievably, found he could smile at O'Shea. "You know what she's doing right now?"

Higgins raced his car through the busy Chicago traffic, leading a parade of five other dark sedans—sirens shrieking, lights flashing.

O'Shea grinned back. "Sure I know what she's doing," he said with a laugh. "Man, nothing gets the best of my little girl for long."

"What are you laughing for?" Higgins growled. "What about any of this is amusing?"

"It's not amusing, and if you think I'm not scared to death for her, then you're a fool, Higgins," O'Shea said without venom.

"Then what do you mean?" Higgins directed his question at Paul. "What is she doing right now?"

Paul rubbed his hands over his face to keep from smiling again because it was so wrong to smile. "Our little, helpless, kidnapping victim is trying to save Francis Caldwell's soul."

"I can lead you to the Lord, Francis. I can pray with you and you can have rest for your soul."

"My soul is dead. Long ago." Caldwell cut from the gaping sleeve hole all the way to her collar, then he circled the table to do it again on the other side.

"No, Francis, every man has an immortal soul, put there by God, that exists to love and serve God. 'As the deer pants for streams of water, so my soul pants for you, my God.' It's the nature of every human soul to long for God. You long for God, Francis. You are thirsty for Him."

Caldwell slit more fabric on her shirt. Keren said with all the intensity in her Christian spirit, "I don't believe I would feel the demon in you if there wasn't hope. Francis, look at me!"

By the sheer force of her will, she brought his eyes around. He saw her. She knew Francis, not Pravus for this one instant, was in control and listening.

From her position of absolute helplessness, she said, "I'll help you, Francis. I'll stay with you. I'll stay by your side through all that is to come."

"And you can protect me from the police?" Francis asked bitterly.

"No." Keren wasn't going to lie to him. "No, Francis. When you get rid of the demon, you will still have to face up to all the harm you've done, because you've always had a choice. The demon in you has only had the power over you that you've given him. So they'll lock you up, and you'll find out that prison walls don't keep God out. You can be a Christian anywhere."

Francis looked at her, listening.

Keren said gently, "I can see your thirst, Francis. Let me go. Let me tell you about my Savior. There is joy for you in this life, Francis. How long has it been since you've felt a moment's joy? There is peace and love and victory—true power, Francis."

Francis's eyes flickered and his breathing became uneven. She could see the struggle in him, but she fervently believed what she said. If there was no hope, then she wouldn't have been given this gift of discernment. She prayed silently, not for her own safety, but for Francis's soul.

He laid his hand in hers, where it was bound.

"He loves you, Francis. God loves you, and I love you. That's why I'm here, to tell you He loves you."

Suddenly Francis's hand gripped hers with violent strength.

Then, with a sudden slashing movement, her hand was free. Francis reached across her and unbound her other hand. He released her feet with a final slash of his chisel and handed the sharp metal tool to her.

"This is crazy. I'm crazy." His whole body trembled violently. "The demon has made me into a monster. Stop me."

Keren sat up. "Let's pray together."

As she prayed, Keren saw darkness seep out of him from every pore. The darkness fought to hold him. Francis held her with his gaze. She prayed fiercely as the demon that had Francis in his grip began to take shape and twist as it rose in the air. A low wail of tormented agony erupted from the black cloud that filled the room. It built and built until Keren wanted to cover her ears from the shriek of fury. The evil wrapped itself around her throat.

The shriek turned to a roar and a window shattered as the black cloud streaked away and vanished.

"It's gone. I felt the weight lift off me."

"Yes, it's gone. Now we need to pray. You need to accept Jesus into your heart. Simply believe in Him to have eternal life."

His hand tightened on hers. The power of being set free didn't gleam in his eyes like it should. "Without the demon, I can see clearly for the first time in years, and all I can see is an evil world—a father who couldn't love me."

"But *God* loves you. You can't have lived through what just happened here and not believe in Him. God has shown Himself to you."

"Yes, He has." A smile twisted Francis's lips. "And God took away all my strength."

"Francis, it's important that you turn to God." Keren thought of the verse that said if a demon left a man but God did not enter in, then more demons would return, more powerfully than ever. "You can't deny His love. You've experienced it in a beautiful way."

"I did experience it. I do believe it. But I don't accept." Francis jerked as if something—or someone—struck him.

"Francis, no, listen to me. Listen to God." Whatever went on inside of Francis, she had to fight her way past it to reach him.

"I liked myself." Francis's voice changed again. His eyes gleamed until Keren could see the flames burning in his soul.

"It's my choice, and I *don't* choose the path your God has for me." He reached for her.

Keren threw herself backward, diving off the table. She landed with a *thud* on her neck and shoulder. She rolled to her feet as Francis rounded the table, a roar of evil joy coming from him.

He slammed into her. They both reeled backward. The apartment wall kept her on her feet. She ran for the door.

Francis was on her, knocking her to the floor. He landed all his weight on her back. Flipping her over, he straddled her stomach. His hands closed on her throat. She knocked his grip away with an upward sweep of her arms, caught the front of his shirt, and rolled, throwing him over her head. On her feet instantly, she turned just as he charged forward and backed her into the wall. His hands tightened on her neck.

She caught his wrists to take the pressure off her windpipe. He wasn't that big. She was trained in self-defense.

He bore down on her. She pushed against the strangling grip. Fighting to draw in a breath, she used every ounce of her strength against him. With a sudden twist, she broke his grip and shoved him sideways. His head hit the wall with a stunning *crack*.

She dived away from him, clawing at her ankle holster. She pulled the gun free and brought it up just as Francis grabbed the chisel that had fallen to the floor. He hurled it at her with the same deadly accuracy he'd used on LaToya.

The razor-sharp chisel hit her arm. The stabbing pain made her drop the gun.

Francis was already on it, raising it with a wicked laugh.

The door behind them flew open. Francis turned, his gun's aim shifting. Higgins was the first in the door. Keren dropped to the floor as Higgins fired.

Francis's body jerked and staggered into a wall. Higgins fired again. The smell of sulfur was like brimstone, overwhelming everything in the room.

Paul ran into the room. Keren noticed he had her gun, the one Francis had knocked out of her hand when they'd found Rosita, tucked in his waistband. O'Shea was right behind him with his sidearm out and ready.

Francis sank to his knees, clutching his bleeding chest. Blood poured from two bullet wounds. He turned to look into Keren's eyes, the evil fading.

Keren ignored the chisel in her arm and crawled to his side. "It's not too late."

"Yes, it is." Francis's chest was soaked and red. He slid sideways against the wall until he slumped onto his back. "I made my choice. I lived with it, and I'll die with it." A look of horror crossed over his face as if now he was realizing just what his choice meant for him, for all eternity.

"Francis, please, listen to me."

Suddenly Francis's eyes popped open, and a look of pure satisfied evil was on his flaccid face. A voice, deep and ugly, came from Francis, even though his mouth didn't move and his chest had quit rising and falling.

"Francis isn't here."

Paul lifted Keren away from the dead man and pulled her into his arms.

"Be careful of her arm," O'Shea shouted.

Higgins was calling for an ambulance.

Paul carefully picked her up and strode out of the room.

She wrapped her arms around his neck and cried.

CHAPTER TWENTY-SEVEN

Keren still couldn't stand the thought of going back to her apartment, and she hadn't had any luck finding a new one, so she worked all day and kept long hours at night with LaToya. The coma wasn't as deep as before and LaToya occasionally stirred and responded to sound without fully waking up, but Keren hoped and prayed it would happen soon.

Keren's arm, where the chisel had stabbed her, was healing.

The lieutenant had put her on sick leave, but she'd prevailed on him to let her do something, using the argument that she would go out of her ever-loving mind if she didn't keep busy.

For now she was assigned to desk duty. She'd been forbidden from anything active until her doctor released her.

The long days and short nights caught up with her as she kept her bedside vigil.

"Keren?"

Keren's eyes flickered open. Her vision was filled with Paul. She hadn't seen him for days.

"How's the arm?" His movements as gentle as his voice, he lowered himself into the chair beside Keren.

"Fine, if I'm careful."

"Which you never are." Paul sounded grumpy, but he didn't have much room to talk. He'd stayed with her at the hospital until she'd been treated, then he'd vanished. It had been four days.

Keren straightened in her chair and ran a hand over her face in case she'd been drooling in her sleep. She couldn't imagine what a mess her hair must be.

Which reminded her. . . "You put a tracking device in my hair tie?"

"Yeah." He smirked, completely unrepentant.

"Why didn't you just tell me it was there? Why the sneaking around?"

"You're stubborn, and it was pretty obvious that Caldwell had decided to come for you and Rosita at some point. I gave Rosie the necklace and told her to keep it on at all times."

"Why didn't you do that for me?"

"I didn't trust you. You're kind of bent on taking care of yourself."

"When did you put it on me?"

"That morning." Paul rubbed both hands over his face. "I thought I had time. I knew you were at risk, but I was being a coward. I was hiding. I had the tracker, but I hadn't even given it to you yet. I almost left it too late."

"Just that morning?" Keren's eyes narrowed. "When you kissed me? You kissed me as an excuse to get close enough to—"

"No, I didn't kiss you for any other reason than because I wanted to. But I'd intended to get it to you somehow that day. I'd have just flat out told you if I couldn't figure out a way to sneak it into your barrette. I had it made so it matched one of the pins that held the barrette in."

"Why didn't you have one on?"

"I did."

She fell silent at that and stared and thought how much she'd missed his faith and support, and even his strange split personality.

"What?" he asked.

"I didn't say anything."

"You smiled."

"Oh, did I?" Keren said in a sleep-roughened voice. "I was just thinking of Pastor Jekyll and Detective Hyde."

Paul furrowed his brow. "Who?"

"You. How are you doing with your split personality? Did you get yourself back? Did you ever figure out who 'yourself' is?"

Paul sprawled back in his chair. "It took some doing. I spent days in prayer, trying to rediscover the calm, unselfish Pastor P."

"Any luck?" Keren knew she couldn't be with the calm, unselfish Pastor P. Her life would destroy him. And she didn't want to be with Paul the cop. He was a jerk.

Paul leaned forward to brace his forearms on his knees and turned his head sideways to look at her. "I never exactly found him. I don't know for sure if I really wanted to."

"Why not?" Keren crossed her arms and relaxed back into her chair with her legs stretched out in front of her.

Paul quit looking at her and stared at the floor between his splayed knees. "I refuse to believe that Pastor P wasn't real. He was. I needed to serve with my whole heart for a while after I left the police force. But all this taught me there is strength in my anger. You remember when I came charging into that room with you and Caldwell?"

"Yes, my knight in shining armor, racing to my rescue." Keren grinned.

Paul turned to look at her with a squinty-eyed glare. "Except Higgins got there first. Higgins saved you—what a grandstander."

"I kind of like him. I mean, he did save my life."

Paul shook his head. "I had your gun."

"I noticed."

"I picked it up in that room where you dropped it."

"Excuse me," Keren said with a stern frown. "It was knocked

out of my hands. I would never *drop* my gun."

Paul nodded and tried to look serious. "Of course you wouldn't."

"Don't forget it," she growled.

"I wanted to use it. I was frantic, furious, completely insane worrying about you."

"Poor baby."

"And on the way to rescue you, O'Shea gave me a little talking to about how terrific you were and how deeply you embraced your faith."

"O'Shea said all that?" She thought of her taciturn partner.

"Well, yeah. He said it in about five words, with a lot of grunting, but I got the message."

"That sounds like him," Keren said fondly.

"Anyway he said enough. And I knew the truth of those words I'd said so many times, 'To live is Christ and to die is gain.' I gave you up to God. I quit worrying. We still drove at top speed, don't get me wrong. But the point is, I still felt all the strength of my anger, but it wasn't out of control. I need to respect it, even use it once in a while. I had finally healed enough that I could quit fearing that part of myself."

"I'm glad." Keren leaned forward until she rested her forearms on her knees in a replica of Paul's pose. She turned her head to look at him. They were inches apart.

He erased those inches when he kissed her.

A very sweet minute later, Paul said, "You did lean close like that so I could kiss you, right?"

"Right," Keren whispered.

"The thing is, I'm always going to run the Lighthouse. It's a calling, and I can't turn my back on it."

Keren nodded. "And I'm always going to be a cop. It's a calling, and I can't turn my back on it."

"But I wouldn't necessarily have to *live* above the shelter. There's a really beautiful little Christian school about three miles from the mission. I'd like our kids to go there. And if we lived close to the school, that'd be more convenient."

Keren's smile widened until she laughed just a little. She never took her eyes off him. She was afraid if she blinked, her dreams might disappear.

He laughed back, just a little, and he kept his eyes on her, too.

"If that is a marriage proposal, it's the worst one I've ever heard."

"Oh yeah? Well, how many of them have you heard?"

She waited and watched and loved. "A couple. One was really romantic."

"The guy who dumped you when he found out you had a spiritual gift he didn't like?"

"Yeah."

Paul arched one eyebrow. "A lot of good all his romance did you. You want poetry? Marry Robert Frost."

"I don't want him, I want you."

Paul reached across the inches between them and clasped her hand in his. He looked at her until she felt like he had taken her inside of himself. He lifted her hand and kissed it. "I love you, Keren. I've been waiting until I got myself centered in my faith before I came to talk to you."

"Your faith was never in danger, Paul."

Paul gave a quick jerk of his head. "Absolutely not. But that didn't mean I couldn't get pretty mixed up for a while. Not about believing in Jesus. But about where I was meant to be, what I was being led to do with my life." He bounced their hands gently between them. "What I was supposed to do with you."

"Had trouble with me, did you?" she asked.

Paul shrugged and let go of her hand and reached into the pocket of the dark blue sweatpants he was wearing. He pulled a little velvet box out of his pocket. "Not so much trouble that I didn't go out and get you this."

He handed her the box and she glanced from the box to him and back to the box about five times before she regained control of her eyeballs. Then, she still wasn't in control of them because they started leaking.

He brushed his thumb across her cheek and murmured, "I hope those are happy tears."

"V-e-ry." Her voice broke. She cleared her throat and tried again. "Very happy."

"Will you marry me, Keren? I love you. I think you're so wonderful. The perfect woman for me. But more than that, I think God had you in mind for me from the moment of our births. I feel like I've found the other half of myself. I can't imagine my life without you."

"That's the most beautiful proposal I've ever heard."

"Really?"

Keren nodded. "You're really getting better at it." She took a swipe at her tears. "We'll probably fight. We have been almost from the moment we met."

"What we were fighting was this." Paul leaned over and kissed her again. A real kiss, the kind of kiss a Christian man shouldn't give a Christian woman if he wasn't planning to marry her.

Her arms went around his neck. He lifted her off her chair and settled her on his lap. He pulled away first, to give her a chance to open the velvet box.

She smiled and opened it.

"It's not very big, Keren. I'm not a rich man and I never will be. But we'll have enough. The Lord will provide." He lifted the solitaire diamond out of its velvet bed. "And it's offered with love."

She extended her hand so he could slip it on.

He said, "Not yet. You haven't said the words yet."

Keren looked away from the beautiful ring and smiled at him. She said with a sassy arch of her eyebrows, "And exactly what words are those, Rev.?"

"How many times have I told you not to call me Rev.?"

"Try 'I love you,'" a groggy voice broke in.

Paul and Keren jerked their heads up and looked at the source of that advice. LaToya, her eyelids heavy, gave them a weak smile.

"LaToya." Keren jumped off Paul's lap, not all that sure how she'd gotten there.

Paul rounded the bed so they were on opposite sides of her.

LaToya said, "Don't let me interrupt. I was enjoying being a Peeping Tom. Then you started getting sidetracked, and I thought you needed help."

"You're awake." Paul reached for her hand. He held it gently. "We've been so worried about you."

LaToya's eyes fell shut. "You didn't look all that worried to me."

"Where's the CALL button? We need to get a doctor in here." Paul looked along the side of the bed.

"I'll go find someone." Keren disappeared out of the room.

"She seems nice." LaToya squeezed his hand.

"Yeah, and I was about to have her all sewn up, when you started talking."

From behind him, Keren said, "Don't give up. You can sew me up, yet."

Paul turned just as two nurses came rushing into the room. He let himself be shoved out of the way.

"You'd better hand over the ring," Keren said. "Before we forget what we were talking about."

"We won't forget." Paul turned to her and pulled her into his arms. "I think I'm going to enjoy shutting that smart mouth."

As his head dipped to kiss her, she gave him the words he'd been fishing for. "I love you, Paul. I want to marry you and send our children to that little Christian school. I want that ring."

"It's not big," he warned.

"It's a beautiful ring." Keren poked him in the shoulder. "I don't ever want to hear a word against it."

"Yes ma'am," Paul said.

"I want to spend my spare time helping at the mission." She thought they might as well talk a few things through.

"I'd really appreciate that."

"But the thing I really want is. . .you."

Paul hesitated long enough to get the ring on her finger, then he kissed her.

Rosita chose that moment to appear for her daily visit. When she saw Paul and Keren in each other's arms and LaToya awake, she looked like she didn't know who to talk to first.

Keren stepped away from Paul.

"Don't quit on my account," Rosita said, with the first genuine smile Keren had seen on her face since she'd been kidnapped.

"Do you have any interest in a long engagement, Keren-happuch?" Paul asked.

"Not on your life." Keren shook her head. "I'd like my folks to come and I'd like my pastor to marry us."

"How about this Saturday?"

"That's four days!" Keren shouted.

Rosita said, "LaToya 'n' me wanna be bridesmaids."

One of the nurses said, "You can get a blood test right down the hall."

The other nurse said, "Kerenhappuch?"

Keren slugged Paul for that. He gently rubbed Keren's sore arm as if worried that punching him might hurt her.

"When will Rosita get out?" Paul asked the nurse.

The nurse gave him a stern look, but a smile lurked behind her glaring eyes. "If she's not out by Saturday, it wouldn't be the first wedding we held at someone's bedside."

Paul looked at Keren. She said, "Oh why not? I guess I can be ready by Saturday. Can O'Shea come?"

Paul said, "I already asked him to be my best man."

"You talked to O'Shea about this before you talked to me?" Keren snapped.

Paul kissed her quiet, and, when she had forgiven him—or maybe forgotten what was the problem—the two of them turned to smile at their friends.

Keren said as she looked at LaToya's smiling face, "The plague has really finally ended."

"Not the way we'd have hoped. It sounds like you led Francis as close to the Lord as anyone can," Paul said with a solemn shake of his head.

"He had to make the last step himself." Keren frowned. "And even now, even seeing what I saw, I can dance around in my head and hope God gave him one more last chance before his soul departed his body."

Paul looked at Keren.

She read such love in his eyes that her heart pounded and her knees went weak and she had to hold on to him tight.

" 'It is not good for the man to be alone.' " Paul planted a kiss on her temple, then her nose, then her lips. He quit just when it was getting good. "That has never been so true as it is for me right now."

Keren smiled at the ancient words that were God's blessing on the first marriage. The room and all its distractions melted away. " 'I will make a helper suitable for him,'" she added with a sassy smile. "That's me. I'll help you, Rev."

"I'm counting on it," Paul said. "Let's go call our parents. And we're getting married whether they can come or not."

"Getting us married'll be the first thing I help you with."

With a quick nod at a glowing Rosita, who waved them away and went to watch over LaToya, they left the room. They left behind the sadness of the plague that had brought them together.

In the hall, they had a moment alone. Paul turned her to face him and pulled her into his arms. "Your courage is something that will humble me for the rest of my life. The way you faced a demon. . .the way you tried to help a man so many people would have killed. . ."

He slung his arm around her shoulders and they headed for the exit and their future. "So, you think you'll spend much time fighting for your life when you should be picking the kids up from school?"

"I'm planning to request a transfer to properties crimes. I'll chase demon-possessed embezzlers for a change."

"Bet you'll be surprised how many of them there are." Paul tried to take her keys when she pulled them out of her pocket.

She held them out of his reach. "I'm driving until you can produce a valid driver's license."

"I'm in a hurry. I want to run the siren on our way to city hall to get the license." He kissed her until she was completely cooperative. But by then he seemed to be feeling pretty agreeable himself, and she got away and slid behind the wheel.

Paul climbed in the passenger side. "We're gonna have fun."

The car roared to life and Keren flicked on the siren and tore out of the hospital parking lot.

Mary Nealy is the suspense genre pen name for bestselling and award-winning author Mary Connealy, who is best known for her humorous Old West romances. She makes her home with her husband on a farm in Nebraska near her four grown daughters.